The Prose Tales of Alexander Pushkin

Alexander Pushkin

The Prose Tales of Alexander Pushkin

ISBN: 978-1-64439-713-8

CONTENTS

CONTENTS

THE CAPTAIN'S DAUGHTER

CHAPTER I

THE SERGEANT OF THE GUARDS

My father, Andrei Petrovitch Grineff, after having served in his youth under Count Münich,[1] quitted the service, in the year 17—, with the rank of senior major. He settled down upon his estate in the district of Simbirsk, where he married Avdotia Vassilevna U——, the daughter of a poor nobleman of the neighbourhood. Nine children were the result of this marriage. All my brothers and sisters died in their infancy. I was enrolled as a sergeant in the Semenovsky Regiment, through the influence of Prince B——, a major in the Guards, and a near relation of our family. I was considered as being on leave of absence until the completion of my course of studies. In those days our system of education was very different from that in vogue at the present time. At five years of age I was given into the hands of our gamekeeper, Savelitch, whose sober conduct had rendered him worthy of being selected to take charge of me. Under his instruction, at the age of twelve I could read and write Russian, and I was by no means a bad judge of the qualities of a greyhound. About that time my father engaged a Frenchman, a Monsieur Beaupré, who had been imported from Moscow, together with the yearly stock of wine and Provence oil. Savelitch was not by any means pleased at his arrival.

"Heaven be thanked!" he muttered to himself; "the child is washed, combed, and well-fed. What need is there for spending money and engaging a Mossoo, as if there were not enough of our own people!"

Beaupré had been a hairdresser in his own country, then a soldier in Prussia, then he had come to Russia pour être outchitel,[2] without very well understanding the meaning of the word. He was a good sort of fellow, but extremely flighty and thoughtless. His chief weakness was a passion for the fair sex; but his tenderness not

---

[1] A celebrated German general who entered the service of Russia during the reign of Peter the Great.
[2] Outchitel. A tutor.

unfrequently met with rebuffs, which would cause him to sigh and lament for the whole twenty-four hours. Moreover, to use his own expression, he was no enemy of the bottle, or, in other words, he loved to drink more than was good for him. But as, with us, wine was only served out at dinner, and then in small glasses only, and as, moreover, the teacher was generally passed over on these occasions, my Beaupré very soon became accustomed to Russian drinks, and even began to prefer them to the wines of his own country, as being more beneficial for the stomach. We soon became very good friends, and although, by the terms of the contract, he was engaged to teach me French, German, and all the sciences, yet he much preferred learning from me to chatter in Russian, and then each of us occupied himself with what seemed best to him. Our friendship was of the most intimate character, and I wished for no other mentor. But fate soon separated us, owing to an event which I will now proceed to relate.

The laundress, Palashka, a thick-set woman with a face scarred by the small-pox, and the one-eyed cowkeeper, Akoulka, made up their minds together one day and went and threw themselves at my mother's feet, accusing themselves of certain guilty weaknesses, complaining, with a flood of tears, that the Mossoo had taken advantage of their inexperience, and had effected their ruin. My mother did not look upon such matters in the light of a joke, so she consulted my father upon the subject. An inquiry into the matter was promptly resolved upon. He immediately sent for the rascally Frenchman. He was informed that Monsieur was engaged in giving me my lesson. My father came to my room. At that particular moment Beaupré was lying on the bed, sleeping the sleep of innocence. I was occupied in a very different manner. I ought to mention that a map had been obtained from Moscow, in order that I might be instructed in geography. It hung upon the wall without ever being made use of, and as it was a very large map, and the paper thick and of good quality, I had long been tempted to appropriate it to my own use. I resolved to make it into a kite, and, taking advantage of Beaupré's slumber, I set to work. My father entered the room just at the moment when I was adjusting a tail to the Cape of Good Hope. Seeing me so occupied with geography, my father saluted me with a box on the ear, then stepped towards Beaupré, and waking him very unceremoniously, overwhelmed him with reproaches. In his confusion, Beaupré wanted to rise up from the bed, but he was unable to do so: the unfortunate Frenchman was hopelessly intoxicated. There was only one course to take after so many acts of misdemeanour. My father seized hold of him by the

2

collar, lifted him off the bed, hustled him out of the room, and dismissed him that very same day from his service—to the unspeakable delight of Savelitch. Thus ended my education.

I now lived the life of a spoiled child, frightening the pigeons, and playing at leap-frog with the boys on the estate. I continued to lead this kind of life until I was sixteen years of age. Then came the turning-point in my existence.

One day in autumn, my mother was boiling some honey preserves in the parlour, and I was looking on and licking my lips as the liquid simmered and frothed. My father was sitting near the window, reading the "Court Calendar," which he received every year. This book always had a great effect upon him; he used to read it with especial interest, and the reading of it always stirred his bile in the most astonishing manner. My mother, who was perfectly well acquainted with his whims and peculiarities, always endeavoured to keep this unfortunate book out of the way as much as she possibly could, and, on this account, his eyes would not catch a glimpse of the volume for months together. But when he did happen to find it, he would sit with it in his hands for hours at a stretch.... As I have said, my father was reading the "Court Calendar," every now and then shrugging his shoulders, and muttering to himself: "Lieutenant-General!... He used to be a sergeant in my company!... Knight of both Russian Orders!... How long is it since we——"

At last my father flung the "Calendar" down upon the sofa, and sank into a reverie—a proceeding that was always of evil augury.

Suddenly he turned to my mother:

"Avdotia Vassilevna,[3] how old is Petrousha?"[4]

"He is getting on for seventeen," replied my mother: "Petrousha was born in the same year that aunt Nastasia Gerasimovna[5] lost her eye, and——"

"Very well," said my father, interrupting her; "it is time that he entered the service. He has had quite enough of running about the servants' rooms and climbing up to the dovecots."

The thought of soon having to part with me produced such an effect upon my mother, that she let the spoon fall into the saucepan, and the tears streamed down her cheeks. As for myself, it would be difficult to describe the delight that I felt. The thought of the service was associated in my mind with thoughts of freedom and the pleasures of a life in St. Petersburg. I imagined myself an officer in the Guards, that being, in my opinion, the summit of human felicity.

---

[3] Avdotia, daughter of Basil.
[4] Diminutive of Peter.
[5] Anastasia, daughter of Gerasim.

3

My father loved neither to change his intentions, nor to delay putting them into execution. The day for my departure was fixed. On the evening before, my father informed me that he intended to write to my future chief, and asked for pens and paper.

"Do not forget, Andrei Petrovitch,"[6] said my mother, "to send my salutations to Prince B——, and say that I hope he will take our Petrousha under his protection."

"What nonsense!" exclaimed my father, frowning. "Why should I write to Prince B——"

"Why, you said just now that you wanted to write to Petrousha's chief."

"Well, and what then?"

"Why, Prince B—— is Petrousha's chief. You know Petrousha is enrolled in the Semenovsky Regiment."

"Enrolled! What care I whether he is enrolled or not? Petrousha is not going to St. Petersburg. What would he learn by serving in St. Petersburg? To squander money and indulge in habits of dissipation. No, let him enter a regiment of the Line; let him learn to carry knapsack and belt, to smell powder, to become a soldier, and not an idler in the Guards. Where is his passport? Bring it here."

My mother went to get my passport, which she preserved in a small box along with the shirt in which I was christened, and delivered it to my father with a trembling hand. My father read it through very attentively, placed it in front of him upon the table, and commenced to write his letter.

I was tortured with curiosity. Where was I to be sent to, if I was not going to St. Petersburg? I kept my eyes steadfastly fixed upon the pen, which moved slowly over the paper. At last he finished the letter, enclosed it in a cover along with my passport, took off his spectacles, and, calling me to him, said:

"Here is a letter for Andrei Karlovitch R——, my old comrade and friend. You are going to Orenburg to serve under his command."

All my brilliant hopes were thus brought to the ground! Instead of a life of gaiety in St. Petersburg, there awaited me a tedious existence in a dreary and distant country. The service, which I had thought of with such rapture but a moment before, now presented itself to my eyes in the light of a great misfortune. But there was no help for it, and arguing the matter would have been of no avail.

---

[6] The Russians usually address each other by their Christian name and that of their father. Thus Andrei Petrovitch means simply Andrew, son of Peter.

Early the next morning a travelling carriage drew up before the door; my portmanteau was placed in it, as well as a small chest containing a tea-service and a tied-up cloth full of rolls and pies—the last tokens of home indulgence. My parents gave me their blessing. My father said to me:

"Good-bye, Peter! Serve faithfully whom you have sworn to serve; obey your superior officers; do not run after their favours; be not too eager in volunteering for service, but never shirk a duty when you are selected for it; and remember the proverb: 'Take care of your coat while it is new, and of your honour while it is young.'"

My mother, with tears in her eyes, enjoined me to take care of my health, at the same time impressing upon Savelitch to look well after the child. A cloak made of hare-skin was then put over my shoulders, and over that another made of fox-skin. I seated myself in the carriage with Savelitch, and started off on my journey, weeping bitterly.

That same night I arrived at Simbirsk, where I was compelled to remain for the space of twenty-four hours, to enable Savelitch to purchase several necessary articles which he had been commissioned to procure. I stopped at an inn. In the morning Savelitch sallied out to the shops. Tired of looking out of the window into a dirty alley, I began to wander about the rooms of the inn. As I entered the billiard-room, my eyes caught sight of a tall gentleman of about thirty-five years of age, with long, black moustaches; he was dressed in a morning-gown, and had a cue in his hand and a pipe between his teeth. He was playing with the marker, who drank a glass of brandy when he scored, but crept on all-fours beneath the table when he failed. I stopped to look at the game. The longer it continued, the more frequent became the crawling on all-fours, until at last the marker crept beneath the table and remained there.

The gentleman uttered a few strong expressions over him, as a sort of funeral oration, and then invited me to play a game with him. I declined, on the score that I did not know how to play. This evidently seemed very strange to him, and he looked at me with an air of commiseration. However, we soon fell into conversation. I learned that his name was Ivan Ivanovitch Zourin; that he was a captain in a Hussar regiment; that he was then stopping in Simbirsk, waiting to receive some recruits, and that he was staying at the same inn as myself.

Zourin invited me to dine with him, in military fashion, upon whatever Heaven should be pleased to set before us. I accepted his invitation with pleasure. We sat down to table. Zourin drank a great deal, and pressed me to do the same, saying that it was necessary for me to get accustomed to the ways of the service. He related to me several military anecdotes, which convulsed me with laughter, and when we rose from the table we had become intimate friends Then he offered to teach me how to play at billiards.

"It is an indispensable game for soldiers like us," said he. "When on the march, for instance, you arrive at some insignificant village, what can you do to occupy the time? You cannot always be thrashing the Jews. You involuntarily make your way to the inn to play at billiards, and to do that, you must know how to play."

I was completely convinced, and I commenced to learn the game with great assiduity. Zourin encouraged me with loud-voiced praise, being astonished at my rapid progress; and after a few lessons he proposed that we should play for money, for the smallest sums possible, not for the sake of gain, but merely for the sake of not playing for nothing, which, according to his opinion, was an exceedingly bad habit.

I agreed to his proposal, and Zourin ordered a supply of punch, which he persuaded me to partake of, saying that it was necessary to become accustomed to it in the service; for what would the service be without punch! I followed his advice. In the meantime we continued our game. The more frequently I had recourse to the punch, the more emboldened I became. The balls kept continually flying in the wrong direction; I grew angry, abused the marker—who counted the points, Heaven only knows how,—increased the stakes from time to time—in a word, I behaved like a boy just out of leading-strings. In the meanwhile the time had passed away without my having observed it. Zourin glanced at the clock, laid down his cue, and informed me that I had lost a hundred roubles.[7] I was considerably confounded by this piece of information. My money was in the hands of Savelitch. I began to make some excuses. Zourin interrupted me:

"Pray, do not be uneasy. I can wait; and now let us go to Arinoushka."[8]

What more shall I add? I finished the day as foolishly as I had commenced it. We took supper with Arinoushka. Zourin kept continually filling my glass, observing as he did so, that it was necessary to become accustomed to it in the service. When I rose from the table, I was scarcely able to stand on my legs; at midnight, Zourin conducted me back to the inn.

Savelitch came to the doorstep to meet us. He uttered a groan

---

[7] The rouble, at that time, was worth about three shillings and four-pence.
[8] Diminutive of Arina.

on perceiving the indubitable signs of my zeal for the service.

"What has happened to you?" he said, in a voice of lamentation. "Where have you been drinking so? Oh, Lord! never did such a misfortune happen before!"

"Hold your tongue, you old greybeard!" I replied, in an unsteady voice; "you are certainly drunk. Go to sleep ... and put me to bed."

The next morning I awoke with a violent headache, and with a confused recollection of the events of the day before. My reflections were interrupted by Savelitch, who brought me a cup of tea.

"You are beginning your games early, Peter Andreitch,"[9] he said, shaking his head. "And whom do you take after? As far as I know, neither your father nor grandfather were ever drunkards; as for your mother, I will say nothing; she has never drunk anything except kvas[10] since the day she was born. And who is to blame for all this? Why, that cursed Mossoo, who was ever running to Antipevna with: 'Madame, je vous prie, vodka.'[11] You see what a pretty pass your je vous prie has brought you to! There's no denying that the son of a dog taught you some nice things! It was worth while to hire such a heathen for your tutor, as if our master had not enough of his own people!"

I felt ashamed of myself. I turned my back to him, and said:

"Go away, Savelitch; I do not want any tea."

But it was a difficult matter to quiet Savelitch when he had set his mind upon preaching a sermon.

"You see now, Peter Andreitch, what it is to get drunk. You have a headache, and you do not want to eat or drink anything. A man who gets drunk is good for nothing. Have some cucumber pickle with honey; or perhaps half a glass of fruit wine would be better still. What do you say?"

At that moment a boy entered the room and handed me a note from Zourin. I opened it and read the following lines:

"DEAR PETER ANDREIVITCH,

"Be so good as to send me, by my boy, the hundred roubles which you lost to me yesterday. I am in great need of money.

"Yours faithfully,

"IVAN ZOURIN."

---

[9] Peter, son of Andrew.
[10] A sour but refreshing drink made from rye-meal and malt.
[11] Brandy.

7

There was no help for it. I assumed an air of indifference, and turning to Savelitch, who was my treasurer and caretaker in one, I ordered him to give the boy a hundred roubles.

"What? why?" asked the astonished Savelitch.

"I owe them to him," I replied, with the greatest possible coolness.

"Owe!" ejaculated Savelitch, becoming more and more astonished. "When did you get into his debt? It looks a very suspicious piece of business. You may do as you like, my lord, but I shall not give the money."

I thought that, if in this decisive moment I did not gain the upper hand of the obstinate old man, it would be difficult for me to liberate myself from his tutelage later on; so, looking haughtily at him, I said:

"I am your master, and you are my servant. The money is mine. I played and lost it because I chose to do so; and I advise you not to oppose my wishes, but to do what you are ordered."

Savelitch was so astounded at my words, that he clasped his hands and stood as if petrified.

"What are you standing there like that for?" I exclaimed angrily.

Savelitch began to weep.

"Father, Peter Andreitch," he stammered in a quivering voice, "do not break my heart with grief. You are the light of my life, so listen to me—to an old man: write to this robber, and tell him that you were only joking, that we have not got so much money. A hundred roubles! Merciful Heaven! Tell him that your parents have strictly forbidden you to play for anything except nuts——"

"That will do; let me have no more of your chatter! Give me the money, or I will put you out by the neck!"

Savelitch looked at me with deep sadness, and went for the money. I pitied the poor old man; but I wanted to assert my independence and to show that I was no longer a child.

The money was paid to Zourin. Savelitch hastened to get me away from the accursed inn. He made his appearance with the information that the horses were ready. With an uneasy conscience, and a silent feeling of remorse, I left Simbirsk without taking leave of my teacher of billiards, and without thinking that I should ever see him again.

CHAPTER II

THE GUIDE

My reflections during the journey were not very agreeable. My loss, according to the value of money at that time, was of no little importance. I could not but confess, within my own mind, that my behaviour at the Simbirsk inn was very stupid, and I felt guilty in the presence of Savelitch.' All this tormented me. The old man sat in gloomy silence upon the seat of the vehicle, with his face averted from me, and every now and then giving vent to a sigh. I wanted at all hazards to become reconciled to him, but I did not know how to begin. At last I said to him:

"Come, come, Savelitch, that will do, let us be friends. I was to blame; I see myself that I was in the wrong. I acted very foolishly yesterday, and I offended you without cause. I promise that I will act more wisely for the future, and listen to your advice. Come, don't be angry, but let us be friends again."

"Ah! father, Peter Andreitch," he replied, with a deep sigh, "I am angry with myself; I alone am to blame. How could I leave you alone in the inn! But what else could be expected? We are led astray by sin. The thought came into my mind to go and see the clerk's wife, who is my gossip.[12] But so it was: I went to my gossip, and ill-luck came of it. Was there ever such a misfortune! How shall I ever be able to look in the face of my master and mistress? What will they say when they know that their child is a drunkard and a gambler?"

In order to console poor Savelitch, I gave him my word that I would never again spend a single copeck[13] without his consent. He calmed down by degrees, although every now and again he still continued muttering, with a shake of the head, "A hundred roubles! It's no laughing matter!"

I was nearing the place of my destination. On every side of me extended a dreary-looking plain, intersected by hills and ravines. Everything was covered with snow. The sun was setting. The kibitka[14] was proceeding along the narrow road, or, to speak more precisely, along the track made by the peasants' sledges Suddenly

---

[12] Savelitch uses the word here in its old meaning of fellow-sponsor.
[13] A tenth of a penny.
[14] A kind of rough travelling cart.

9

the driver began gazing intently about him, and at last, taking off his cap, he turned to me and said:

"My lord, will you not give orders to turn back?"

"Why?"

"The weather does not look very promising: the wind is beginning to rise; see how it whirls the freshly fallen snow along."

"What does that matter?"

"And do you see that yonder?"

And the driver pointed with his whip towards the east.

"I see nothing, except the white steppe and the clear sky."

"There—away in the distance: that cloud."

I perceived, indeed, on the edge of the horizon, a white cloud, which I had taken at first for a distant hill. The driver explained to me that this small cloud presaged a snowstorm.

I had heard of the snowstorms of that part of the country, and I knew that whole trains of waggons were frequently buried in the drifts. Savelitch was of the same opinion as the driver, and advised that we should return. But the wind did not seem to me to be very strong: I hoped to be able to reach the next station in good time, and I gave orders to drive on faster.

The driver urged on the horses at a gallop, but he still continued to gaze towards the east. The horses entered into their work with a will. In the meantime the wind had gradually increased in violence. The little cloud had changed into a large, white, nebulous mass, which rose heavily, and gradually began to extend over the whole sky. A fine snow began to fall, and then all at once this gave place to large heavy flakes. The wind roared; the snowstorm had burst upon us. In one moment the dark sky became confounded with the sea of snow; everything had disappeared.

"Well, my lord," cried the driver, "this is a misfortune; it is a regular snowstorm!"

I looked out of the kibitka; all was storm and darkness. The wind blew with such terrific violence that it seemed as if it were endowed with life. Savelitch and I were covered with snow: the horses ploughed their way onward at a walking pace, and soon came to a standstill.

"Why don't you go on?" I called out impatiently to the driver.

"But where am I to drive to?" he replied, jumping down from his seat; "I haven't the slightest idea as to where we are; there is no road, and it is dark all round."

I began to scold him. Savelitch took his part.

"You ought to have taken his advice," he said angrily. "You should have returned to the posting-house; you could have had some tea and could have slept there till the morning; the storm would have blown over by that time, and then you could have proceeded on your journey. And why such haste? It would be all very well if we were going to a wedding!"

Savelitch was right. But what was to be done? The snow still continued to fall. A drift began to form around the kibitka. The horses stood with dejected heads, and every now and then a shudder shook their frames. The driver kept walking round them, and, being unable to do anything else, busied himself with adjusting the harness. Savelitch grumbled. I looked round on every side, hoping to discover some sign of a house or a road, but I could distinguish nothing except the confused whirling snowdrifts Suddenly I caught sight of something black.

"Hillo! driver," I cried; "look! what is that black object yonder?"

The driver looked carefully in the direction indicated.

"God knows, my lord," said he, seating himself in his place again; "it is neither a sledge nor a tree, and it seems to move. It must be either a man or a wolf."

I ordered him to drive towards the unknown object, which was gradually drawing nearer to us. In about two minutes we came up to it and discovered it to be a man.

"Hi! my good man," cried the driver to him; "say, do you know where the road is?"

"The road is here; I am standing on a firm track," replied the wayfarer. "But what of it?"

"Listen, peasant," said I to him; "do you know this country? Can you lead me to a place where I can obtain a night's lodging?"

"I know the country very well," replied the peasant. "Heaven be thanked, I have crossed it and re-crossed it in every direction. But you see what sort of weather it is: it would be very easy to miss the road. You had much better stay here and wait; perhaps the storm will blow over, and the sky become clear, then we shall be able to find the road by the help of the stars."

His cool indifference encouraged me. I had already resolved to abandon myself to the will of God and to pass the night upon the steppe, when suddenly the peasant mounted to the seat of our vehicle and said to the driver:

"Thank Heaven, there is a house not far off; turn to the right and go straight on."

"Why should I go to the right?" asked the driver in a dissatisfied tone. "Where do you see a road? I am not the owner of these horses that I should use the whip without mercy."

The driver seemed to me to be in the right.

"In truth," said I, "why do you think that there is a house not far off?"

11

"Because the wind blows from that direction," replied the wayfarer, "and I can smell smoke; that is a sign that there is a village close at hand."

His sagacity and nicety of smell astonished me. I ordered the driver to go on. The horses moved heavily through the deep snow. The kibitka advanced very slowly, at one moment mounting to the summit of a ridge, at another sinking into a deep hollow, now rolling to one side, and now to the other. It was very much like being in a ship on a stormy sea. Savelitch sighed and groaned, and continually jostled against me. I let down the cover of the kibitka, wrapped myself up in my cloak, and fell into a slumber, lulled by the music of the storm, and rocked by the motion of the vehicle.

I had a dream which I shall never forget, and in which I still see something prophetic when I compare it with the strange events of my life. The reader will excuse me for mentioning the matter, for probably he knows from experience that man is naturally given to superstition in spite of the great contempt entertained for it.

I was in that condition of mind when reality and imagination become confused in the vague sensations attending the first stage of drowsiness. It seemed to me that the storm still continued, and that we were still wandering about the wilderness of snow.... All at once I caught sight of a gate, and we entered the courtyard of our mansion. My first thought was a fear that my father would be angry with me for my involuntary return to the paternal roof, and would regard it as an act of intentional disobedience. With a feeling of uneasiness I sprang out of the kibitka, and saw my mother coming down the steps to meet me, with a look of deep affliction upon her face.

"Hush!" she said to me; "your father is on the point of death, and wishes to take leave of you."

Struck with awe, I followed her into the bedroom. I looked about me; the room was dimly lighted, and round the bed stood several persons with sorrow-stricken countenances. I approached very gently; my mother raised the curtain and said:

"Andrei Petrovitch, Petrousha has arrived; he has returned because he heard of your illness; give him your blessing."

I knelt down and fixed my eyes upon the face of the sick man. But what did I see?... Instead of my father, I saw lying in the bed a black-bearded peasant, who looked at me with an expression of gaiety upon his countenance. Greatly perplexed, I turned round to my mother and said to her:

"What does all this mean? This is not my father. Why should I ask this peasant for his blessing?"

"It is all the same, Petrousha," replied my mother; "he is your stepfather; kiss his hand and let him bless you." I would not consent

12

to it. Then the peasant sprang out of bed, grasped the axe which hung at his back,[15] and commenced flourishing it about on every side. I wanted to run away, but I could not; the room began to get filled with dead bodies; I kept stumbling against them, and my feet continually slipped in pools of blood. The dreadful peasant called out to me in a gentle voice, saying:

"Do not be afraid; come and receive my blessing." Terror and doubt took possession of me.... At that moment I awoke; the horses had come to a standstill. Savelitch took hold of my hand, saying:

"Get out, my lord, we have arrived."

"Where are we?" I asked, rubbing my eyes.

"At a place of refuge. God came to our help and conducted us straight to the fence of the house. Get out as quickly as you can, my lord, and warm yourself."

I stepped out of the kibitka. The storm still raged, although with less violence than at first. It was as dark as if we were totally blind. The host met us at the door, holding a lantern under the skirt of his coat, and conducted me into a room, small, but tolerably clean. It was lit up by a pine torch. On the wall hung a long rifle, and a tall Cossack cap.

The host, a Yaikian Cossack by birth, was a peasant of about sixty years of age, still hale and strong. Savelitch brought in the tea-chest, and asked for a fire in order to prepare some tea, which I seemed to need at that moment more than at any other time in my life. The host hastened to attend to the matter.

"Where is the guide?" I said to Savelitch.

"Here, your Excellency," replied a voice from above. I glanced up at the loft, and saw a black beard and two sparkling eyes.

"Well, friend, are you cold?"

"How could I be otherwise than cold in only a thin tunic! I had a fur coat, but why should I hide my fault?—I pawned it yesterday with a brandy-seller; the cold did not seem to be so severe."

At that moment the host entered with a smoking tea-urn; I offered our guide a cup of tea; the peasant came down from the loft. His exterior seemed to me somewhat remarkable. He was about forty years of age, of middle height, thin and broad-shouldered. In his black beard streaks of grey were beginning to make their appearance; his large, lively black eyes were incessantly on the roll. His face had something rather agreeable about it, although an expression of vindictiveness could also be detected upon it. His hair was cut close round his head. He was dressed in a ragged tunic and

---

[15] The Russian peasant usually carries his axe behind him.

13

Tartar trousers. I gave him a cup of tea; he tasted it, and made a wry face.

"Your Excellency," said he, "be so good as to order a glass of wine for me; tea is not the drink for us Cossacks."

I willingly complied with his request. The landlord brought a square bottle and a glass from a cupboard, went up to him, and, looking into his face, said:

"Oh! you are again in our neighbourhood! Where have you come from?"

My guide winked significantly, and made reply:

"Flying in the garden, pecking hempseed; the old woman threw a stone, but it missed its aim. And how is it with—you?"

"How is it with us?" replied the landlord, continuing the allegorical conversation, "they were beginning to ring the vespers, but the pope's wife would not allow it: the pope is on a visit, and the devils are in the glebe."

"Hold your tongue, uncle," replied my rover; "when there is rain, there will be mushrooms; and when there are mushrooms, there will be a pannier; but now" (and here he winked again) "put your axe behind your back; the ranger is going about. Your Excellency, I drink to your health!"

With these words he took hold of the glass, made the sign of the cross, and drank off the liquor in one draught; then, bowing to me, he returned to the loft.

At that time I could not understand anything of this thieves' slang, but afterwards I understood that it referred to the Yaikian army, which had only just then been reduced to submission after the revolt of 1772. Savelitch listened with a look of great dissatisfaction. He glanced very suspiciously, first at the landlord, then at the guide. The inn, or umet, as it was called in those parts, was situated in the middle of the steppe, far from every habitation or village, and had very much the appearance of a rendezvous for thieves. But there was no help for it. We could not think of continuing our journey. The uneasiness of Savelitch afforded me very great amusement. In the meantime I made all necessary arrangements for passing the night comfortably, and then stretched myself upon a bench. Savelitch resolved to avail himself of the stove;[16] our host lay down upon the floor. Soon all in the house were snoring, and I fell into a sleep as sound as that of the grave.

When I awoke on the following morning, at a somewhat late hour, I perceived that the storm was over. The sun was shining. The snow lay like a dazzling shroud over the boundless steppe. The

---

[16] The usual sleeping place of the Russian peasant.

horses were harnessed. I paid the reckoning to the host, the sum asked of us being so very moderate that even Savelitch did not dispute the matter and commence to haggle about the payment as was his usual custom; moreover, his suspicions of the previous evening had completely vanished from his mind. I called for our guide, thanked him for the assistance he had rendered us, and ordered Savelitch to give him half a rouble for brandy.

Savelitch frowned.

"Half a rouble for brandy?" said he; "why so? Because you were pleased to bring him with you to this inn? With your leave, my lord, but we have not too many half roubles to spare. If we give money for brandy to everybody we have to deal with, we shall very soon have to starve ourselves."

I could not argue with Savelitch. According to my own promise, the disposal of my money was to be left entirely to his discretion. But I felt rather vexed that I was not able to show my gratitude to a man who, if he had not rescued me from certain destruction, had at least delivered me from a very disagreeable position.

"Well," said I, coldly, "if you will not give him half a rouble, give him something out of my wardrobe; he is too thinly clad. Give him my hare-skin pelisse."

"In the name of Heaven, father, Peter Andreitch!" said Savelitch, "why give him your pelisse? The dog will sell it for drink at the first tavern that he comes to."

"It is no business of yours, old man," said my stroller, "whether I sell it for drink or not. His Excellency is pleased to give me a cloak from off his own shoulders; it is his lordly will, and it is your duty, as servant, to obey, and not to dispute."

"Have you no fear of God, you robber!" said Savelitch, in an angry tone. "You see that the child has not yet reached the age of discretion, and yet you are only too glad to take advantage of his good-nature, and rob him. What do you want with my master's pelisse? You will not be able to stretch it across your accursed shoulders."

"I beg of you not to show off your wit," I said to my guardian. "Bring the pelisse hither immediately!"

"Gracious Lord!" groaned Savelitch, "the pelisse is almost brand-new! If it were to anybody deserving of it, it would be different, but to give it to a ragged drunkard!"

However, the pelisse was brought. The peasant instantly commenced to try it on. And, indeed, the garment, which I had grown out of, and which was rather tight for me, was a great deal too small for him. But he contrived to get it on somehow, though not without bursting the seams in the effort. Savelitch very nearly

15

gave vent to a groan when he heard the stitches giving way. The stroller was exceedingly pleased with my present. He conducted me to the kibitka, and said, with a low bow:

"Many thanks, your Excellency! May God reward you for your virtue. I shall never forget your kindness."

He went his way, and I set out again on my journey, without paying any attention to Savelitch, and I soon forgot all about the storm of the previous day, the guide, and my pelisse.

On arriving at Orenburg, I immediately presented myself to the general. He was a tall man, but somewhat bent with age. His long hair was perfectly white. His old faded uniform recalled to mind the warrior of the time of the Empress Anne, and he spoke with a strong German accent.

I gave him the letter from my father. On hearing the name, he glanced at me quickly.

"Mein Gott!" said he, "it does not seem so very long ago since Andrei Petrovitch was your age, and now what a fine young fellow he has got for a son! Ach! time, time!"

He opened the letter and began to read it half aloud, making his own observations upon it in the course of his reading.

"'Esteemed Sir, Ivan Karlovitch, I hope that your Excellency'—Why all this ceremony? Pshaw! Isn't he ashamed of himself? To be sure, discipline before everything, but is that the way to write to an old comrade?—'Your Excellency has not forgotten'—Hm!—'and—when—with the late Field Marshal Mün—in the campaign—also Caroline'—Ha, brother! he still remembers our old pranks, then?—'Now to business.—I send you my young hopeful'—Hm!—'Hold him with hedgehog mittens.'—What are hedgehog mittens? That must be a Russian proverb.—What does 'hold him with hedgehog mittens' mean?" he repeated, turning to me.

"It means," I replied, looking as innocent as I possibly could, "to treat a person kindly, not to be too severe, and to allow as much liberty as possible."

"Hm! I understand—'And do not give him too much liberty.'—No, it is evident that 'hedgehog mittens' does not mean that.—'Enclosed you will find his passport.'—Where is it then? Ah! here it is.—'Enrol him in the Semenovsky Regiment.'—Very well, very well, everything shall be attended to.—'Allow me without ceremony to embrace you as an old comrade and friend.'—Ah! at last he has got to it.—'Etcetera, etcetera.'—'Well, my little father,' said he, finishing the reading of the letter, and putting my passport on one side, 'everything shall be arranged; you shall be an officer in the Regiment, and so that you may lose no time, start to-morrow for the fortress of Bailogorsk, where you will be under the command of

Captain Mironoff, a good and honest man. There you will learn real service, and be taught what real discipline is. Orenburg is not the place for you, there is nothing for you to do there; amusements are injurious to a young man. Favour me with your company at dinner to-day."

"This is getting worse and worse," I thought to myself. "Of what use will it be to me to have been a sergeant in the Guards almost from my mother's womb! Whither has it led me? To the Regiment, and to a dreary fortress on the borders of the Kirghis-Kaisaks steppes!"

I dined with Andrei Karlovitch, in company with his old adjutant. A strict German economy ruled his table, and I believe that the fear of being obliged to entertain an additional guest now and again was partly the cause of my being so promptly banished to the garrison.

The next day I took leave of the general, and set out for the place of my destination.

CHAPTER III

THE FORTRESS

The fortress of Bailogorsk was situated about forty versts[17] from Orenburg. The road to it led along the steep bank of the Yaik.[18] The river was not yet frozen, and its leaden-coloured waves had a dark and melancholy aspect as they rose and fell between the dreary banks covered with the white snow. Beyond it stretched the Kirghis steppes. I sank into reflections, most of them of a gloomy nature. Garrison life had little attraction for me. I endeavoured to picture to myself Captain Mironoff, my future chief; and I imagined him to be a severe, ill-tempered old man, knowing nothing except what was connected with his duty, and ready to arrest me and put me on bread and water for the merest trifle.

In the meantime it began to grow dark, and we quickened our pace.

---

[17] A verst is two-thirds of an English mile.
[18] A tributary of the Oural.

17

"Is it far to the fortress?" I inquired of our driver.

"Not far," he replied, "you can see it yonder."

I looked around on every side, expecting to see formidable bastions, towers, and ramparts, but I could see nothing except a small village surrounded by a wooden palisade. On one side stood three or four hayricks, half covered with snow; on the other a crooked looking windmill, with its bark sails hanging idly down.

"But where is the fortress?" I asked in astonishment.

"There it is," replied the driver, pointing to the village, and, as he spoke, we entered into it.

At the gate I saw an old cast-iron gun; the streets were narrow and crooked; the cottages small, and for the most part covered with thatch. I expressed a wish to be taken to the Commandant, and, in about a minute, the kibitka stopped in front of a small wooden house, built on an eminence, and situated near the church, which was likewise of wood.

Nobody came out to meet me. I made my way to the entrance and then proceeded to the ante-room. An old pensioner, seated at a table, was engaged in sewing a blue patch on the elbow of a green uniform coat. I ordered him to announce me.

"Go inside, little father," replied the pensioner; "our people are at home."

I entered into a very clean room, furnished in the old-fashioned style. In one corner stood a cupboard containing earthenware utensils; on the wall hung an officers diploma, framed and glazed, and around it were arranged a few rude wood engravings, representing the "Capture of Kustrin and Otchakoff,"[19] the "Choice of the Bride," and the "Burial of the Cat." At the window sat an old woman in a jerkin, and wearing a handkerchief round her head. She was unwinding thread which a one-eyed old man, dressed in an officer's uniform, held in his outstretched hands.

"What is your pleasure, little father?" she asked, continuing her occupation.

I replied that I had come to enter the service, and, in accordance with the regulations, to notify my arrival to the Captain in command. And with these words I turned towards the one-eyed old man, whom I supposed to be the Commandant; but the old lady interrupted me in the speech which I had so carefully prepared beforehand.

---

[19] Taken from the Turks in 1737 by the Russian troops under Count Münich.

18

"Ivan Kouzmitch[20] is not at home," said she; "he has gone to visit Father Gerasim. But it is all the same, I am his wife."

She summoned a maid-servant and told her to call an orderly officer. The little old man looked at me out of his one eye with much curiosity.

"May I ask," said he, "in what regiment you have deigned to serve?"

I satisfied his curiosity.

"And may I ask," he continued, "why you have exchanged the Guards for this garrison?"

I replied that such was the wish of the authorities.

"Probably for conduct unbecoming an officer of the Guards?" continued the indefatigable interrogator.

"A truce to your foolish chatter," said the Captain's wife to him; "you see that the young man is tired after his journey. He has something else to do than to listen to your nonsense." Then turning to me she added: "You are not the first, and you will not be the last. It is a hard life here, but you will soon get to like it. It is five years ago since Shvabrin Alexei Ivanitch was sent here to us for a murder. Heaven knows what it was that caused him to go wrong. You see, he went out of the town with a lieutenant; they had taken their swords with them, and they began to thrust at one another, and Alexei Ivanitch stabbed the lieutenant, and all before two witnesses! But what would you? Man is not master of sin."

At this moment the orderly officer, a young and well-built Cossack, entered the room.

"Maximitch," said the Captain's wife to him, "conduct this officer to his quarters, and see that everything is attended to."

"I obey, Vassilissa Egorovna," replied the orderly. "Is not his Excellency to lodge with Ivan Polejaeff?"

"What a booby you are, Maximitch!" said the Captain's wife. "Polejaeff's house is crowded already; besides, he is my gossip, and remembers that we are his superiors. Take the officer—what is your name, little father?"[21]

"Peter Andreitch."

"Take Peter Andreitch to Simon Kouzoff. The rascal allowed his horse to get in my kitchen-garden.... And is everything right, Maximitch?"

"Everything, thank God!" replied the Cossack; "only Corporal

---

[20] Ivan (John), son of Kouzma.
[21] Little father (batyushka). A familiar idiom peculiar to the Russian language.

19

Prokhoroff has been having a squabble at the bath with Ustinia Pegoulina, on account of a can of hot water."

"Ivan Ignatitch," said the Captain's wife to the one-eyed old man, "decide between Prokhoroff and Ustinia as to who is right and who is wrong, and then punish both. Now, Maximitch, go, and God be with you. Peter Andreitch, Maximitch will conduct you to your quarters."

I bowed and took my departure. The orderly conducted me to a hut, situated on the steep bank of the river, at the extreme end of the fortress. One half of the hut was occupied by the family of Simon Kouzoff; the other was given up to me. It consisted of one room, of tolerable cleanliness, and was divided into two by a partition.

Savelitch began to set the room in order, and I looked out of the narrow window. Before me stretched a gloomy steppe. On one side stood a few huts, and two or three fowls were wandering about the street. An old woman, standing on a doorstep with a trough in her hands, was calling some pigs, which answered her with friendly grunts. And this was the place in which I was condemned to spend my youth! Grief took possession of me; I came, away from the window and lay down to sleep without eating any supper, in spite of the exhortations of Savelitch, who kept repeating in a tone of distress:

"Lord of heaven! he will eat nothing! What will my mistress say if the child falls ill?"—

The next morning I had scarcely begun to dress when the door opened, and a young officer, somewhat short in stature, with a swarthy and rather ill-looking countenance, though distinguished by extraordinary vivacity, entered the room.

"Pardon me," he said to me in French, "for coming without ceremony to make your acquaintance. I heard yesterday of your arrival, and the desire to see at last a fresh human face took such possession of me, that I could not wait any longer. You will understand this when you have lived here a little while."

I conjectured that this was the officer who had been dismissed from the Guards on account of the duel. We soon became acquainted. Shvabrin was by no means a fool. His conversation was witty and entertaining. With great liveliness he described to me the family of the Commandant, his society, and the place to which fate had conducted me. I was laughing with all my heart when the old soldier who had been mending his uniform in the Commandant's ante-chamber, came to me, and, in the name of Vassilissa Egorovna, invited me to dinner. Shvabrin declared that he would go with me.

On approaching the Commandant's house, we perceived on the square about twenty old soldiers, with long pig-tails and three-cornered hats. They were standing to the front. Before them stood the Commandant, a tall and sprightly old man, in a nightcap and flannel dressing-gown. Observing us, he came forward towards us, said a few kind words to me, and then went on again with the drilling of his men. We were going to stop to watch the evolutions, but he requested us to go to Vassilissa Egorovna, promising to join us in a little while. "Here," he added, "there is nothing for you to see."

Vassilissa Egorovna received us with unfeigned gladness and simplicity, and treated me as if she had known me all my life. The pensioner and Palashka spread the tablecloth.

"What is detaining my Ivan Kouzmitch so long to-day?" said the Commandant's wife. "Palashka, go and call your master to dinner.... But where is Masha?"[22]

At that moment there entered the room a young girl of about eighteen years of age, with a round, rosy face, and light brown hair, brushed smoothly back behind her ears, which were tinged with a deep blush. She did not produce a very favourable impression upon me at the first glance. I regarded her with prejudiced eyes. Shvabrin had described Masha, the Captain's daughter, as a perfect idiot. Maria Ivanovna[23] sat down in a corner and began to sew. Meanwhile, the cabbage-soup was brought in. Vassilissa Egorovna, not seeing her husband, sent Palashka after him a second time.

"Tell your master that the guests are waiting, and that the soup is getting cold. Thank Heaven, the drill will not run away! he will have plenty of time to shout himself hoarse."

The Captain soon made his appearance, accompanied by the little one-eyed old man.

"What is the meaning of this, little father?" said his wife to him; "the dinner has been ready a long time, and you would not come."

"Why, you see, Vassilissa Egorovna," said Ivan Kouzmitch, "I was occupied with my duties; I was teaching my little soldiers."

"Nonsense!" replied his wife; "it is all talk about your teaching the soldiers. The service does not suit them, and you yourself don't understand anything about it. It would be better for you to stay at home and pray to God. My dear guests, pray take your places at the table."

We sat down to dine. Vassilissa Egorovna was not silent for a single moment, and she overwhelmed me with questions. Who were my parents? Were they living? Where did they live? How much were

---

[22] Diminutive of Maria or Mary.
[23] Mary, daughter of Ivan (i.e., Masha).

they worth? On hearing that my father owned three hundred souls:[24]

"Really now!" she exclaimed; "well, there are some rich people in the world! As for us, my little father, we have only our one servant-girl, Palashka; but, thank God, we manage to get along well enough! There is only one thing that we are troubled about. Masha is an eligible girl, but what has she got for a marriage portion? A clean comb, a hand-broom, and three copecks—Heaven have pity upon her!—to pay for a bath. If she can find a good man, all very well; if not, she will have to be an old maid."

I glanced at Maria Ivanovna; she was blushing all over, and tears were even falling into her plate. I began to feel pity for her, and I hastened to change the conversation.

"I have heard," said I, as appropriately as I could, "that the Bashkirs are assembling to make an attack upon your fortress."

"And from whom did you hear that, my little father?" asked Ivan Kouzmitch.

"They told me so in Orenburg," I replied.

"All nonsense!" said the Commandant; "we have heard nothing about them for a long time. The Bashkirs are a timid lot, and the Kirghises have learnt a lesson. Don't be alarmed, they will not attack us; but if they should venture to do so, we will teach them such a lesson that they will not make another move for the next ten years."

"And are you not afraid," continued I, turning to the Captain's wife, "to remain in a fortress exposed to so many dangers?"

"Habit, my little father," she replied. "It is twenty years ago since they transferred us from the regiment to this place, and you cannot imagine how these accursed heathens used to terrify me. If I caught a glimpse of their hairy caps now and then, or if I heard their yells, will you believe it, my father, my heart would leap almost into my mouth. But now I am so accustomed to it that I would not move out of my place if anyone came to tell me that the villains were prowling round the fortress."

"Vassilissa Egorovna is a very courageous lady," observed Shvabrin earnestly; "Ivan Kouzmitch can bear witness to that."

"Yes, I believe you," said Ivan Kouzmitch; "the wife is not one of the timid ones."

"And Maria Ivanovna," I asked, "is she as brave as you?"

"Masha brave?" replied her mother. "No, Masha is a coward. Up to the present time she has never been able to hear the report of a gun without trembling all over. Two years ago, when Ivan Kouzmitch took the idea into his head to fire off our cannon on my

---

[24] The technical name for serfs.

22

name-day,[25] my little dove was so frightened that she nearly died through terror. Since then we have never fired off the accursed cannon."

We rose from the table. The Captain and his wife went to indulge in a nap, and I accompanied Shvabrin to his quarters, where I spent the whole evening.

CHAPTER IV

THE DUEL

Several weeks passed by, and my life in the fortress of Bailogorsk became not only endurable, but even agreeable. In the house of the Commandant I was received as one of the family. Both husband and wife were very worthy persons. Ivan Kouzmitch, who had risen from the ranks, was a simple and unaffected man, but exceedingly honest and good-natured. His wife managed things generally for him, and this was quite in harmony with his easy-going disposition. Vassilissa Egorovna looked after the business of the service as well as her own domestic affairs, and ruled the fortress precisely as she did her own house. Maria Ivanovna soon ceased to be shy in my presence. We became acquainted. I found her a sensible and feeling girl. In an imperceptible manner I became attached to this good family, even to Ivan Ignatitch, the one-eyed garrison lieutenant, whom Shvabrin accused of being on terms of undue intimacy with Vassilissa Egorovna, an accusation which had not a shadow of probability to give countenance to it; but Shvabrin did not trouble himself about that.

I was promoted to the rank of officer. My duties were not very heavy. In this God-protected fortress there was neither parade, nor drill, nor guard-mounting. The Commandant sometimes instructed the soldiers for his own amusement, but he had not yet got so far as teaching them which was the right-hand side and which the left. Shvabrin had several French books in his possession. I began to read them, and this awakened within me a taste for literature. In the

<hr />

[25] The Russians do not keep the actual day of their birth, but their name-day—that is, the day kept in honour of the saint after whom they are called.

23

morning I read, exercised myself in translating, and sometimes even attempted to compose verses. I dined nearly always at the Commandants, where I generally spent the rest of the day, and where sometimes of an evening came Father Gerasim, with his wife, Akoulina Pamphilovna, the greatest gossip in the whole neighbourhood. It is unnecessary for me to mention that Shvabrin and I saw each other every day, but his conversation began to be more disagreeable the more I saw of him. His continual ridiculing of the Commandant's family, and especially his sarcastic observations concerning Maria Ivanovna, annoyed me exceedingly. There was no other society in the fortress, and I wished for no other.

In spite of the predictions, the Bashkirs did not revolt. Tranquillity reigned around, our fortress. But the peace was suddenly disturbed by civil dissensions.

I have already mentioned that I occupied myself with literature. My essays were tolerable for those days, and Alexander Petrovitch Soumarokoff,[26] some years afterwards, praised them very much. One day I contrived to write a little song with which I was much pleased. It is well-known that, under the appearance of asking advice, authors frequently endeavour to secure a well-disposed listener. And so, writing out my little song, I took it to Shvabrin, who was the only person in the whole fortress who could appreciate a poetical production. After a short preamble, I drew my manuscript out of my pocket, and read to him the following verses:

"I banish thoughts of love, and try
My fair one to forget;
And, to be free again, I fly
From Masha with regret.

"My troubled soul no rest can know,
No peace of mind for me;
For wheresoever I may go,
Those eyes I still shall see.

"Take pity, Masha, on this heart
Oppressed by grief and care;
And let compassion rend apart
The clouds of dark despair."

"What do you think of it?" I asked Shvabrin, expecting that

---

[26] A Russian dramatic poet, once celebrated, but now almost forgotten. His most popular works were two tragedies, "Khoreff," and "Pemetrius the Pretender."

praise which I considered I was justly entitled to. But, to my great disappointment, Shvabrin, who was generally complaisant; declared very peremptorily that the verses were not worth much.

"And why?" I asked, hiding my vexation.

"Because," he replied, "such verses are worthy of my instructor Tredyakovsky,[27] and remind me very much of his love couplets."

Then he took the manuscript from me and began unmercifully to pull to pieces every verse and word, jeering at me in the most sarcastic manner. This was more than I could endure, and snatching my manuscript out of his hand, I told him that I would never show him any more of my compositions. Shvabrin laughed at my threat.

"We shall see," said he, "if you will keep your word. A poet needs a listener, just as Ivan Kouzmitch needs his decanter of brandy before dinner. And who is this Masha to whom you declare your tender passion and your amorous distress? Can it be Maria Ivanovna?"

"That is not your business," replied I, frowning; "it is nothing to do with you who she is. I want neither your opinion nor your conjectures."

"Oho! my vain poet 'and discreet lover!'" continued Shvabrin, irritating me more and more. "But listen to a friend's advice; if you wish to succeed, I advise you not to have recourse to writing verses."

"What do you mean, sir? Please explain yourself."

"With pleasure. I mean that if you wish Masha Mironoff to meet you at dusk, instead of tender verses, you must make her a present of a pair of earrings."

My blood began to boil.

"Why have you such an opinion of her?" I asked, with difficulty restraining my anger.

"Because," replied he, with a fiendish smile, "I know from experience her ways and habits."

"You lie, scoundrel!" I exclaimed with fury. "You lie in the most shameless manner!"

Shvabrin changed colour.

"This shall not be overlooked," said he, pressing my hand. "You shall give me satisfaction." "With pleasure, whenever you like," I replied, delighted beyond measure.

At that moment I was ready to tear him in pieces.

I immediately hastened to Ivan Ignatitch, and found him with a needle in his hand; in obedience to the commands of the Commandant's wife he was stringing mushrooms for drying during the winter.

---

[27] A minor poet of the last century.

"Ah, Peter Andreitch," said he, on seeing me, "you are welcome. May I ask on what business Heaven has brought you here?"

In a few words I explained to him that, having had a quarrel with Shvabrin, I came to ask him—Ivan Ignatitch—to be my second.

Ivan Ignatitch listened to me with great attention, keeping his one eye fixed upon me all the while.

"You wish to say," he said to me, "that you want to kill Shvabrin, and that you would like me to be a witness to it? Is that so, may I ask?

"Exactly so."

"In the name of Heaven, Peter Andreitch, whatever are you thinking of! You have had a quarrel with Shvabrin. What a great misfortune! A quarrel should not be hung round one's neck. He has insulted you, and you have insulted him; he gives you one in the face, and you give him one behind the ear; a second blow from him, another from you—and then each goes his own way; in a little while we bring about a reconciliation.... Is it right to kill one's neighbour, may I ask? And suppose that you do kill him—God be with him! I have no particular love for him. But what if he were to let daylight through you? How about the matter in that case? Who would be the worst off then, may I ask?"

The reasonings of the discreet lieutenant produced no effect upon me; I remained firm in my resolution.

"As you please," said Ivan Ignatitch; "do as you like. But why should I be a witness to it? People fight,—what is there wonderful in that, may I ask? Thank Heaven! I have fought against the Swedes and the Turks, and have seen enough of every kind of fighting."

I endeavoured to explain to him, as well as I could, the duty of a second; but Ivan Ignatitch could not understand me at all.

"Have your own way," said he; "but if I ought to mix myself up in the matter at all, it should be to go to Ivan Kouzmitch and report to him, in accordance with the rules of the service, that there was a design on foot to commit a crime within the fortress, contrary to the interest of the crown, and to request him to take the necessary measures——"

I felt alarmed, and implored Ivan Ignatitch not to say anything about the matter to the Commandant; after much difficulty I succeeded in talking him over, he gave me his word, and then I took leave of him.

I spent the evening as usual at the Commandant's house. I endeavoured to appear gay and indifferent, so as not to excite suspicion, and in order to avoid importunate questions; but I confess that I had not that cool assurance which those who find themselves in my position nearly always boast about. That evening I

26

was disposed to be tender and sentimental. Maria Ivanovna pleased me more than usual. The thought that perhaps I was looking at her for the last time, imparted to her in my eyes something touching. Shvabrin likewise put in an appearance. I took him aside and informed him of my interview with Ivan Ignatitch.

"What do we want seconds for?" said he, drily; "we can do without them."

We agreed to fight behind the hayricks which stood near the fortress, and to appear on the ground at seven o'clock the next morning.

We conversed together in such an apparently amicable manner that Ivan Ignatitch was nearly betraying us in the excess of his joy.

"You should have done that long ago," he said to me, with a look of satisfaction; "a bad reconciliation is better than a good quarrel."

"What's that, what's that, Ivan Ignatitch?" said the Commandant's wife, who was playing at cards in a corner. "I did not hear what you said."

Ivan Ignatitch, perceiving signs of dissatisfaction upon my face, and remembering his promise, became confused, and knew not what reply to make. Shvabrin hastened to his assistance.

"Ivan Ignatitch," said he, "approves of our reconciliation."

"And with whom have you been quarrelling, my little father?"

"Peter Andreitch and I have had rather a serious fall out."

"What about?"

"About a mere trifle—about a song, Vassilissa Egorovna."

"A nice thing to quarrel about, a song! But how did it happen?"

"In this way. Peter Andreitch composed a song a short time ago, and this morning he began to sing it to me, and I began to hum my favourite ditty:

'Daughter of the Captain,
Walk not out at midnight.'

Then there arose a disagreement. Peter Andreitch grew angry, but then he reflected that everyone likes to sing what pleases him best, and there the matter ended."

Shvabrin's insolence nearly made me boil over with fury; but nobody except myself understood his coarse insinuations; at least, nobody paid any attention to them. From songs the conversation turned upon poets, and the Commandant observed that they were all rakes and terrible drunkards, and advised me in a friendly manner to have nothing to do with poetry, as it was contrary to the rules of the service, and would lead to no good.

27

Shvabrin's presence was insupportable to me. I soon took, leave of the Commandant and his family, and returned home. I examined my sword, tried the point of it, and then lay down to sleep, after giving Savelitch orders to wake me at seven o'clock.

The next morning, at the appointed hour, I stood ready behind the hayricks, awaiting my adversary. He soon made his appearance.

"We may be surprised," he said to me, "so we must make haste."

We took off our uniforms, remaining in our waistcoats, and drew our swords. At that moment Ivan Ignatitch and five of the old soldiers suddenly made their appearance from behind a hayrick, and summoned us to go before the Commandant. We obeyed with very great reluctance; the soldiers surrounded us, and we followed behind Ivan Ignatitch, who led the way in triumph, striding along with majestic importance.

We reached the Commandant's house. Ivan Ignatitch threw open the door, exclaiming triumphantly:

"Here they are!"

Vassilissa Egorovna came towards us.

"What is the meaning of all this, my dears? A plot to commit murder in our fortress! Ivan Kouzmitch, put them under arrest immediately! Peter Andreitch! Alexei Ivanitch! Give up your swords—give them up at once! Palashka, take the swords into the pantry. Peter Andreitch, I did not expect this of you! Are you not ashamed? As regards Alexei Ivanitch, he was turned out of the Guards for killing a man; he does not believe in God. Do you wish to be like him?"

Ivan Kouzmitch agreed with everything that his wife said, and added:

"Yes, Vassilissa Egorovna speaks the truth; duels are strictly forbidden by the articles of war."

In the meanwhile Palashka had taken our swords and carried them to the pantry. I could not help smiling. Shvabrin preserved his gravity.

"With all due respect to you," he said coldly to her, "I cannot but observe that you give yourself unnecessary trouble in constituting yourself our judge. Leave that to Ivan Kouzmitch; it is his business."

"What do you say, my dear!" exclaimed the Commandant's wife. "Are not husband and wife, then, one soul and one body? Ivan Kouzmitch! what are you staring at? Place them at once in separate corners on bread and water, so that they may be brought to their proper senses, and then let Father Gerasim impose a penance upon

28

them, that they may pray to God for forgiveness, and show themselves repentant before men."

Ivan Kouzmitch knew not what to do. Maria Ivanovna was exceedingly pale. Gradually the storm blew over; the Commandant's wife recovered her composure, and ordered us to embrace each other. Palashka brought back our swords to us. We left the Commandant's house to all appearance perfectly reconciled. Ivan Ignatitch accompanied us.

"Were you not ashamed," I said angrily to him, "to go and report us to the Commandant, after having given me your word that you would not do so?"

"As true as there is a heaven above us, I did not mention I a word about the matter to Ivan Kouzmitch," he replied. "Vassilissa Egorovna got everything out of me. She arranged the whole business without the Commandant's knowledge. However, Heaven be thanked that it has all ended in the way that it has!"

With these words he returned home, and Shvabrin and I remained alone.

"Our business cannot end in this manner," I said to him. "Certainly not," replied Shvabrin; "your blood shall answer for your insolence to me; but we shall doubtless be watched. For a few days, therefore, we must dissemble. Farewell, till we meet again."

And we parted as if nothing were the matter.

Returning to the Commandant's house I seated myself, as usual, near Maria Ivanovna. Ivan Kouzmitch was not at home. Vassilissa Egorovna was occupied with household matters. We were conversing together in an under tone. Maria Ivanovna reproached me tenderly for the uneasiness which I had caused them all by my quarrel with Shvabrin.

"I almost fainted away," said she, "when they told us that you intended to fight with swords. What strange beings men are! For a single word, which they would probably forget a week afterwards, they are ready to murder each other and to sacrifice not only their life, but their conscience and the happiness of those——But I am quite sure that you did not begin the quarrel. Without doubt, Alexei Ivanitch first began it."

"Why do you think so, Maria Ivanovna?"

"Because—he is so sarcastic. I do not like Alexei Ivanitch. He is very disagreeable to me; yet it is strange: I should not like to displease him. That would cause me great uneasiness."

"And what do you think, Maria Ivanovna—do you please him or not?"

Maria Ivanovna blushed and grew confused.

"I think," said she, "I believe that I please him."

"And why do you think so?"

"Because he once proposed to me."

"Proposed! He proposed to you? And when?"

"Last year; two months before your arrival."

"And you refused?"

"As you see. Alexei Ivanitch is, to be sure, a sensible man and of good family, and possesses property; but when I think that I should have to kiss him under the crown[28] in the presence of everybody— no! not for anything in the world!"

Maria Ivanovna's words opened my eyes and explained a great many things. I now understood why Shvabrin calumniated her so remorselessly. He had probably observed our mutual inclination towards each other, and endeavoured to produce a coolness between us. The words which had been the cause of our quarrel appeared to me still more abominable, when, instead of a coarse and indecent jest, I was compelled to look upon them in the light of a deliberate calumny. The wish to chastise the insolent slanderer became still stronger within me, and I waited impatiently for a favourable opportunity for putting it into execution.

I did not wait long. The next day, when I was occupied in composing an elegy, and sat biting my pen while trying to think of a rhyme, Shvabrin tapped at my window. I threw down my pen, took up my sword, and went out to him.

"Why should we delay any longer?" said Shvabrin; "nobody is observing us. Let us go down to the river; there no one will disturb us."

We set out in silence. Descending a winding path, we stopped at the edge of the river and drew our swords. Shvabrin was more skilful in the use of the weapon than I, but I was stronger and more daring, and Monsieur Beaupré, who had formerly been a soldier, had given me some lessons in fencing which I had turned to good account. Shvabrin had not expected to find in me such a dangerous adversary. For a long time neither of us was able to inflict any injury upon the other; at last, observing that Shvabrin was beginning to relax his endeavours, I commenced to attack him with increased ardour, and almost forced him back into the river. All at once I heard my name pronounced in a loud tone. I looked round and perceived Savelitch hastening down the path towards me.... At that same moment I felt a sharp thrust in the breast, beneath the right shoulder, and I fell senseless to the ground.

---

[28] Crowns are held above the heads of the bride and bridegroom during the marriage ceremony in Russia.

CHAPTER V

LOVE

On recovering consciousness I for some time could neither understand nor remember what had happened to me. I was lying in bed in a strange room, and felt very weak. Before me stood Savelitch with a candle in his hand. Someone was carefully unwinding the bandages which were wrapped round my chest and shoulder. Little by little my thoughts became more collected. I remembered my duel and conjectured that I was wounded. At that moment the door creaked.

"Well, how is he?" whispered a voice which sent a thrill through me.

"Still in the same condition," replied Savelitch with a sigh; "still unconscious, and this makes the fifth day that he has been like it."

I wanted to turn round, but I was unable to do so.

"Where am I? Who is here?" said I with an effort. Maria Ivanovna approached my bed and leaned over me. "Well, how do you feel?" said she.

"God be thanked!" replied I in a weak voice. "Is it you, Maria Ivanovna? Tell me——"

I had not the strength to continue and I became silent. Savelitch uttered a shout and his face beamed with delight.

"He has come to himself again! He has come to himself again!" he kept on repeating. "Thanks be to Thee, O Lord! Come, little father, Peter Andreitch! What a fright you have given me! It is no light matter; this is the fifth day——"

Maria Ivanovna interrupted him.

"Do not speak to him too much, Savelitch," said she, "he is still very weak."

She went out of the room and closed the door very quietly after her. My thoughts became agitated. And so I was in the house of the Commandant; Maria Ivanovna had been to see me. I wanted to ask Savelitch a few questions, but the old man shook his head and stopped his ears. Filled with vexation, I closed my eyes and soon fell asleep.

When I awoke I called Savelitch, but instead of him I saw Maria Ivanovna standing before me; she spoke to me in her angelic voice. I cannot describe the delightful sensation which took possession of me at that moment. I seized her hand, pressed it to my lips, and watered it with my tears. Maria did not withdraw it.... and suddenly her lips touched my cheek, and I felt a hot fresh kiss imprinted upon it. A fiery thrill passed through me.

"Dear, good Maria Ivanovna," I said to her, "be my wife, consent to make me happy."

She recovered herself.

"For Heaven's sake, calm yourself," said she, withdrawing her hand from my grasp; "you are not yet out of danger: your wound may re-open. Take care of yourself, if only for my sake."

With these words she left the room, leaving me in a transport of bliss. Happiness saved me. "She will be mine! She loves me!" This thought filled my whole being.

From that moment I grew hourly better. The regimental barber attended to the dressing of my wound, for there was no other doctor in the fortress, and, thank heaven, he did not assume any airs of professional wisdom. Youth and nature accelerated my recovery. The whole family of the Commandant attended upon me. Maria Ivanovna scarcely ever left my side. As will naturally be supposed, I seized the first favourable opportunity for renewing my interrupted declaration of love, and this time Maria Ivanovna listened to me more patiently.

Without the least affectation she confessed that she was favourably disposed towards me, and said that her parents, without doubt, would be pleased at her good fortune.

"But think well," she added; "will there not be opposition on the part of your relations?"

This set me thinking. I was not at all uneasy on the score of my mother's affection; but, knowing my father's disposition and way of thinking, I felt that my love would not move him very much, and that he would look upon it as a mere outcome of youthful folly.

I candidly confessed this to Maria Ivanovna, but I resolved, nevertheless, to write to my father as eloquently as possible, to implore his paternal blessing. I showed the letter to Maria Ivanovna, who found it so convincing and touching, that she entertained no doubts about the success, of it, and abandoned herself to the feelings of her tender heart with all the confidence of youth and love.

With Shvabrin I became reconciled during the first days of my convalescence. Ivan Kouzmitch, reproaching me for,' having engaged in the duel, said to me:

"See now, Peter Andreitch, I ought really to put you under arrest, but you have been punished enough already without that. As for Alexei Ivanitch, he is confined under guard in the corn magazine, and Vassilissa Egorovna has got his sword under lock and key. He will now have plenty of time to reflect and repent."

I was too happy to cherish any unfriendly feeling in my heart. I began to intercede for Shvabrin, and the good Commandant, with the consent of his wife, agreed to restore him to liberty.

Shvabrin came to me; he expressed deep regret for all that had happened, confessed that he alone was to blame, and begged of me to forget the past. Not being by nature of a rancorous disposition, I readily forgave him the quarrel which he had caused between us, and the wound which I had received at his hands. In his slander I saw nothing but the chagrin of wounded vanity and slighted love, and l generously extended pardon to my unhappy rival.

I soon recovered my health and was able to return to my own quarters. I waited impatiently for a reply to my letter, not daring to hope, and endeavouring to stifle the sad presentiment that was ever uppermost within me. To Vassilissa Egorovna and her husband I had not yet given an explanation; but my proposal would certainly not come as a surprise to them. Neither Maria Ivanovna nor I had endeavoured to hide our feelings from them, and we felt assured of their consent beforehand.

At last, one morning, Savelitch came to me carrying a letter in his hand. I seized it with trembling fingers. The address was in the handwriting of my father. This prepared me for something serious, for the letters I received from home were generally written by my mother, my father merely adding a few lines at the end as a postscript. For a long time I could not make up my mind to break the seal, but kept reading again and again the solemn superscription:

"To my son, Peter Andreitch Grineff,

"Government[29] of Orenburg,

"Fortress of Bailogorsk."

I endeavoured to discover from the handwriting the disposition of mind which my father was in when the letter was written. At last I resolved to open it, and I saw at the very first glance that all my hopes were shipwrecked. The letter ran as follows:—

"MY SON PETER,

"Your letter, in which you ask for our paternal blessing and our consent to your marriage with Maria Ivanovna, the daughter of Mironoff, reached us the 15th inst., and not only do I intend to refuse to give you my blessing and my

[29] For administrative purposes Russia is divided into seventy-two governments, exclusive of Finland, which enjoys a separate administration.

33

consent, but, furthermore, I intend to come and teach you a lesson for your follies, as I would a child, notwithstanding your officer's rank; for you have shown yourself unworthy to carry the sword which was entrusted to you for the defence of your native country, and not for the' purpose of fighting duels with fools like yourself. I shall write at once to Andrei Karlovitch to ask him to transfer you from the fortress of Bailogorsk to some place farther away, where you will be cured of your folly. Your mother, on hearing of your duel and your wound, was taken ill through grief, and she is now confined to her bed. I pray to God that He may correct you, although I hardly dare to put my trust in His great goodness.

"Your father—A. G."

The reading of this letter excited within me various feelings. The harsh expressions which my father had so unsparingly indulged in afflicted me deeply. The contempt with which he referred to Maria Ivanovna appeared to me as indecent as it was unjust. The thought of my being transferred from the fortress of Bailogorsk to some other military station terrified me, but that which grieved me more than everything else was the' intelligence of my mother's illness. I was very much displeased with Savelitch, not doubting that my parents had obtained information of my duel through him. After pacing up and down my narrow room for some time, I stopped before him and said, as I looked frowningly at him:

"It seems that you are not satisfied that, thanks to you, I should be wounded and for a whole month lie at the door of death, but you wish to kill my mother also."

Savelitch gazed at me as if he were thunderstruck.

"In the name of Heaven, master," said he, almost sobbing, "what do you mean? I the cause of your being wounded! God knows that I was running to screen you with my own breast from the sword of Alexei Ivanovitch! My accursed old age prevented me from doing so. But what have I done to your mother?"

"What have you done?" replied I. "Who asked you to write and denounce me? Have you then been placed near me to act as a spy upon me?"

"I write and denounce you?" replied Savelitch, with tears in his eyes. "O Lord, King of Heaven! Be pleased to read what my master has written to me—you will then see whether I have denounced you or not."

And with these words he took from his pocket a letter and handed it to me.

It ran as follows:—

"You ought to be ashamed of yourself, you old hound, for not having—in spite of my strict injunctions to you to do so—written to me and informed me of the conduct of my son, Peter Andreitch, and leaving it to strangers to acquaint me with his follies. Is it thus that you fulfil your duty and your master's will? I will send you to tend the pigs, you old hound, for concealing the truth and for indulging the young man. On receipt of this, I command you to write back to me without delay, and inform me of the present state of his health, of the exact place of his wound, and whether he has been well attended to."

It was evident that Savelitch was perfectly innocent, and that I had insulted him with my reproaches and suspicions for no reason at all. I asked his pardon; but the old man was inconsolable.

"That I should have lived to come to this!" he kept on repeating; "these are the thanks that I receive from my master. I am an old hound, a keeper of pigs, and I am the cause of your being wounded. No, little father, Peter Andreitch, it is not I, but that accursed mossoo who is to blame: it was he who taught you to thrust with those iron spits and to stamp your foot, as if by thrusting and stamping one could protect himself from a bad man. It was very necessary to engage that mossoo and so throw good money to the winds!"

But who then had taken upon himself the trouble to denounce my conduct to my father? The general? But he did not appear to trouble himself in the least about me; and Ivan Kouzmitch had not considered it necessary to report my duel to him. I became lost in conjecture. My suspicions settled upon Shvabrin. He alone could derive any advantage from the denunciation, the result of which might be my removal from the fortress and separation from the Commandant's family. I went to inform Maria Ivanovna of everything. She met me on the steps leading up to the door.

"What has happened, to you?" said she, on seeing me; "how pale you are!"

"It is all over," replied I, and I gave her my father's letter.

She now grew pale in her turn. Having read the letter, she returned it to me with a trembling hand, and said, with a quivering voice:

"Fate ordains that I should not be your wife.... Your parents will not receive me into their family. God's will be done! God knows better than we do, what is good for us. There is nothing to be done, Peter Andreitch; may you be happy——"

"It shall not be!" I exclaimed, seizing hold of her hand. "You love me; I am prepared for everything. Let us go and throw ourselves at the feet of your parents; they are simple people, not hard-hearted and proud. They will give us their blessing; we will get married ... and then, with time, I feel quite certain that we shall succeed in bringing my father round; my mother will be on our side; he will forgive me——"

"No, Peter Andreitch," replied Masha, "I will not marry you without the blessing of your parents. Without their blessing you will not be happy. Let us submit to the will of God. If you meet with somebody else, if you love another God be with you, Peter Andreitch, I will pray for you both——"

Then she burst into tears and left me. I wanted to follow her into her room, but I felt that I was not in a condition to control myself, and I returned home to my quarters.

I was sitting down, absorbed in profound thoughtfulness, when Savelitch interrupted my meditations.

"Here, sir," said he, handing me a written sheet of paper: "see whether I am a spy upon my master, and whether I try to cause trouble between father and son."

I took the paper out of his hand. It was the reply of Savelitch to the letter which he had received. Here it is, word for word:

"LORD ANDREI PETROVITCH, our gracious father,

"I have received your gracious letter, in which you are pleased to be angry with me, your slave, telling me that I ought to be ashamed of myself for not fulfilling my master's orders. I am not an old hound, but your faithful servant, and I do obey my master's orders, and I have always served you zealously till my grey hairs. I did not write anything to you about Peter Andreitch's wound, in order that I might not alarm you without a reason, and now I hear that our lady, our mother, Avdotia Vassilevna, is ill from fright, and I am going to pray to God to restore her to health. Peter Andreitch was wounded under the right shoulder, in the breast, exactly under a rib, to the depth of nearly three inches, and he was put to bed in the Commandant's house, whither we carried him from the bank of the river, and he was healed by Stepan Paramonoff, the barber of this place, and now, thank God, Peter Andreitch is well, and I have nothing but good to write about him. His superior officers, I hear, are satisfied with him; and Vassilissa Egorovna treats him as if he were her own son. And because such an accident occurred to him, the young man ought not to be reproached: the horse has

four legs, and yet he stumbles. And if it please you to write that I should go and feed the pigs, let your lordly will be done. Herewith I humbly bow down before you.
"Your faithful slave,

"ARKHIP SAVELITCH."

I could not help smiling several times while reading the good old man's letter. I was not in a condition to reply to my father, and Savelitch's letter seemed to me quite sufficient to calm my mother's fears.

From this time my situation changed. Maria Ivanovna scarcely ever spoke to me, nay, she even tried to avoid me. The Commandant's house began to become insupportable to me. Little by little I accustomed myself to remaining at home alone. Vassilissa Egorovna reproached me for it at first, but perceiving my obstinacy, she left me in peace. Ivan Kouzmitch I only saw when the service demanded it; with Shvabrin I rarely came into contact, and then against my will, all the more so because I observed in him a secret enmity towards me, which confirmed me in my suspicions. My life became unbearable to me. I sank into a profound melancholy, which was enhanced by loneliness and inaction. My love grew more intense in my solitude, and became more and more tormenting to me. I lost all pleasure in reading and literature. I grew dejected. I was afraid that I should either go out of my mind or that I should give way to dissipation. But an unexpected event, which exercised an important influence upon my after life, suddenly occurred to give to my soul a powerful and salutary shock.

CHAPTER VI

POUGATCHEFF

Before I proceed to write a description of the strange events of which I was a witness, I must say a few words concerning the condition of the government of Orenburg towards the end of the year 1773.

This rich and extensive government was inhabited by horde? of

37

half-savage people, who had only recently acknowledged the sovereignty of the Russian Czars. Their continual revolts, their disinclination to a civilized life and an existence regulated by laws, their fickleness and cruelty, demanded on the part of the government a constant vigilance in order to keep them in subjection. Fortresses had been erected in convenient places, and were garrisoned for the most part by Cossacks, who had formerly held possession of the shores of the Yaik. But these Yaikian Cossacks, whose duty it was to preserve peace and to watch over the security of this district, had themselves for some time past become very troublesome and dangerous to the government. In the year 1772 an insurrection broke out in their principal city. The causes of it were the severe measures taken by General Traubenberg to bring the army into a state of obedience. The result was the barbarous murder of Traubenberg, the selection of new leaders, and finally the suppression of the revolt by grapeshot and cruel punishments.

This happened a little while before my arrival at the fortress of Bailogorsk. All was now quiet, or at least appeared so; but the authorities believed too easily in the pretended repentance of the cunning rebels, who nursed their hatred in secret and only waited for a favourable opportunity to recommence the struggle.

I now return to my narrative.

One evening (it was in the beginning of October in the year. 1773) I was sitting indoors alone, listening to the moaning of the autumn wind, and gazing out of the window at the clouds, as they sailed rapidly over the face of the moon. A message was brought to me to wait upon the Commandant. I immediately repaired to his quarters. I there found Shvabrin, Ivan Ignatitch, and the Cossack orderly. Neither Vassilissa Egorovna nor Maria Ivanova was in the room. The Commandant greeted me with a pre-occupied air. He closed the door, made us all sit-down except the orderly, who remained standing near the door, drew a paper out of his pocket, and said to us:—

"Gentlemen, we have here important news! Hear what the general writes."

Then he put on his spectacles and read as follows:

"To the Commandant of the Fortress of Bailogorsk, Captain Mironoff. (*Confidential.*)

"I hereby inform you that the fugitive and schismatic Don Cossack, Emelian Pougatcheff, after having been guilty of the unpardonable insolence of assuming the name

38

of the deceased Emperor Peter III.,[30] has collected a band of evil-disposed persons, has excited disturbances in the settlements along the banks of the Yaik, and has already taken and destroyed several fortresses, pillaging and murdering on every side. Therefore, on the receipt of this letter, you, Captain, will at once take the necessary measures to repel the above-mentioned villain and impostor, and, if possible, to completely annihilate him, if he should turn his arms against the fortress entrusted to your care."

"Take the necessary measures," said the Commandant, taking off his spectacles and folding up the letter; "you see that it is very easy to say that. The villain is evidently strong in numbers, whereas we have but 130 men altogether, not counting the Cossacks, upon whom we can place very little dependence—without intending any reproach to you, Maximitch." The orderly smiled. "Still, there is no help for it, but to do the best we can, gentlemen. Let us be on our guard and establish night patrols; in case of attack, shut the gates and assemble the soldiers. You, Maximitch, keep a strict eye on your Cossacks. See that the cannon be examined and thoroughly cleaned. Above all things, keep what I have said a secret, so that nobody in the fortress may know anything before the time."

After giving these orders, Ivan Kouzmitch dismissed us. I walked away with Shvabrin, reflecting upon what we had heard.

"How do you think that this will end?" I asked him.

"God knows," he replied; "we shall see. I do not see anything to be alarmed about at present. If, however——"

Then he began to reflect and to whistle abstractedly a French air.

In spite of all our precautions, the news of the appearance of Pougatcheff soon spread through the fortress. Although Ivan Kouzmitch entertained the greatest respect for his wife, he would not for anything in the world have confided to her a secret entrusted to him in connection with the service. After having received the general's letter, he contrived in a tolerably dexterous manner to get

---

[30] Husband of the Empress Catherine II. The latter, whom the Emperor had threatened to divorce, having won over to her side a considerable portion of the army, had compelled her unpopular consort to sign an act of abdication in 1762. Having been removed as a prisoner to Ropscha, it was shortly afterwards announced that He had died of colic, though the truth was, he had been strangled to death by Alexis Orloff, one of Catherine's numerous admirers.

Vassilissa Egorovna out of the way, telling her that Father Gerasim had received some extraordinary news from Orenburg, which he kept a great secret. Vassilissa Egorovna immediately wished to go and pay a visit to the pope's wife and, by the advice of Ivan Kouzmitch, she took Masha with her, lest she should feel dull by herself.

Ivan Kouzmitch, being thus left sole master of the situation, immediately sent for us, having locked Palashka in the pantry, so that she might not be able to overhear what we had to say.

Vassilissa Egorovna returned home, without having succeeded in getting anything out of the pope's wife, and she learned that, during her absence, a council of war had been held in Ivan Kouzmitch's house, and that Palashka had been under lock and key. She suspected that she had been duped by her husband, and she began to assail him with questions. But Ivan Kouzmitch was prepared for the attack. He was not in the least perturbed, and boldly made answer to his inquisitive consort:

"Hark you, mother dear, our women hereabouts have taken a notion into their heads to heat their ovens with straw, and as some misfortune might be the outcome of it, I gave strict orders that the women should not heat their ovens with straw, but should burn brushwood and branches of trees instead."

"But why did you lock up Palashka, then?" asked his wife. "Why was the poor girl compelled to sit in the kitchen till we returned?"

Ivan Kouzmitch was not prepared for such a question; he became confused, and stammered out something very incoherent. Vassilissa Egorovna perceived her husband's perfidy, but, knowing that she would get nothing out of him just then, she abstained from asking any further questions and turned the conversation to the subject of the pickled; cucumbers, which Akoulina Pamphilovna knew how to prepare in such an excellent manner. But all that night Vassilissa Egorovna could not sleep a wink, nor could she understand what it was that was in her husband's head that; she was not permitted to know.

The next day, as she was returning home from mass, she saw Ivan Ignatitch, who was busily engaged in clearing the cannon of pieces of rag, small stones, bits of bone, and rubbish of every sort, which had been deposited there by the little boys of the place.

"What mean these warlike preparations?" thought the Commandant's wife. "Can it be that they fear an attack on the part of the Kirghises? But is it possible that Ivan Kouzmitch could conceal such a trifle from me?"

She called Ivan Ignatitch to her with the firm determination of learning from him the secret which tormented her woman's curiosity.

Vassillissa Egorovna began by making a few observations to him about household matters, like a judge who commences an examination with questions foreign to the matter in hand, in order to lull the suspicions of the person accused. Then, after a silence of a few moments, she heaved a deep sigh, and said, shaking her head:

"Oh, Lord God! What news! What will be the end of all this?"

"Well, well, mother!" replied Ivan Ignatitch; "God is merciful; we have soldiers enough, plenty of powder, and I have cleaned the cannon. Perhaps we shall be able to offer a successful resistance to this Pougatcheff; if God will only not abandon us, we shall be safe enough here."

"And what sort of a man is this Pougatcheff?" asked the Commandant's wife.

Then Ivan Ignatitch perceived that he had said more ban he ought to have done, and he bit his tongue. But it was now too late. Vassilissa Egorovna compelled him to inform her of everything, having given him her word that she would not mention the matter to anybody.

Vassilissa Egorovna kept her promise and said not a word to anybody, except to the pope's wife, and to her only because her cow was still feeding upon the steppe, and might be captured by the brigands.

Soon everybody was talking about Pougatcheff. The reports concerning him varied very much. The Commandant sent his orderly to glean as much information as possible about him in all the neighbouring villages and fortresses. The orderly returned after an absence of two days, and reported that, at about sixty versts from the fortress, he had seen a large number of fires upon the steppe, and that he had heard from the Bashkirs that an immense force was advancing. He could not say anything more positive, because he had feared to venture further.

An unusual agitation now began to be observed among the Cossacks of the fortress; in all the streets they congregated in small groups, quietly conversing among themselves, and dispersing whenever they caught sight of a dragoon or any other soldier belonging to the garrison. They were closely watched by spies. Youlai, a converted Calmuck, made an important communication to the commandant. The orderly's report, according to Youlai, was a false one; on his return the treacherous Cossack announced to his companions that he had been among the rebels, and had been presented to their leader, who had given him his hand and had conversed with him for a long time. The Commandant immediately

41

placed the orderly under arrest, and appointed Youlai in his place. This change was the cause of manifest dissatisfaction among the Cossacks. They murmured loudly, and Ivan Ignatitch, who executed the Commandant's instructions, with his own ears heard them say:

"Just wait a little while, you garrison rat!"

The Commandant had intended interrogating the prisoner that very same day, but the orderly had made his escape, no doubt with the assistance of his partisans.

A fresh event served to increase the Commandant's uneasiness. A Bashkir, carrying seditious letters, was seized. On this occasion the Commandant again decided upon assembling his officers, and therefore he wished once more to get Vassilissa Egorovna out of the way under some plausible pretext. But as Ivan Kouzmitch was a most upright and sincere man, he could find no other method than that employed on the previous occasion.

"Listen, Vassilissa Egorovna," he said to her, coughing to conceal his embarrassment: "they say that Father Gerasim has received——"

"That's enough, Ivan Kouzmitch," said his wife, interrupting him: "you wish to assemble a council of war to talk about Emelian Pougatcheff without my being present; but you shall not deceive me this time."

Ivan Kouzmitch opened his eyes.

"Well, little mother," he said, "if you know everything, you may remain; we shall speak in your presence."

"Very well, my little father," replied she; "you should not try to be so cunning; send for the officers."

We assembled again. Ivan Kouzmitch, in the presence of his wife, read to us Pougatcheff's proclamation, drawn up probably by some half-educated Cossack. The robber announced therein his intention of immediately marching upon our fortress; he invited the Cossacks and soldiers to join him, and advised the superior officers not to offer any resistance, threatening them with death in the event of their doing so. The proclamation was couched in coarse but vigorous language, and could not but produce a powerful impression upon the minds of simple people.

"What a rascal!" exclaimed the Commandant's wife; "that he should propose such a thing to us. To go out to meet him and lay our flags at his feet! Ah! the son of a dog! He does not know then that we have been forty years in the service, and that, thanks to God, we have seen a good deal during that time. Is it possible that there are commandants who would be cowardly enough to yield to a robber like him?"

"There ought not to be," replied Ivan Kouzmitch; "but it is reported that the scoundrel has already taken several fortresses."

"He seems to have great power," observed Shvabrin.

"We shall soon find out the real extent of his power," said the Commandant. "Vassilissa Egorovna, give me the key of the loft. Ivan Ignatitch, bring hither the Bashkir, and tell Youlai to fetch a whip."

"Wait a moment, Ivan Kouzmitch," said his wife, rising from her seat. "Let me take Masha somewhere out of the house; otherwise she will hear the cries and will feel frightened. And I myself, to tell the truth, am no lover of inquisitions. So good-bye for the present."

Torture, in former times, was so rooted in our judicial proceedings, that the benevolent ukase[31] ordering its abolition remained for a long time a dead letter. It was thought that the confession of the criminal was indispensable for his full conviction—an idea not only unreasonable, but even contrary to common sense from a jurisprudential point of view; for if the denial of the accused person be not accepted as proof of his innocence, the confession that has been wrung from him ought still less to be accepted as a proof of his guilt. Even in our days I sometimes hear old judges regretting the abolition of the barbarous custom. But in those days nobody had any doubt about the necessity of torture, neither the judges nor even the accused persons themselves. Therefore it was that the Commandant's order did not astonish or alarm any of us. Ivan Ignatitch went to fetch the Bashkir, who was confined in the loft, under lock and key, and a few minutes afterwards he was led prisoner into the ante-room. The Commandant ordered the captive to be brought before him.—

The Bashkir stepped with difficulty across the threshold (for his feet were in fetters) and, taking off his high cap, remained standing near the door. I glanced at him and shuddered. Never shall I forget that man. He appeared to be about seventy years of age, and had neither nose nor ears. His head was shaved, and instead of a beard he had a few grey hairs upon his chin; he was of short stature, thin and bent; but his small eyes still flashed fire.

"Ah, ah!" said the Commandant, recognizing by these dreadful marks one of the rebels punished in the year 1741, "I see you are an old wolf; you have already been caught in our traps. It is not the first time that you have rebelled, since your head is planed so smoothly. Come nearer; speak, who sent you here?"

The old Bashkir remained silent and gazed at the Commandant with an air of complete stolidity.

---

[31] Torture was abolished in 1768 by an edict of Catherine II.

"Why do you not answer?" continued Ivan Kouzmitch. "Don't you understand Russian? Youlai, ask him in your language, who sent him to our fortress."

Youlai repeated the Commandant's question in the Tartar language. But the Bashkir looked at him with the same expression and answered not a word.

"By heaven!" exclaimed the Commandant, "you shall answer me. My lads! take off that ridiculous striped gown of his, and tickle his back. Youlai, see that it is carried out properly."

Two soldiers began to undress the Bashkir. The face of the unhappy man assumed an expression of uneasiness. He looked round on every side, like a poor little animal f that has been captured by children. But when one of the soldiers seized his hands to twine them round his neck, and raised the old man upon his shoulders, and Youlai grasped the whip and began to flourish it round his head, then the Bashkir uttered a feeble groan, and, raising his head, opened his mouth, in which, instead of a tongue, moved a short stump.

When I reflect that this happened during my lifetime, and that I now live under the mild government of the Emperor Alexander, I cannot but feel astonished at the rapid progress of civilization, and the diffusion of humane ideas. Young man! if these lines of mine should fall into your hands, remember that those changes which proceed from an amelioration of manners and customs are much better and more lasting than those which are the outcome of acts of violence.

We were all horror-stricken.

"Well," said the Commandant, "it is evident that we shall get nothing out of him. Youlai, lead the Bashkir back to the loft; and let us, gentlemen, have a little further talk about the matter."

We were yet considering our position, when Vassilissa Egorovna suddenly rushed into the room, panting for breath, and beside herself with excitement.

"What has happened to you?" asked the astonished Commandant.

"I have to inform you of a great misfortune!" replied Vassilissa Egorovna. "Nijniosern was taken this morning. Father Gerasim's servant has just returned from there. He saw how they took it. The Commandant and all the officers are hanged, and all the soldiers are taken prisoners. In a little while the villains will be here."

This unexpected intelligence produced a deep impression upon me. The Commandant of the fortress of Nijniosem, a quiet and modest young man, was an acquaintance of mine; two months before he had visited our fortress when on his way from Orenburg along with his young wife, and had stopped for a little while in the house of Ivan Kouzmitch. Nijniosern was about twenty-five versts from our fortress. We might therefore expect to be attacked by Pougatcheff at any moment. The fate in store for Maria Ivanovna presented itself vividly to my imagination, and my heart sank within me.

"Listen, Ivan Kouzmitch," said I to the Commandant; "our duty is to defend the fortress to the last gasp; there is no question about that. But we must think about the safety of the women. Send them on to Orenburg, if the road be still open, or to some safer and more distant fortress where these villains will not be able to make their way."

Ivan Kouzmitch turned round to his wife and said to her:

"Listen, mother; would it not be just as well if we sent you away to some place farther off until we have settled matters with these rebels?"

"What nonsense!" said the Commandant's wife. "Where is there a fortress that would be safe from bullets? Why is Bailogorsk not safe? Thank God, we have lived in it for two-and-twenty years! We have seen Bashkirs and Kirghises; perhaps we shall also escape the clutches of Pougatcheff."

"Well, mother," replied Ivan Kouzmitch, "stay if you like, if you have such confidence in our fortress. But what shall we do with Masha? All well and good if we offer a successful resistance, or can hold out till we obtain help; but what if the villains should take the fortress?"

"Why, then——"

But at this juncture Vassilissa Egorovna began to stammer and then remained silent, evidently agitated by deep emotion.

"No, Vassilissa Egorovna," continued the Commandant, observing that his words had produced an impression upon her, perhaps for the first time in his life, "Masha must not remain here. Let us send her to Orenburg, to her godmother; there are plenty of soldiers and cannon there, and the walls are of stone. And I would advise you to go there with her; for although you are an old woman, think what might happen to you if the fortress should be taken by storm."

"Very well," replied the Commandant's wife; "let it be so: we will send Masha away. As for me, you need not trouble yourself about asking me to go; I will remain here. Nothing shall make me part from you in my old age to go and seek a lonely grave in a strange country. Together we have lived, together we will die."

"Well, you are right," said the Commandant; "but let us not delay any longer. Go and get Masha ready for the journey. She must set out at daybreak to-morrow, and we shall let her have an escort, although we have not too many men in the fortress to be able to spare any of them. But where is Masha?"

"Along with Akoulina Pamphilovna," replied the Commandant's wife. "She fainted away when she heard of the capture of Nijniosern; I am afraid that she will be ill. Lord God of heaven, what have we lived to see!"

Vassilissa Egorovna went to prepare for her daughter's departure. The consultation with the Commandant was then continued; but I no longer took any part in it, nor did I listen to anything that was said. Maria Ivanovna appeared at supper, her face pale and her eyes red with weeping. We supped in silence, and rose from the table sooner than usual; then taking leave of the family, we all returned to our respective quarters. But I intentionally forgot my sword, and went back for it: I had a presentiment that I should find Maria alone. True enough I met her in the doorway, and she handed me my sword.

"Farewell, Peter Andreitch!" she said to me, with tears in her eyes; "they are going to send me to Orenburg. May you be well and happy. God may be pleased to ordain that we should see each other again; if not——"

Here she burst out sobbing. I clasped her in my arms.

"Farewell, my angel!" said I. "Farewell, my darling, my heart's desire! Whatever may happen to me, rest assured that my last thought and last prayer shall be for you."

Masha still continued to weep, resting her head upon my breast. I kissed her fervently, and hastily quitted the room.

CHAPTER VII

THE ASSAULT

That night I neither slept nor undressed. It was my intention to proceed early in the morning to the gate of the fortress through which Maria Ivanovna would have to pass, so that I might take leave of her for the last time. I felt within myself a great change; the agitation of my soul was far less burdensome to me than the melancholy into which I had lately fallen. With the grief of separation there was mingled a vague, but sweet hope, an impatient expectation of danger, a feeling of noble ambition.

The night passed away imperceptibly. I was just about to leave the house when my door opened, and the corporal entered the room with the information that our Cossacks had quitted the fortress during the night, taking Youlai by force along with them, and that strange people were riding round the fortress. The thought that Maria Ivanovna would not be able to get away filled me with alarm. I hurriedly gave some orders to the corporal, and then hastened at once to the Commandant's quarters.

Day had already begun to dawn. I was hurrying along the street when I heard someone call out my name. I stopped.

"Where are you going?" said Ivan Ignatitch, overtaking me. "Ivan Kouzmitch is on the rampart, and he has sent me for you. Pougatch[32] has come."

"Has Maria Ivanovna left the fortress?" I asked, with a trembling heart.

"She was unable to do so," replied Ivan Ignatitch; "the road to Orenburg is cut off and the fortress is surrounded. It is a bad look-out, Peter Andreitch."

We made our way to the rampart, an elevation formed by nature and fortified by a palisade. The inhabitants of the fortress were already assembled there. The garrison stood drawn up under arms. The cannon had been dragged thither the day before. The Commandant was walking up and down in front of his little troop. The approach of danger had inspired the old warrior with unusual vigour. On the steppe, not very far from the fortress, about a score of men could be seen riding about on horseback. They seemed to be Cossacks, but among them were some Bashkirs, who were easily recognized by their hairy caps, and by their quivers.

The Commandant walked along the ranks of his little army, saying to the soldiers:

"Now, my children, let us stand firm to-day for our mother the Empress and let us show the whole world that we are brave people, and true to our oath."

The soldiers responded to his appeal with loud shouts. Shvabrin stood near me and attentively observed the enemy. The people riding about on the steppe, perceiving some movement in the fortress, gathered together in a group and began conversing among themselves. The Commandant ordered Ivan Ignatitch to point the cannon at them, and then applied the match to it with his own hand. The ball whistled over their heads, without doing any

---

[32] A pun on the name of the rebel chief. Literally, "a scarecrow."

harm. The horsemen dispersed, galloping out of sight almost immediately, and the steppe was deserted.

At that moment Vassilissa Egorovna appeared upon the rampart, followed by Masha, who was unwilling to leave her.

"Well," said the Commandant's wife, "how goes the battle? Where is the enemy?"

"The enemy is not far off," replied Ivan Kouzmitch. "God grant that all may go well!... Well, Masha, do you feel afraid?"

"No, papa," replied Maria Ivanovna; "I feel more afraid being at home alone."

Then she looked at me and made an effort to smile. I involuntarily grasped the hilt of my sword, remembering that I had received it from her hand the evening before—as if for the protection of my beloved. My heart throbbed. I imagined myself her champion. I longed to prove that I was worthy of her confidence, and waited impatiently for the decisive moment.

All of a sudden some fresh bodies of mounted men made their appearance from behind an elevation situated about half a mile from the fortress, and soon the steppe was covered with crowds of persons armed with lances and quivers. Among them, upon a white horse, was a man in a red caftan[33], holding a naked sword in his hand; this was Pougatcheff himself. He stopped his horse, and the others gathered round him, and, in obedience to his order as it seemed, four men detached themselves from the crowd and galloped at full speed towards the fortress. We recognized among them some of our traitors. One of them held a sheet of paper above his head, while another bore upon the top of his lance the head of Youlai, which he threw over the palisade among us. The head of the poor Calmuck fell at the feet of the Commandant.

The traitors cried out:

"Do not fire! Come out and pay homage to the Czar. The Czar is here!"

"Look out for yourselves!" cried Ivan Kouzmitch, "Ready, lads—fire!"

Our soldiers fired a volley. The Cossack who held the letter staggered and fell from his horse; the others galloped back. I turned and looked at Maria Ivanovna. Terror-stricken by the sight of the bloodstained head of Youlai, and stunned by the din of the discharge, she seemed perfectly paralyzed. The Commandant called the corporal and ordered him to fetch the paper from the hands of the fallen Cossack. The corporal went out into the plain, and returned leading by the bridle the horse of the dead man. He

---

[33] A kind of overcoat.

handed the letter to the Commandant. Ivan Kouzmitch read it to himself and then tore it into pieces. In the meantime we could see the rebels preparing for the attack. Soon the bullets began to whistle about our ears, and several arrows fell close to us, sticking in the ground and in the palisade.

"Vassilissa Egorovna!" said the Commandant; "women have no business here. Take Masha away; you see that the girl is more dead than alive."

Vassilissa Egorovna, tamed by the bullets, cast a glance at the steppe, where a great commotion was observable, and then turned round to her husband and said to him:

"Ivan Kouzmitch, life and death are in the hands of God; bless Masha. Masha, come near to your father."

Masha, pale and trembling, approached Ivan Kouzmitch, knelt down before him, and bowed herself to the ground. The old Commandant made the sign of the cross over her three times, then raised her up, and kissing her, said in a voice of deep emotion:

"Well, Masha, be happy. Pray to God; He will never forsake you. If you find a good man, may God give you love and counsel. Live together as your mother and I have lived. And now, farewell, Masha. Vassilissa Egorovna, take her away quickly."

Masha threw her arms round his neck and sobbed aloud.

"Let us kiss each other also," said the Commandant's wife, weeping. "Farewell, my Ivan Kouzmitch. Forgive me if I have ever vexed you in any way!"

"Farewell, farewell, little mother!" said the Commandant, embracing the partner of his joys and sorrows for so many years. "Come now, that is enough! Make haste home; and if you can manage it, put a sarafan[34] on Masha."

The Commandant's wife walked away along with her daughter. I followed Maria Ivanovna with my eyes; she turned round and nodded her head to me.

Ivan Kouzmitch then returned to us, and bestowed all his attention upon the enemy. The rebels gathered round their leader and suddenly dismounted from their horses.

"Stand firm now," said the Commandant, "the assault is going to begin."

At that moment frightful yells and cries rose in the air; the

---

[34] A wide open robe without sleeves, beneath which is worn a full long-sleeved gown. It is usually made of velvet, richly embroidered, he embroidery varying according to the rank of the wearer. It is the custom among the Russians to bury the dead in their richest dress.

rebels dashed forward towards the fortress. Our cannon was loaded with grape-shot.

The Commandant allowed them to come very close, and then suddenly fired again. The grape fell into the very midst of the crowd. The rebels recoiled and then dispersed on every side. Their leader alone remained facing us. He heaved his sword and seemed to be vehemently exhorting his followers to return to the attack. The shrieks and yells, which had ceased for a minute, were immediately renewed.

"Now, lads!" said the Commandant; "open the gate, beat the drum, and let us make a sally. Forward, and follow me!"

The Commandant, Ivan Ignatitch, and I were outside the wall of the fortress in a twinkling; but the timid garrison did not move.

"Why do you hold back, my children?" cried Ivan Kouzmitch. "If we are to die, let us die doing our duty!"

At that moment the rebels rushed upon us and forced an entrance into the fortress. The drum ceased to beat; the garrison flung down their arms. I was thrown to the ground, but I rose up and entered the fortress along with the rebels. The Commandant, wounded in the head, was surrounded by a crowd of the robbers, who demanded of him the keys. I was about to rush to his assistance, but several powerful Cossacks seized hold of me and bound me with their sashes, exclaiming:

"Just wait a little while and see what you will get, you traitors to the Czar!"

They dragged us through the streets; the inhabitants came out of their houses with bread and salt;[35] the bells began to ring. Suddenly among the crowd a cry was raised that the Czar was in the square waiting for the prisoners to take their oath of allegiance to him. The throng pressed towards the market-place, and our captors dragged us thither also.

Pougatcheff was seated in an armchair on the steps of the Commandant's house. He was attired in an elegant Cossack caftan, ornamented with lace. A tall cap of sable, with gold tassels, came right down to his flashing eyes. His face seemed familiar to me. He was surrounded by the Cossack chiefs. Father Gerasim, pale and trembling, stood upon the steps with a cross in his hands, and seemed to be silently imploring mercy for the victims brought forward. In the square a gallows was being hastily erected. As we approached, the Bashkirs drove back the crowd, and we were

---

[35] The customary offering to a Russian emperor on entering a town. The act is indicative of submission.

brought before Pougatcheff. The bells had ceased ringing, and a deep silence reigned around.

"Which is the Commandant?" asked the pretender.

Our orderly stepped forward out of the crowd and pointed to Ivan Kouzmitch.

Pougatcheff regarded the old man with a menacing look, and said to him:

"How dared you oppose me—your emperor?"

The Commandant, weakened by his wound, summoned ill his remaining strength and replied in a firm voice:

"You are not my emperor; you are a robber and a pretender, that is what you are!"

Pougatcheff frowned savagely and waved his white handkerchief. Several Cossacks seized the old captain and dragged him towards the gallows. Astride upon the cross-beam could be seen the mutilated Bashkir whom we had examined the day before. He held in his hand a rope, and a minute afterwards I saw poor Ivan Kouzmitch suspended in the air. Then Ivan Ignatitch was brought before Pougatcheff.

."Take the oath of fealty," said Pougatcheff to him, "to the Emperor Peter Fedorovitch!"

"You are not our emperor," replied Ivan Ignatitch, repeating the words of his captain; "you, uncle, are a robber and a pretender!"

Pougatcheff again waved his handkerchief, and the good lieutenant was soon hanging near his old chief.

It was now my turn. I looked defiantly at Pougatcheff, prepared to repeat the answer of my brave comrades, when, to my inexpressible astonishment, I perceived, among the rebels, Shvabrin, his hair cut close, and wearing a Cossack kaftan. He stepped up to Pougatcheff and whispered a few words in his ear.

"Let him be hanged!" said Pougatcheff, without even looking at me.

The rope was thrown round my neck. I began to repeat a prayer to myself, expressing sincere repentance for all my sins, and imploring God to save all those who were dear to me. I was led beneath the gibbet.

"Don't be afraid, don't be afraid," said my executioners, wishing sincerely, perhaps, to encourage me.

Suddenly I heard a cry:

"Stop, villains! hold!"

The executioners paused. I looked round. Savelitch was on his knees at the feet of Pougatcheff.

"Oh, my father!" said my poor servant, "why should you wish for the death of this noble child? Let him go you will get a good ransom for him; if you want to make an example of somebody for the sake of terrifying others order me to be hanged—an old man!"

Pougatcheff gave a sign, and I was immediately unbound and set at liberty.

"Our father pardons you," said the rebels who had charge of me.

I cannot say that at that moment I rejoiced at my deliverance, neither will I say that I was sorry for it. My feelings were too confused. I was again led before the usurper and compelled to kneel down in front of him. Pougatcheff stretched out to me his sinewy hand.

"Kiss his hand, kiss his hand!" exclaimed voices on every side of me.

But I would have preferred the most cruel punishment to such contemptible degradation.

"My little father, Peter Andreitch," whispered Savelitch standing behind me and nudging my elbow, "do not be obstinate. What will it cost you? Spit[36] and kiss the brig——pshaw! kiss his hand!"

I did not move. Pougatcheff withdrew his hand, saying with a smile:

"His lordship seems bewildered with joy. Lift him up!"

I was raised to my feet and released. I then stood by to observe the continuation of the terrible comedy.

The inhabitants began to take the oath of allegiance. They approached one after another, kissed the crucifix and then bowed to the usurper. Then came the turn of the soldiers of the garrison. The regimental barber, armed with his blunt scissors, cut off their hair. Then, after shaking their heads, they went and kissed the hand of Pougatcheff, who declared them pardoned, and then enrolled them among his followers.

All this lasted for about three hours. At length Pougatcheff rose up from his armchair and descended the steps, accompanied by his chiefs. A white horse, richly caparisoned, was led forward to him. Two Cossacks took hold of him under the arms and assisted him into the saddle. He informed Father Gerasim that he would dine with him. At that moment a woman's scream was heard. Some of the brigands were dragging Vassilissa Egorovna, with her hair dishevelled and her clothes half torn off her body, towards the steps. One of them had already arrayed himself in her gown. The others were carrying off beds, chests, tea-services, linen, and all kinds of furniture.

---

[36] A sign of contempt among Russians and Orientals.

"My fathers!" cried the poor old woman, "have pity upon me and let me go. Kind fathers! take me to Ivan Kouzmitch."

Suddenly she caught sight of the gibbet and recognized her husband.

"Villains!" she cried, almost beside herself; "what have you done to him? My Ivan Kouzmitch! light of my life! brave soldier heart! Neither Prussian bayonets nor Turkish bullets have touched you; not in honourable fight have you yielded up your life; you received your death at the hand of a runaway galley-slave!"

"Make the old witch hold her tongue!" said Pougatcheff.

A young Cossack struck her on the head with his sabre, and she fell dead at the foot of the steps. Pougatcheff rode off; the crowd followed him.

CHAPTER VIII

AN UNINVITED GUEST

The square was deserted. I remained standing in the same place, unable to collect my thoughts, bewildered as I was by so many terrible emotions.

Uncertainty with respect to the fate of Maria Ivanovna tortured me more than anything else. Where was she? What had become of her? Had she contrived to hide herself? Was her place of refuge safe?

Filled, with these distracting thoughts, I made my way to the Commandant's house. It was empty. The chairs, tables, and chests were broken, the crockery dashed to pieces, and everything in confusion. I ran up the little staircase which led to Maria's room, and which I now entered for the first time in my life. Her bed had been ransacked by the robbers; the wardrobe was broken open and plundered; the small lamp was still burning before the empty image case.37 There was also left a small mirror hanging on the partition wall.... Where was the mistress of his humble, virginal cell? A terrible thought passed through my mind; I imagined her in the

---

37 The small wardrobe, with glass doors, in which the sacred images are kept, and which forms a domestic altar.

hands of the robbers.... My heart sank within me.... I wept bitterly, most bitterly, and called aloud the name of my beloved.... At that moment I heard a slight noise, and from behind the ward-robe appeared Palasha, pale and trembling.

"Ah, Peter Andreitch!" said she, clasping her hands, "What a day! what horrors!"

"And Maria Ivanovna?" I asked impatiently. "What has become of Maria Ivanovna?"

"The young lady is alive," replied Palasha; "she is hiding in the house of Akoulina Pamphilovna."

"With the priest's wife!" I exclaimed in alarm. "My God! Pougatcheff is there!"

I dashed out of the room, and in the twinkling of an eye I was in the street and hurrying off to the clergyman's house, without devoting the slightest attention to anything else. Shouts, songs, and bursts of laughter resounded from within.... Pougatcheff was feasting with his companions. Palasha had followed me thither. I sent her to call out Akoulina Pamphilovna secretly. In about a minute the priest's wife came out to me in the vestibule, with an empty bottle in her hand.

"In Heaven's name! where is Maria Ivanovna?" I asked with indescribable agitation.

"The dear little dove is lying down on my bed behind the partition," replied the priest's wife. "But a terrible misfortune had very nearly happened, Peter Andreitch! Thanks be to God, however, everything has passed off happily. The villain had just sat down to dine, when the poor child uttered a moan!... I felt as if I should have died. He heard it. 'Who is that moaning in your room, old woman?'—I bowed myself to the ground, and replied: 'My niece, Czar; she has been lying ill for about a fortnight.'—'And is your niece young?'—'She is young, Czar.' —'Show me your niece then, old woman.' My heart sank within me, but there was no help for it. 'Very well, Czar; but the girl will not have the strength to get up and come before your Grace.'—'Never mind, old woman, I will go and see her myself.' And the villain went behind the partition and, will you believe it?—actually drew aside the curtain and looked at her with his hawk-like eyes—but nothing came of it,—God helped us! Will you believe it? I and the father were prepared for a martyr's death. Fortunately, my little dove did not recognize him. Lord God! what have we lived to see! Poor Ivan Kouzmitch! who would have thought it!... And Vassilissa Egorovna? And Ivan Ignatitch? What was he killed for? And how came they to spare you? And what do you think of Shvabrin? He has had his hair cut, and is now feasting inside along with them! He is a very sharp fellow, there is no gainsaying that! When I spoke of my sick niece—will you believe it?—he looked at me as if he would have stabbed me; but he did not betray me. I am thankful to him for that, anyway."

At that moment I heard the drunken shouts of the guests and the voice of Father Gerasim. The guests were demanding wine, and the host was calling for his wife.

"Go back home, Peter Andreitch," said the priest's wife, somewhat alarmed; "I cannot stop to speak to you now; I must go and wait upon the drunken scoundrels. It might be unfortunate for you if you fell into their hands. Farewell, Peter Andreitch. What is to be, will be; perhaps God will not abandon us!"

The priest's wife went back inside the house. Somewhat more easy in mind, I returned to my quarters. As I crossed the square I saw several Bashkirs assembled round the gibbets, engaged in dragging off the boots of those who had been hanged. With difficulty I repressed my indignation, feeling convinced that if I gave expression to it, it would have been perfectly useless. The brigands invaded every part of the fortress, and plundered the officers' houses. On every side resounded the shouts of the drunken mutineers. I reached home. Savelitch met me on the threshold.

"Thank God!" he exclaimed when he saw me; "I was beginning to think that the villains had seized you again. Ah! my little father, Peter Andreitch, will you believe it, the robbers have plundered us of everything—clothes, linen, furniture, plate—they have not left us a single thing. But what does it matter? Thank God! they have spared your life. But, my lord, did you recognize their leader?"

"No, I did not recognize him. Who is he then?"

"How, my little father! Have you forgotten that drunken scoundrel who swindled you out of the pelisse at the inn? A brand new hareskin pelisse; and the beast burst the seams in putting it on."

I was astounded. In truth, the resemblance of Pougatcheff to my guide was very striking. I felt convinced that Pougatcheff and he were one and the same person, and then I understood why he had spared my life. I could not but feel surprised at the strange connection of events—a child's pelisse, given to a roving vagrant, had saved me from the hangman's noose, and a drunkard, who had passed his life in wandering from one inn to another, was now besieging fortresses and shaking the empire!

"Will you not eat something?" asked Savelitch, still faithful to his old habits. "There is nothing in the house; but I will go and search, and get something ready for you."

When I was left alone, I began to reflect. What was I to do? To remain in the fortress now that it was in the hands of the villain, or to join his band, was unworthy of an officer. Duty demanded that I should go wherever my services might still be of use to my fatherland in the present critical position of its affairs.... But love strongly urged me to remain near Maria Ivanovna and be her protector and defender. Although I foresaw a speedy and inevitable change in the course of affairs, yet I could not help trembling when I thought of the danger of her situation.

My reflections were interrupted by the arrival of one of the Cossacks, who came to inform me that "the great Czar required me to appear before him."

"Where is he?" I asked, preparing to obey.

"In the Commandant's house," replied the Cossack. "After dinner our father took a bath, but at present he is resting. Ah! your Excellency, it is very evident that he is a distinguished person; at dinner he deigned to eat two roasted sucking pigs, then he entered the bath, where the I water was so hot that even Tarass Kourotchkin could not bear it; he had to give the besom to Tomka Bikbaieff, and only came to himself through having cold water poured over him. There is no denying it; all his ways are majestic.... And I was told that in the bath he showed his Czar's signs upon his breast: on one side a two-headed eagle as large as a five-copeck piece, and on the other his own likeness."

I did not consider it necessary to contradict the Cossack's statement, and I accompanied him to the Commandant's house, trying to imagine beforehand what kind of a reception I should meet with from Pougatcheff, and endeavouring to guess how it would end. The reader will easily understand that I did not by any means feel easy within myself.

It was beginning to get dark when I reached the Commandant's house. The gibbet, with its victims, loomed black and terrible before me. The body of the poor Commandant's wife still lay at the bottom of the steps, near which two Cossacks stood on guard. The Cossack who accompanied me went in to announce me, and, returning almost immediately, conducted me into the room where, the evening before, I had taken a tender farewell of Maria Ivanovna.

An unusual spectacle presented itself to my gaze. At a table, covered with a cloth and loaded with bottles and glasses, sat Pougatcheff and some half-a-score of Cossack chiefs, in coloured caps and shirts, heated with wine, with flushed faces and flashing eyes. I did not see among then: Shvabrin and his fellow traitor, the orderly.

"Ah! your Excellency!" said Pougatcheff, seeing me, "Welcome; honour to you and a place at our banquet."

The guests moved closer together. I sat down silently at the end of the table. My neighbour, a young Cossack, tall and handsome, poured out for me a glass of wine, which, however, I did not touch. I began to observe the company with curiosity. Pougatcheff occupied the seat of honour, his elbows resting on the table, and his broad fist propped under his black beard. His features, regular and sufficiently agreeable, had nothing fierce about them. He frequently turned to speak to a man of about fifty years of age, addressing him sometimes as Count, sometimes as Timofeitch, sometimes as uncle. All those present treated each other as comrades, and did not show any particular respect for their leader. The conversation was upon the subject of the assault of the morning, of the success of the revolt, and of their future operations. Each one boasted of what he had done, expressed his opinion, and fearlessly contradicted Pougatcheff. And in this strange council of war it was resolved to march upon Orenburg; a bold movement, and which was to be very nearly crowned with success! The march was fixed for the following day.

"Now, lads," said Pougatcheff, "before we retire to rest, let us have my favourite song. Choumakoff, begin!"

My neighbour sang, in a shrill voice, the following melancholy peasants' song, and all joined in the chorus:

> "Stir not, mother, green forest of oak,
> Disturb me not in my meditation;
> For to-morrow before the court I must go,
> Before the stern judge, before the Czar himself.
> The great Lord Czar will begin to question me:
> 'Tell me, young man, tell me, thou peasant's son,
> With whom have you stolen, with whom have you robbed?
> Did you have many companions with you?'
> 'I will tell you, true-believing Czar,
> The whole truth I will confess to you.
> My companions were four in number:
> My first companion was the dark night,
> My second companion was a steel knife,
> My third companion was my good horse,
> My fourth companion was my taut bow,
> My messengers were my tempered arrows.'
> Then speaks my hope, the true-believing Czar:
> 'Well done! my lad, brave peasant's son;
> You knew how to steal, you knew how to reply:
> Therefore, my lad, I will make you a present
> Of a very high structure in the midst of a field—
> Of two upright posts with a cross-beam above.'"

It is impossible to describe the effect produced upon me by this popular gallows song, trolled out by men destined for the gallows. Their ferocious countenances, their sonorous voices, and the melancholy expression which they imparted to the words, which in themselves were not very expressive, filled me with a sort of poetical terror.

The guests drank another glass, then rose from the table and took leave of Pougatcheff.

I wanted to follow them, but Pougatcheff said to me:

"Sit down; I want to speak to you."

We remained face to face.

For some moments we both continued silent. Pougatcheff looked at me fixedly, every now and then winking his left eye with a curious expression of craftiness and drollery. At last he burst out laughing, and with such unfeigned merriment, that I, too, looking at him, began to laugh, without knowing why.

"Well, your lordship," he said to me, "confess now, you were in a terrible fright when my fellows put the rope round your neck. I do not believe that the sky appeared bigger than a sheepskin to you just then.... You would have been strung up to the crossbeam if it had not been for your servant. I knew the old fellow at once. Well, would your lordship have thought that the man who conducted you to the inn, was the great Czar himself?"

Here he assumed an air of mystery and importance.

"You have been guilty of a serious offence against me," continued he, "but I pardoned you on account of your virtue, and because you rendered me a service when I was compelled to hide myself from my enemies. But you will see something very different presently! You will see how I will reward you when I enter into possession of my kingdom! Will you promise to serve me with zeal?"

The rascal's question, and his insolence, appeared to me so amusing, that I could not help smiling.

"Why do you smile?" he asked, frowning. "Perhaps you do not believe that I am the great Czar? Is that so?—answer plainly."

I became confused. To acknowledge a vagabond as emperor was quite out of the question; to do so seemed to me unpardonable cowardice. To tell him to his face that he was an impostor was to expose myself to certain death, and that which I was prepared to say beneath the gibbet before the eyes of the crowd, in the first outburst of my indignation, appeared to me now a useless boast. I hesitated. In gloomy silence Pougatcheff awaited my reply. At last (and even now I remember that moment with self-satisfaction) the sentiment of duty triumphed over my human weakness. I replied to Pougatcheff:

"Listen, I will tell you the whole truth. Judge yourself: can I acknowledge you as emperor? You, as a sensible man, would know that it would not be saying what I really thought."

"Who am I, then, in your opinion?"

"God only knows; but whoever you may be, you are playing a dangerous game."

Pougatcheff threw a rapid glance at me.

"Then you do not believe," said he, "that I am the Emperor Peter? Well, be it so. But is not success the reward of the bold? Did not Grishka Otrepieff[38] reign in former days? Think of me what you please, but do not leave me. What does it matter to you one way or the other? Whoever is pope is father. Serve me faithfully and truly, and I will make you a field-marshal and a prince. What do you say?"

"No," I replied with firmness. "I am by birth a nobleman; I have taken the oath of fealty to the empress: I cannot serve you. If you really wish me well, send me back to Orenburg."

Pougatcheff reflected.

"But if I let you go," said he, "will you at least promise not to serve against me?"

"How can I promise you that?" I replied. "You yourself know that it does not depend upon my own will. If I am ordered to march against you, I must go—there is no help for it. You yourself are now a chief; you demand obedience from your followers. How would it seem, if I refused to serve when my services were needed? My life is in your hands: if you set me free, I will thank you; if you put me to death, God will be your judge; but I have told you the truth."

My frankness struck Pougatcheff.

"Be it so," said he, slapping me upon the shoulder. "One should either punish completely or pardon completely. Go then where you like, and do what you like. Come to-morrow to say good-bye to me, and now go to bed. I feel very drowsy myself."

I left Pougatcheff and went out into the street. The night was calm and cold. The moon and stars were shining brightly, lighting

---

38 The first false Demetrius, the Perkin Warbeck of Russia. The real Demetrius was the son of Ivan the Terrible (Ivan IV.), and is generally believed to have been assassinated by order of Boris Godunoff, a nobleman of Tartar origin, who was afterwards elected Czar. Otrepieff's story was that his physician had pretended to comply with the orders of Boris, but had substituted the son of a serf for him. Being supported in his claims by the Poles, the pretender succeeded in gaining the throne, but his partiality for everything Polish aroused the national jealousy of the Russians, and he was slain by the infuriated populace of Moscow, after a brief reign of one year.

up the square and the gibbet. In the fortress all was dark and still. Only in the tavern was a light visible, where could be heard the noise of late revellers.

I glanced at the pope's house. The shutters and doors were closed. Everything seemed quiet within.

I made my way to my own quarters and found Savelitch grieving about my absence. The news of my being set at liberty filled him with unutterable joy.

"Thanks be to Thee, Almighty God!" said he, making the sign of the cross. "At daybreak to-morrow we will leave the fortress and go wherever God will direct us. I have prepared something for you; eat it, my little father, and then rest yourself till the morning, as if you were in the bosom of Christ."

I followed his advice and, having eaten with a good appetite, I fell asleep upon the bare floor, worn out both in body and mind.

CHAPTER IX

THE PARTING

Early next morning I was awakened by the drum. I went to the place of assembly. There Pougatcheff's followers were already drawn up round the gibbet, where the victims of the day before were still hanging. The Cossacks were on horseback, the soldiers were under arms. Flags were waving. Several cannon, among which I recognized our own, were mounted on travelling gun-carriages. All the inhabitants were gathered together there, awaiting the usurper. Before the steps of the Commandant's house a Cossack stood holding by the bridle a magnificent white horse of Kirghis breed. I looked about for the corpse of the Commandant's wife. It had been pushed a little on one side and covered with a mat. At length Pougatcheff came out of the house. The crowd took off their caps. Pougatcheff stood still upon the steps and greeted his followers. One of the chiefs gave him a bag filled with copper coins, and he began to scatter them by handfuls. The crowd commenced scrambling for them with eager cries, and there was no lack of pushing and scuffling in the attempts to get possession of them. Pougatcheff's chief followers assembled round him. Among them stood Shvabrin.

Our eyes met; in mine he could read contempt, and he turned away with an expression of genuine hate and affected scorn. Pougatcheff, seeing me among the crowd, nodded his head to me and called me to him.

"Listen," said he to me, "set off at once for Orenburg and tell the governor and all the generals from me, that they may expect me in about a week. Advise them to receive me with filial love and submission; otherwise they shall not escape a terrible punishment. A pleasant journey, your lordship!"

Then turning round to the crowd and pointing to Shvabrin, he said:

"There, children, is your new Commandant. Obey him in everything; he is answerable to me for you and for the fortress."

I heard these words with alarm: Shvabrin being made governor of the fortress, Maria Ivanovna remained in his power! Great God! what would become of her!

Pougatcheff descended the steps. His horse was brought to him. He vaulted nimbly into the saddle, without waiting for the Cossacks, who were going to help him to mount.

At that moment I saw my Savelitch emerge from the midst of the crowd; he approached Pougatcheff and gave him a sheet of paper. I could not imagine what was the meaning of this proceeding on his part.

"What is this?" asked Pougatcheff, with an air of importance.

"Read it, then you will see," replied Savelitch. Pougatcheff took the paper and examined it for a long time with a consequential look.

"Why do you write so illegibly?" said he at last. "Our lucid eyes[39] cannot decipher a word. Where is my chief secretary?"

A young man, in the uniform of a corporal, immediately ran up to Pougatcheff.

"Read it aloud," said the usurper, giving him the paper.

I was exceedingly curious to know what my follower could have written to Pougatcheff about. The chief secretary, in a loud voice, began to spell out as follows:

"Two dressing-gowns, one of linen and one of striped silk, six roubles."

"What does this mean?" said Pougatcheff, frowning.

"Order him to read on," replied Savelitch coolly.

The chief secretary continued:

"One uniform coat of fine green cloth, seven roubles.

---

[39] An allusion to the customary form of speech on presenting a petition to the Czar: "I strike the earth with my forehead, and present my petition to your lucid eyes."

"One pair of white cloth breeches, five roubles.

"Twelve Holland linen shirts with ruffles, ten roubles.

"A chest and tea-service, two roubles and a half...."

"What is all this nonsense?" exclaimed Pougatcheff. "What are these chests and breeches with ruffles to do with me?"

Savelitch cleared his throat and began to explain.

"This, my father, you will please to understand is a list of my master's goods that have been stolen by those scoundrels——"

"What scoundrels?" said Pougatcheff, threateningly.

"I beg your pardon, that was a slip on my part," replied Savelitch. "They were not scoundrels, but your fellows, who have rummaged and plundered everything. Do not be angry: the horse has got four legs, and yet he stumbles. Order him to read to the end."

"Read on to the end," said Pougatcheff.

The secretary continued:

"One chintz counterpane, another of taffety quilted with cotton wool, four roubles.

"A fox-skin pelisse, covered with red flannel, forty roubles.

"Likewise a hare-skin morning-gown, presented to your Grace at the inn on the steppe, fifteen roubles."

"What's that'!" exclaimed Pougatcheff, his eyes flashing fire.

I confess that I began to feel alarmed for my poor servant. He was about to enter again into explanations, but Pougatcheff interrupted him.

"How dare you pester me with such nonsense!" he cried, snatching the paper out of the secretary's hands and flinging it in Savelitch's face. "Stupid old man! You have been robbed; what a misfortune! Why, old greybeard, you ought to be eternally praying to God for me and my lads, that you and your master are not hanging yonder along with the other traitors to me.... A hare-skin morning-gown! Do you know that I could order you to be flayed alive and have your skin made into a morning-gown?"

"As you please," replied Savelitch; "but I am not a free man, and must be answerable for my lord's goods."

Pougatcheff was evidently in a magnanimous humour. He turned round and rode off without saying another word. Shvabrin and the chiefs followed him. The troops marched out of the fortress in order. The crowd pressed forward to accompany Pougatcheff. I remained in the square alone with Savelitch. My servant held in his hand the list of my things and stood looking at it with an air of deep regret.

Seeing me on such good terms with Pougatcheff, he thought that he might take advantage of the circumstance; but his sage scheme did not succeed. I was on the point of scolding him for his misplaced zeal, but I could not restrain myself from laughing.

"Laugh away, my lord," replied Savelitch: "laugh away; but when the time comes for you to procure a new outfit, we shall see if you will laugh then."

I hastened to the priest's house to see Maria Ivanovna. The priest's wife met me with sad news. During the night Maria Ivanovna had been seized with a violent attack of fever. She lay unconscious and in a delirium. The priest's wife conducted me into her room. I softly approached her bed. The change in her face startled me. She did not recognize me. For a long time I stood beside her without paying any heed either to Father Gerasim or to his good wife, who endeavoured to console me. Gloomy thoughts took possession of me. The condition of the poor defenceless orphan, left alone in the midst of the lawless rebels, as well as my own powerlessness, terrified me. But it was the thought of Shvabrin more than anything else that filled my imagination with alarm. Invested with power by the usurper, and entrusted with the command of the fortress, in which the unhappy girl—the innocent object of his hatred—remained, he was capable of any villainous act. What was I to do? How should I help her? How could I rescue her out of the hands of the brigands? There remained only one way. I resolved to set out immediately for Orenburg, in order to hasten the deliverance of Bailogorsk, and, as far as possible, to co-operate in the undertaking. I took leave of the priest and of Akoulina Pamphilovna, recommending to their care her whom I already considered as my wife. I seized the hand of the poor girl and kissed it, bedewing it with my tears.

"Farewell," said the pope's wife to me, accompanying me to the door "farewell, Peter Andreitch. Perhaps we shall see each other again in happier times. Do not forget us, and write to us often. Poor Maria Ivanovna has nobody now, except you, to console and protect her."

On reaching the square, I stopped for a moment and looked at the gibbet, then, bowing my head before it, I quitted the fortress and took the road to Orenburg, accompanied by Savelitch, who had not left my side.

I was walking on, occupied with my reflections, when suddenly I heard behind me the trampling of horses' feet. Looking round, I saw, galloping out of the fortress, a Cossack, holding a Bashkir horse by the rein and making signs to me from afar. I stopped and soon recognized our orderly. Galloping up to us, he dismounted from his own horse, and giving me the rein of the other, said:

"Your lordship! our father sends you a horse, and a pelisse from

63

his own shoulders." (To the saddle was attached a sheepskin pelisse.) "Moreover," continued the orderly with some hesitation, "he sends you—half-a-rouble—but I have lost it on the road; be generous and pardon me."

Savelitch eyed him askance and growled out:

"You lost it on the road! What is that chinking in your pocket, then, you shameless rascal!"

"What is that chinking in my pocket?" replied the orderly, without being in the least confused. "God be with you, old man! It is a horse's bit, and not half-a-rouble."

"Very well," said I, putting an end to the dispute. "Give my thanks to him who sent you; and as you go back, try and find the lost half-rouble and keep it for drink-money."

"Many thanks, your lordship," replied he, turning his horse round; "I will pray to God for you without ceasing." With these words he galloped back again, holding one hand to his pocket, and in about a minute he was hidden from sight.

I put on the pelisse and mounted the horse, taking Savelitch up behind me.

"Now do you see, my lord," said the old man, "that I did not give the petition to the rascal in vain? The robber felt ashamed of himself. Although this lean-looking Bashkir jade and this sheepskin pelisse are not worth half of what the rascals stole from us, and what you chose to give him yourself, they may yet be of some use to us; from a vicious dog, even a tuft of hair."

CHAPTER X

THE SIEGE

In approaching Orenburg, we saw a crowd of convicts, with shaven heads, and with faces disfigured by the hangman's pincers. They were at work on the fortifications, under the direction of the soldiers of the garrison. Some were carrying away in wheel-barrows the earth and refuse which filled the moat, others with shovels were digging up the ground; on the rampart the masons were carrying stones and repairing the walls. The sentinels stopped us at the gate and demanded our passports. As soon as the sergeant heard that I came from Bailogorsk, he took me straight to the General's house.

I found him in the garden. He was inspecting the apple-trees, which the autumn winds had stripped of their leaves, and, with the help of an old gardener, was carefully covering them with straw. His face expressed tranquillity, health, and good-nature. He was much pleased to see me, and began questioning me about the terrible events of which I had been an eye-witness. I related everything to him. The old man listened to me with attention, and continued the meantime to lop off the dry twigs.

"Poor Mironoff!" said he, when I had finished my sad story; "I feel very sorry for him, he was a good officer; and Madame Mironoff was a good woman,—how clever she was at pickling mushrooms! And what has become of Masha, the Captain's daughter?"

I replied that she was still at the fortress in the hands of the pope and his wife.

"That is bad, very bad. Nobody can place any dependence upon the discipline of robbers. What will become of the poor girl?"

I replied that the fortress of Bailogorsk was not far off and that, without doubt, his Excellency would not delay in sending thither a detachment of soldiers to deliver the poor inhabitants.

The General shook his head dubiously.

"We shall see, we shall see," said he, "we have plenty of time to talk about that. Do me the pleasure of taking a cup of tea with me: a council of war is to be held at my house this evening. You may be able to give us some trustworthy information concerning this rascal Pougatcheff and his army. And now go and rest yourself for a little while."

I went to the quarter assigned to me, where Savelitch had already installed himself, and where I awaited with impatience the appointed time. The reader will easily imagine that I did not fail to make my appearance at the council which was to have such an influence upon my fate At the appointed hour I repaired to the General's house.

I found with him one of the civil officials of the town, the director of the custom-house, if I remember rightly, a stout, red-faced old man in a silk coat. He began to question me about the fate of Ivan Kouzmitch, whom he called his gossip, and frequently interrupted my discourse with additional questions and moral observations, which, if they did not prove him to be a man well versed in military matters, showed at least that he possessed sagacity and common sense. In the meantime the other persons who had been invited to the council had assembled. When they were all seated, and a cup of tea had been handed round to each, the

General entered into a clear and detailed account of the business in question.

"And now, gentlemen," continued he, "we must decide in what way we are to act against the rebels: offensively or defensively? Each of these methods has its advantages and disadvantages. Offensive warfare holds out a greater prospect of a quicker extermination of the enemy; defensive action is safer and less dangerous.... Therefore let us commence by putting the question to the vote in legal order, that is, beginning with the youngest in rank. Ensign," continued he, turning to me, "will you please favour us with your opinion?"

I rose, and after having described, in a few words, Pougatcheff and his followers, I expressed my firm opinion that the usurper was not in a position to withstand disciplined troops.

My opinion was received by the civil officials with evident dissatisfaction. They saw in it only the rashness and temerity of a young man. There arose a murmur, and I distinctly heard the word "greenhorn" pronounced in a whisper. The General turned to me and said with a smile:

"Ensign, the first voices in councils of war are generally in favour of adopting offensive measures. We will now continue and hear what others have to say. Mr. Counsellor of the College, tell us your opinion."

The little old man in the silk coat hastily swallowed his third cup of tea, into which he had poured some rum, and then replied:

"I think, your Excellency, that we ought to act neither offensively nor defensively."

"How, Sir Counsellor?" replied the astonished General. "Tactics present no other methods of action; offensive action or defensive...."

"Your Excellency, act diplomatically."

"Ah! your idea is a very sensible one. Diplomatic action is allowed by the laws of tactics, and we will profit by your advice. We might offer for the head of the rascal ... seventy or even a hundred roubles ... out of the secret funds...."

"And then," interrupted the Director of the Customs, "may I become a Kirghis ram, and not a College Counsellor, if these robbers do not deliver up to us their leader, bound hand and foot."

"We will think about it, and speak of it again," replied the General. "But, in any case, we must take military precautions. Gentlemen, give your votes in regular order."

The opinions of all were contrary to mine. All the civil officials expatiated upon the untrustworthiness of the troops, the uncertainty of success, the necessity of being cautious, and the like. All agreed' that it was more prudent to remain behind the stone walls of the fortress under the protection of the cannon, than to try the fortune of arms in the open field. At length the General, having heard all their opinions, shook the ashes from his pipe and spoke as follows:

"Gentlemen, I must declare to you that, for my part, I am entirely of the same opinion as the ensign; because this opinion is founded upon sound rules of tactics, which nearly always give the preference to offensive action rather than to defensive."

Then he paused and began to fill his pipe. My vanity triumphed. I cast a proud glance at the civil officials, who were whispering among themselves with looks of displeasure and uneasiness.

"But, gentlemen," continued the General, heaving a deep sigh, and emitting at the same time a thick cloud of tobacco smoke, "I dare not take upon myself such a great responsibility, when it is a question of the safety of the provinces confided to me by Her Imperial Majesty, my Most Gracious Sovereign. Therefore it is that I fall in with the views of the majority, who have decided that it is safer and more prudent to await the siege inside the town, and to repel the attack of the enemy by the use of artillery and—if possible—by sallies."

The officials in their turn now glanced at me ironically. The council separated. I could not but deplore the weakness of this estimable soldier, who, contrary to his own conviction, resolved to follow the advice of ignorant and inexperienced persons.

Some days after this memorable council we heard that Pougatcheff, faithful to his promise, was marching on Orenburg. From the lofty walls of the town I observed the army of the rebels. It seemed to me that their numbers had increased since the last assault, of which I had been a witness. They had with them also some pieces of artillery which had been taken by Pougatcheff from the small fortresses that had been conquered by him. Remembering the decision of the council, I foresaw a long incarceration within the walls of Orenburg, and I was almost ready to weep with vexation.

I do not intend to describe the siege of Orenburg, which belongs to history and not to family memoirs. I will merely observe that this siege, through want of caution on the part of the local authorities, was a disastrous one for the inhabitants, who had to endure hunger and every possible privation. It can easily be imagined that life in Orenburg was almost unbearable. All awaited in melancholy anxiety the decision of fate; all complained of the famine, which was really terrible. The inhabitants became accustomed to the cannon-balls falling upon their houses; even Pougatcheff's assaults no longer produced any excitement. I was dying of ennui. Time wore on. I received no letters from Bailogorsk.

All the roads were cut off. Separation from Marla Ivanovna became insupportable to me. Uncertainty with respect to her fate tortured me. My only diversion consisted in making excursions outside the city. Thanks to the kindness of Pougatcheff, I had a good horse, with which I shared my scanty allowance of food, and upon whose back I used to ride out daily beyond the walls and open fire upon Pougatcheff's partisans. In these skirmishes the advantage was generally on the side of the rebels, who had plenty to eat and drink, and possessed good horses. Our miserable cavalry were unable to cope with them. Sometimes our famished infantry made a sally; but the depth of the snow prevented their operations being successful against the flying cavalry of the enemy. The artillery thundered in vain from the summit of the ramparts, and had it been in the field, it could not have advanced on account of our emaciated horses. Such was our style of warfare! And this was what the civil officials of Orenburg called prudence and foresight!

One day, when we had succeeded in dispersing and driving off a tolerably large body of the enemy, I came up with a Cossack who had remained behind his companions, and I was just about to strike him with my Turkish sabre, when he suddenly took off his cap and cried out:

"Good day, Peter Andreitch; how do you do?"

I looked at him and recognized our orderly. I cannot say how delighted I was to see him.

"Good day, Maximitch," said I to him. "How long is it since you left Bailogorsk?"

"Not long, Peter Andreitch; I only returned from there yesterday. I have a letter for you."

"Where is it?" cried I, perfectly beside myself with excitement.

"I have it here," replied Maximitch, placing his hand upon his bosom. "I promised Palasha that I would give it to you somehow."

He then gave me a folded paper and immediately galloped off. I opened it and, deeply agitated, read the following lines:

"It has pleased God to deprive me suddenly of both father and mother: I have now on earth neither a relation nor a protector. I therefore turn to you, because I know that you have always wished me well, and that you are ever ready to help others. I pray to God that this letter may reach you in some way! Maximitch has promised to give it to you. Palasha has also heard from Maximitch that he has frequently seen you from a distance in the sorties, and that you do not take the least care of yourself, not thinking about those who pray to God for you in tears. I was ill a

68

long time, and, when I recovered, Alexei Ivanovitch, who commands here in place of my deceased father, compelled Father Gerasim to deliver me up to him, threatening him with Pougatcheff's anger if he refused. I live in our house which is guarded by a sentry. Alexei Ivanovitch wants to compel me to marry him. He says that he saved my life because he did not reveal the deception practised by Akoulina Pamphilovna, who told the rebels that I was her niece. But I would rather die than become the wife of such a man as Alexei Ivanovitch. He treats me very cruelly, and threatens that if I do not change my mind and agree to his proposal, he will conduct me to the rebels' camp, where I shall suffer the same fate as Elizabeth Kharloff.[40] I have begged Alexei Ivanovitch to give me time to reflect. He has consented to give me three days longer, and if at the end of that time I do not agree to become his wife, he will show me no further mercy. Oh, Peter Andreitch! you are my only protector; save a poor helpless girl! Implore the General and all the commanders to send us help as soon as possible, and come yourself if you can.

"I remain your poor obedient orphan,

"MARIA MIRONOFF."

The reading of this letter almost drove me out of my mind. I galloped back to the town, spurring my poor horse without mercy. On the way I turned over in my I mind one plan and another for the rescue of the poor girl, but I could not come to any definite conclusion. On reaching the town I immediately repaired to the General's, and presented myself before him without the least delay.

He was walking up and down the room, smoking his meerschaum pipe. On seeing me he stopped. Probably; he was struck by my appearance, for he anxiously inquired the reason of my hasty visit.

"Your Excellency," said I to him, "I come to you as I would to my own father: for Heaven's sake, do not refuse my request; the happiness of my whole life depends upon it!"

"What is the matter?" asked the astonished old soldier. "What can I do for you? Speak!"

"Your Excellency, allow me to take a battalion of soldiers and a company of Cossacks to recapture the fortress of Bailogorsk."

The General looked at me earnestly, imagining, without doubt,

---

[40] A Commandant's daughter, whom Pougatcheff outraged and then put to death.

that I had taken leave of my senses—and, for the matter of that, he was not very far out in his supposition.

"How?—what? Recapture the fortress of Bailogorsk?" said he at last.

"I will answer for the success of the undertaking," I replied with ardour; "only let me go."

"No, young man," said he, shaking his head. "At such a great distance the enemy would easily cut off your communication with the principal strategical point, and gain a complete victory over you. Communication being cut off...."

I became alarmed when I perceived that he was about to enter upon a military dissertation, and I hastened to interrupt him.

"The daughter of Captain Mironoff has written a letter to me," I said to him; "she asks for help: Shvabrin wants to compel her to become his wife."

"Indeed! Oh, this Shvabrin is a great rascal, and if he should fall into my hands I will order him to be tried within twenty-four hours, and we will have him shot on the parapet of the fortress. But in the meantime we must have patience."

"Have patience!" I cried, perfectly beside myself. "But in the meantime he will force Maria Ivanovna to become his wife!"

"Oh!" exclaimed the General. "But even that would be no great misfortune for her. It would be better for her to become the wife of Shvabrin, he would then take her under his protection; and when we have shot him we will soon find a sweetheart for her, please God. Pretty widows do not remain single long; I mean that a widow finds a husband much quicker than a spinster."

"I would rather die," said I in a passion, "than resign her to Shvabrin."

"Oh, oh!" said the old man, "now I understand. You are evidently in love with Maria Ivanovna, and that alters the case altogether. Poor fellow! But, for all that, I cannot give you a battalion of soldiers and fifty Cossacks. Such an expedition would be the height of folly, and I cannot take the responsibility of it upon myself."

I cast down my head; despair took possession of me. Suddenly a thought flashed through my mind: what it was, the reader will discover in the following chapter, as the old romance writers used to say.

CHAPTER XI

THE REBEL ENCAMPMENT

I left the General and hastened to my own quarters. Savelitch received me with his usual admonitions.

"What pleasure do you find, my lord, in fighting against drunken robbers? Is that the kind of occupation for a nobleman? All hours are not alike, and you will sacrifice your life for nothing. It would be all well and good if you were fighting against the Turks or the Swedes, but it is a shame to mention the name of the enemy that you are dealing with now."

I interrupted him in his speech by the question:

"How much money have I left?"

"You have a tolerably good sum still left," he replied, with a look of satisfaction. "In spite of their searching and rummaging, I succeeded in hiding it from the robbers." So saying, he drew from his pocket a long knitted purse, filled with silver pieces.

"Well, Savelitch," said I to him, "give me half of what you have, and keep the rest yourself. I am going to Fortress Bailogorsk."

"My little father, Peter Andreitch!" said my good old servant in a trembling voice; "do not tempt God! How can you travel at the present time, when none of the roads are free from the robbers? Have compassion upon your parents, if you have no pity for yourself. Where do you Want to go? And why? Wait a little while. The troops will soon be here and will quickly make short work of the robbers. Then you may go in whatever direction you like." But my resolution was not to be shaken.

"It is too late to reflect," I said to the old man. "I must go, I cannot do otherwise than go. Do not grieve, Savelitch: God is merciful, perhaps we may see each other again. Have no scruples about spending the money, and don't be sparing of it. Buy whatever you require, even though you have to pay three times the value of it. I give this money to you. If in three days I do not return——"

"What are you talking about, my lord?" said Savelitch, interrupting me. "Do you think that I could let you go alone? Do not imagine anything of the kind. If you have resolved to go, I will accompany you, even though it be on foot; I will not leave you. The idea of my sitting down behind a stone wall without you! Do you think then that I have gone out of my mind? Do as you please, my lord, but I will not leave you."

I knew that it was useless to dispute with Savelitch, and I

allowed him to prepare for the journey. In half an hour I was seated upon the back of my good horse, while Savelitch was mounted upon a lean and limping jade, which one of the inhabitants of the town had given to him for nothing, not having the means to keep it any longer. We reached the gates of the town; the sentinels allowed us to pass, and we left Orenburg behind us.

It was beginning to grow dark. My road led past the village of Berd, one of Pougatcheff's haunts. The way was covered with snow, but over the whole of the steppe could be seen the footprints of horses, renewed every day. I rode forward at a quick trot. Savelitch could hardly keep pace with me, and kept calling out:

"Not so fast, my lord, for Heaven's sake, not so fast! My accursed hack cannot keep up with your long-legged devil. Where are you off to in such a hurry? It would be all very well if we were going to a feast, but we are more likely going to run our heads into a noose.... Peter Andreitch ... little father ... Peter Andreitch! Lord God! the child is rushing to destruction!"

We soon caught sight of the fires of Berd glimmering in the distance. We approached some ravines, which served as natural defences to the hamlet. Savelitch still followed me, and did not cease to utter his plaintive entreaties. I hoped to be able to ride round the village without being observed, when suddenly I perceived through the darkness, straight in front of me, five peasants armed with clubs; it was the advanced guard of Pougatcheff's camp. They challenged us. Not knowing the password, I wanted to ride on without saying anything; but they immediately surrounded me, and one of them seized hold of my horse's bridle. I drew my sword and struck the peasant on the head. His cap saved him, but he staggered and let the reins fall from his hand. The others grew frightened and took to their heels; I seized the opportunity, and, setting spurs to my horse, I galloped off.

The increasing darkness of the night might have saved me from further dangers, but, turning round all at once, I perceived that Savelitch was no longer with me. The poor old man, with his lame horse, had not been able to get clear of the robbers. What was to be done? After waiting a few minutes for him, and feeling convinced that he had been stopped, I turned my horse round to hasten to his assistance.

Approaching the ravine, I heard in the distance confused cries, and the voice of my Savelitch. I quickened my pace, and soon found myself in the midst of the peasants who had stopped me a few minutes before. Savelitch was among them. With loud shouts they threw themselves upon me and dragged me from my horse in a twinkling. One of them, apparently the leader of the band, informed us that he was going to conduct us immediately before the Czar. I "And our father," added he, "will decide whether you shall be hanged immediately or wait till daylight."

I offered no resistance; Savelitch followed my example, and the sentinels led us away in triumph.

We crossed the ravine and entered the village. In all the huts fires were burning. Noise and shouts resounded on every side. In the streets I met a large number of people; but nobody observed us in the darkness, and no one recognized in me an officer from Orenburg. We were conducted straight to a cottage which stood at the corner where two streets met. Before the door stood several wine-casks and two pieces of artillery.

"This is the palace," said one of the peasants; "we will announce you at once."

He entered the cottage. I glanced at Savelitch: the old man was making the sign of the cross and muttering his prayers to himself.

I waited a long time; at last the peasant returned and said to me:

"Come inside; our father has given orders for the officer to be brought before him."

I entered the cottage, or the palace, as the peasants called it. It was lighted by two tallow candles, and the walls were covered with gilt paper; otherwise, the benches, the table, the little wash-hand basin suspended by a cord, the towel hanging on a nail, the oven-fork in the corner, the broad shelf loaded with pots—everything was the same as in an ordinary cottage. Pougatcheff was seated under the holy picture,[41] dressed in a red caftan and wearing a tall cap, and with his arms set akimbo in a very self-important manner. Around him stood several of his principal followers, with looks of feigned respect and submission upon their faces. It was evident that the news of the arrival of an officer from Orenburg had awakened a great curiosity among the rebels, and that they had prepared to receive me with as much pomp as possible. Pougatcheff recognized me at the first glance. His assumed importance vanished all at once.

"Ah! your lordship!" said he gaily. "How do you do?"

"What, in Heaven's name, has brought you here?"

I replied that I was travelling on my own business, and that his people had stopped me.

"What business?" asked he.

I knew not what to reply. Pougatcheff, supposing that I did not

---

41 The picture of some saint, usually painted on wood. There is generally one of them hung in the corner of every room in the houses of the Russians.

like to explain in the presence of witnesses, turned to his companions and ordered them to go out of the room. All obeyed, except two, who did not stir from their places.

"Speak boldly before them," said Pougatcheff, "I do not hide anything from them."

I glanced stealthily at the impostor's confidants. One of them, a weazen-faced, crooked old man, with a short grey beard, had nothing remarkable about him except a blue riband, which he wore across his grey tunic. But never shall I forget his companion. He was a tall, powerful, broad-shouldered man, and seemed to me to be about forty-five years of age. A thick red beard, grey piercing eyes, a nose without nostrils, and reddish scars upon his forehead and cheeks, gave to his broad, pock-marked face an indescribable expression. He had on a red shirt, a Kirghis robe, and Cossack trousers. The first, as I learned afterwards, was the runaway corporal Bailoborodoff; the other, Afanassy Sokoloff, surnamed Khlopousha,[42] a condemned criminal, who had three times escaped from the mines of Siberia. In spite of the feelings of agitation which so exclusively occupied my mind at that time, the society in the midst of which I so unexpectedly found myself awakened my curiosity in a powerful degree. But Pougatcheff soon recalled me to myself by his question:

"Speak! on what business did you leave Orenburg?"

A strange thought came into my head: it seemed to me that Providence, by conducting me a second time into the presence of Pougatcheff, gave me the opportunity of carrying my project into execution. I determined to take advantage of it, and, without any further reflection, I replied to Pougatcheff's question:

"I was going to the fortress of Bailogorsk to rescue an orphan who is oppressed there."

Pougatcheff's eyes sparkled.

"Which of my people dares to oppress the orphan?" cried he. "Were he seven feet high he should not escape my judgment. Speak! who is the culprit?"

"Shvabrin is the culprit," replied I. "He holds captive the young girl whom you saw ill at the priest's house, and wants to force her to marry him."

"I will soon put Shvabrin in his right place," said Pougatcheff fiercely. "He shall learn what it is to oppress my people according to his own will and pleasure. I will have him hanged."

"Allow me to speak a word," said Khlopousha in a hoarse; voice.

---

[42] The name of a celebrated bandit of the last century, who for a long time offered resistance to the Imperial troops.

"You were in too great a hurry in appointing Shvabrin to the command of the fortress, and now you are in too great a hurry to hang him. You have already offended the Cossacks by placing a nobleman over them as their chief; do not now alarm the nobles by hanging them at the first accusation."

"They ought neither to be pitied nor favoured," said the little old man with the blue riband. "To hang Shvabrin would be no great misfortune, neither would it be amiss to put this officer through a regular course of questions. Why has he deigned to pay us a visit? If he does not recognize you as Czar, he cannot come to seek justice from you; and if he does recognize you, why has he remained up to the present time in Orenburg along with your enemies? Will you not order him to be conducted to the court-house, and have a fire lit there?[43] It seems to me that his Grace is sent to us from the generals in Orenburg."

The logic of the old rascal seemed to me to be plausible enough. A shudder passed through the whole of my body, when I thought into whose hands I had fallen. Pougatcheff observed my agitation.

"Well, your lordship," said he to me, winking his eyes; "my Field-Marshal, it seems to me, speaks to the point. What do you think?"

Pougatcheff's raillery restored my courage. I calmly replied that I was in his power, and that he could deal with me in whatever way he pleased.

"Good," said Pougatcheff. "Now tell me, in what condition is your town?"

"Thank God!" I replied, "everything is all right."

"All right!" repeated Pougatcheff, "and the people are dying of hunger!"

The impostor spoke the truth; but in accordance with the duty imposed upon me by my oath, I assured him that what he had heard were only idle reports, and that in Orenburg there was a sufficiency of all kinds of provisions.

"You see," observed the little old man, "that he deceives you to your face. All the deserters unanimously declare that famine and sickness are rife in Orenburg, that they are eating carrion there and think themselves fortunate to get it to eat; and yet his Grace assures us that there is plenty of everything there. If you wish to hang Shvabrin, then hang this young fellow on the same gallows, that they may have nothing to reproach each other with."

The words of the accursed old man seemed to produce an effect

---

43 For the purpose of torture.

upon Pougatcheff. Fortunately, Khlopousha began to contradict his companion.

"That will do, Naoumitch," said he to him: "you only think of strangling and hanging. What sort of a hero are you? To look at you, one is puzzled to imagine how your body and soul contrive to hang together. You have one foot in the grave yourself, and you want to kill others. Haven't you enough blood on your conscience?"

"And what sort of a saint are you?" replied Bailoborodoff. "Whence this compassion on your side?"

"Without doubt," replied Khlopousha, "I also am a sinner, and this hand"—here he clenched his bony fist and, pushing back his sleeve, disclosed his hairy arm—"and this hand is guilty of having shed Christian blood. But I killed my enemy, and not my guest; on the open highway or in a dark wood, and not in the house, sitting behind the stove; with the axe and club, and not with old woman's chatter."

The old man turned round and muttered the words: "Slit nostrils!"

"What are you muttering, you old greybeard?" cried Khlopousha. "I will give you slit nostrils. Just wait a little, and your turn will come too. Heaven grant that your nose may smell the pincers.... In the meantime, take care that I don't pull out your ugly beard by the roots." "Gentlemen, generals!" said Pougatcheff loftily, "there has been enough of this quarrelling between you. It would be no great misfortune if all the Orenburg dogs were hanging by the heels from the same crossbeam; but it would be a very great misfortune if our own dogs were to begin devouring each other. So now make it up and be friends again."

Khlopousha and Bailoborodoff said not a word, but glared furiously at each other. I felt the necessity of changing the subject of a conversation which might end in a very disagreeable manner for me, and turning to Pougatcheff, I said to him with a cheerful look:

"Ah! I had almost forgotten to thank you for the horse and pelisse. Without you I should never have reached the town, and I should have been frozen to death on the road."

My stratagem succeeded. Pougatcheff became good-humoured again.

"The payment of a debt is its beauty," said he, winking his eyes. "And now tell me, what have you to do with this young girl whom Shvabrin persecutes? Has she kindled a flame in your young heart, eh?"

"She is my betrothed," I replied, observing a favourable change in the storm, and hot deeming it necessary to conceal the truth.

"Your betrothed!" exclaimed Pougatcheff. "Why did you not say so before? We will marry you, then, and have some merriment at your wedding!"

Then turning to Bailoborodoff:

"Listen, Field-Marshal!" said he to him: "his lordship and I are old friends; let us sit down to supper; morning's judgment is wiser than that of evening—so we will see to-morrow what is to be done with him."

I would gladly have declined the proposed honour, but there was no help for it. Two young Cossack girls, daughters of the owner of the cottage, covered the table with a white cloth, and brought in some bread, fish-soup, and several bottles of wine and beer, and for the second time I found myself seated at the same table with Pougatcheff and his terrible companions.

The drunken revel, of which, I was an involuntary witness, continued till late into the night. At last, intoxication began; to overcome the three associates. Pougatcheff fell off to sleep where he was sitting: his companions rose and made signs to me to leave him where he was. I went out with them. By order of Khlopousha, the sentinel conducted me; to the justice-room, where I found Savelitch, and where they left me shut up with him. My servant was so astonished at all he saw and heard, that he could not ask me a single question. He lay down in the dark, and continued to sigh and moan for a long time; but at length he began to snore, and I gave myself up to meditations, which hindered me from obtaining sleep for a single minute during the whole of the night.

The next morning, Pougatcheff gave orders for me to be brought before him. I went to him. In front of his door stood a kibitka, with three Tartar horses harnessed to it. The crowd filled the street. I encountered Pougatcheff in the hall. He was dressed for a journey, being attired in a fur cloak and a Kirghis cap. His companions of the night before stood around him, exhibiting an appearance of submission, which contrasted strongly with everything that I had witnessed the previous evening. Pougatcheff saluted me in a cheerful tone, and ordered me to sit down beside him in the kibitka.

We took our seats.

"To the fortress of Bailogorsk!" said Pougatcheff to the broad-shouldered Tartar who drove the vehicle. My heart beat violently. The horses broke into a gallop, the little bell tinkled, and the kibitka flew over the snow.

"Stop! stop!" cried a voice which I knew only too well, and I saw Savelitch running towards us.

Pougatcheff ordered the driver to stop.

"Little father, Peter Andreitch!" cried my servant; "do not leave me in my old age among these scoun——"

"Ah, old greybeard!" said Pougatcheff to him. "It is God's will that we should meet again. Well, spring up behind."

"Thanks, Czar, thanks, my own father!" replied Savelitch, taking his seat. "May God give you a hundred years of life and good health for deigning to cast your eyes upon and console an old man. I will pray to God for you all the days of my life, and I will never again speak about the hareskin pelisse."

This allusion to the hareskin pelisse might have made Pougatcheff seriously angry. Fortunately, the usurper did not hear, or pretended not to hear, the misplaced remark. The horses again broke into a gallop; the people in the streets stood still and made obeisance. Pougatcheff bowed his head from side to side. In about a minute we had left the village behind us and were flying along over the smooth surface of the road.

One can easily imagine what my feelings were at that moment. In a few hours I should again set eyes upon her whom I had already considered as lost to me for ever. I pictured to myself the moment of our meeting.... I thought also of the man in whose hands lay my fate, and who, by a strange concourse of circumstances, had become mysteriously connected with me. I remembered the thoughtless cruelty and the bloodthirsty habits of him, who now constituted himself the deliverer of my beloved. Pougatcheff did not know that she was the daughter of Captain Mironoff; the exasperated Shvabrin might reveal everything to him; it was also possible that Pougatcheff might find out the truth in some other way.... Then what would become of Maria Ivanovna? A shudder passed through my frame, and my hair stood on end.

Suddenly Pougatcheff interrupted my meditations, by turning to me with the question:

"What is your lordship thinking of?"

"What should I not be thinking of," I replied. "I am an officer and a gentleman; only yesterday I was fighting against you, and now to-day I am riding side by side with you in the same carriage, and the happiness of my whole life depends upon you."

"How so?" asked Pougatcheff. "Are you afraid?"

I replied that, having already had my life spared by him,

I hoped, not only for his mercy, but even for his assistance.

"And you are right; by God, you are right!" said the impostor. "You saw that my fellows looked askant at you; and this morning the old man persisted in his statement that you were a spy, and that it was necessary that you should be interrogated by means of torture and then hanged. But I would not consent to it," he added, lowering his voice, so that Savelitch and the Tartar should not be able to hear him, "because I remembered your glass of wine and hareskin pelisse. You see now that I am not such a bloodthirsty creature as your brethren maintain."

I recalled to mind the capture of the fortress of Bailogorsk but I did not think it advisable to contradict him, and so I made no reply.

"What do they say of me in Orenburg?" asked Pougatcheff, after a short interval of silence.

"They say that it will be no easy matter to get the upper hand of you; and there is no denying that you have made yourself felt."

The face of the impostor betokened how much his vanity was gratified by this remark.

"Yes," said he, with a look of self-satisfaction, "I wage war to some purpose. Do you people in Orenburg know about the battle of Youzeiff?[44] Forty general officers killed, four armies taken captive. Do you think the King of Prussia could do as well as that?"

The boasting of the brigand appeared to me to be somewhat amusing.

"What do you think about it yourself?" I said to him: "do you think that you could beat Frederick?"

"Fedor Fedorovitch?[45] And why not? I beat your generals, and they have beaten him. My arms have always been successful up till now. But only wait awhile, you will see something very different when I march to Moscow."

"And do you intend marching to Moscow?"

The impostor reflected for a moment and then said in a low voice:

"God knows. My road is narrow; my will is weak. My followers do not obey me. They are scoundrels. I must keep a sharp look-out; at the first reverse they will save their own necks at the expense of my head."

"That is quite true," I said to Pougatcheff. "Would it not be better for you to separate yourself from them in good time, and throw yourself upon the mercy of the Empress?"

Pougatcheff smiled bitterly.

"No," replied he: "it is too late for me to repent now. There would be no pardon for me. I will go on as I have begun. Who knows? Perhaps I shall be successful. Grishka Otrepieff was made Czar at Moscow."

"And do you know what his end was? He was flung out of a

---

[44] An engagement in which Pougatcheff had the advantage.
[45] The name given to Frederick the Great by the Russian soldiers.

window, his body was cut to pieces and burnt, and then his ashes were placed in a cannon and scattered to the winds!"

"Listen," said Pougatcheff with a certain wild inspiration. "I will tell you a tale which was told to me in my childhood by an old Calmuck. 'The eagle once said to the crow: "Tell me, crow, why is it that you live in this bright world for three hundred years, and I only for thirty-three years?" "Because, little father," replied the crow, "you drink live blood, and I live on carrion."—The eagle reflected for a little while and then said: "Let us both try and live on the same food."—"Good! agreed!" The eagle and the crow flew away. Suddenly they caught sight of a fallen horse, and they alighted upon it. The crow began to pick its flesh and found it very good. The eagle tasted it once, then a second time, then shook its pinions and said to the crow: "No, brother crow; rather than live on carrion for three hundred years, I would prefer to drink live blood but once, and trust in God for what might happen afterwards!"' What do you think of the Calmuck's story?"

"It is very ingenious," I replied. "But to live by murder and robbery is, in my opinion, nothing else than living on carrion."

Pougatcheff looked at me in astonishment and made no reply. We both became silent, each being wrapped in his own thoughts. The Tartar began to hum a plaintive song. Savelitch, dozing, swayed from side to side. The kibitka glided along rapidly over the smooth frozen road.... Suddenly I caught sight of a little village on the steep bank of the Yaik, with its palisade and belfry, and about a quarter of an hour afterwards we entered the fortress of Bailogorsk.

CHAPTER XII

THE ORPHAN

The kibitka drew up in front of the Commandant's house. The inhabitants had recognized Pougatcheff's little bell, and came crowding around us. Shvabrin met the impostor at the foot of the steps. He was dressed as a Cossack, and had allowed his beard to grow. The traitor helped Pougatcheff to alight from the kibitka, expressing, in obsequious terms, his joy and zeal. On seeing me, he became confused; but quickly recovering himself, he stretched out his hand to me, saying:

"And are you also one of us? You should have been so long ago!"

I turned away from him and made no reply.

My heart ached when we entered the well-known room, on the wall of which still hung the commission of the late Commandant, as a mournful epitaph of the past. Pougatcheff seated himself upon the same sofa on which Ivan Kouzmitch was accustomed to fall asleep, lulled by the scolding of his wife. Shvabrin himself brought him some brandy. Pougatcheff drank a glass, and said to him, pointing to me:

"Give his lordship a glass."

Shvabrin approached me with his tray, but I turned away from him a second time. He seemed to have become quite another person. With his usual sagacity, he had certainly perceived that Pougatcheff was dissatisfied with him. He cowered before him, and glanced at me with distrust.

Pougatcheff asked some questions concerning the condition of the fortress, the reports referring to the enemy's army, and the like. Then suddenly and unexpectedly he said to him:

"Tell me, my friend, who is this young girl that you hold a prisoner here? Show her to me."

Shvabrin turned as pale as death.

"Czar," said he, in a trembling voice... "Czar, she is not a prisoner ... she is ill ... she is in bed."

"Lead me to her," said the impostor, rising from his seat.

Refusal was impossible. Shvabrin conducted Pougatcheff to Maria Ivanovna's room. I followed behind them.

Shvabrin stopped upon the stairs.

"Czar," said he: "you may demand of me whatever you please; but do not permit a stranger to enter my wife's bedroom."

I shuddered.

"So you are married!" I said to Shvabrin, ready to tear him to pieces.

"Silence!" interrupted Pougatcheff: "that is my business. And you," he continued, turning to Shvabrin, "keep your airs and graces to yourself: whether she be your wife or whether she be not, I will take to her whomsoever I please. Your lordship, follow me."

At the door of the room Shvabrin stopped again, and said in a faltering voice:

"Czar, I must inform you that she is in a high fever, and has been raving incessantly for the last three days."

"Open the door!" said Pougatcheff.

Shvabrin began to search in his pockets and then said that he had not brought the key with him. Pougatcheff pushed the door with his foot; the lock gave way, the door opened, and we entered.

I glanced round the room—and nearly fainted away. On the floor, clad in a ragged peasant's dress, sat Maria Ivanovna, pale, thin, and with dishevelled hair. Before her stood a pitcher of water, covered with a piece of bread. Seeing me, she shuddered and uttered a piercing cry. What I felt at that moment I cannot describe.

Pougatcheff looked at Shvabrin and said with a sarcastic smile:

"You have a very nice hospital here!"

Then approaching Maria Ivanovna:

"Tell me, my little dove, why does your husband punish you in this manner?"

"My husband!" repeated she. "He is not my husband. I will never be his wife! I would rather die, and I will die, if I am not set free."

Pougatcheff cast a threatening glance at Shvabrin.

"And you have dared to deceive me!" he said to him. "Do you know, scoundrel, what you deserve?"

Shvabrin fell upon his knees.... At that moment contempt extinguished within me all feelings of hatred and resentment. I looked with disgust at the sight of a nobleman grovelling at the feet of a runaway Cossack.

Pougatcheff relented.

"I forgive you this time," he said to Shvabrin: "but bear in mind that the next time you are guilty of an offence, I will remember this one also."

Then he turned to Maria Ivanovna and said to her kindly:

"Go, my pretty girl; I give you your liberty. I am the Czar."

Maria Ivanovna glanced rapidly at him, and intuitively divined that before her stood the murderer of her parents. She covered her face with both hands and fainted away. I hastened towards her; but at that moment my old acquaintance, Palasha, very boldly entered the room, and began to attend to her young mistress. Pougatcheff quitted the apartment, and we all three entered the parlour.

"Well, your lordship," said Pougatcheff smiling, "we have set the pretty girl free! What do you say to sending for the pope and making him marry his niece to you? If you like, I will act as father, and Shvabrin shall be your best man. We will then smoke and drink and make ourselves merry to our hearts' content!"

What I feared took place. Shvabrin, hearing Pougatcheff's proposal, was beside himself with rage.

"Czar!" he exclaimed, in a transport of passion, "I am guilty; I have lied to you; but Grineff is deceiving you also. This young girl is not the pope's niece: she is the daughter of Ivan Mironoff, who was hanged at the taking of the fortress."

Pougatcheff glanced at me with gleaming eyes.

"What does this mean?" he asked in a gloomy tone.

"Shvabrin has told you the truth," I replied in a firm voice.

"You did not tell me that," replied Pougatcheff, whose face had become clouded.

"Judge of the matter yourself," I replied: "could I, in the presence of your people, declare that she was the daughter of Mironoff? They would have torn her to pieces! Nothing would have saved her!"

"You are right," said Pougatcheff smiling. "My drunkards would not have spared the poor girl; the pope's wife did well to deceive them."

"Listen," I continued, seeing him so well disposed; "I know not what to call you, and I do not wish to know.... But God is my witness that I would willingly repay you with my life for what you have done for me. But do not demand of me anything that is against my honour and my Christian conscience. You are my benefactor. End as you have begun: let me go away with that poor orphan wherever God will direct us. And wherever you may be, and whatever may happen to you, we will pray to God every day for the salvation of your soul...."

Pougatcheff's fierce soul seemed touched.

"Be it as you wish!" said he. "Punish thoroughly or pardon thoroughly: that is my way. Take your beautiful one, take her wherever you like, and may God grant you love and counsel!"

Then he turned to Shvabrin and ordered him to give me a safe conduct for all barriers and fortresses subjected to his authority. Shvabrin, completely dumbfounded, stood as if petrified. Pougatcheff then went off to inspect the fortress. Shvabrin accompanied him, and I remained behind under the pretext of making preparations for my departure.

I hastened to Maria's room. The door was locked. I knocked.

"Who is there?" asked Palasha.

I called out my name. The sweet voice of Maria Ivanovna sounded from behind the door:

"Wait a moment, Peter Andreitch. I am changing my dress. Go to Akoulina Pamphilovna; I shall be there presently."

I obeyed and made my way to the house of Father Jerasim. He and his wife came forward to meet me Savelitch had already informed them of what had happened.

"You are welcome, Peter Andreitch," said the pope's wife. "God has ordained that we should meet again. And how are you? Not a day has passed without our talking about you. And Maria Ivanovna, the poor little dove, what has she not suffered while you have been away! But tell us, little father, how did you manage to arrange matters with Pougatcheff? How was it that he did not put you to death? The villain be thanked for that, at all events!"

"Enough, old woman," interrupted Father Gerasim. "Don't babble about everything that you know. There is; no salvation for chatterers. Come in, Peter Andreitch, I beg of you. It is a long, long time since we saw each other." The pope's wife set before me everything that she had in the house, without ceasing to chatter away for a single moment. She related to me in what manner Shvabrin had compelled them to deliver Maria Ivanovna up to him; how the poor girl wept and did not wish to be parted from them; how she had kept up a constant communication with them; by means of Palashka[46] (a bold girl who compelled the orderly himself to dance to her pipe); how she had advised Maria Ivanovna to write a letter to me, and so forth.

I then, in my turn, briefly related to them my story. The pope and his wife made the sign of the cross on hearing that; Pougatcheff had become acquainted with their deception.

"The power of the Cross defend us!" ejaculated Akoulina Pamphilovna. "May God grant that the cloud will pass over. Well, well, Alexei Ivanitch, you are a very nice fellow: there is no denying that!"

At that moment the door opened, and Maria Ivanovna entered the room with a smile upon her pale face. She had doffed her peasant's dress, and was attired as before, plainly and becomingly.

I grasped her hand and for some time could not utter a single word. We were both silent from fulness of heart. Our hosts felt that their presence was unnecessary to us, and so they withdrew. We were left by ourselves. Everything else was forgotten. We talked and talked and could not say enough to each other. Maria related to me all that had happened to her since the capture of the fortress; she described to me all the horror of her situation, all the trials which she had experienced at the hands of the detestable Shvabrin. We recalled to mind the happy days of the past, and we could not prevent the tears coming into our eyes. At last I began to explain to her my project. For her to remain in the fortress, subjected to Pougatcheff and commanded by Shvabrin, was impossible. Neither could I think of taking her to Orenburg, just then undergoing all the calamities of a siege. She had not a single relative in the whole world. I proposed to her that she should seek shelter with my

---

[46] Diminutive of Palasha.

parents. She hesitated at first: my father's unfriendly disposition towards her frightened her. I made her mind easy on that score. I knew that my father would consider himself bound in honour to receive into his house the daughter of a brave and deserving soldier who had lost his life in the service of his country.

"Dear Maria Ivanovna," I said at last: "I look upon you as my wife. Strange circumstances have united us together indissolubly; nothing in the world can separate us."

Maria Ivanovna listened to me without any assumption of affectation. She felt that her fate was linked with mine. But she repeated that she would never be my wife, except with the consent of my parents. I did not contradict her. We kissed each other fervently and passionately, and in this manner everything was resolved upon between us.

About an hour afterwards, the orderly brought me my safe conduct, inscribed with Pougatcheff's scrawl, and informed me that his master wished to see me. I found him ready to st out on his road. I cannot describe what I felt on taking leave of this terrible man, this outcast, so villainously cruel to all except myself alone. But why should I not tell the truth? At that moment I felt drawn towards him by a powerful sympathy. I ardently wished to tear him away! from the midst of the scoundrels, whom he commanded, and save his head while there was yet time. Shvabrin, and the crowd gathered around us, prevented me from giving expression to all that filled my heart.

We parted as friends. Pougatcheff, catching sight of Akoulina Pamphilovna among the crowd, threatened her with his finger and winked significantly; then he seated himself in his kibitka[47] and gave orders to return to Berd; and when the horses started off, he leaned once out of the carriage, and cried out to me: "Farewell, your lordship! Perhaps we shall see each other again!"

We did indeed see each other again, but under what circumstances!

Pougatcheff was gone. I stood for a long time gazing across the white steppe, over which his troika went gliding rapidly. The crowd dispersed. Shvabrin disappeared. I returned to the pope's house. Everything was ready for our departure; I did not wish to delay any longer. Our luggage had already been deposited in the Commandant's old travelling carriage. The horses were harnessed in a twinkling. Maria Ivanovna went to pay a farewell visit to the graves of her parents, who were buried behind the church. I wished to accompany her, but she begged of me to let her go alone. After a

---

[47] An open vehicle drawn by three horses yoked abreast.

few minutes she returned silently weeping. The carriage was ready. Father Gerasim and his wife came out upon the steps. Maria Ivanovna, Palasha and I took our places inside the kibitka, while Savelitch seated himself in the front.

"Farewell, Maria Ivanovna, my little dove; farewell, Peter Andreitch, my fine falcon!" said the pope's good wife. "A safe journey, and may God bless you both and make you happy!"

We drove off. At the window of the Commandant's house I perceived Shvabrin standing. His face wore an expression of gloomy malignity. I did not wish to triumph over a defeated enemy, so I turned my eyes the other way.

At last we passed out of the gate, and left the fortress of Bailogorsk behind us for ever.

CHAPTER XIII

THE ARREST

United so unexpectedly with the dear girl, about whom I was so terribly uneasy that very morning, I could scarcely believe the evidence of my senses, and imagined that everything that had happened to me was nothing but an empty dream. Maria Ivanovna gazed thoughtfully, now at me, now at the road, and seemed as if she had not yet succeeded in recovering her senses. We were both silent. Our hearts were too full of emotion. The time passed almost imperceptibly, and after journeying for about two hours, we reached the next fortress, which was also subject to Pougatcheff. Here we changed horses. By the rapidity with which this was effected, and by the obliging manner of the bearded Cossack who had been appointed Commandant by Pougatcheff, I perceived that, thanks to the gossip of our driver, I was taken for a favourite of their master.

We continued our journey. It began to grow dark. We approached a small town, where, according to the bearded Commandant, there was a strong detachment on its way to join the impostor. We were stopped by the sentries. In answer to the challenge: "Who goes there?" our driver replied in a loud voice: "The Czar's friend with his little, wife."

Suddenly a troop of hussars surrounded us, uttering the most terrible curses.

"Step down, friend of the devil!" said a moustached sergeant-major. "We will make it warm for you and your little wife!"

I got out of the kibitka and requested to be brought before their commander. On seeing my officer's uniform, the soldiers ceased their imprecations, and the sergeant conducted me to the major.

Savelitch followed me, muttering:

"So much for your being a friend of the Czar! Out of the frying-pan into the fire. Lord Almighty! how is all this going to end?"

The kibitka followed behind us at a slow pace.

In about five minutes we arrived at a small, well-lighted house. The sergeant-major left me under a guard and entered to announce me. He returned immediately and informed me that his Highness had no time to receive me, but that he had ordered that I should be taken to prison, and my wife conducted into his presence.

"What does this mean?" I exclaimed in a rage. "Has he taken leave of his senses?"

"I do not know, your lordship," replied the sergeant-major. "Only his Highness has ordered that your lordship should be taken to prison, and her ladyship conducted into his presence, your lordship!"

I dashed up the steps. The sentinel did not think of detaining me, and I made my way straight into the room, where six Jiussar officers were playing at cards. The major was dealing. What was my astonishment when, looking at him attentively, I recognized Ivan Ivanovitch Zourin, who had once beaten me at play in the Simbirsk tavern.

"Is it possible?" I exclaimed. "Ivan Ivanovitch! Is it really you?"

"Zounds! Peter Andreitch! What chance has brought you here? Where have you come from? How is it with you, brother? Won't you join in a game of cards?"

"Thank you, but I would much rather you give orders for quarters to be assigned to me."

"What sort of quarters do you want? Stay with me."

"I cannot: I am not alone."

"Well, bring your comrade with you."

"I have no comrade with me; I am with a—lady."

"A lady! Where did you pick her up? Aha, brother mine!"

And with these words, Zourin whistled so significantly that all the others burst out laughing, and I felt perfectly confused.

"Well," continued Zourin: "let it be so. You shall have quarters. But it is a pity.... We should have had one of our old sprees.... I say, boy! Why don't you bring in Pougatcheff's lady friend? Or is she obstinate? Tell her that she need not be afraid, that the gentleman is very kind and will do her no harm—then bring her in by the collar."

"What do you mean?" said I to Zourin. "What lady-friend of Pougatcheff's are you talking of? It is the daughter of the late Captain Mironoff. I have released her from captivity, and I am now conducting her to my father's country seat, where I am going to leave her."

"What! Was it you then who was announced to me just now? In the name of Heaven! what does all this mean?"

"I will tell you later on. For the present, I beg of you to set at ease the mind of this poor girl, who has been terribly frightened by your hussars."

Zourin immediately issued the necessary orders. He went out himself into the street to apologize to Maria Ivanovna for the involuntary misunderstanding, and ordered the sergeant-major to conduct her to the best lodging in the town. I remained to spend the night with him.

We had supper, and when we two were left together, I related to him my adventures. Zourin listened to me with the greatest attention. When I had finished, he shook his head, and said:

"That is all very well, brother; but there is one thing which is not so; why the devil do you want to get married? As an officer and a man of honour, I do not wish to deceive you; but, believe me, marriage is all nonsense. Why should you saddle yourself with a wife and be compelled to dandle children? Scout the idea. Listen to me: shake off this Captain's daughter. I have cleared the road to Simbirsk, and it is quite safe. Send her to-morrow by herself to your parents, and you remain with my detachment. There is no need for you to return to Orenburg. If you should again fall into the hands of the rebels, you may not escape from them so easily a second time. In this way your love folly will die a natural death, and everything will end satisfactorily."

Although I did not altogether agree with him, yet I felt that duty and honour demanded my presence in the army of the Empress. I resolved to follow Zourin's advice: to send Maria Ivanovna to my father's estate, and to remain with his detachment.

Savelitch came in to help me to undress; I told him that he was to get ready the next day to accompany Maria Ivanovna on her journey. He began to make excuses.

"What do you say, my lord? How can I leave you? Who will look after you? What will your parents say?"

Knowing the obstinate disposition of my follower, I resolved to get round him by wheedling and coaxing him.

"My dear friend, Arkhip Savelitch!" I said to him: "do not refuse me; be my benefactor. I do not require a servant here, and I should not feel easy if Maria Ivanovna were to set out on her journey without you. By serving her you will be serving me, for I am firmly resolved to marry her, as soon as circumstances will permit."

Here Savelitch clasped his hands with an indescribable look of astonishment.

"To marry!" he repeated: "the child wants to marry! But what will your father say? And your mother, what will she think?"

"They will give their consent, without a doubt, when they know Maria Ivanovna," I replied. "I count upon you. My father and mother have great confidence in you; you will therefore intercede for us, won't you?"

The old man was touched.

"Oh, my father, Peter Andreitch!" he replied, "although you are thinking of getting married a little too early, yet Maria Ivanovna is such a good young lady, that it would be a pity to let the opportunity escape. I will do as you wish. I will accompany her, the angel, and I will humbly say to your parents, that such a bride does not need a dowry."

I thanked Savelitch, and then lay down to sleep in the same room with Zourin. Feeling very much excited, I began to chatter. At first Zourin listened to my remarks very willingly; but little by little his words became rarer and more disconnected, and at last, instead of replying to' one of my questions, he began to snore. I stopped talking and soon followed his example.

The next morning I betook myself to Maria Ivanovna. I communicated to her my plans. She recognized the reasonableness of them, and immediately agreed to carry them out. Zourin's detachment was to leave the town that day. There was no time to be lost. I at once took leave of Maria Ivanovna, confiding her to the care of Savelitch, and giving her a letter to my parents.

Maria burst into tears.

"Farewell, Peter Andreitch," said she in a gentle voice. "God alone knows whether we shall ever see each other again or not; but I will never forget you; till my dying day you alone shall live in my heart!"

I was unable to reply. There was a crowd of people around us, and I did not wish to give way to my feelings before them. At last she departed. I returned to Zourin, silent and depressed. He endeavoured to cheer me up, and I tried to divert my thoughts; we spent the day in noisy mirth, and in the evening we set out on our march.

It was now near the end of February. The winter, which had rendered all military movements extremely difficult, was drawing to its close, and our generals began to make preparations for combined action. Pougatcheff was still under the walls of Orenburg, but our divisions united and began to close in from every side upon the rebel camp. On the appearance of our troops, the revolted villages returned to their allegiance; the rebel bands everywhere retreated before us, and everything gave promise of a speedy and successful termination to the campaign.

Soon afterwards Prince Golitzin defeated Pougatcheff under the walls of the fortress of Tatischtscheff, routed his troops, relieved Orenburg, and to all appearances seemed to have given the final and decisive blow to the rebellion. Zourin was sent at this time against a band of rebellious Bashkirs, who, however, dispersed before we were able to come up with them. The spring found us in a little Tartar village. The rivers overflowed their banks, and the roads became impassable. We consoled ourselves for our inaction with the thought that there would soon be an end to this tedious petty warfare with brigands and savages.

But Pougatcheff was not yet taken. He soon made his appearance in the manufacturing districts of Siberia, where he collected new bands of followers and once more commenced his marauding expeditions. Reports of fresh successes on his part were soon in circulation. We heard of the destruction of several Siberian fortresses. Then came the news of the capture of Kazan, and the march of the impostor to Moscow, which greatly disturbed the leaders of the army, who had fondly imagined that the power of the despised rebel had been completely broken. Zourin received orders to cross the Volga.

I will not describe our march and the conclusion of the war. I will only say that the campaign was as calamitous as it possibly could be. Law and order came to an end everywhere, and the landholders concealed themselves in the woods. Bands of robbers scoured the country in all directions; the commanders of isolated detachments punished and pardoned as they pleased; and the condition of the extensive territory in which the conflagration raged, was terrible.... Heaven grant that we may never see such, a senseless and merciless revolt again!

Pougatcheff took to flight, pursued by Ivan Ivanovitch Michelson. We soon heard of his complete overthrow. At last Zourin received news of the capture of the impostor, and, at the same time, orders to halt. The war was ended. At last it was possible for me to return to my parents. The thought of embracing them, and of seeing Maria Ivanovna, again, of whom I had received no information, filled me with delight. I danced about like a child. Zourin laughed and said with a shrug of his shoulders:

90

"No good will come of it! If you get married, you are lost!"

In the meantime a strange feeling poisoned my joy: the thought of that evil-doer, covered with the blood of so many innocent victims, and of the punishment that awaited him, troubled me involuntarily.

"Emelia, Emelia!"[48] I said to myself with vexation, "why did you not dash yourself against the bayonets, or fall beneath the bullets? That was the best thing you could have done."[49]

And how could I feel otherwise? The thought of him was inseparably connected with the thought of the mercy which he had shown to me in one of the most terrible moments of my life, and with the deliverance of my bride from the hands of the detested Shvabrin.

Zourin granted me leave of absence. In a few days' time I should again be in the midst of my family, and should once again set eyes upon the face of my Maria Ivanovna.... Suddenly an unexpected storm burst upon me.

On the day of my departure, and at the very moment when I was preparing to set out, Zourin came to my hut, holding in his hand a paper, and looking exceedingly troubled. A pang went through my heart. I felt alarmed, without knowing why. He sent my servant out of the room, and said that he had something to tell me.

"What is it?" I asked with uneasiness.

"Something rather disagreeable," replied he, giving me the paper. "Read what I have just received."

I read it: it was a secret order to all the commanders of detachments to arrest me wherever I might be found, and to send me without delay under a strong guard to Kazan, to appear before the Commission instituted for the trial of Pougatcheff.

The paper nearly fell from my hands.

"There is no help for it," said Zourin, "my duty is to obey orders. Probably the report of your intimacy with Pougatcheff has in some way reached the ears of the authorities. I hope that the affair will have no serious consequences, and that you will be able to justify yourself before the Commission. Keep up your spirits and set out at once."

My conscience was clear, and I did not fear having to appear before the tribunal; but the thought that the hour of my meeting

---

[48] Diminutive of Emelian.

[49] After having advanced to the gates of Moscow, Pougatcheff was defeated, and being afterwards sold by his accomplices for 100,000 roubles, he was imprisoned in an iron cage and carried to Moscow, where he was executed in the year 1775.

with Maria might be deferred for several months, filled me with misgivings.

The telega[50] was ready. Zourin took a friendly leave of me, and I took my place in the vehicle. Two hussars with drawn swords seated themselves, one on each side of me, and we set out for our destination.

CHAPTER XIV

THE SENTENCE

I felt convinced that the cause of my arrest was my absenting myself from Orenburg without leave. I could easily justify myself on that score: for sallying out against the enemy had not only not been prohibited, but had even been encouraged. I might be accused of undue rashness instead of disobedience of orders. But my friendly intercourse with Pougatcheff could be proved by several witnesses, and could not but at least appear very suspicious. During the whole of the journey I thought of the examination that awaited me, and mentally prepared the answers that I should make. I resolved to tell the plain unvarnished truth before the court, feeling convinced that this was the simplest and, at the same time, the surest way of justifying myself.

I arrived at Kazan—the town had been plundered and set on fire. In the streets, instead of houses, there were to be seen heaps of burnt stones, and blackened walls without roofs or windows. Such were the traces left by Pougatcheff! I was conducted to the fortress which had escaped the ravages of the fire. The hussars delivered me over to the officer of the guard. The latter ordered a blacksmith to be sent for. Chains were placed round my feet and fastened together. Then I was taken to the prison and left alone in a dark and narrow dungeon, with four blank walls and a small window protected by iron gratings.

Such a beginning boded no good to me. For all that, I did not lose hope nor courage. I had recourse to the consolation of all those in affliction, and after having tasted for the first time the sweet

---

[50] An open vehicle without springs.

92

comforting of prayer poured out from a pure but sorrow-stricken heart, I went off into a calm sleep, without thinking of what might happen to me.

The next morning the gaoler awoke me with the announcement that I was to appear before the Commission. Two soldiers conducted me through a courtyard to the Commandant's house: they stopped in the ante-room and allowed me to enter the inner room by myself.

I found myself in a good-sized apartment At the table, which was covered with papers, sat two men: an elderly general, of a cold and stem aspect, and a young captain of the Guards, of about twenty-eight years of age, and of very agreeable and affable appearance. Near the window, at a separate table, sat the secretary, with a pen behind his ear, and bending over his paper, ready to write down my depositions.

The examination began. I was asked my name and profession. The General inquired if I was the son of Andrei Petrovitch Grineff, and on my replying in the affirmative, he exclaimed in a stem tone:

"It is a pity that such an honourable man should have such an unworthy son!"

I calmly replied that whatever were the accusations against me, I hoped to be able to refute them by the candid avowal of the truth.

My assurance did not please him.

"You are very audacious, my friend," said he, frowning: "but we have dealt with others like you."

Then the young officer asked me under what circumstances and at what time I had entered Pougatcheff's service, and in what affairs I had been employed by him.

I replied indignantly, that, as an officer and a nobleman, I could never have entered Pougatcheff's service, and could never have received any commission from him whatever.

"How comes it then," continued the interrogator, "that the nobleman and officer was the only one spared by the impostor, while all his comrades were cruelly murdered? How comes it that this same officer and nobleman could revel with the rebellious scoundrels, and receive from the leader of the villains presents, consisting of a pelisse, a horse, and half a rouble? Whence came such strange friendship, and upon what does it rest, if not upon treason, or at least upon abominable and unpardonable cowardice?"

I was deeply offended by the words of the officer of the Guards, and I began to defend myself with great warmth. I related how my acquaintance with Pougatcheff began upon the steppe during a snow-storm, how he had recognized me at the capture of the fortress of Bailogorsk and spared my life. I admitted that I had

93

received a pelisse and a horse from the impostor, but that I had defended the fortress of Bailogorsk against the rebels to the last extremity. In conclusion I appealed to my General, who could bear witness to my zeal during the disastrous siege of Orenburg.

The stern old man took up from the table an open letter and began to read it aloud:

"In reply to your Excellency's inquiry respecting Ensign Grineff, who is charged with being implicated in the present insurrection and with entering into communication with the leader of the robbers, contrary to the rules of the service and the oath of allegiance, I have the honour to report that the said Ensign Grineff formed part of the garrison in Orenburg from the beginning of October 1773 to the twenty-fourth of February of the present year, on which date he quitted the town, and since that time he has not made his appearance again. We have heard from some deserters that he was in Pougatcheff's camp, and that he accompanied him to the fortress of Bailogorsk, where he had formerly been garrisoned. With respect to his conduct, I can only...."

Here the General interrupted his reading and said to me harshly:

"What do you say now by way of justification?"

I was about to continue as I began and explain the state of affairs between myself and Maria Ivanovna as frankly as all the rest, but suddenly I felt an invincible disgust at the thought of doing so. It occurred to my mind, that if I mentioned her name, the Commission would summon her to appear, and the thought of connecting her name with the vile doings of hardened villains, and of herself being confronted with them—this terrible idea produced such an impression upon me, that I became confused and maintained silence.

My judges, who seemed at first to have listened to my answers with a certain amount of good-will, were once more prejudiced against me on perceiving my confusion. The officer of the Guards demanded that I should be confronted with my principal accuser. The General ordered that the "rascal of yesterday" should be summoned. I turned round quickly towards the door, to await the appearance of my accuser. After a few moments I heard the clanking of chains, the door opened, and—Shvabrin entered the room. I was astonished at the change in his appearance. He was terribly thin and pale. His hair, but a short time ago as black as pitch, was now quite grey; his long beard was unkempt. He repeated all his accusations in a weak but determined voice. According to his account, I had been sent by Pougatcheff to Orenburg as a spy; every day I used to ride out to the advanced posts, in order to transmit written information of all that took place within the town; that at last I had gone quite over to the side of the usurper and had accompanied him from fortress to fortress, endeavouring in every way to injure my companions in crime, in order to occupy their places and profit the better by the rewards of the impostor.

I listened to him in silence, and I rejoiced on account of one thing: the name of Maria was not mentioned by the scoundrel, whether it was that his self-love could not bear the thought of one who had rejected him with contempt, or that within his heart there was a spark of that self-same feeling which had induced me to remain silent. Whatever it was, the name of the daughter of the Commandant of Bailogorsk was not pronounced in the presence of the Commission. I became still more confirmed in my resolution, and when the judges asked me what I had to say in answer to Shvabrin's evidence, I replied that I still stood by my first statement and that I had nothing else to add in justification of myself.

The General ordered us to be led away. We quitted the room together. I looked calmly at Shvabrin, but did not say a word to him. He looked at me with a malicious smile, lifted up his fetters and passed out quickly in front of me. I was conducted back to prison, and was not compelled to undergo a-second examination.

I was not a witness of all that now remains for me to impart to the reader; but I have heard it related so often, that the most minute details are indelibly engraven upon my memory, and it seems to me as if I had taken a part in them unseen.

Maria Ivanovna was received by my parents with that sincere kindness which distinguished people in the olden time. They regarded it as a favour from God that the opportunity was afforded them of sheltering and consoling the poor orphan. They soon became sincerely attached to her, because it was impossible to know her and not to love her. My love for her no longer appeared mere folly to my father, and my mother had one wish only, that her Peter should marry the pretty Captain's daughter.

The news of my arrest filled all my family with consternation. Maria Ivanovna had related so simply to my parents my strange acquaintance with Pougatcheff, that not only had they felt quite easy about the matter, but had often been obliged to laugh heartily at the whole story. My father would not believe that I could be implicated in an infamous rebellion, the aim of which was the destruction of the throne and the extermination of the nobles. He questioned Savelitch severely. My retainer did not deny that I had been the guest of Pougatcheff, and that the villain had acted very generously towards me, but he affirmed with a solemn oath that he had never heard a word about treason. My old parents became easier in mind, and waited impatiently for more favourable news. Maria Ivanovna, however, was in a state of great agitation, but she kept silent, as she was modest and prudent in the highest degree.

Several weeks passed.... Then my father unexpectedly received from St. Petersburg a letter from our relative, Prince B——. The letter was about me. After the usual compliments, he informed him that the suspicions which had been raised concerning my participation in the plots of the rebels, had unfortunately been shown to be only too well founded; that capital punishment would have been meted out to me, but that the Empress, in consideration of the faithful services and the grey hairs of my father, had resolved to be gracious towards his criminal son, and, instead of condemning him to suffer an ignominious death, had ordered that he should be sent to the most remote part of Siberia for the rest of his life.

This unexpected blow nearly killed my father. He lost his usual firmness, and his grief, usually silent, found vent in bitter complaints.

"What!" he cried, as if beside himself: "my son has taken part in Pougatcheff's plots! God of Justice, that I should live to see this! The Empress spares his life! Does that make it any better for me? It is not death at the hands of the executioner that is so terrible: my great-grandfather died upon the scaffold for the defence of that which his conscience regarded as sacred;[51] my father suffered with Volinsky and Khrouschtcheff.[52] But that a nobleman should be false to his oath, should associate with robbers, with murderers and with runaway slaves!... Shame and disgrace upon our race!"

Frightened by his despair, my mother dared not weep in his presence; she endeavoured to console him by speaking of the uncertainty of reports, and the little dependency to be placed upon the opinions of other people. But my father was inconsolable.

Maria Ivanovna suffered more than anybody. Being firmly convinced that I could have justified myself if I had only wished to do so, she guessed the reason of my silence, and considered herself the cause of my misfortune. She hid from everyone her tears and sufferings, and was incessantly thinking of the means by which I might be saved.

One evening my father was seated upon the sofa turning over the leaves' of the "Court Calendar," but his thoughts were far away, and the reading of the book failed to produce upon him its usual

---

[51] One of Poushkin's ancestors was condemned to death by Peter the Great.
[52] Chiefs of the Russian party against Biren, the unscrupulous German Favourite of the Empress Anne. They were put to death under circumstances of great cruelty.

effect. He was whistling an old march. My mother was silently knitting a woollen waistcoat, and from time to time her tears ran down upon her work. All at once, Maria Ivanovna, who was also at work in the same room, declared that it was absolutely necessary that she should go to St. Petersburg, and she begged of my parents to furnish her with the means of doing so. My mother was very much hurt at this resolution.

"Why do you wish to go to St. Petersburg?" said she. "Is it possible, Maria Ivanovna, that you want to forsake us also?"

Maria replied that her fate depended upon this journey, that she was going to seek help and protection from powerful persons, as the daughter of a man who had fallen a victim to his fidelity.

My father lowered his head; every word that recalled to mind the supposed crime of his son, was painful to him, and seemed like a bitter reproach.

"Go, my child," he said to her at last with a sigh; "we do not wish to stand in the way of your happiness. May God give you an honest man for a husband, and not an infamous traitor."

He rose and left the room.

Maria Ivanovna, left alone with my mother, confided to her a part of her plan. My mother, with tears in her eyes, embraced her and prayed to God that her undertaking might be crowned with success. Maria Ivanovna made all her preparations, and a few days afterwards she set out on her road with the faithful Palasha and the equally faithful Savelitch, who, forcibly separated from me, consoled himself at least with the thought that he was serving my betrothed.

Maria Ivanovna arrived safely at Sofia, and learning that the Court was at that time at Tsarskoe Selo, she resolved to stop there. At the post-house, a small recess behind a. partition was assigned to her. The postmaster's wife came immediately to chat with her, and she informed Maria that she was niece to one of the stove-lighters of the Court, and she initiated her into all the mysteries of Court life. She told her at what hour the Empress usually got up, when she took coffee, and when she went out for a walk; what great lords were then with her; what she had deigned to say the day before at table, and whom she had received in the evening. In a word, the conversation of Anna Vlassievna was as good as a volume of historical memoirs, and would be very precious to the present generation.

Maria Ivanovna listened to her with great attention. They went together into the palace garden. Anna Vlassievna related the history of every alley and of every little bridge, and after seeing all that they wished to see, they returned to the post-house, highly satisfied with each other.

The next day, early in the morning, Maria Ivanovna awoke, dressed herself, and quietly betook herself to the palace garden. It was a lovely morning; the sun was gilding the tops of the linden trees, already turning yellow beneath the cold breath of autumn. The broad lake glittered in the light. The swans, just awake, came sailing majestically out from under the bushes overhanging the banks. Maria Ivanovna walked towards a delightful lawn, where a monument had just been erected in honour of the recent victories gained by Count Peter Alexandrovitch Roumyanzoff.[53] Suddenly a little white dog of English breed ran barking towards her. Maria grew frightened and stood still. At the same moment she heard an agreeable female voice call out:

"Do not be afraid, it will not bite."

Maria saw a lady seated on the bench opposite the monument. Maria sat down on the other end of the bench. The lady looked at her attentively; Maria on her side, by a succession of stolen glances, contrived to examine the stranger from head to foot. She was attired in a white morning gown, a light cap, and a short mantle. She seemed to be about forty years of age. Her face, which was full; and red, wore an expression of calmness and dignity, and her blue eyes and smiling lips had an indescribable charm about them. The lady was the first to break silence.

"You are doubtless a stranger here?" said she.

"Yes, I only arrived yesterday from the country."

"Did you come with your parents?"

"No, I came alone."

"Alone! But you are very young to travel alone."

"I have neither father nor mother."

"Perhaps you have come here on some business?"

"Yes, I have come to present a petition to the Empress."

"You are an orphan: probably you have come to complain of some injustice."

"No, I have come to ask for mercy, not justice."

"May I ask you who you are?"

"I am the daughter of Captain Mironoff."

"Of Captain Mironoff! the same who was Commandant of one of the Orenburg fortresses?"

"The same, Madam."

The lady appeared moved.

"Forgive me," said she, in a still kinder voice, "for interesting

---

[53] A famous Russian general who distinguished himself in the war against the Turks.

98

myself in your business; but I am frequently at Court; explain to me the nature of your request, and perhaps I may be able to help you."

Maria Ivanovna arose and thanked her respectfully. Everything about this unknown lady drew her towards her and inspired her with confidence. Maria drew from her pocket a folded paper and gave it to her unknown protectress, who read it to herself.

At first she began reading with an attentive and benevolent expression; but suddenly her countenance changed, and Maria, whose eyes followed all her movements, became frightened by the severe expression of that face, which a moment before had been so calm and gracious.

"You are supplicating for Grineff?" said the lady in a cold tone. "The Empress cannot pardon him. He went over to the usurper, not out of ignorance and credulity, but as a depraved and dangerous scoundrel."

"Oh! it is not true!" exclaimed Maria.

"How, not true?" replied the lady, her face flushing.

"It is not true; as God is above us, it is not true! I know all, I will tell you everything. It was for my sake alone that he exposed himself to all the misfortunes that have overtaken him. And if he did not justify himself before the Commission, it was only because he did not wish to implicate me."

She then related with great warmth all that is already known to the reader.

The lady listened to her attentively.

"Where are you staying?" she asked, when Maria had finished her story; and hearing that it was with Anna Vlassievna, she added with a smile:

"Ah, I know. Farewell; do not speak to anybody about our meeting. I hope that you will not have to wait long for an answer to your letter."

With these words she rose from her seat and proceeded down a covered alley, while Maria Ivanovna returned to Anna Vlassievna, filled with joyful hopes.

Her hostess scolded her for going out so early; the autumn air, she said, was not good for a young girl's health. She brought an urn, and over a cup of tea she was about to begin her endless discourse about the Court, when suddenly a carriage with armorial bearings stopped before the door, and a lackey entered with the announcement that the Empress summoned to her presence the daughter of Captain Mironoff.

Anna Vlassievna was perfectly amazed.

"Good Lord!" she exclaimed: "the Empress summons you to Court. How did she get to know anything about you? And how will you present yourself before Her Majesty, my little mother? I do not think that you even know how to walk according to Court manners.... Shall I conduct you? I could at any rate give you a little caution. And how can you go in your travelling dress? Shall I send to the nurse for her yellow gown?"

The lackey announced that it was the Empress's pleasure that Maria Ivanovna should go alone and in the dress that she had on. There was nothing else to be done: Maria took her seat in the carriage and was driven off, accompanied by the counsels and blessings of Anna Vlassievna.

Maria felt that our fate was about to be decided; her heart beat violently. In a few moments the carriage stopped at the gate of the palace. Maria descended the steps with trembling feet. The doors flew open before her. She traversed a large number of empty but magnificent rooms, guided by the lackey. At last, coming to a closed door, he informed her that she would be announced directly, and then left her by herself.

The thought of meeting the Empress face to face so terrified her, that she could scarcely stand upon her feet. In about a minute the door was opened, and she was ushered into the Empress's boudoir.

The Empress was seated at her toilette-table, surrounded by a number of Court ladies, who respectfully made way for Maria Ivanovna. The Empress turned round to her with an amiable smile, and Maria recognized in her the lady with whom she had spoken so freely a few minutes before. The Empress bade her approach, and said with a smile:

"I am glad that I am able to keep my word and grant your petition. Your business is arranged. I am convinced of the innocence of your lover. Here is a letter which you will give to your future father-in-law."

Maria took the letter with trembling hands and, bursting into tears, fell at the feet of the Empress, who raised her up and kissed her upon the forehead.

"I know that you are not rich," said she; "but I owe a debt to the daughter of Captain Mironoff. Do not be uneasy about the future. I will see to your welfare."

After having consoled the poor orphan in this way, the Empress allowed her to depart. Maria left the palace in the same carriage that had brought her thither. Anna Vlassievna, who was impatiently awaiting her return, overwhelmed her with questions, to which Maria returned very vague answers. Although dissatisfied with the weakness of her memory, Anna Vlassievna ascribed it to her provincial bashfulness, and magnanimously excused her. The same day Maria, without even desiring to glance at St. Petersburg, set out on her return journey.

The memoirs of Peter Andreitch Grineff end here. But from a family Tradition we learn that he was released from his imprisonment towards the end of the year 1774 by order of the Empress, and that he was present at the execution of Pougatcheff, who recognized him in the crowd and nodded to him with his head, which, a few moments afterwards, was shown lifeless and bleeding to the people.[54] Shortly afterwards, Peter Andreitch and Maria Ivanovna were married. Their descendants still flourish in the government of Simbirsk. About thirty versts from ----, there is a village belonging to ten landholders. In the house of one of them, there may still be seen, framed and glazed, the autograph letter of Catherine II. It is addressed to the father of Peter Andreitch, and contains the justification of his son, and a tribute of praise to the heart and intellect of Captain Mironoff's daughter.

---

[54] It is said that even at the present day the peasants in the south-east of Russia are firmly convinced that Pougatcheff was really the Emperor Peter III., and not an impostor.

DOUBROVSKY

CHAPTER I

Some years ago, there lived on one of his estates a Russian gentleman of the old school named Kirila Petrovitch Troekouroff. His wealth, distinguished birth, and connections gave him great weight in the government where his property was situated. Completely spoilt by his surroundings, he was in the habit of giving way to every impulse of his passionate nature, to every caprice of his sufficiently narrow mind. The neighbours were ready to gratify his slightest whim; the government officials trembled at his name. Kirila Petrovitch accepted all these signs of servility as homage due to him. His house was always full of guests, ready to amuse his lordship's leisure, and to join his noisy and sometimes boisterous mirth. Nobody dared to refuse his invitations or, on certain days, omit to put in an appearance at the village of Pokrovskoe. Kirila Petrovitch was very hospitable, and in spite of the extraordinary vigour of his constitution, he suffered two or three times a week from surfeit, and became tipsy every evening.

Very few of the young women of his household escaped the amorous attentions of this old man of fifty. Moreover, in one of the wings of his house lived sixteen girls engaged in needlework. The windows of this wing were protected by wooden bars, the doors were kept locked, and the keys retained by Kirila Petrovitch. The young recluses at an appointed hour went into the garden for a walk under the surveillance of two old women. From time to time Kirila Petrovitch married some of them off, and new comers took their places. He treated his peasants and domestics in a severe and arbitrary fashion, in spite of which they were very devoted to him: they loved to boast of the wealth and influence of their master, and in their turn took many a liberty with their neighbours, trusting to his powerful protection.

The ordinary occupations of Troekouroff consisted in driving over his vast domains, passing his nights in prolonged revels, and playing practical jokes, specially invented from time to time, the victims being generally new acquaintances, though his old friends did not always escape, one only—Andrei Gavrilovitch Doubrovsky—excepted.

This Doubrovsky, a retired lieutenant of the Guards, was his nearest neighbour, and possessed seventy serfs. Troekouroff, haughty in his dealings with people of the highest rank, respected

Doubrovsky, in spite of his humble fortune. They had been friends in the service, and Troekouroff knew from experience the impatience and decision of his character. The celebrated events of the year 1762[55] separated them for a long time. Troekouroff, a relative of the Princess Dashkoff,[56] received rapid promotion; Doubrovsky with his reduced fortune, was compelled to leave the service and settle down in the only village that remained to him. Kirila Petrovitch, hearing of this, offered him his protection but Doubrovsky thanked him and remained poor and independent. Some years later, Troekouroff, having obtained the rank of general, and retired to his estate, they met again and were delighted with each other. After that they saw each other every day, and Kirila Petrovitch, who had never deigned to visit anybody in his life, came quite as a matter of course to the little house of his old comrade. Being of the same age, born in the same rank of society, and having received the same education, they resembled each other somewhat in character and inclinations. In some respects their fates had been similar: both had married for love, both had soon become widowers, and both had been left with an only child. The son of Doubrovsky was studying at St. Petersburg; the daughter of Kirila Petrovitch grew up under the eyes of her father, and Troekouroff often said to Doubrovsky:

"Listen, brother Andrei Gavrilovitch; if your Volodka[57] should be successful, I will give him Masha[58] for his wife, in spite of his being as naked as a goshawk."

Andrei Gavrilovitch used to shake his head, and generally replied:

"No', Kirila Petrovitch; my Volodka is no match for Maria Kirilovna. A poor petty noble, such as he, would do better to marry a poor girl of the petty nobility, and be the head of his house, rather than become the bailiff of some spoilt little woman."

Everybody envied the good understanding existing between the haughty Troekouroff and his poor neighbour, and wondered at the boldness of the latter when, at the table of Kirila Petrovitch, he expressed his own opinion frankly, and did not hesitate to maintain an opinion contrary to that of his host Some attempted to imitate him and ventured to overstep the limits of the license accorded them; but Kirila Petrovitch taught them such a lesson, that they

---

[55] Alluding to the deposition and assassination of Peter III., and the accession of his wife Catherine II.
[56] One of Catherine's partisans in the revolution of 1762.
[57] Diminutive of Vladimir.
[58] Diminutive of Maria or Mary.

never afterwards felt any desire to repeat the experiment. Doubrovsky alone remained beyond the range of this general law. But an unexpected incident deranged and altered all this.

One day, in the beginning of autumn, Kirila Petrovitch prepared to go out hunting. Orders had been given the evening before for the huntsmen and gamekeepers to be ready at five o'clock in the morning. The tent and kitchen had been sent on beforehand to the place where Kirila Petrovitch was to dine. The host and his guests went to the kennel, where more than five hundred harriers and greyhounds lived in luxury and warmth, praising the generosity of Kirila Petrovitch in their canine language. There was also a hospital for the sick dogs, under the care of staff-surgeon Timoshka, and a separate place where the bitches brought forth and suckled their pups. Kirila Petrovitch was proud of this magnificent establishment, and never missed an opportunity of boasting about it, before his guests, each of whom had inspected it at least twenty times. He walked through the kennel, surrounded by his guests and accompanied by Timoshka and the head gamekeepers, pausing before some of the compartments, either to ask, after the health of some sick dog, to make some observation more or less just and severe, or to call some dog to him; by name and speak caressingly to it. The guests considered it their duty to go into raptures over Kirila Petrovitch's kennel; Doubrovsky alone remained silent and frowned. He was an ardent sportsman; but his modest fortune only permitted him to keep two harriers and one greyhound, and he could not restrain a certain feeling of envy at the sight of this magnificent establishment.

"Why do you frown, brother?" Kirila Petrovitch asked him. "Does not my kennel please you?"

"No," replied Doubrovsky abruptly: "the kennel, is marvellous, but I doubt whether your people live as well as your dogs."

One of the gamekeepers took offence.

"Thanks to God and our master, we have nothing to complain of," said he; "but if the truth must be told, there are certain nobles who would not do badly if they exchanged their manor-house for one of the compartments of this kennel: they would be better fed and feel warmer."

Kirila Petrovitch burst out laughing at this insolent remark from his servant, and the guests followed his example, although they felt that the gamekeeper's joke I might apply to them also. Doubrovsky turned pale and said not a word. At that moment a basket, containing I some new-born puppies, was brought to Kirila Petrovitch; he chose two out of the litter and ordered the rest to be drowned. In the meantime Andrei Gavrilovitch had disappeared without anybody having observed it.

On returning with his guests from the kennel, Kirila Petrovitch sat down to supper, and it was only then that he noticed the absence of Doubrovsky. His people informed him that Andrei Gavrilovitch had gone home. Troekouroff immediately gave orders that he was to be overtaken and brought back without fail. He had never gone hunting without Doubrovsky, who was a fine and experienced connoisseur in all matters relating to dogs, and an infallible umpire in all possible disputes connected with sport. The servant who had galloped after him, returned while they were still seated at table, and informed his master that Andrei Gavrilovitch had refused to listen to him and would not return. Kirila Petrovitch, as usual, was heated with liquor, and becoming very angry, he sent the same servant a second time to tell Andrei Gavrilovitch that if he did not return at once to spend the night at Pokrovskoe, he, Troekouroff, would break off all friendly intercourse with him for ever. The servant galloped off again. Kirila Petrovitch rose from the table, dismissed his guests retired to bed.

The next day his first question was: "Is Andrei Gavrilovitch here?" A triangular-shaped letter was handed to him. Kirila Petrovitch ordered his secretary to read it aloud, and the following is what he heard:

"Gracious Sir!

"I do not intend to return to Pokrovskoe until you send the dog-feeder Paramoshka to me with an apology: I shall retain the liberty of punishing or for forgiving him. I cannot put up with jokes from your servants, nor do I intend to put up with them from you, as I am not a buffoon, but a gentleman of ancient family. I remain your obedient servant,

"ANDREI DOUBROVSKY."

According to present ideas of etiquette, such a letter would be very unbecoming; it irritated Kirila Petrovitch, not by its strange style, but by its substance.

"What!" exclaimed Troekouroff, springing barefooted out of bed; "send my people to him with an apology! And he to be at liberty to punish or pardon them! What can he be thinking of? Does he know with whom he is dealing? I'll teach him a lesson! He shall know what it is to oppose Troekouroff!"

Kirila Petrovitch dressed himself and set out for the hunt with

105

his usual ostentation. But the chase was not successful; during the whole of the day one hare only was seen, and that escaped. The dinner in the field, under the tent, was also a failure, or at least it was not to the taste of Kirila Petrovitch, who struck the cook, abused the guests, and on the return journey rode intentionally, with all his suite, through the fields of Doubrovsky.

CHAPTER II

Several days passed, and the animosity between the two neighbours did not subside. Andrei Gavrilovitch returned no more to Pokrovskoe, and Kirila Petrovitch, feeling dull without him, vented his spleen in the most insulting expressions, which, thanks to the zeal of the neighbouring nobles, reached Doubrovsky revised and augmented. A fresh incident destroyed the last hope of a reconciliation.

One day, Doubrovsky was going the round of his little estate, when, on approaching a grove of birch trees, he heard the blows of an axe, and a minute afterwards the crash of a falling tree; he hastened to the spot and found some of the Pokrovskoe peasants stealing his wood. Seeing him, they took to flight; but Doubrovsky, with the assistance of his coachman, caught two of them, whom he brought home bound. Moreover, two horses, belonging to the enemy, fell into the hands of the conqueror.

Doubrovsky was exceedingly angry. Before this, Troekouroff's people, who were well-known robbers, had never dared to play tricks within the boundaries of his property, being aware of the friendship which existed between him and their master. Doubrovsky now perceived that they were taking advantage of the rupture which had occurred between him and his neighbour, and he resolved, contrary to all ideas of the rules of war, to teach his prisoners a lesson with the rods which they themselves had collected in his grove, and to send the horses to work and to incorporate them with his own cattle.

The news of these proceedings reached the ears of Kirila Petrovitch that very same day. He was almost beside himself with rage, and in the first moment of his passion, he wanted to take all his domestics and make an attack upon Kistenevka (for such was

106

the name of his neighbour's village), raze it to the ground, and besiege the landholder in his own residence. Such exploits were not rare with him; but his thoughts soon took another direction. Pacing with heavy steps up and down the hall, he glanced casually out of the window, and saw a troika in the act of stopping at his, gate. A man in a leather travelling-cap and a frieze cloak stepped out of the telega and proceeded towards the wing occupied by the bailiff. Troekouroff recognized the assessor Shabashkin, and gave orders for him to be sent in to him. A minute afterwards Shabashkin stood before Kirila Petrovitch, and bowing repeatedly, waited respectfully to hear what he had to say to him.

"Good day—what is your name?" said Troekouroff: "Why have you come?"

"I was going to the town, Your Excellency," replied Shabashkin, "and I called on Ivan Demyanoff to know if there; were any orders."

"You have come at a very opportune moment—what is; your name? I have need of you. Take a glass of brandy and listen to me."

Such a friendly welcome agreeably surprised the assessor: he declined the brandy, and listened to Kirila Petrovitch with all possible attention.

"I have a neighbour," said Troekouroff, "a small proprietor, a rude fellow, and I want to take his property from him.... What do you think of that?"

"Your Excellency, are there any documents—?"

"Don't talk nonsense, brother,[59] what documents are you talking about? The business in this case is to take his property away from him, with or without documents. But stop! This estate belonged to us at one time. It was bought from a certain Spitsin, and then sold to Doubrovsky's father. Can't you make a case out of that?"

"It would be difficult, Your Excellency: probably the sale was effected in strict accordance with the law."

"Think, brother; try your hardest."

"If, for example, Your Excellency could in some way obtain from your neighbour the contract, in virtue of which he holds possession of his estate, then, without doubt—"

"I understand, but that is the misfortune: all his papers were burnt at the time of the fire."

"What! Your Excellency, his papers were burnt? What could be better? In that case, take proceedings according to law; without the slightest doubt you will receive complete satisfaction."

---

[59] Superiors in Russia frequently make use of this term in addressing their inferiors.

"You think so? Well, see to it, I rely upon your zeal, and you can rest assured of my gratitude."

Shabashkin, bowing almost to the ground, took his departure; from that day he began to devote all his energies to the business intrusted to him and, thanks to his prompt action, exactly a fortnight afterwards Doubrovsky received from the town a summons to appear in court and to produce the documents, in virtue of which he held possession of the village of Kistenevka.

Andrei Gavrilovitch, greatly astonished by this unexpected request, wrote that very same day a somewhat rude reply, in which he explained that the village of Kistenevka became his on the death of his father, that he held it by right of inheritance, that Troekouroff had nothing to do with the matter, and that all adventitious pretensions to his property were nothing but the outcome of chicanery and roguery. Doubrovsky had no experience in litigation. He generally followed the dictates of common sense, a guide rarely safe, and nearly always insufficient.

This letter produced a very agreeable impression on the mind of Shabashkin; he saw, in the first place, that Doubrovsky knew very little about legal matters; and, in the second, that it would not be difficult to place such a passionate and indiscreet man in a very disadvantageous position.

Andrei Gavrilovitch, after a more careful consideration of the questions addressed to him, saw the necessity of replying more circumstantially. He wrote a sufficiently pertinent paper, but in the end this proved insufficient also.

The business dragged on. Confident in his own right, Andrei Gavrilovitch troubled himself very little about the matter; he had neither the inclination nor the means to scatter money about him, and he began to deride the mercenary consciences of the scribbling fraternity. The idea of being made the victim of treachery never entered his head. Troekouroff, on his side, thought as little of winning the case he had devised. Shabashkin took the matter in hand for him, acting in his name, threatening and bribing the judges and quoting and interpreting the ordinances in the most distorted manner possible.

At last, on the 9th day of February, in the year 18—, Doubrovsky received, through the town police, an invitation to appear at the district court to hear the decision in the matter of the disputed property between himself—Lieutenant Doubrovsky, and General-in-Chief Troekouroff, and to sign his approval or disapproval of the verdict. That same day Doubrovsky set out for the town. On the road he was overtaken by Troekouroff. They glared haughtily at each other, and Doubrovsky observed a malicious smile upon the face of his adversary.

Arriving in town, Andrei Gavrilovitch stopped at the house of an acquaintance, a merchant, with whom he spent the night, and the next morning he appeared before the Court. Nobody paid any attention, to him. After him arrived Kirila Petrovitch. The members of the Court received him with every manifestation of the deepest submission, and an armchair was brought to him out of consideration for his rank, years and corpulence. He sat down; Andrei Gavrilovitch stood leaning against the wall. A deep silence ensued, and the secretary began in a sonorous voice to read the decree of the Court.

When the secretary had ceased reading, the assessor arose and, with a low bow, turned to Troekouroff, inviting him to sign the paper which he held out to him. Troekouroff, quite triumphant, took the pen and wrote beneath the decision of the Court his complete satisfaction.

It was now Doubrovsky's turn. The secretary handed the paper to him, but Doubrovsky stood immovable, with his head bent down. The secretary repeated his invitation: "To subscribe his full and complete satisfaction, or his manifest dissatisfaction, if he felt in his conscience that his case was just, and intended to appeal against the decision of the Court."

Doubrovsky remained silent ... Suddenly he raised his head, his eyes sparkled, he stamped his foot, pushed back the secretary, with such force, that he fell, seized the inkstand, hurled it at the assessor, and cried in a wild voice:

"What! you don't respect the Church of God! Away, you race of Shem!"

Then turning to Kirila Petrovitch:

"Has such a thing ever been heard of, Your Excellency?" he continued. "The huntsmen lead greyhounds into the Church of God! The dogs are running about the church! I will teach them a lesson presently!"

Everybody was terrified. The guards rushed in on hearing the noise, and with difficulty overpowered him. They led him out and placed him in a sledge. Troekouroff went out after him, accompanied by the whole Court Doubrovsky's sudden madness had produced a deep impression upon his imagination; the judges, who had counted upon his gratitude, were not honoured by receiving a single affable word from him. He returned immediately to Pokrovskoe, secretly tortured by his conscience, and not at all satisfied with the triumph of his hatred. Doubrovsky, in the meantime, lay in bed. The district doctor—not altogether a blockhead—bled him and applied leeches and mustard-plasters to him. Towards evening he began to feel better, and the next day he was taken to Kistenevka, which scarcely belonged to him any longer.

CHAPTER III

Some time elapsed, but the health of the stricken Doubrovsky showed no signs of improvement. It is true that the fits of madness did not recur, but his strength became visibly less. He forgot his former occupations, rarely left his room, and for days together remained absorbed in his own reflections. Egorovna, a kind-hearted old woman who had once tended his son, now became his nurse. She waited upon him like a child, reminded him when it was time to eat and sleep, fed him and even put him to bed. Andrei Gavrilovitch obeyed her, and had no intercourse with anybody else. He was not in a condition to think about his affairs or to look after his property, and Egorovna saw the necessity of informing young Doubrovsky, who was then serving in one of the regiments of Foot Guards stationed in St. Petersburg, of everything that had happened. And so, tearing a leaf from the account-book, she dictated to Khariton the cook, the only literate person in Kistenevka, a letter, which she sent off that same day to the town post.

But it is time for the reader to become acquainted with the real hero of this story.

Vladimir Doubrovsky had been educated at the cadet school and, on leaving it, had entered the Guards as sub-lieutenant. His father spared nothing that was necessary to enable him to live in a becoming manner, and the young man received from home a great deal more than he had any right to expect. Being imprudent and ambitious, he indulged in extravagant habits, ran into debt, and troubled himself very little about the future. Occasionally the thought crossed his mind that sooner or later he would be obliged to take to himself a rich bride.

One evening, when several officers were spending a few hours with him, lolling on the couches and smoking pipes with amber mouth-pieces, Grisha,[60] his valet, handed him a letter, the address

---

[60] Diminutive of Gregory.

and seal of which immediately attracted the young man's attention. He hastily opened it and read the following:

"Our Lord Vladimir Andreivitch, I, your old nurse, venture to inform you of the health of your papa. He is very poorly, sometimes he wanders in his talk, and the whole day long he sits like a stupid child—but life and death are in the hands of God. Come to us, my bright little falcon, and, we will send horses to meet you at Pesotchnoe. We hear that the Court is going to hand us over to Kirila Petrovitch Troekouroff, because it is said that we belong to him, although we have always belonged to you, and have always heard so ever since we can remember. You might, living in St. Petersburg, inform our Father the Czar of this, and he will not allow us to be wronged. It has been raining here for the last fortnight, and the shepherd Rodia died about Michaelmas Day. I send my maternal blessing to Grisha. Does he serve you well? I remain your faithful nurse,

"ARINA EGOROVNA BOUZIREVA."

Vladimir Doubrovsky read these somewhat unintelligible lines several times with great agitation. He had lost his mother during his childhood, and, hardly knowing his father, had been taken to St. Petersburg when he was eight years of age. In spite of that, he was romantically attached to his father, and having had but little opportunity of enjoying the pleasures of family life, he loved it all the more in consequence.

The thought of losing his father pained him exceedingly, and the condition of the poor invalid, which he guessed from his nurse's letter, horrified him. He imagined his father, left in an out-of-the-way village, in the hands of a stupid old woman and her fellow servants, threatened by some misfortune, and expiring without help in the midst of tortures both mental and physical. Vladimir Andreivitch reproached himself with criminal neglect. Not having received any news of his father for a long time, he had not even thought of making inquiries about him, supposing him to be travelling about or engaged in the management of his estate. That same evening he began to take the necessary steps for obtaining leave of absence, and two days afterwards he set out in the stage coach, accompanied by his faithful Grisha.

Vladimir Andreivitch neared the post station at which he was to take the turning for Kistenevka. His heart was filled with sad forebodings; he feared that he would no longer find his father alive.

He pictured to himself the dreary kind of life that "awaited him in the village: the loneliness, solitude, poverty and cares of business of which he knew nothing. Arriving at the station, he went to the postmaster and asked for fresh horses. The postmaster, having inquired where he was going, informed him that horses sent from Kistenevka had been waiting for him for the last four days. Soon appeared before Vladimir Andreivitch the old coachman Anton, who used formerly to take him over the stables and look after his pony. Anton's eyes filled with tears on seeing his young master, and bowing to the ground, he told him that his old master was still alive, and then hastened to harness the horses. Vladimir Andreivitch declined the proffered breakfast, and hastened to depart. Anton drove him along the cross country roads, and conversation began between them.

"Tell me, if you please, Anton, what is this business between my father and Troekouroff?"

"God knows, my little father Vladimir Andreivitch; our master, they say, had a dispute with Kirila Petrovitch, and the latter summoned him before the judge, though very often he himself is the judge. It is not the business of servants to discuss the affairs of their masters, but it was useless of your father to contend against Kirila Petrovitch: better had it been if he had not opposed him."

"It seems, then, that this Kirila Petrovitch does just what he pleases among you?"

"He certainly does, master: he does not care a rap for the assessor, and the chief of police runs on errands for him. The nobles repair to his house to do homage to him, for as the proverb says: 'Where there is a trough, there will the pigs be also.'"

"Is it true that he wants to take our estate from us?"

"Oh, master, that is what we have heard. A few days ago, the sexton from Pokrovskoe said at the christening held at the house of our overseer: 'You do well to enjoy yourselves while you are able, for you'll not have much chance of doing so when Kirila Petrovitch takes you in hand;' and Nikita the blacksmith said to him: 'Savelitch, don't distress your fellow sponsor, don't disturb the guests. Kirila Petrovitch is what he is, and Andrei Gavrilovitch is the same—and we are all God's and the Czar's.' But you cannot sew a button upon another person's mouth."

"Then you do not wish to pass into the possession of Troekouroff?"

"Into the possession of Kirila Petrovitch! The Lord save and preserve us! His own people fare badly enough, and if he got possession of strangers, he would strip off, not only their skin, but their flesh also. No, may God grant long life to Andrei Gavrilovitch;

112

and if God should take him to Himself, we want nobody but you, our benefactor. Do not give us up, and we will stand by you."

With these words, Anton flourished his whip, shook the reins, and the horses broke into a brisk trot.

Touched by the devotion of the old coachman, Doubrovsky became silent and gave himself up to his own reflections. More than an hour passed; suddenly Grisha roused him by exclaiming: "There is Pokrovskoe!" Doubrovsky raised his head. They were just then driving along the bank of a broad lake, out of which flowed a small stream winding among the hills. On one of these, above a thick green wood, rose the green roof and belvedere of a. huge stone house, together with a five-domed church with an ancient belfry; round about were scattered the village huts with their gardens and wells. Doubrovsky recognized these places; he remembered that on that very hill he had played with little Masha Troekouroff, who was two years younger than he, and who even then gave promise of being very beautiful. He wanted to make inquiries of Anton about her, but a certain bashfulness restrained him.

On approaching the castle, he perceived a white dress flitting among the trees in the garden. At that moment Anton whipped the horses, and impelled by that vanity, common to village coachmen as to drivers in general, he drove at full speed over the bridge and past the garden. On emerging from the village, they ascended the hill, and Vladimir perceived the little wood of birch trees, and to the left, in an open place, a small grey house with a red roof. His heart began to beat—before him was Kistenevka, the humble abode of his father.

About ten minutes afterwards he drove into the courtyard He looked around him with indescribable emotion: twelve years had elapsed since he last saw 'his native place. The little birches, which had just then been planted near the wooden fence, had now become tall trees with long branches. The courtyard, formerly ornamented with three regular flower-beds, between which ran a broad path carefully swept, had been converted into a meadow, in which was grazing a tethered horse. The dogs began to bark, but recognizing Anton, they became silent and commenced wagging their shaggy tails. The servants came rushing out of the house and surrounded the young master with loud manifestations of joy. It was with difficulty that he was able to make his way through the enthusiastic crowd. He ran up the well-worn steps; in the vestibule he was met by Egorovna, who tearfully embraced him.

"How do you do, how do you do, nurse?" he repeated, pressing the good old woman to his heart. "And my father? Where is he? How is he?"

At that moment a tall old man, pale and thin, in a dressing-gown and cap, entered the room, dragging one foot after the other with difficulty.

"Where is Volodka?" said he in a weak voice, and Vladimir embraced his father with affectionate emotion.

The joy proved too much for the sick man; he grew weak, his legs gave way beneath him, and he would have fallen, if his son had not held him up.

"Why did you get out of bed?" said Egorovna to him. "He cannot stand upon his feet, and yet he wants to do the same as other people."

The old man was carried back to his bedroom. He tried to converse with his son, but he could not collect his thoughts, and his words had no connection with each other. He became silent and fell into a kind of somnolence. Vladimir was struck by his condition. He installed himself in the bedroom and requested to be left alone with his father. The household obeyed, and then all turned towards Grisha and led him away to the servants' hall, where they gave him a hearty welcome according to the rustic custom, the while they wearied him with questions and compliments.

CHAPTER IV

A few days after his arrival, young Doubrovsky wished to turn his attention to business, but his father was not in a condition to give him the necessary explanations, and Andrei Gavrilovitch had no confidential adviser. Examining his papers, Vladimir only found the first letter of the assessor and a rough copy of his father's reply to it. From these he could not obtain any clear idea of the lawsuit, and he determined to await the result, trusting in the justice of his father's cause.

Meanwhile the health of Andrei Gavrilovitch grew worse from hour to hour. Vladimir foresaw that his end was not far off, and he never left the old man, now fallen into complete childishness.

In the meantime the period of delay had expired and no appeal had been presented. Kistenevka therefore belonged to Troekouroff. Shabashkin came to him, and with a profusion of salutations and congratulations, inquired when His Excellency intended to enter into possession of his newly-acquired property—would he go and do so himself, or would he deign to commission somebody else to act as his representative?

Kirila Petrovitch felt troubled. By nature he was not avaricious; his desire for revenge had carried him too far, and he now felt the rebukings of his conscience. He knew in what condition his adversary, the old comrade of his youth, lay, and his victory brought no joy to his heart. He glared sternly at Shabashkin, seeking for some pretext to vent his displeasure upon him, but not finding a suitable one, he said to him in an angry tone:

"Be off! I do not want you!"

Shabashkin, seeing that he was not in a good humour, bowed and hastened to withdraw, and Kirila Petrovitch, left alone, began to pace up and down, whistling: "Thunder of victory resound!" which, with him, was always a sure sign of unusual agitation of mind.

At last he gave orders for the droshky[61] to be got ready, wrapped himself up warmly (it was already the end of September), and, himself holding the reins, drove out of the courtyard.

He soon caught sight of the house of Andrei Gavrilovitch. Contradictory feelings filled his soul. Satisfied vengeance and love of power had, to a certain extent, deadened his more noble sentiments, but at last these latter prevailed. He resolved to effect a reconciliation with his old neighbour, to efface the traces of the quarrel and restore to him his property. Having eased his soul with this good intention, Kirila Petrovitch set off at a gallop towards the residence of his neighbour and drove straight into the courtyard.

At that moment the invalid was sitting at his bedroom window. He recognized Kirila Petrovitch—and his face assumed an expression of terrible emotion: a livid flush replaced his usual pallor, his eyes gleamed and he uttered a few unintelligible sounds. His son, who was sitting there examining the account books, raised his head and was struck by the change in his father's condition. The sick man pointed with his finger towards the courtyard with an expression of rage and horror. At that moment the voice and heavy tread of Egorovna were heard:

"Master, master! Kirila Petrovitch has come! Kirila Petrovitch is on the steps!" she cried.... "Lord God! What is the matter? What has happened to him?"

Andrei Gavrilovitch had hastily gathered up the skirts of his dressing-gown and was preparing to rise from his armchair. He succeeded in getting upon his feet—and then suddenly fell. His son rushed towards him; the old man lay insensible and without breathing: he had been attacked by paralysis.

---

[61] A low four-wheeled carriage.

"Quick, quick! hasten to the town for a doctor!" cried Vladimir.

"Kirila Petrovitch is asking for you," said a servant, entering the room.

Vladimir gave him a terrible look.

"Tell Kirila Petrovitch to take himself off as quickly as possible, before I have him turned out—go!"

The servant gladly left the room to execute his master's orders. Egorovna raised her hands to heaven.

"Little father," she exclaimed in a piping voice, "you; will lose your head! Kirila Petrovitch will eat us all up."

"Silence, nurse," said Vladimir angrily: "send Anton at once to the town for a doctor."

Egorovna left the room. There was nobody in the antechamber; all the domestics had run out into the courtyard' to look at Kirila Petrovitch. She went out on the steps and heard the servant deliver his young master's reply. Kirila Petrovitch heard it, seated in the droshky; his face became darker than night; he smiled contemptuously, looked threateningly at the assembled domestics, and then drove slowly out of the courtyard. He glanced up at the window where, a minute before, Andrei Gavrilovitch had been sitting, but he was no longer there. The nurse remained standing on the steps, forgetful of her master's injunctions. The domestics were noisily talking of what had just occurred. Suddenly Vladimir appeared in the midst of them, and said abruptly:

"There is no need for a doctor—my father is dead!" General consternation followed these words. The domestics rushed to the room of their old master. He was lying in the armchair in which Vladimir had placed him; his right arm hung down to the ground, his head was bent forward upon his chest—there was not the least sign of life in his body, which, not yet cold, was already disfigured by death. Egorovna set up a howl. The domestics surrounded the corpse, which was left to their care, washed it, dressed it in a uniform made in the year 1797, and laid it out on the same stable at which for so many years they had waited upon their master.

CHAPTER V

The funeral took place the third day. The body of the poor old man lay in the coffin, covered with a shroud and surrounded by candles. The dining-room was filled with domestics, ready to carry out the corpse. Vladimir and the servants raised the coffin. The priest went in front, followed by the clerk, chanting the prayers for the dead. The master of Kistenevka crossed the threshold of his house for the last time. The coffin was carried through the wood— the church lay just behind it. The day was clear and cold; the autumn leaves were falling from the trees. On emerging from the wood, they saw before them the wooden church of Kistenevka and the cemetery shaded by old lime trees. There reposed the body of Vladimir's mother; there, beside her tomb, a new grave had been dug the day before. The church was full of the Kistenevka peasantry, come to render the last homage to their master. Young Doubrovsky stood in the chancel; he neither wept nor prayed, but the expression of his face was terrible. The sad ceremony came to an end. Vladimir approached first to take leave of the corpse, after him came the domestics. The lid was brought and nailed upon the coffin. The women wept aloud, and the men frequently wiped away their tears with their fists. Vladimir and three of the servants carried the coffin to the cemetery, accompanied by the whole village. The coffin was lowered into the grave, all present threw upon it a handful of earth, the pit was filled up, the crowd saluted for the last time and then dispersed. Vladimir hastily departed, got ahead of everybody, and disappeared into the Kistenevka wood.

Egorovna, in the name of her master, invited the pope and all the clergy to a funeral dinner, informing them that her young master did not intend being present.

Then Father Anissim, his wife Fedorovna and the clerk took their way to the manor-house, discoursing with Egorovna upon the virtues of the deceased and upon what, in all probability, awaited his heir. The visit of Troekouroff and the reception given to him were already known to the whole neighbourhood, and the local politicians predicted that serious consequences would result from it.

"What is to be, will be," said the pope's wife: "but it will be a pity if Vladimir Andreivitch does not become our master. He is a fine young fellow, there is no denying that."

"And who is to be our master if he is not to be?" interrupted Egorovna. "Kirila Petrovitch need not put himself out—he has; not got a coward to deal with. My young falcon will know how to defend himself, and with God's help, he will not lack friends. Kirila Petrovitch is too overweening; and yet he slunk away with his tail between his legs when my Grishka[62] cried out to him: 'Be off, you old cur! Clear out of the place!'"

"Oh! Egorovna," said the clerk, "however could he bring his tongue to utter such words? I think I would rather bring myself to face the devil, than look askant at Kirila Petrovitch. As you look at him, you become terrified, and your very backbone seems to curve!"

"Vanity, vanity!" said the priest: "the service for the dead will some day be chanted for Kirila Petrovitch, as today for Andrei Gavrilovitch; the funeral may perhaps be more imposing, and more guests may be invited; but are not all equal in the sight of God?"

"Oh, father, we wanted to invite all the neighbourhood, but Vladimir Andreivitch did not wish it. Don't be alarmed, we have plenty to entertain people with.... but what would you have had us do? At all events, if there are not many people, I can treat you well, my dear friends."

This enticing promise and the hope of finding a toothsome pie, caused the talkers to quicken their steps, and they safely reached the manor-house, where the table was already laid and brandy served out.

Meanwhile Vladimir advanced further into the depth of the wood, endeavouring by exercise and fatigue to deaden the affliction of his soul. He walked on without taking any notice of the road; the branches constantly grazed and scratched him, and his feet continually sank into the swamp—he observed nothing. At last he reached a small glade surrounded by trees on every side; a little stream wound silently through the trees, half-stripped of their leaves by the autumn. Vladimir stopped, sat down upon the cold turf, and thoughts, each more gloomy than the other, oppressed his soul.... He felt his loneliness very keenly; the future appeared to him enveloped in terrible clouds. Troekouroff's enmity foreboded fresh misfortunes for him. His modest heritage might pass from him into the hands of a stranger, in which case beggary awaited him. For a long time he sat quite motionless in the same place, observing the gentle flow of the stream, bearing along on its surface a few withered leaves, and vividly representing to him the analogy of life. At last he observed that it began to grow dark; he arose and sought for the road home, but for a long time he wandered about the unknown wood before he stumbled upon the path which led straight up to the gate of his house.

He had not gone far before he met the priest coming towards

---

[62] Diminutive of Gregory.

him with all his clergy. The thought immediately occurred to him that this foreboded misfortune.[63] He involuntarily turned aside and disappeared behind the trees. The priests had not observed him, and they continued talking very earnestly among themselves.

"Fly from evil and do good," said the priest to his wife. "There is no need for us to remain here; it does not concern us, however the business may end."

The priest's wife made some reply, but Vladimir could not hear what she said.

Approaching the house, he saw a crowd of people; peasants and servants of the household were flocking into the courtyard. In the distance Vladimir could hear an unusual noise and murmur of voices. Near the coach-house stood two troikas. On the steps several unknown men in uniform were seemingly engaged in conversation.

"What does this mean?" he asked angrily of Anton, who ran forward to meet him. "Who are these people, and what do they want?"

"Oh, father Vladimir Andreivitch," replied Anton, out of breath, "the Court has come. They are giving us over to Troekouroff, they are taking us from your Honour!..."

Vladimir hung down his head; his people surrounded their unhappy master.

"You are our father," they cried, kissing his hands.

"We want no other master but you. We will die, but we will not leave you. Give us the order, Your Lordship, and we will soon settle matters with the Court."

Vladimir looked at them, and dark thoughts rose within him.

"Keep quiet," he said to them: "I will speak to the officers."

"That's it—speak to them, father," shouted the crowd: "put the accursed wretches to shame!"

Vladimir, approached the officials. Shabashkin, with his cap on his head, stood with his arms akimbo, looking proudly around him. The sheriff, a tall stout man, of about fifty years of age, with a red face and a moustache, seeing Doubrovsky approach, cleared his throat and called out in a hoarse voice:

"And therefore I repeat to you what I have already said: by the decision of the district Court, you now belong to Kirila Petrovitch Troekouroff, who is here represented by M. Shabashkin. Obey him in everything that he orders you; and you, women, love and honour him, as he loves you."

At this witty joke the sheriff began to laugh. Shabashkin and the

---

[63] To meet a priest is considered a bad omen in Russia.

other officials followed his example. Vladimir boiled over with indignation.

"Allow me to ask, what does all this mean?" he inquired, with pretended calmness, of the jocular sheriff.

"It means," replied the witty official, "that we have come to place Kirila Petrovitch Troekouroff in possession of this property, and to request certain others to take themselves off for good and all!"

"But I think that you could have communicated all this to me first, rather than to my peasants, and announced to the landholder the decision of the authorities——"

"The former landowner, Andrei Gavrilovitch, is dead according to the will of God; but who are you?" said Shabashkin, with an insolent look. "We do not know you, and we don't want to know you."

"Your Honour, that is our young master," said a voice in the crowd.

"Who dared to open his mouth?" said the sheriff, in a terrible tone. "That your master? Your master is Kirila Petrovitch Troekouroff.... do you hear, idiots?"

"Nothing of the kind!" said the same voice.

"But this is a revolt!" shrieked the sheriff. "Hi, bailiff, this way!"

The bailiff stepped forward.

"Find out immediately who it was that dared to answer me. I'll teach him a lesson!"

The bailiff turned towards the crowd and asked who had spoken. But all remained silent. Soon a murmur was heard at the back; it gradually grew louder, and in a minute it broke out into a terrible wail. The sheriff lowered his voice and was about to try to persuade them to be calm.

"Why do you stand looking at him?" cried the servants: "Come on, lads, forward!" And the crowd began to move.

Shabashkin and the other members of the Court rushed into the vestibule, and closed the door behind them.

"Seize them, lads!" cried the same voice, and the crowd pressed forward.

"Hold!" cried Doubrovsky: "idiots! what are you doing? You will ruin yourselves and me, too. Go home all of you, and leave me to myself. Don't fear, the Czar is merciful: I will present a petition to him—he will not let us be made the victims of an injustice. We are all his children. But how can he take your part, if you begin rebelling and plundering?"

This speech of young Doubrovsky's, his sonorous voice and imposing appearance, produced the desired effect. The crowd

120

became quiet and dispersed; the courtyard became empty, the officials of the Court still remained inside the house. Vladimir sadly ascended the steps. Shabashkin opened the door, and with obsequious bows began to thank Doubrovsky for his generous intervention.

Vladimir listened to him with contempt and made no reply.

"We have resolved," continued the assessor, "with your permission, to remain here for the night, as it is already dark, and your peasants might attack us on the road. Be kind enough to order some hay to be put down for us on the parlour floor, as soon as it is daylight, we will take our departure."

"Do what you please," replied Doubrovsky drily: "I am no longer master here."

With these words he entered into his fathers room and locked the door behind him.

CHAPTER VI

"And so, all is finished!" said Vladimir to himself. "This morning I had a corner and a piece of bread; to-morrow I must leave the house where I was born. My father, with the ground where he reposes, will belong to that hateful man, the cause of his death and of my ruin!"... Vladimir clenched his teeth and fixed his eyes upon the portrait of his mother. The artist had represented her leaning upon a balustrade, in a white morning dress, with a rose in her hair.

"And that portrait will fall into the hands of the enemy of my family," thought Vladimir. "It will be thrown into a lumber room together with broken chairs, or hung up in the ante-room, to become an object of derision for his dog-keepers; and in her bedroom, in the room where my father died, will be installed his bailiff, or his harem. No, no! he shall not have possession of the house of mourning, from which he is driving me out."

Vladimir clenched his teeth again; terrible thoughts rose up in his mind. The voices of the officials reached him; they were giving their orders, demanding first one thing and then another, and disagreeably disturbing him in the midst of his painful meditations.

At last all became quiet.

Vladimir unlocked the drawers and boxes and began to examine the papers of the deceased. They consisted for the most part of farming accounts and letters connected with various matters of business. Vladimir tore them up without reading them. Among them he came across a packet with the inscription: "Letters from my wife." A prey to deep emotion, Vladimir began to read them. They had been written during the Turkish campaign, and were addressed to the army from Kistenevka. Madame Doubrovsky described to her husband her life in the country and her business concerns, complained with tenderness of the separation, and implored him to return home as soon as possible to the arms of his loving wife. In one of these letters, she expressed to him her anxiety concerning the health of little Vladimir; in another she rejoiced over his early intelligence, and predicted for him a happy and brilliant future. Vladimir was so absorbed in his reading, that he forgot everything else in the world as his mind conjured up visions of domestic happiness, and he did not observe how the time was passing: the clock upon the wall struck eleven. Vladimir placed the letters in his pocket, took up a candle and left the room. In the parlour the officials were sleeping on the floor. Upon the table were tumblers which they had emptied, and a strong smell of rum pervaded the entire room. Vladimir turned from them with disgust, and passed into the anteroom. There all was dark. Somebody, seeing the light, crouched into a corner. Turning the light towards him, Vladimir recognized Arkhip the blacksmith.

"Why are you here?" he asked, in surprise.

"I wanted—I came to find out if they were all in the house," replied Arkhip, in a low faltering voice.

"And why have you got your axe?"

"Why have I got my axe? Can anybody go about nowadays without an axe? These officials are such impudent knaves, that one never knows——"

"You are drunk; throw the axe down and go to bed."

"I drunk? Father Vladimir Andreivitch, God is my witness that not a single drop of brandy has passed my lips, nor has the thought of such a thing entered my mind. Was ever such a thing heard of? These clerks have taken it into their heads to rule over us and to drive our master out of the manor-house.... How they snore, the wretches! I should like to put an end to the whole lot of them at once."

Doubrovsky frowned.

"Listen, Arkhip," said he, after a short pause: "Get such ideas out of your head. It is not the fault of the officials. Light the lantern and follow me."

122

Arkhip took the candle out of his master's hand, found the lantern behind the stove, lit it, and then both of them softly descended the steps and proceeded around the courtyard. The watchman began beating upon an iron plate; the dogs commenced to bark.

"Who is on the watch?" asked Doubrovsky.

"We, little father," replied a thin voice: "Vassilissa and Loukeria."

"Go home," said Doubrovsky to them, "you are not wanted."

"You can have a holiday," added Arkhip.

"Thank you, benefactor," replied the women, and they immediately returned home.

Doubrovsky walked on further. Two men approached him: they challenged him, and Doubrovsky recognized the voices of Anton and Grisha.

"Why are you not in bed and asleep?" he asked them.

"This is no time for us to think of sleep," replied Anton. "Who would have thought that we should ever have come to this?"

"Softly," interrupted Doubrovsky. "Where is Egorovna?"

"In the manor-house, in her room," replied Grisha.

"Go and bring her here, and make all our people get out of the house; let not a soul remain in it except the officials; and you, Anton, get the cart ready."

Grisha departed; a minute afterwards he returned with his mother. The old woman had not undressed that night; with the exception of the officials, nobody closed an eye.

"Are all here?" asked Doubrovsky. "Has anybody been left in the house?"

"Nobody, except the clerks," replied Grisha.

"Bring here some hay or some straw," said Doubrovsky. The servants ran to the stables and returned with armfuls of hay.

"Put it under the steps—that's it. Now, my lads, a light!"

Arkhip opened the lantern and Doubrovsky kindled a torch.

"Wait a moment," said he to Arkhip: "I think, in my hurry, that I locked the doors of the hall. Go quickly and open them."

Arkhip ran to the vestibule: the doors were open. He locked them, muttering in an undertone: "It's likely that I'll leave them open!" and then returned to Doubrovsky.

Doubrovsky applied the torch to the hay, which burst into a blaze, the flames rising to a great height and illuminating the whole courtyard.

"Alas!" cried Egorovna plaintively: "Vladimir Andreivitch, what are you doing?"

"Silence!" said Doubrovsky. "Now, children, farewell; I am going where God may direct me. Be happy with your new master."

"Our father, our benefactor!" cried the peasants, "we will die—but we will not leave you, we will go with you."

The horses were ready. Doubrovsky took his seat in the cart with Grisha; Anton whipped the horses and they drove out of the courtyard.

In one moment the whole house was enveloped in flames. The floors cracked and gave way; the burning beams began to fall; a red smoke rose above the roof, and there arose piteous groans and cries of "Help, help!"

"Shout away!" said Arkhip, with a malicious smile, contemplating the fire.

"Dear Arkhip," said Egorovna to him, "save them, the scoundrels, and God will reward you."

"Let them shout," replied the blacksmith.

At that moment the officials appeared at the window, endeavouring to burst the double sash. But at the same instant the roof fell in with a crash—and the cries ceased.

Soon all the peasants came pouring into the courtyard. The women, screaming wildly, hastened to save their effects; the children danced about admiring the conflagration. The sparks flew up in a fiery shower, setting light to the huts.

"Now everything is right!" said Arkhip. "How it burns! It must be a grand sight from Pokrovskoe."

At that moment a new apparition attracted his attention. A cat ran along the roof of a burning barn, without knowing where to leap from. Flames surrounded it on every side. The poor creature cried for help with plaintive mewings; the children screamed with laughter on seeing its despair.

"What are you laughing at, you little demons?" said the blacksmith, angrily. "Do you not fear God? One of God's creatures is perishing, and you rejoice over it." Then placing a ladder against the burning roof, he mounted up towards the cat. She understood his intention, and, with grateful eagerness, clutched hold of his sleeve. The half-burnt blacksmith descended with his burden.

"And now, lads, good bye," he said to the dismayed peasants: "there is nothing more for me to do here. May you be happy. Do not think too badly of me."

The blacksmith took his departure. The fire raged for some time longer, and at last went out. Piles of red-hot embers glowed brightly in the darkness of the night, while round about them wandered the burnt-out inhabitants of Kistenevka.

CHAPTER VII

The next day the news of the fire spread through all the neighbourhood. Everybody explained it in a different way. Some maintained that Doubrovsky's servants, having got drunk at the funeral, had set fire to the house through carelessness; others blamed the officials, who were drunk also in their new quarters. Some guessed the truth, and affirmed that the author of the terrible calamity was Doubrovsky himself, urged on to the committal of the deed by the promptings of resentment and despair. Many maintained that he had himself perished in the flames with the officials and all his servants.

Troekouroff came the next day to the scene of the conflagration, and conducted the inquest himself. It was stated that the sheriff, the assessor of the land Court, the attorney and his clerk, as well as Vladimir Doubrovsky, the nurse Egorovna, the servant Grisha, the coachman Anton, and the blacksmith Arkhip had disappeared—nobody knew where. All the servants declared that the officials perished at the moment when the roof fell in. Their charred remains in fact were discovered. The women, Vassilissa and Loukeria, said that they had seen Doubrovsky and Arkhip the blacksmith a few minutes before the fire. The blacksmith Arkhip, according to the general showing, was alive, and was probably the principal, if not the sole author of the fire. Strong suspicions fell upon Doubrovsky. Kirila Petrovitch sent to the Governor a detailed account of all that had happened, and a new suit was commenced.

Soon other reports furnished fresh food for curiosity and gossip. Brigands appeared and spread terror throughout the whole neighbourhood. The measures taken against them proved unavailing. Robberies; each more daring than the other, followed one after another. There was no security either on the roads or in the villages. Several troikas, filled with brigands, traversed the whole province in open daylight, stopping travellers and the mail The villages were visited by them, and the manor-houses were attacked and set on fire. The chief of the band had acquired a great reputation for intelligence, daring, and a sort of generosity. Wonders were related of him. The name of Doubrovsky was upon every lip. Everybody was convinced that it was he, and nobody else, who commanded the daring robbers. One thing was remarkable: the domains and property of Troekouroff were spared. The brigands had not attacked a single barn of his, nor stopped a single load belonging to him. With his usual arrogance, Troekouroff attributed this exception to the fear which he had inspired throughout the whole province, as well as to the excellent police which he had organized in his villages. At first the neighbours smiled at the presumption of Troekouroff, and everyone expected that the uninvited guests would visit Pokrovskoe, where they would find something worth having, but at last they were compelled to agree and confess that the brigands showed him unaccountable respect. Troekouroff triumphed, and at the news of each fresh exploit on the part of Doubrovsky, he indulged in ironical remarks at the expense of the Governor, the sheriffs, and the regimental commanders, who always allowed the brigand chief to escape with impunity.

Meanwhile the 1st of October arrived, the day of the annual church festival in Troekouroff's village. But before we proceed to describe further events, we must acquaint the reader with some personages who are new to him, or whom we merely mentioned at the beginning of our story.

CHAPTER VIII

The reader has probably already divined that the daughter of Kirila Petrovitch, of whom we have as yet said but very little, is the heroine of our story. At the period about which we are writing, she was seventeen years old, and in the full bloom of her beauty. Her father loved her to the verge of folly, but treated her with his characteristic wilfulness, at one time endeavouring to gratify her slightest whims, at another terrifying her by his coarse and sometimes brutal behaviour. Convinced of her attachment, he could yet never gain her confidence. She was accustomed to conceal from him her thoughts and feelings, because she never knew in what manner they would be received. She had no companions, and had grown up in solitude. The wives and daughters of the neighbours rarely visited at the house of Kirila Petrovitch, whose usual conversation and amusements demanded the companionship of men, and not the presence of ladies. Our beauty rarely appeared among the guests who were invited to her father's house. The extensive library, consisting for the most part of works of French writers of the eighteenth century, was given over to her charge. Her father never read anything except the "Perfect Cook," and could not guide her in the choice of books, and Masha, after having dipped into works of various kinds, had naturally given her preference to romances. In this manner she went on completing her education, first begun under the direction of Mademoiselle Micheau, in whom Kirila Petrovitch reposed great confidence, and whom he was at last obliged to send away secretly to another estate, when the results of this friendship became too apparent.

Mademoiselle Micheau left behind her a rather agreeable recollection. She was a good-natured girl, and had never misused the influence which she evidently exercised over Kirila Petrovitch, in which she differed from the other confidants, whom he constantly kept changing. Kirila Petrovitch himself seemed to like her more than the others, and a dark-eyed, roguish-looking little fellow of nine, recalling the southern features of Mademoiselle Micheau, was being brought up by him and was recognized as his son, notwithstanding the fact that quite a number of bare-footed lads ran about in front of his windows, who were as like Kirila Petrovitch as one drop of water is to another, and who were inscribed as forming part of his household. Kirila Petrovitch had sent to Moscow for a French tutor for his little son, Sasha,[64] and this tutor came to Pokrovskoe at the time of the events that we are now describing.

This tutor, by his prepossessing appearance and simple manners, produced a very agreeable impression upon the mind of Kirila Petrovitch. He presented to the latter his credentials, and a letter from one of Troekouroff's relations, with whom he had lived as tutor for four years. Kirila Petrovitch examined all these, and was dissatisfied only with the youthfulness of the Frenchman, not because he considered this agreeable defect incompatible with the patience and experience necessary for the unhappy calling of a tutor, but because he had doubts of his own, which he immediately resolved to have cleared up. For this purpose he ordered Masha to be sent to him. Kirila Petrovitch did not speak French, and she acted as interpreter for him.

"Come here, Masha: tell this Monsieur that I accept him only on condition that he does not venture to pay court to my girls, for if he should do so, the son of a dog, I'll... Translate that to him, Masha."

Masha blushed, and turning to the tutor, told him in French that her father counted upon his modesty and orderly conduct.

The Frenchman bowed to her, and replied that he hoped to merit esteem, even if favour were not shown to him. Masha translated his reply word for word.

---

[64] Diminutive of Alexander.

"Very well, very well," said Kirila Petrovitch, "he needs neither favour nor esteem. His business is to look after Sasha and teach him grammar and geography—translate that to him."

Maria Kirilovna softened the rude expressions of her father in translating them, and Kirila Petrovitch dismissed his Frenchman to the wing of the house in which his room was situated.

Masha had not given a thought to the young Frenchman. Brought up with aristocratic prejudices, a tutor, in her eyes, was only a sort of servant or artizan; and servants or artizans did not seem to her to be men at all. Nor did she observe the impression that she had produced upon Monsieur Desforges, nor his confusion, nor his agitation, nor the tremor in his voice. For several days afterwards, she met him very frequently, but without honouring him with much attention. In an unexpected manner, however, she received quite a new impression with respect to him.

In the courtyard of Kirila Petrovitch there were usually kept several young bears, and they formed one of the chief amusements of the master of Pokrovskoe. While they were young, they were brought every day into the parlour, where Kirila Petrovitch used to spend whole hours in amusing himself with them, setting them at cats and young dogs. When they were grown up, they were attached to a chain, to await being baited in earnest. Sometimes they were brought out in front of the windows of the manor-house, and an empty wine-cask, studded with nails, was put before them. The bear would sniff it, then touch it gently, and getting its paws pricked, it would become angry and push the cask with greater force, and so wound itself still more. The beast would then work itself into a perfect frenzy, and fling itself upon the cask, growling furiously, until they removed from the poor animal the object of its vain rage. Sometimes a pair of bears were harnessed to a telega, then, willingly or unwillingly, guests were placed in it, and the bears were allowed to gallop wherever chance might direct them. But the best joke of Kirila Petrovitch's was as follows:

A starving bear used to be shut up in an empty room and fastened by a rope to a ring screwed into the wall. The rope was nearly the length of the room, so that only the opposite corner was out of the reach of the ferocious beast. A novice was generally brought to the door of this room, and, as if by accident, pushed in along with the bear; the door was then locked, and the unhappy victim was left alone with the shaggy hermit. The poor guest, with torn skirts and scratched hands, soon sought the safe corner, but he was sometimes compelled to stand for three whole hours, pressed against the wall, watching the savage beast, two steps from him, leaping and standing on its hind legs, growling, tugging at the rope and endeavouring to reach him. Such were the noble amusements of a Russian gentleman!

Some days after the arrival of the French tutor, Troekouroff thought of him, and resolved to give him a taste of the bear's room. For this purpose, he summoned him one morning, and conducted him along several dark corridors; suddenly a side door opened—two servants pushed the Frenchman into the room and locked the door after him. Recovering from his surprise, the tutor perceived the chained bear. The animal began to snort and to sniff at his visitor from a distance, and suddenly raising himself upon his hind legs, he advanced towards him.... The Frenchman was not alarmed; he did not retreat but awaited the attack. The bear drew near; Desforges drew from his pocket a small pistol, inserted it in the ear of the hungry animal, and fired. The bear rolled over. Everybody was attracted to the spot by the report, the door was opened, and Kirila Petrovitch entered, astonished at the result of his joke.

Kirila Petrovitch wanted an explanation of the whole affair. Who had warned Desforges of the joke, or how came he to have a loaded pistol in his pocket? He sent for Masha. Masha came and interpreted her father's questions to the Frenchman.

"I never heard even of the existence of the bear," replied Desforges, "but I always carry a pistol about with me, because I do not intend to put up with an offence for which, on account of my calling, I cannot demand satisfaction."

Masha looked at him in astonishment and translated his words to Kirila Petrovitch. Kirila Petrovitch made no reply; he ordered the bear to be removed and its skin to be taken off; then turning to his people, he said:

"What a brave fellow! There is nothing of the coward about him. By the Lord, he is certainly no coward!"

From that moment he took a liking to Desforges, and never thought again of putting him to the proof.

But this incident produced a. still greater impression upon Maria Kirilovna. Her imagination had been struck: she had seen the dead bear, and Desforges standing calmly over it and talking tranquilly to her. She saw that bravery and proud self-respect did not belong exclusively to one class, and from that moment she began to show regard for the young tutor, and this regard increased from day to day. A certain intimacy sprang up between them. Masha had a beautiful voice and great musical ability; Desforges proposed to give her lessons. After that it will not be difficult for the reader to understand that Masha fell in love with him without acknowledging it to herself.

CHAPTER IX

On the eve of the festival, of which we have already spoken, the guests began to arrive at Pokrovskoe. Some were accommodated at the manor-house and in the wings attached to it; others in the house of the bailiff; a third party was quartered upon the priest; and the remainder upon the better class of peasants. The stables were filled with the horses of the visitors, and the yards and coach-houses were crowded with vehicles of every sort. At nine o'clock in the morning the bells rang for mass, and everybody repaired to the new stone church, built by Kirila Petrovitch and annually enriched by his offerings. The church was soon crowded with such a number of distinguished worshippers, that the simple peasants could find no room within the edifice, and had to stand beneath the porch and inside the railings. The mass had not yet begun: they were waiting for Kirila Petrovitch. He arrived at last in a caliche drawn by six horses, and walked proudly to his place, accompanied by Maria Kirilovna. The eyes of both men and women were turned upon her— the former were astonished at her beauty, the latter examined her dress with great attention.

The mass began. The household singers sang in the choir, and Kirila Petrovitch joined in with them. He prayed without looking either to the right or to the left, and with proud humility he bowed himself to the ground when the deacon in a loud voice mentioned the name of the founder of the church.

The mass came to an end.[65] Kirila Petrovitch was the first to kiss the crucifix. All the others followed him; the neighbours approached him with respect, the ladies surrounded Masha. Kirila Petrovitch, on issuing from the church, invited everybody to dine with him, then he seated himself in the caliche and drove home. All the guests followed after him.

The rooms began to fill with the visitors; every moment new faces appeared, and it was with difficulty that the host could be approached. The ladies sat decorously in a semicircle, dressed in antiquated fashion, in dresses of faded but expensive material, all covered with pearls and brilliants. The men crowded round the caviar[66] and the vodka,[67] conversing among themselves with great animation. In the dining-room the table was laid for eighty persons;

---

[65] At the end of the service in the Russian Church, all the members of the congregation kiss the crucifix.
[66] The roes of sturgeons prepared and salted.
[67] Brandy.

the servants were bustling about, arranging the bottles and decanters and adjusting the table-cloths.

At last the house-steward announced that dinner was ready. Kirila Petrovitch went first and took his seat at the table; the ladies followed after him, and took their places with an air of great gravity, observing a sort of precedence as they did so. The young ladies crowded together like a timid herd of kids, and took their places next to one another. Opposite to them sat the gentlemen. At the end of the table sat the tutor by the side of the little Sasha.

The servants began to pass the plates round according to the rank of the guests; when they were in doubt about the latter point, they allowed themselves to be guided by instinct, and their guesses were nearly always correct. The noise of the plates and spoons mingled with the loud talk of the guests. Kirila Petrovitch looked gaily round his table and thoroughly enjoyed the happiness of being able to provide such a hospitable entertainment. At that moment a calèche, drawn by six horses, drove into the yard.

"Who is that?" asked the host.

"Anton Pafnoutitch," replied several voices.

The doors opened, and Anton Pafnoutitch Spitsin, a stout man of about fifty years of age, with a round pockmarked face, adorned with a treble chin, rolled into the-dining-room, bowing, smiling, and preparing to make his excuses.

"A cover here!" cried Kirila Petrovitch. "Pray sit down, Anton Pafnoutitch, and tell us what this means: you were not at my mass, and you are late for dinner. This is not like you. You are devout, and you love good cheer."

"Pardon me," replied Anton Pafnoutitch, fastening his serviette in the button-hole of his coat: "pardon me, little father Kirila Petrovitch, I started early on my journey, but I had not gone ten versts, when suddenly the tire of the front wheel snapped in two. What was to be done? Fortunately it was not far from the village. But by the time we had arrived there, and had found a blacksmith, and had got everything put to rights, three hours had elapsed. It could not be helped. To take the shortest route through the wood of Kistenevka, I did not dare, so we came the longest way round."

"Ah, ah!" interrupted Kirila Petrovitch, "it is evident that you do not belong to the brave ten. What are you afraid of?"

"How, what am I afraid of, little father Kirila Petrovitch? And Doubrovsky? I might have fallen into his clutches. He is a young man who never misses his aim—he lets nobody off; and I am afraid he would have flayed me twice over, had he got hold of me."

"Why, brother, such a distinction?"

"Why, father Kirila Petrovitch? Have you forgotten the lawsuit

131

of the late Andrei Gavrilovitch? Was it not I who, to please you, that is to say, according to conscience and justice, showed that Doubrovsky held possession of Kistenevka without having any right to it, and solely through your condescension; and did not the deceased—God rest his soul!—vow that he would settle with me in his own way, and might not the son keep his father's word? Hitherto the Lord has been merciful to me. Up to the present they have only plundered one of my barns, but one of these days they may find their way to the manor-house."

"Where they would find a rich booty," observed Kirila Petrovitch: "I have no doubt that the little red cash-box is as full as it can be."

"Not so, father Kirila Petrovitch; there was a time when it was full, but now it is perfectly empty."

"Don't tell lies, Anton Pafnoutitch. We know you. Where do you spend money? At home you live like a pig, you never receive anybody, and you fleece your peasants. You do nothing with your money but hoard it up."

"You are only joking, father Kirila Petrovitch," murmured Anton Pafnoutitch, smiling; "but I swear to you that we are ruined," and Anton Pafnoutitch swallowed his host's joke with a greasy piece of fish pasty.

Kirila Petrovitch left him and turned to the new sheriff, who was his guest for the first time and who was sitting at the other end of the table, near the tutor.

"Well, Mr. Sheriff, give us a proof of your cleverness: catch Doubrovsky for us."

The sheriff looked disconcerted, bowed, smiled, stammered, and said at last:

"We will try, Your Excellency."

"H'm! 'we will try!' You have been trying for a long time to rid our country of brigands. Nobody knows how to set about the business. And, after all, why try to catch him? Doubrovsky's robberies are a blessing to the sheriffs: what with investigations, travelling expenses, and the money they put into their pockets. He will never be caught Why should such a benefactor be put down? Isn't that true, Mr. Sheriff?"

"Perfectly true, Your Excellency," replied the completely confused sheriff.

The guests roared with laughter.

"I like the fellow for his frankness," said Kirila Petrovitch: "but it is a pity that our late sheriff is no longer with us. If he had not been burnt, the neighbourhood would have been quieter. And what news of Doubrovsky? Where was he last seen?"

132

"At my house, Kirila Petrovitch," said a female voice: "last Tuesday he dined with me."

All eyes were turned towards Anna Savishna Globova, a very simple widow, beloved by everybody for her kind and cheerful disposition. Everyone prepared to listen to her story with the deepest interest.

"You must know that three weeks ago I sent my steward to the post with a letter for my Vaniusha.[68] I do not spoil my son, and moreover I haven't the means of spoiling him, even if I wished to do so. However, you know very well that an officer of the Guards must live in a suitable style, and I share my income with Vaniusha as well as I can. Well, I sent two thousand roubles to him; and although the thought of Doubrovsky came more than once into my mind, I thought to myself: the town is not far off—only seven, versts altogether, perhaps God will order all things for the best. But what happens? In the evening my steward returns, pale, tattered, and on foot. 'What is the matter? What has happened to you?' I exclaimed. 'Little mother Anna Savishna,' he replied, 'the brigands have robbed and almost killed me. Doubrovsky himself was there, and he wanted to hang me, but he afterwards had pity upon me and let me go. But he plundered me of everything—money, horse, and cart,' A faintness came over me. Heavenly Lord! What will become of my Vaniusha? There was nothing to be done. I wrote a fresh letter, telling him all that had happened, and sent him my blessing without a farthing of money. One week passed, and then another. Suddenly, one day, a calèche drove into my courtyard. Some general asked to see me: I gave orders for him to be shown in. He entered the room, and I saw before me a man of about thirty-five years of age, dark, with black hair, moustache and beard—the exact portrait of Koulneff. He introduced himself to me as a friend and comrade of my late husband, Ivan Andreivitch. He happened to be passing by, and he could not resist paying a visit to his old friend's widow, knowing that I lived there. I invited him to dine, and I set before him what God had sent me. We spoke of this and that, and at last we began to talk about Doubrovsky. I told him of my trouble. My general frowned. 'That is strange,' said he: 'I have heard that Doubrovsky does not attack everybody, but only people who are well known to be rich, and that even then he leaves them a part of their possessions and does not plunder them of everything. As for murdering people, nobody has yet accused him of that. Is there not some roguery here? Oblige me by sending for your steward.'

---

[68] Diminutive of Ivan.

"The steward was sent for, and quickly made his appearance. But as soon as he caught sight of the general he stood as if petrified.

"'Tell me, brother, in what manner did Doubrovsky plunder you, and how was it that he wanted to hang you?' My steward began to tremble and fell at the general's feet.

"'Little father, I am guilty. The evil one led me astray. I have lied.'

"'If that is so,' replied the general, 'have the goodness to relate to your mistress how it all happened, and I will listen.'

"My steward could not recover himself.

"'Well, then,' continued the general, 'tell us where you met Doubrovsky.'

"'At the two pine trees, little father, at the two pine trees.'

"'What did he say to you?'

"'He asked me who I was, where I was going, and why.'

"'Well, and after that?'

"'After that he demanded the letter and the money from me, and I gave them to him.'

"'And he?'

"'Well, and he ... little father, pardon me!'

"'Well, what did he do?'

"'He returned me the money and the letter, and said 'Go, in the name of God, and put this in the post.'

"'Well!'

"'Little father, pardon me!'

"'I will settle with you, my pigeon,' said the general sternly. 'And you, madam, order this scoundrel's trunk to be searched, and then give him into my hands; I will teach him a lesson.'

"I guessed who his Excellency was, but I did not make any observation. The coachmen tied the steward to the box of the calèche; the money was found; the general remained to dine with me, and departed immediately afterwards, taking with him my steward. The steward was found the next day in the wood, tied to an oak, and as ragged as a lime tree."

Everybody listened in silence to Anna Savishna's story, especially the young ladies. Many of them secretly wished well to Doubrovsky, seeing in him a romantic hero, particularly Maria Kirilovna, an impulsive, sentimental girl, imbued with the mysterious horrors of Mrs. Anne Radcliffe.[69]

"And do you think, Anna Savishna, that it was Doubrovsky himself who visited you?" asked Kirila Petrovitch. "You are very

---

[69] A now almost forgotten romance writer, whose "Romance of the Forest," "Mysteries of Udolpho," and "Italian," were very popular a century ago.

much mistaken. I do not know who your guest may have been, but I feel quite sure that it was not Doubrovsky."

"How, little father, not Doubrovsky? But who is it then, if not he, who stops travellers on the high road in order to search them?"

"I don't know; but I feel confident that it is not Doubrovsky. I remember him as a child; I do, not know whether his hair has turned black, but at that time he was a curly flaxen-haired boy. But I do know for a positive fact, that Doubrovsky is five years older than my Masha, and that consequently he is not thirty-five, but about twenty-three."

"Exactly so, Your Excellency," observed the sheriff: "I have in my pocket the description of Vladimir Doubrovsky. In that it is distinctly stated that he is twenty-three years of age."

"Ah!" said Kirila Petrovitch. "By the way, read it, and we will listen: it will not be a bad thing for us to know his description. Perhaps he may fall into our clutches, and if so, he will not escape in a hurry."

The sheriff drew from his pocket a rather dirty sheet of paper, unfolded it with an air of great importance, and began to read in a monotonous tone:

"Description of Doubrovsky, based upon the depositions of his former servants:

"Twenty-three years of age, medium height, clear complexion, shaves his beard, has brown eyes, flaxen hair, straight nose. Does not seem to have any particular marks."

"And is that all?" said Kirila Petrovitch.

"That is all," replied the sheriff, folding up the paper.

"I congratulate you, Mr. Sheriff. A very valuable document With that description it will not be difficult for you to find Doubrovsky! Who is not of medium height? Who has not flaxen hair, a straight nose and brown eyes? I would wager that you would talk for three hours at a stretch to Doubrovsky himself, and you would never guess in whose company you were. There is no denying that these officials have wise heads."

The sheriff, meekly replacing the paper in his pocket, silently busied himself with his goose and cabbage. Meanwhile the servants had already gone the round of the guests several times, filling up each one's glass. Several bottles of Caucasus wine had been opened with a great deal of noise, and had been thankfully accepted under the name of champagne. Faces began to glow, and the conversation grew louder, more incoherent and more lively.

"No," continued Kirila Petrovitch, "we shall never see another sheriff like the late Taras Alexeievitch! He was not the man to be thrown off the scent very easily. I am very sorry that the fellow was

135

burnt, for otherwise not one of the band would have got away from him. He would have laid his hands upon the whole lot of them, and not even Doubrovsky himself would have escaped. Taras Alexeievitch would perhaps have taken money from him, but he would not have let him go. Such was the way of the deceased. Evidently there is nothing else to be done but for me to take the matter in hand and go after the brigands with my people. I will begin by sending out twenty men to scour the wood. My people are not cowards. Each of them would attack a bear single-handed, and they certainly would not fall back before a brigand."

"How is your bear, father Kirila Petrovitch?" asked Anton Pafnoutitch, being reminded by these words of his shaggy acquaintance and of certain pleasantries of which he had once been the victim.

"Misha[70] wishes you a long life,[71] replied Karila Petrovitch: "he died a glorious death at the hands of the enemy. There is his conqueror!" Kirila Petrovitch pointed to the french tutor. "He has avenged your—if you will allow me to say so—do you remember?"

"How should I not remember?" said Anton Pafnoutitch, scratching his head: "I remember it only too well. So Misha is dead. I am very sorry for Misha—upon my word, I am very sorry! How amusing he was! How intelligent! You will not find another bear like him. And why did monsieur kill him?"

Kirila Petrovitch began, with great satisfaction, to relate the exploit of his Frenchman, for he possessed the happy faculty of boasting of everything that was about him. The guests listened with great attention to the story of Misha's death, and gazed in astonishment at Desforges, who, not suspecting that his bravery was the subject of conversation, sat tranquilly in his place, giving advice to his restive pupil.

The dinner, after lasting about three hours, came to an end; the host placed his serviette upon the table, and everybody rose and repaired to the parlour, where awaited them coffee, cards, and a continuation of the carouse so excellently begun in the dining-room.

---

[70] Diminutive of Michael—the familiar name for a bear in Russia.
[71] A Russian figure of speech which signifies that the person spoken of is dead.

CHAPTER X

About seven o'clock in the evening, some of the guests wished to depart, but the host, merry with punch, ordered the gates to be locked, and declared that nobody should leave the house until the next morning. Music soon resounded, the doors of the saloon were thrown open and the ball began. The host and his familiar acquaintances sat in a corner, draining glass after glass, and admiring the gaiety of the young people. The old ladies played at cards. The gentlemen, as is always the case, except where a brigade of uhlans is stationed, were less in number than the ladies, and all the men, suitable for partners, were soon engaged for the dance. The tutor particularly distinguished himself among them; all the ladies wanted to have him as a partner, as they found it so exceedingly easy to waltz with him. He danced several times with Maria Kirilovna, and the ladies observed them with great interest. At last, about midnight, the tired host stopped the dancing, ordered supper to be served, and then betook himself off to bed.

The retirement of Kirila Petrovitch gave to the company more freedom and animation. The gentlemen ventured to sit near the ladies; the girls laughed and spoke in whispers to their neighbours; the ladies spoke in loud voices across the table; the gentlemen drank, disputed, and laughed boisterously. In a word, the supper was exceedingly merry, and left behind it a very agreeable impression.

One man only did not share in the general joy. Anton Pafnoutitch sat gloomy and silent in his place, ate absently, and seemed extremely uneasy. The conversation about the brigands had worked upon his imagination. We shall soon see that he had good cause to fear them.

Anton Pafnoutitch, in invoking God as a witness that the little red cash-box was empty, had not lied and sinned. The little red cash-box was really empty. The bank notes, which had at one time been in it, had been transferred to a leather pouch, which he carried on his breast under his shirt. This precaution alone quieted his distrust of everybody and his constant fear. Being compelled to spend the night in a strange house, he was afraid that he might be lodged in some solitary room, where thieves could easily break in. He looked round in search of a trustworthy companion, and at last his choice fell upon Desforges. His appearance,—indicative of strength,—but especially the bravery shown by him in his encounter with the bear, which poor Anton Pafnoutitch could never think of without a shudder, decided his choice. When they rose from the table, Anton Pafnoutitch began moving round the young Frenchman, clearing his throat and coughing, and at last he turned to him and addressed him:

"Hm! hm! Couldn't I spend the night in your room, mossoo, because you see——"

"Que desire monsieur?" asked Desforges, with a polite bow.

"Ah! what a pity, mossoo, that you have not yet learnt Russian. Je vais moa chez vous coucher. Do you understand?"

"Monsieur, très volontiers," replied Desforges, "veuillez donner des ordres en conséquence."

Anton Pafnoutitch, well satisfied with his knowledge of the French language, went off at once to make the necessary arrangements.

The guests began to wish each other good night, and each retired to the room assigned to him, while Anton Pafnoutitch accompanied the tutor to the wing. The night was dark. Desforges lighted the way with a lantern. Anton Pafnoutitch followed him boldly enough, pressing the hidden treasure occasionally against his breast, in order to convince himself that his money was still there.

On arriving at the wing, the tutor lit a candle and both began to undress; in the meantime Anton Pafnoutitch was walking about the room, examining the locks and windows, and shaking his head at the unassuring inspection. The doors fastened with only one bolt, and the windows had not yet their double frames.[72] He tried to complain to Desforges, but his knowledge of the French language was too limited to enable him to express himself with sufficient clearness. The Frenchman did not understand him, and Anton Pafnoutitch was obliged to cease his complaints. Their beds stood opposite each other; they both lay down, and the tutor extinguished the light.

"Pourquoi vous toucher; pourquoi vous toucher?" cried Anton Pafnoutitch, conjugating the Russian verb to extinguish, after the French manner. "I cannot dormir in the dark."

Desforges did not understand his exclamations, and wished him good night.

"Accursed pagan!" muttered Spitsin, wrapping himself up in the bedclothes: "he couldn't do without extinguishing the light. So much the worse for him. I cannot sleep without a light—Mossoo, mossoo," he continued: "Je ve avec vous parler."

But the Frenchman did not reply, and soon began to snore.

"He is snoring, the French brute," thought Anton Pafnoutitch,

---

[72] The Russians put double frames to their windows in winter.

"while I can't even think of going to sleep. Thieves might walk in at any moment through the open doors or climb in through the window, and the firing of a cannon would not wake him, the beast!"

"Mossoo! mossoo!—the devil take you!"

Anton Pafnoutitch became silent. Fatigue and the effects of wine gradually overcame his fear. He began to doze, and soon fell into a deep sleep. A strange sensation aroused him. He felt in his sleep that someone was gently pulling him by the collar of his shirt. Anton Pafnoutitch opened his eyes and, by the pale light of an autumn morning, he saw Desforges standing before him. In one hand the Frenchman held a pocket pistol, and with the other he was unfastening the strings of the precious leather pouch. Anton Pafnoutitch felt faint.

"Qu'est ce que c'est, Mossoo, qu'est ce que c'est?" said he, in a trembling voice.

"Hush! Silence!" replied the tutor in pure Russian.

"Silence! or you are lost. I am Doubrovsky."

CHAPTER XI

We will now ask the permission of the reader to explain the last incidents of our story, by referring to the circumstances that preceded them, and which we have not yet had time to relate.

At the station of ——, at the house of the postmaster, of whom we have already spoken, sat a traveller in a corner, looking very modest and resigned, and having the appearance of a plebeian or a foreigner, that is to say, of a man having no voice in connection with the post route. His britchka[73] stood in the courtyard, waiting for the wheels to be greased. Within it lay a small portmanteau, evidence of a very modest fortune. The traveller ordered neither tea nor coffee, but sat looking out of the window and whistling, to the great annoyance of the postmistress sitting behind the partition.

"The Lord has sent us a whistler," said she, in a low voice. "How he does whistle! I wish he would burst, the accursed pagan!"

"What does it matter?" said her husband. "Let him whistle!"

---

[73] A kind of open four-wheeled carriage, with a top and shutters to close at pleasure.

"What does it matter?" retorted his angry spouse; "don't you know the saying?"

"What saying? That whistling drives money away? Oh, Pakhomovna, whether he whistles or not, we shall get precious little money out of him."

"Then let him go, Sidoritch. What pleasure have you in keeping him here? Give him the horses, and let him go to the devil."

"He can wait, Pakhomovna. I have only three troikas in the stable, the fourth is resting. Besides, travellers of more importance may arrive at any moment, and I don't wish to risk my neck for a Frenchman.... Hallo! there you are! Don't you hear the sound of galloping! What a rate! Can it be a general?"

A caliche stopped in front of the steps. The servant jumped down from the box, opened the door, and a moment afterwards a young man in a military cloak and white cap entered the station. Behind him followed his servant, carrying a small box which he placed upon the window-ledge.

"Horses!" said the officer, in an imperious voice.

"Directly!" replied the postmaster: "your road-pass, if you please."

"I have no road-pass: I am not going to take the main road.... Besides, don't you recognize me?"

The postmaster hastened to hurry the postilions. The young man began to pace up and down the room. Then he went behind the partition, and inquired of the postmistress in a low voice:

"Who is that traveller?"

"God knows!" replied the postmistress: "some Frenchman or other. He has been five hours waiting for horses, and has done nothing but whistle the whole of the time. He has quite wearied me, the heathen!"

The young man spoke to the traveller in French.

"Where are you going to?" he asked.

"To the neighbouring town," replied the Frenchman: "and from there I am going to a landed proprietor who has engaged me as tutor without ever having seen me. I thought I should have reached the place to-day, but the postmaster has evidently decided otherwise. In this country it is difficult to procure horses, monsieur l'officier."

"And to which of the landed proprietors about here have you engaged yourself?" asked the officer.

"To Troekouroff," replied the Frenchman.

"To Troekouroff? Who is this Troekouroff?"

"Ma foi, monsieur. I have heard very little good of him. They say that he is a proud and wilful noble, and so harsh towards the members of his household, that nobody can live on good terms with him: that all tremble at his name, and that with his tutors he stands upon no ceremony whatever."

"And you have decided to engage yourself to such a monster?"

"What is to be done, monsieur l'officier? He proposes to give me good wages: three thousand roubles a year and everything found. Perhaps I may be more fortunate than the others. I have an aged mother: one half of my salary I will send to her for her support, and out of the rest of my money I shall be able in five years to save a small capital sufficient to make me independent for the rest of my life. Then, bon soir, I return to Paris and set up in business."

"Does anybody at Troekouroff's know you?" asked the officer.

"Nobody," replied the tutor. "He engaged me at Moscow, through one of his friends, whose cook is a countryman of mine, and who recommended me. I must tell you that I did not intend to be a tutor, but a confectioner; but I was told that in your country the profession of tutor is more lucrative."

The officer reflected.

"Listen to me," he said to the Frenchman: "What would you say if, instead of this engagement, you were offered ten thousand roubles, ready money, on condition that you returned immediately to Paris?"

The Frenchman looked at the officer in astonishment, smiled, and shook his head.

"The horses are ready," said the postmaster, entering the room at that moment.

The servant confirmed this statement.

"Presently," replied the officer: "leave the room for a moment." The postmaster and the servant withdrew "I am not joking," he continued in French. "I can give you ten thousand roubles; I only want your absence and your papers."

So saying, he opened his small box and took out of it several bank notes. The Frenchman opened his eyes. He did not know what to think.

"My absence ... my papers!" he repeated in astonishment. "Here are my papers ... but you are surely joking. What do you want my papers for?"

"That does not concern you. I ask you, do you consent or not?"

The Frenchman, still unable to believe his own ears, handed his papers to the young officer, who rapidly examined them.

"Your passport ... very well; your letter of recommendation ... let us see; the certificate of your birth ... capital! Well, here is your money; return home. Farewell."

141

The Frenchman stood as if glued to the spot. The officer came back.

"I had almost forgotten the most important thing of all. Give me your word of honour that all this will remain a secret between us.... Your word of honour."

"My word of honour," replied the Frenchman. "But my papers? What shall I do without them?"

"In the first town you come to, announce that you have been robbed by Doubrovsky. They will believe you, and give you fresh papers. Farewell: God grant you a safe and speedy return to Paris, and may you find your mother in good health."

Doubrovsky left the room, mounted the caliche, and galloped off.

The postmaster stood looking out of the window, and when the caliche had driven off, he turned to his wife, exclaiming:

"Pakhomovna, do you know who that was? That was Doubrovsky!"

The postmistress rushed towards the window, but it was too late. Doubrovsky was already a long way off. Then she began to scold her husband.

"You have no fear of God. Why did you not tell me sooner, I should at least have had a glimpse of Doubrovsky. But now I shall have to wait long enough before I get a chance of seeing him again. Shameless creature that you are!"

The Frenchman stood as if petrified. The agreement with the officer, the money—everything seemed like a dream to him. But the bundle of bank notes was there in his pocket, eloquently confirming the reality of the wonderful adventure.

He resolved to hire horses to take him to the next town. The postilion drove him very slowly, and he reached the town at nightfall.

On approaching the barrier, where, in place of a sentinel, stood a dilapidated sentry-box, the Frenchman told the postilion to stop, got out of the britchka and proceeded on foot, explaining by signs to the driver that he might keep the vehicle and the portmanteau and buy brandy with them. The driver was as much astonished at his generosity as the Frenchman himself had been by Doubrovsky's proposal. But concluding that the "German"[74] had taken leave of his senses, the driver thanked him with a very profound bow, and not caring about entering the town, he made his way to a house of entertainment that was well known to him, and the proprietor of which was a friend of his. There he passed the whole night, and the

---

[74] A general name for all foreigners in Russia.

142

next morning he started back on his return journey with the troika, without the britchka and without the portmanteau, but with a swollen face and red eyes.

Doubrovsky, having possession of the Frenchman's papers, boldly appeared, as we have already seen, at the house of Troekouroff, and there established himself. Whatever, were his secret intentions—we shall know them later on—there was nothing in his behaviour to excite suspicion. It is true that he did not occupy himself very much with the education of little Sasha, to whom he allowed full liberty, nor was he very exacting in the matter of his lessons, which were only given for form's sake, but he paid great attention to the musical studies of his fair pupil, and frequently sat for hours beside her at the piano.

Everybody liked the young tutor: Kirila Petrovitch for his boldness and dexterity in the hunting-field; Maria Kirilovna for his unbounded zeal and slavish attentiveness; Sasha for his tolerance, and the members of the household for his kindness and generosity, apparently incompatible with his means. He himself seemed to be attached to the whole family, and already regarded himself as a member of it.

About a month had elapsed from the time of his entering upon the calling of tutor to the date of the memorable fête, and nobody suspected that the modest young Frenchman was in reality the terrible brigand whose name was a source of terror to all the landed proprietors of the neighbourhood. During all this time, Doubrovsky had never quitted Pokrovskoe, but the reports of his depredations did not cease for all that, thanks to the inventive imagination of the country people. It is possible, too, that his band may have continued their exploits during the absence of the chief.

Passing the night in the same room with a man whom he could only regard as a personal enemy, and one of the principal authors of his misfortune, Doubrovsky had not been able to resist temptation. He knew of the existence of the pouch, and had resolved to take possession of it.

We have seen how he frightened poor Anton Pafnoutitch by his unexpected transformation from a tutor into a brigand.

143

CHAPTER XII

At nine o'clock in the morning, the guests who had passed the night at Pokrovskoe repaired one after the other to the sitting-room, where the tea-urn was already boiling, and before which sat Maria Kirilovna in a morning gown, and Kirila Petrovitch in a frieze coat and slippers, drinking his tea out of a large cup like a wash-hand basin.

The last to appear was Anton Pafnoutitch; he was so pale, and seemed so troubled, that everybody was struck by his appearance, and Kirila Petrovitch inquired after his health. Spitsin replied in an evasive manner, glaring with horror at the tutor, who sat there as if nothing had happened. A few minutes afterwards a servant entered and announced to Spitsin that his carriage was ready. Anton Pafnoutitch hastened to take his leave of the company, and then hurried out of the room and started off immediately. The guests and the host could not understand what had happened to him, and Kirila Petrovitch came to the conclusion that he was suffering from an attack of indigestion.

After tea and the farewell breakfast, the other guests began to take their leave, and soon Pokrovskoe became empty, and everything went on in the usual manner.

Several days passed, and nothing remarkable had happened. The life of the inhabitants of Pokrovskoe became very monotonous. Kirila Petrovitch went out hunting every day; while Maria Kirilovna devoted her time to reading, walking, and especially to musical exercises. She was beginning to understand her own heart, and acknowledged to herself with involuntary vexation that she was not indifferent to the good qualities of the young Frenchman. He, on his side, never overstepped the limits of respect and strict decorum, and thereby quieted her pride and her timid suspicions. With more and more confidence she gave herself up to the alluring habit of seeing him. She felt dull without Desforges, and in his presence she was constantly occupied with him, wishing to know his opinion of everything, and always agreeing with him. She was not yet in love with him perhaps; but at the first accidental obstacle or unexpected reverse of destiny, the flame of passion would burst forth within her heart.

One day, on entering the parlour, where the tutor awaited her, Maria Kirilovna observed with astonishment that he looked pale and troubled. She opened the piano and sang a few notes; but Doubrovsky, under the pretext of a headaches, apologized, interrupted the lesson, closed the music, and slipped a note into her hand. Maria Kirilovna, without pausing to reflect, took it, and repented almost at the same moment for having done so. But Doubrovsky was no longer in the room. Maria Kirilovna went to her room, unfolded the note, and read as follows:

"Be in the arbour near the brook this evening, at seven o'clock: it is necessary that I should speak to you."

Her curiosity was strongly excited. She had long expected a declaration, desiring it and dreading it at one and the same time. It would have been agreeable to her to hear the confirmation of what she divined; but she felt that it would have been unbecoming to hear such a declaration from a man who, on account of his position, ought never to aspire to win her hand. She resolved to go to the meeting-place, but she hesitated about one thing: in what manner she ought to receive the tutor's declaration—with aristocratic indignation, with friendly admonition, with good-humoured banter, or with silent sympathy. In the meantime she kept constantly looking at the clock. It grew-; dark: candles were brought in. Kirila Petrovitch sat down to play at "Boston"[75] with some of his neighbours who had come to pay him a visit. The clock struck a quarter to seven, and Maria Kirilovna walked quietly out on to the steps, looked round on every side, and then hastened into the garden.

The night was dark, the sky was covered with clouds, and it was impossible to see anything at a distance of two paces; but Maria Kirilovna went forward in the darkness along paths that were quite familiar to her, and in a few minutes she reached the arbour. There she paused in order to draw breath and to present herself before Desforges with an air of calm indifference. But Desforges already stood before her.

"I thank you," he said in a low, sad voice, "for having granted my request. I should have been in despair if you had not complied with it."

Maria Kirilovna answered him in the words she had prepared beforehand.

"I hope you will not cause me to repent of my condescension."

He was silent, and seemed to be collecting himself.

"Circumstances demand—I am obliged to leave you," he said at last. "It may be that you will soon hear—but before going away, I must have an explanation with you."

---

[75] A card game that was very popular on the Continent at the beginning of the present century.

Maria Kirilovna made no reply. In these words she saw the preface to the expected declaration.

"I am not what you suppose," continued he, lowering his head: "I am not the Frenchman Desforges—I am Doubrovsky."

Maria Kirilovna uttered a cry.

"Do not be alarmed, for God's sake! You need not be afraid of my name. Yes, I am that unhappy person, whom your father, after depriving him of his last crust of bread, drove out of his paternal home and sent on to the highway to rob. But you need not be afraid, either on your own account or on his. All is over.... I have forgiven him; you have saved him. My first crime of blood was to have been accomplished upon him. I prowled round his house, determining where the fire should burst out, where I should enter his bedroom, and how I should cut him off from all means of escape; at that moment you passed by me like a heavenly vision, and my heart was subdued. I understood that the house, in which you dwelt, was sacred; that not a single person, connected with you by the ties of blood, could lie beneath my curse. I looked upon vengeance as madness, and dismissed the thought of it from my mind. Whole days I wandered around the gardens of Pokrovskoe, in the hope of seeing your white robe in the distance. In your incautious walks I followed you, stealing from bush to bush, happy in the thought that for you there was no danger, where I was secretly present. At last an opportunity presented itself.... I established myself in your house. Those three weeks were for me days of happiness; the recollection of them will be the joy of my sad life.... To-day I received news which renders it impossible for me to remain here any longer. I part from you to-day—at this very moment.... But before doing so, I felt that it was necessary that I should reveal myself to you, so that you might not curse me nor despise me. Think sometimes of Doubrovsky. Know that he was born for another fate, that his soul was capable of loving you, that never——"

Just then a loud whistle resounded, and Doubrovsky became silent. He seized her hand and pressed it to his burning lips. The whistle was repeated.

"Farewell," said Doubrovsky: "they are calling me. A moment's delay may destroy me."

He moved away.... Maria Kirilovna stood motionless. Doubrovsky returned and once more took her by the hand.

"If misfortune should ever overtake you, and you are unable to obtain help or protection from anybody, will you promise to apply to me, to demand from me everything that may be necessary for your happiness? Will you promise not to reject my devotion?"

146

Maria Kirilovna wept silently. The whistle resounded for the third time.

"You will destroy me!" cried Doubrovsky: "but I will not leave you until you give me a reply. Do you promise me or not?"

"I promise!" murmured the poor girl.

Greatly agitated by her interview with Doubrovsky, Maria Kirilovna returned from the garden. As she approached the house, she perceived a great crowd of people in the courtyard; a troika was standing in front of the steps, the servants were running hither and thither, and the whole house was in a commotion. In the distance she heard the voice of Kirila Petrovitch, and she hastened to reach her room, fearing that her absence might be noticed. Kirila Petrovitch met her in the hall. The visitors were pressing round our old acquaintance the sheriff, and were overwhelming him with questions. The sheriff, in travelling dress, and armed from head to foot, answered them with a mysterious and anxious air.

"Where have you been, Masha?" asked Kirila Petrovitch. "Have you seen Monsieur Desforges?"

Masha could scarcely answer in the negative.

"Just imagine," continued Kirila Petrovitch: "the sheriff has come to arrest him, and assures me that he is Doubrovsky."

"He answers the description in every respect, Your Excellency," said the sheriff respectfully.

"Oh! brother," interrupted Kirila Petrovitch, "go to—you know where—with your descriptions. I will not surrender my Frenchman to you until I have investigated the matter myself. How can anyone believe the word of Anton Pafnoutitch, a coward and a clown? He must have dreamt that the tutor wanted to rob him. Why didn't he tell me about it the next morning? He never said a word about the matter.

"The Frenchman threatened him, Your Excellency," replied the sheriff, "and made him swear that he would preserve silence."

"A pack of lies!" exclaimed Kirila Petrovitch: "I will have this mystery cleared up immediately. Where is the tutor?" he asked of a servant who entered at that moment.

"He cannot be found anywhere," replied the servant.

"Then search for him!" cried Troekouroff, beginning to entertain doubts.

"Show me your vaunted description," said he to the sheriff, who immediately handed him the paper.

"Hm! hm! twenty-three years old, etc., etc. That is so, but yet that does not prove anything. Well, what about the tutor?"

"He is not to be found," was again the answer.

147

Kirila Petrovitch began to be uneasy; Maria Kirilovna was neither dead nor alive.

"You are pale, Masha," remarked her father to her; "have they frightened you?"

"No, papa," replied Masha; "I have a headache."

"Go to your own room, Masha, and don't be alarmed."

Masha kissed his hand and retired hastily to her room. There she threw herself upon her bed and burst into a hysterical flood of tears. The maids hastened to her assistance, undressed her with difficulty, and with difficulty succeeded in calming her by means of cold water and all possible kinds of smelling salts. They put her to bed and she fell into a slumber.

In the meantime the Frenchman could not be found. Kirila Petrovitch paced up and down the room, loudly whistling his favourite military air. The visitors whispered among themselves; the sheriff looked foolish; the Frenchman was not to be found. Probably he had managed to escape through being warned beforehand. But by whom and how? That remained a mystery.

It was eleven o'clock, but nobody thought of sleep. At last Kirila Petrovitch said angrily to the sheriff:

"Well, do you wish to stop here till daylight? My house is not an inn. It is not by any cleverness on your part, brother, that Doubrovsky will be taken—if he really be Doubrovsky. Return home, and in future be a little quicker. And it is time for you to go home, too," he continued, addressing his guests. "Order the horses to be got ready. I want to go to bed."

In this ungracious manner did Troekouroff take leave of his guests.

CHAPTER XIII

Some time elapsed without anything remarkable happening. But at the beginning of the following summer, many changes occurred in the family arrangements of Kirila Petrovitch.

About thirty versts from Pokrovskoe was the wealthy estate of Prince Vereisky. The Prince had lived abroad for a long time, and his estate was managed by a retired major. No intercourse existed between Pokrovskoe and Arbatova. But at the end of the month of

May, the Prince returned from abroad and took up his abode in his own village, which he had never seen since he was born. Accustomed to social pleasures, he could not endure solitude, and the third day after his arrival, he set out to dine with Troekouroff, with whom he had formerly been acquainted. The Prince was about fifty years of age, but he looked much older. Excesses of every kind had ruined his health, and had placed upon him their indelible stamp. In spite of that, his appearance was agreeable and distinguished, and his having always been accustomed to society gave him a certain affability of demeanour, especially towards ladies. He had a constant need of amusement, and he was a constant victim to ennui.

Kirila Petrovitch was exceedingly gratified by this visit, which he regarded as a mark of respect from a man who knew the world. In accordance with his usual custom, he began to entertain his visitor by conducting him to inspect his establishments and kennels. But the Prince could hardly breathe in the atmosphere of the dogs, and he hurried out, holding a scented handkerchief to his nose. The old garden, with its clipped limes, square pond and regular walks, did not please him; he did not like the English gardens and the so-called natural style, but he praised them and went into ecstasies over everything. The servant came to announce that dinner was served, and they repaired to the dining-room. The Prince limped, being fatigued after his walk, and already repenting for having paid his visit.

But in the dining-hall Maria Kirilovna met them—and the old sensualist was struck by her beauty. Troekouroff placed his guest beside her. The Prince was resuscitated by her presence; he became quite cheerful, and succeeded several times in arresting her attention by the recital of some of his curious stories. After dinner Kirila Petrovitch proposed a ride on horseback, but the Prince excused himself, pointing to his velvet boots and joking about his gout. He proposed a drive in a carriage, so that he should not be separated from his charming neighbour. The carriage was got ready. The two old men and the beautiful young girl took their seats in it, and they started off. The conversation did not flag. Maria Kirilovna listened with pleasure to the flattering compliments and witty remarks of the man of the world, when suddenly Vereisky, turning to Kirila Petrovitch, said to him: "What is the meaning of that burnt building—does it belong to you?"

Kirila Petrovitch frowned: the memories awakened by the burnt manor-house were disagreeable to him. He replied that the land was his now, but that formerly it had belonged to Doubrovsky.

"To Doubrovsky?" repeated Vereisky. "What! to the famous brigand?"

"To his father," replied Troekouroff: "and the father himself was a true brigand."

"And what has become of our Rinaldo? Have they caught him? Is he still alive?"

"He is still alive and at liberty. By the way, Prince, Doubrovsky paid you a visit at Arbatova."

"Yes, last year, I think, he burnt or plundered something or other. Don't you think, Maria Kirilovna, that it would be very interesting to make a closer acquaintance with this romantic hero?"

"Interesting!" said Troekouroff: "she knows him already. He taught her music for three whole weeks, and thank God, took nothing for his lessons."

Then Kirila Petrovitch began to relate the story of the pretended French tutor. Maria Kirilovna felt as if she were sitting upon needles. Vereisky, listening with deep attention, found it all very strange, and changed the subject of conversation. On returning from the drive, he ordered his carriage to be brought, and in spite of the earnest requests of Kirila Petrovitch to stay for the night, he took his departure immediately after tea. Before setting out, however, he invited Kirila Petrovitch to pay him a visit and to bring Maria Kirilovna with him, and the proud Troekouroff promised to do so'; for taking into consideration his princely dignity, his two stars, and the three thousand serfs belonging to his estate, he regarded Prince Vereisky in some degree as his equal.

CHAPTER XIV

Two days after this visit, Kirila Petrovitch set out with his daughter for the abode of Prince Vereisky. On approaching Arbatova, he could not sufficiently admire the clean and cheerful-looking huts of the peasants, and the stone manor-house built in the style of an English castle. In front of the house stretched a close green lawn, upon which were grazing some Swiss cows tinkling their bells. A spacious park surrounded the house on every side. The master met the guests on the steps, and gave his arm to the young beauty. She was then conducted into a magnificent hall, where the table was laid for three. The Prince led his guests to a window, and a charming view opened out before them. The Volga flowed past the windows, and upon its bosom floated laden barges under full sail, and small fishing-boats known by the expressive name of "soul-destroyers." Beyond the river stretched hills and fields, and several little villages animated the landscape.

Then they proceeded to inspect the galleries of pictures bought by the Prince in foreign countries. The Prince explained to Maria Kirilovna their various characteristics, related the history of the painters, and pointed out their merits and defects. He did not speak of pictures in the pretentious language of the pedantic connoisseur, but with feeling and imagination. Maria Kirilovna listened to him with pleasure.

They sat down to table. Troekouroff rendered full justice to the wines of his Amphytrion, and to the skill of his cook; while Maria Kirilovna did not feel at all confused or constrained in her conversation with a man whom she now saw for the second time in her life. After dinner the host proposed to his guests that they should go into the garden. They drank coffee in the arbour on the bank of a broad lake studded with little islands. Suddenly resounded the music of wind instruments, and a six-oared boat drew up before the arbour. They rowed on the lake, round the islands, and visited some of them. On one they found a marble statue; on another, a lonely grotto; on a third, a monument with a mysterious inscription, which awakened within Maria Kirilovna a girlish curiosity not completely satisfied by the polite but reticent explanations of the Prince. The time passed imperceptibly. It began to grow dark. The Prince, under the pretext of the cold and the dew, hastened to return to the house, where the tea-urn awaited them. The Prince requested Maria Kirilovna to discharge the functions of hostess in his bachelor's home. She poured out the tea, listening to the inexhaustible stories of the charming talker. Suddenly a shot was heard, and a rocket illuminated the sky. The Prince gave Maria Kirilovna a shawl, and led her and Troekouroff on to the balcony. In front of the house, in the darkness, different coloured fires blazed up, whirled round, rose up in sheaves, poured out in fountains, fell in showers of rain and stars, went out and then burst into a blaze again. Maria Kirilovna was as delighted as a child. Prince Vereisky was delighted with her enjoyment, and Troekouroff was very well satisfied with him, for he accepted tous les frais of the Prince as signs of respect and a desire to please him.

The supper was quite equal to the dinner in every respect. Then the guests retired to the rooms assigned to them, and the next morning took leave of their amiable host, promising each other soon to meet again.

CHAPTER XV

Aria Kirilovna was sitting in her room, embroidering at her frame before the open window. She did not entangle her threads like Conrad's mistress, who, in her amorous distraction, embroidered a rose with green silk. Under her needle, the canvas repeated unerringly the design of the original; but in spite of that, her thoughts did not follow her work—they were far away.

Suddenly an arm passed silently through the window, placed a letter upon the frame and disappeared before Maria Kirilovna could recover herself. At the same moment a servant entered to call her to Kirila Petrovitch. Trembling very much, she hid the letter under her fichu and hastened to her father in his study.

Kirila Petrovitch was not alone. Prince Vereisky was sitting in the room with him. On the appearance of Maria Kirilovna, the Prince rose and silently bowed, with a confusion that was quite unusual in him.

"Come here, Masha," said Kirila Petrovitch: "I have a piece of news to tell you which I hope will please you very much. Here is a sweetheart for you: the Prince proposes for your hand."

Masha was dumfounded; a deadly pallor overspread her countenance. She was silent. The Prince approached her, took her hand, and with a tender look, asked her if she would consent to make him happy. Masha remained silent.

"Consent? Of course she will consent," said Kirila Petrovitch; "but you know, Prince, it is difficult for a girl to say such a word as that. Well, children, kiss one another and be happy."

Masha stood motionless; the old Prince kissed her hand. Suddenly the tears began to stream down her pale cheeks. The Prince frowned slightly.

"Go, go, go!" said Kirila Petrovitch: "dry your tears and come back to us in a merry humour. They all weep at the moment of being betrothed," he continued, turning to Vereisky; "it is their custom. Now, Prince, let us talk about business, that is to say, about the dowry."

Maria Kirilovna eagerly took advantage of the permission to retire. She ran to her room, locked herself in and gave way to her tears, already imagining herself the wife of the old Prince. He had suddenly become repugnant and hateful to her. Marriage terrified her, like the block, like the grave.

"No, no," She repeated in, despair; "I would rather go into a convent, I would rather marry Doubrovsky...."

Then she remembered the letter and eagerly began to read it, having a presentiment that it was from him. In fact, it was written by him, and contained only the following words:

"This evening, at ten o'clock, in the same place as before."

The moon was shining; the night was calm; the wind rose now and then, and a gentle rustle ran over the garden.

Like a light shadow, the beautiful young girl drew near to the appointed meeting-place. Nobody was yet visible, when suddenly, from behind the arbour, Doubrovsky appeared before her.

"I know all," he said to her in a low, sad voice; "remember your promise."

"You offer me your protection," replied Masha; "do not be angry—but the idea alarms me. In what way can you help me?"

"I can deliver you from a detested man...."

"For God's sake, do not touch him, do not venture to touch him, if you love me. I do not wish to be the cause of any horror...."

"I will not touch him: your wish is sacred for me. He owes his life to you. Never shall a crime be committed in your name. You shall not be stigmatized on account of my misdeeds. But how can I save you from a cruel father?"

"There is still hope; I hope to touch him with my tears—my despair. He is obstinate, but he loves me very dearly."

"Do not put your trust in a vain hope. In those tears he will see only the usual timidity and aversion common to all young girls, when they marry from motives of interest and not from affection. But if he takes it into his head to accomplish your happiness in spite of yourself? If you are conducted to the altar by force, in order that your destiny may be placed for ever in the hands of an old man?"

"Then—then there will be nothing else to do. Come for me—I will be your wife."

Doubrovsky trembled; his pale face became covered with a deep flush, and the next minute he became paler than before. He remained silent for a long time, with his head bent down.

"Muster the full strength of your soul, implore your father, throw yourself at his feet; represent to him all the horror of the future that he is preparing for you, your youth fading away by the side of a feeble and dissipated old man. Tell him that riches will not

153

procure for you a single moment of happiness. Luxury consoles poverty alone, and even in that case only for a brief season. Do not be put off by him, and do not be frightened either by his anger or by his threats, as long as there remains the least shadow of hope. For God's sake do not leave off importuning him. If, however, you have no other resource left, decide upon a plain speaking explanation; tell him that if he remains inexorable, then—then you will find a terrible protector."

Here Doubrovsky covered his face with his hands; he seemed to be choking. Masha wept.

"My miserable, miserable fate!" said he, with a bitter sigh. "For you I would have given my life. To see you from afar, to touch your hand was for me happiness beyond expression; and when there opens up before me the possibility of pressing you to my agitated heart, and saying to you: 'I am yours for ever'—miserable creature that I am! I must fly from such happiness, I must repel it from me with all my strength. I dare not throw myself at your feet and thank Heaven for an incomprehensible, unmerited reward. Oh! how I ought to hate him who—but I feel that now there is no place in my heart for hatred."

He gently passed his arm round her slender figure and pressed her tenderly to his heart. She confidingly leaned her head upon the young brigand's shoulder and both remained silent.... The time flew past.

"It is time," said Masha at last.

Doubrovsky seemed as if awakening from a dream. He took her hand and placed a ring on her finger.

"If you decide upon having recourse to me," said he, "then bring the ring here and place it in the hollow of this oak. I shall know what to do."

Doubrovsky kissed her hand and disappeared among the trees.

CHAPTER XVI

Prince Vereisky's intention of getting married was no longer a secret in the neighbourhood. Kirila Petrovitch received the congratulations of his acquaintances, and preparations were made for the wedding. Masha postponed from day to day the decisive explanation. In the meantime her manner towards her elderly lover was cold and constrained. The Prince did not trouble himself about that; the question of love gave him no concern; her silent consent was quite sufficient for him.

But the time went past. Masha at last decided to act, and wrote a letter to Prince Vereisky. She tried to awaken within his heart a feeling of magnanimity, candidly confessing that she had not the least attachment for him, and entreating him to renounce her hand and even to protect her from the tyranny of her father. She furtively delivered the letter to Prince Vereisky. The latter read it alone, but was not in the least moved by the candour of his betrothed. On the contrary, he perceived the necessity of hastening the marriage, and therefore he showed the letter to his future father-in-law.

Kirila Petrovitch was furious, and it was with difficulty that the Prince succeeded in persuading him not to let Masha see that he was acquainted with the contents of the letter. Kirila Petrovitch promised not to speak about the matter to her, but he resolved to lose no time and fixed the wedding for the next day. The Prince found this very reasonable, and he went to his betrothed and told her that her letter had grieved him very much, but that he hoped in time to gain her affection; that the thought of resigning her was too much for him to bear, and that he had not the strength to consent to his own sentence of death. Then he kissed her hand respectfully and took his departure, without saying a word to her about Kirila Petrovitch's decision.

But scarcely had he left the house, when her father entered and peremptorily ordered her to be ready for the next day. Maria Kirilovna, already agitated by the interview with Prince Vereisky, burst into tears and threw herself at her father's feet.

"Papa!" she cried in a plaintive voice, "papa! do not destroy me. I do not love the Prince, I do not wish to be his wife."

"What does this mean?" said Kirila Petrovitch, fiercely. "Up till the present you have kept silent and consented, and now, when everything is decided upon, you become capricious and refuse to accept him. Don't act the fool; you will gain nothing from me by so doing."

"Do not destroy me!" repeated poor Masha. "Why are you sending me away from you and giving me to a man that I do not love? Do I weary you? I want to stay with you as before. Papa, you will be sad without me, and sadder still when you know that I am unhappy. Papa, do not force me: I do not wish to marry."

Kirila Petrovitch was touched, but he concealed his emotion, and pushing her away from him, said harshly:

"That is all nonsense, do you hear? I know better than you what is necessary for your happiness. Tears will not help you. The day after to-morrow your wedding will take place.

"The day after to-morrow!" exclaimed Masha. "My God! No, no, impossible; it cannot be! Papa, hear me: if you have resolved to destroy me, then I will find a protector that you do not dream of. You will see, and then you will regret having driven me to despair."

"What? What?" said Troekouroff. "Threats! threats to me? Insolent girl! Do you know that I will do with you what you little imagine. You dare to frighten me, you worthless girl! We will see who this protector will be."

"Vladimir Doubrovsky," replied Masha, in despair.

Kirila Petrovitch thought that she had gone out of her mind, and looked at her in astonishment.

"Very well!" said he to her, after an interval of silence; "expect whom you please to deliver you, but, in the meantime, remain in this room—you shall not leave it till the very moment of the wedding."

With these words Kirila Petrovitch went out, locking the door behind him.

For a long time the poor girl wept, imagining all that awaited her. But the stormy interview had lightened her soul, and she could more calmly consider the question of her future and what it behoved her to do. The principal thing was—to free herself from this odious marriage. The lot of a brigand's wife seemed paradise to her in comparison with the fate prepared for her. She glanced at the ring given to her by Doubrovsky. Ardently did she long to see him alone once more before the decisive moment, so that she might concert measures with him. A presentiment told her that in the evening she would find Doubrovsky in the garden, near the arbour; she resolved to go and wait for him there.

As soon as it began to grow dark, Masha prepared to carry out her intention, but the door of her room was locked. Her maid told her from the other side of the door, that Kirila Petrovitch had given orders that she was not to be let out. She was under arrest. Deeply hurt, she sat down by the window and remained there till late in the night, without undressing, gazing fixedly at the dark sky. Towards dawn she began to doze; but her light sleep was disturbed by sad visions, and she was soon awakened by the rays of the rising sun.

CHAPTER XVII

He awoke, and all the horror of her position rose up in her mind. She rang. The maid entered, and in answer to her questions, replied that Kirila Petrovitch had set out the evening before for Arbatova, and had returned very late; that he had given strict orders that she was not to be allowed out of her room and that nobody was to be permitted to speak to her; that otherwise, there were no signs of any particular preparations for the wedding, except that the pope had been ordered not to leave the village under any pretext whatever. After disburdening herself of this news, the maid left Maria Kirilovna and again locked the door.

Her words hardened the young prisoner. Her head burned, her blood boiled. She resolved to inform Doubrovsky of everything, and she began to think of some means by which she could get the ring conveyed to the hole in the sacred oak. At that moment a stone struck against her window; the glass rattled, and Maria Kirilovna, looking out into the courtyard, saw the little Sasha making signs to her. She knew that he was attached to her, and she was pleased to see him.

"Good morning, Sasha; why do you call me?"

"I came, sister, to know if you wanted anything. Papa is angry, and has forbidden the whole house to obey you; but order me to do whatever you like, and I will do it for you."

"Thank you, my dear Sasha. Listen; you know the old hollow oak near the arbour?"

"Yes, I know it, sister."

"Then, if you love me, run there as quickly as you can and put this ring in the hollow; but take care that nobody sees you."

With these words, she threw the ring to him and closed the window.

The lad picked up the ring, and ran off with all his might, and in three minutes he arrived at the sacred tree. There he paused, quite out of breath, and after looking round on every side, placed the ring in the hollow. Having successfully accomplished his mission, he wanted to inform Maria Kirilovna of the fact at once, when suddenly a red-haired ragged boy darted out from behind the arbour, dashed towards the oak and thrust his hand into the hole. Sasha, quicker than a squirrel, threw himself upon him and seized him with both hands.

"What are you doing here?" said he sternly.

"What business is that of yours?" said the boy, trying to disengage himself.

"Leave that ring alone, red head," cried Sasha, "or I will teach you a lesson in my own style."

Instead of replying, the boy gave him a blow in the face with his fist; but Sasha still held him firmly in his grasp, and cried out at the top of his voice:

"Thieves! thieves! help! help!"

The boy tried to get away from him. He seemed to be about two years older than Sasha, and very much stronger; but Sasha was more agile. They struggled together for some minutes; at last the red-headed boy gained the advantage. He threw Sasha upon the ground and seized him by the throat. But at that moment a strong hand grasped hold of his shaggy red hair, and Stepan, the gardener, lifted him half a yard from the ground.

"Ah! you red-headed beast!" said the gardener. "How dare you strike the young gentleman?"

In the meantime, Sasha had jumped to his feet and recovered himself.

"You caught me under the arm-pits," said he, "or you would never have thrown me. Give me the ring at once and be off."

"It's likely!" replied the red-headed one, and suddenly twisting himself round, he disengaged his bristles from Stepan's hand.

Then he started off running, but Sasha overtook him, gave him a blow in the back, and the boy fell. The gardener again seized him and bound him with his belt.

"Give me the ring!" cried Sasha.

"Wait a moment, young master," said Stepan; "we will lead him to the bailiff to be questioned.".

The gardener led the captive into the courtyard of the manor-house, accompanied by Sasha, who glanced uneasily at his trousers, torn and stained with the grass. Suddenly all three found themselves face to face with Kirila Petrovitch, who was going to inspect his stables.

"What is the meaning of this?" he said to Stepan.

Stepan in a few words related all that had happened.

Kirila Petrovitch listened to him with attention.

"You rascal," said he, turning to Sasha: "why did you wrestle with him?"

"He stole a ring out of the hollow tree, papa; make him give up the ring."

"What ring? Out of what hollow tree?"

"The one that Maria Kirilovna ... the ring...." Sasha stammered and became confused. Kirila Petrovitch frowned and said, shaking his head:

"Ah! Maria Kirilovna is mixed up in this. Confess everything, or I will give you such a birching as you have never had in your life."

"As true as heaven, papa, I ... papa ... Maria Kirilovna never told me to do anything, papa."

"Stepan, go and cut me some fine, fresh birch twigs."

"Stop, papa, I will tell you all. I was running about the courtyard to-day, when sister Maria Kirilovna opened the window. I ran towards her, and she accidentally dropped a ring, and I went and hid it in the hollow tree, and ... and this red-headed fellow wanted to steal the ring."

"She did not drop it accidentally,—you wanted to hide it ... Stepan, go and get the birch twigs."

"Papa, wait, I will tell you everything. Sister Maria Kirilovna told me to run to the oak tree and put the ring in the hollow; I ran and did so, but this nasty fellow——"

Kirila Petrovitch turned to the "nasty fellow" and said to him sternly:

"To whom do you belong?"

"I belong to my master Doubrovsky."

Kirila Petrovitch's face grew dark.

"It seems, then, that you do not recognize me as your master. Very well. What were you doing in my garden?"

"I was stealing raspberries."

"Ah, ah! the servant is like his master. As the pope is, so is his parish. And do my raspberries grow upon oak trees? Have you ever heard so?"

The boy did not reply.

"Papa, make him give up the ring," said Sasha.

"Silence, Alexander!" replied Kirila Petrovitch; "don't forget that I intend to settle with you presently. Go to your room. And you, squint-eyes, you seem to me to be a knowing sort of lad; if you confess everything to me, I will not whip you, but will give you a five copeck piece to buy nuts with. Give lip the ring and go."

The boy opened his fist and showed that there was nothing in his hand.

"If you don't, I shall do something to you that you little expect. Now!"

The boy did not answer a word, but stood with his head bent down, looking like a perfect simpleton.

"Very well!" said Kirila Petrovitch: "lock him up somewhere, and see that he does not escape, or I'll skin the whole household."

Stepan conducted the boy to the pigeon loft, locked him in there, and ordered the old poultry woman, Agatha, to keep a watch upon him.

159

"There is no doubt about it: she has kept up intercourse with that accursed Doubrovsky. But if she has really invoked his aid——" thought Kirila Petrovitch, pacing up and down the room, and angrily whistling his favourite air,——"I am hot upon his track, at all events, and he shall not escape me. We shall take advantage of this opportunity.... Hark! a bell; thank God, that is the sheriff. Bring here the boy that is locked up."

In the meantime, a small telega drove into the courtyard, and our old acquaintance, the sheriff, entered the room, all covered with dust.

"Glorious news!" said Kirila Petrovitch: "I have caught Doubrovsky."

"Thank God, Your Excellency!" said the sheriff, his face beaming with delight. "Where is he?"

"That is to say, not Doubrovsky himself, but one of his band. He will be here presently. He will help us to apprehend his chief. Here he is."

The sheriff, who expected to see some fierce-looking brigand, was astonished to perceive a lad of thirteen years of age, of somewhat delicate appearance. He turned to Kirila Petrovitch with an incredulous look, and awaited an explanation. Kirila Petrovitch then began to relate the events of the morning, without, however, mentioning the name of Maria Kirilovna.

The sheriff listened to him attentively, glancing from time to time at the young rogue, who, assuming a look of imbecility, seemed to be paying no attention to all that was going on around him.

"Will Your Excellency allow me to speak to you apart?" said the sheriff at last.

Kirila Petrovitch conducted him into the next room and locked the door after him.

Half an hour afterwards they returned to the hall, where the captive was awaiting the decision respecting his fate.

"The master wished," said the sheriff to him, "to have you locked up in the town gaol, to be whipped, and then to be sent to the convict settlement; but I interceded for you and have obtained your pardon. Untie him!"

The lad was unbound.

"Thank the master," said the sheriff.

The lad went up to Kirila Petrovitch and kissed his hand.

"Run away home," said Kirila Petrovitch to him, "and in future do not steal raspberries from oak trees."

The lad went out, ran merrily down the steps, and without looking behind him, dashed off across the fields in the direction of Kistenevka. On reaching the village, he stopped at a half-ruined hut, the first from the corner, and tapped at the window. The window was opened, and an old woman appeared.

"Grandmother, some bread!" said the boy: "I have eaten nothing since this morning; I am dying of hunger."

"Ah! it is you, Mitia;[76] but where have you been all this time, you little devil?" asked the old woman.

"I will tell you afterwards, grandmother. For God's sake, some bread!"

"Come into the hut, then."

"I haven't the time, grandmother; I've got to run on to another place. Bread, for the Lord's sake, bread!"

"What a fidget!" grumbled the old woman: "there's a piece for you," and she pushed through the window a slice of black bread.

The boy bit it with avidity, and then continued his course, eating it as he went.

It was beginning to grow dark. Mitia made his way along by the corn kilns and kitchen gardens into the Kistenevka wood. On arriving at the two pine trees, standing like advanced guards before the wood, he paused, x looked round on every side, gave a shrill, abrupt whistle, and then listened. A light and prolonged whistle was heard in reply, and somebody came out of the wood and advanced towards him.

CHAPTER XVIII

Kirila Petrovitch was pacing up and down the hall, whistling his favourite air louder than usual. The whole house was in a commotion; the servants were running about, and the maids were busy. In the courtyard there was a crowd of people. In Maria Kirilovna's dressing-room, before the looking-glass, a lady, surrounded by maidservants, was attiring the pale, motionless young bride. Her head bent languidly beneath the weight of her diamonds; she started slightly when a careless hand pricked her, but she remained silent, gazing absently into the mirror.

"Aren't you nearly finished?" said the voice of Kirila Petrovitch at the door.

---

[76] Diminutive of Dimitry (Demetrius).

"In a minute!" replied the lady. "Maria Kirilovna, get up and look at yourself. Is everything right?"

Maria Kirilovna rose, but made no reply. The door was opened.

"The bride is ready," said the lady to Kirila Petrovitch; "order the carriage."

"With God!" replied Kirila Petrovitch, and taking a sacred image from the table, "Approach, Masha," said he, in a voice of emotion; "I bless you...."

The poor girl fell at his feet and began to sob.

"Papa ... papa ..." she said through her tears, and then her voice failed her.

Kirila Petrovitch hastened to give her his blessing. She was raised up and almost carried into the carriage. Her godmother and one of the maidservants got in with her, and they drove off to the church. There the bridegroom was already waiting for them. He came forward to meet the bride, and was struck by her pallor and her strange look. They entered the cold deserted church together, and the door was locked behind them. The priest came out from the altar, and the ceremony at once began.

Maria Kirilovna saw nothing, heard nothing; she had been thinking of but one thing the whole morning: she expected Doubrovsky; nor did her hope abandon her for one moment. But when the priest turned to her with the usual question, she started and felt faint; but still she hesitated, still she expected. The priest, without waiting for her reply, pronounced the irrevocable words.

The ceremony was over. She felt the cold kiss of her hated husband; she heard the flattering congratulations of those present; and yet she could not believe that her life was bound for ever, that Doubrovsky had not arrived to deliver her. The Prince turned to her with tender words—she did not understand them. They left the church; in the porch was a crowd of peasants from Pokrovskoe. Tier glance rapidly scanned them, and again she exhibited her former insensibility. The newly-married couple seated themselves in the carriage and drove off to Arbatova, whither Kirila Petrovitch had already gone on before, in order to welcome the wedded pair there.

Alone with his young wife, the Prince was not in the least piqued by her cold manner. He did not begin to weary her with amorous protestations and ridiculous enthusiasm; his words were simple and required no answer. In this way they travelled about ten versts. The horses dashed rapidly along the uneven country roads, and the carriage scarcely shook upon its English springs. Suddenly were heard cries of pursuit. The carriage stopped, and a crowd of armed men surrounded it. A man in a half-mask opened the door on the side where the young Princess sat, and said to her:

162

"You are free! Alight."

"What does this mean?" cried the Prince. "Who are you that—"

"It is Doubrovsky," replied the Princess.

The Prince, without losing his presence of mind, drew from his side pocket a travelling pistol and fired at the masked brigand. The Princess shrieked, and, filled with horror, covered her face with both her hands. Doubrovsky was wounded in the shoulder; the blood was flowing. The Prince, without losing a moment, drew another pistol; but he was not allowed time to fire; the door was opened, and several strong arms dragged him out of the carriage and snatched the pistol from him. Above him flashed several knives.

"Do not touch him!" cried Doubrovsky, and his terrible associates drew back.

"Your are free!" continued Doubrovsky, turning to the pale Princess.

"No!" replied she; "it is too late! I am married. I am the wife of Prince Vereisky."

"What do you say?" cried Doubrovsky in despair. "No! you are not his wife. You were forced, you could never have consented."

"I have consented, I have taken the oath," she answered with firmness. "The Prince is my husband; give orders for him to be set at liberty, and leave me with him. I have not deceived you. I waited for you till the last moment ... but now, I tell you, now, it is too late. Let us go."

But Doubrovsky no longer heard her. The pain of his wound, and the violent emotion of his mind had deprived him of all power over himself. He fell against the wheel; the brigands surrounded him. He managed to say a few words to them. They placed him on horseback; two of them held him up, a third took the horse by the bridle, and all withdrew from the spot, leaving the carriage in the middle of the road, the servants bound, the horses unharnessed, but without carrying anything away with them, and without shedding one drop of blood in revenge for the blood of their chief.

CHAPTER XIX

In the middle of a dense wood, on a narrow grass-plot, rose a small earthwork, consisting of a rampart and ditch, behind which were some huts and tents. Within the inclosed space, a crowd of

163

persons who, by their varied garments and by their arms, could at once be recognized as brigands, were having their dinner, seated bareheaded around a large cauldron. On the rampart, by the side of a small cannon, sat a sentinel, with his legs crossed under him. He was sewing a patch upon a certain part of his attire, handling his needle with a dexterity that bespoke the experienced tailor, and every now and then raising his head and glancing found on every side.

Although a certain ladle had passed from hand to hand several times, a strange silence reigned among this crowd. The brigands finished their dinner; one after another rose and said a prayer to God; some dispersed among the huts, others strolled away into the wood or lay down to sleep, according to the Russian habit.

The sentinel finished his work, shook his garment, gazed admiringly at the patch, stuck the needle in his sleeve, sat astride the cannon, and began to sing a melancholy old song with all the power of his lungs.

At that moment the door of one of the huts opened, and an old woman in a white cap, neatly and even pretentiously dressed, appeared upon the threshold.

"Enough of that, Stepka,"[77] said she angrily. "The master is sleeping, and yet you must make that frightful noise; you have neither conscience nor pity."

"I beg pardon, Petrovna," replied Stepka. "I won't do it any more. Let our little father sleep on and get well."

The old woman withdrew into the hut, and Stepka began to pace to and fro upon the rampart.

Within the hut, from which the old woman had emerged, lay the wounded Doubrovsky upon a cold bed behind a partition. Before him, upon a small table, lay his pistols, and a sword hung near his head. The mud hut was hung round and covered with rich carpets. In the corner was a lady's silver toilet and mirror. Doubrovsky held in his hand an open book, but his eyes were closed, and the old woman, peeping at him from behind the partition, could not tell whether he was asleep or only thinking.

Suddenly Doubrovsky started. In the fort there was a great commotion, and Stepka came and thrust his head in through the window of the hut.

"Father Vladimir Andreivitch!" he cried; "our men are signalling—they are on our track!"

Doubrovsky leaped from his bed, seized his arms and issued from the hut. The brigands were noisily crowding together in the

---

[77] Diminutive of Stepan (Stephen).

inclosure, but on the appearance of their chief a deep silence reigned.

"Are all here?" asked Doubrovsky.

"All except the patrols," was the reply.

"To your places!" cried Doubrovsky, and the brigands took up each his appointed place.

At that moment, three of the patrols ran up to the gate of the fort. Doubrovsky went to meet them.

"What is it?" he asked.

"The soldiers are in the wood," was the reply; "they are surrounding us."

Doubrovsky ordered the gate to be locked, and then went himself to examine the cannon. In the wood could be heard the sound of many voices, every moment drawing nearer and nearer. The brigands waited in silence. Suddenly three or four soldiers appeared from the wood, but immediately fell back again, firing their guns as a signal to their comrades.

"Prepare for battle!" cried Doubrovsky. There was a movement among the brigands, then all was silent again.

Then was heard the noise of an approaching column; arms glittered among the trees, and about a hundred and fifty soldiers dashed out of the wood and rushed with a wild shout towards the rampart. Doubrovsky applied the match to the cannon; the shot was successful—one soldier had his head shot off, and two others were wounded. The troops were thrown into confusion, but the officer in command rushed forward, the soldiers followed him and jumped down into the ditch. The brigands fired down at them with muskets and pistols, and then, with axes in their hands, they began to defend the rampart, up which the infuriated soldiers were now climbing, leaving twenty of their comrades wounded in the ditch below. A hand to hand struggle began. The soldiers were already upon the rampart, the brigands were beginning to give way; but Doubrovsky advanced towards the officer in command, presented his pistol at his breast, and fired. The officer fell backwards to the ground. Several soldiers raised him in their arms and hastened to carry him into the wood; the others, having lost their chief, stopped fighting. The emboldened brigands took advantage of this moment of hesitation, and surging forward, hurled their assailants back into the ditch. The besiegers began to run; the brigands with fierce yells started in pursuit of them. The victory was decisive. Doubrovsky, trusting to the complete confusion of the enemy, stopped his followers and shut himself up in the fortress, doubled the sentinels, forbade anyone to absent himself, and ordered the wounded to be collected.

This last event drew the serious attention of the government to the daring exploits of Doubrovsky. Information was obtained of his place of retreat, and a detachment of soldiers was sent to take him, dead or alive. Several of his band were captured, and from these it was ascertained that Doubrovsky was no longer among them. A few days after the battle that we have just described, he collected all his followers and informed them that it was his intention to leave them for ever, and advised them to change their mode of life:

"You have become rich under my command. Each of you has a passport with which he will be able to make his way safely to some distant province, where he can pass the rest of his life in ease and honest labour. But you are all rascals, and probably do not wish to abandon your trade."

After this speech he left them, taking with him only one of his followers. Nobody knew what became of him. At first the truth of this testimony was doubted, for the devotion of the brigands to their chief was well known, and it was supposed that they had concocted the story to secure his safety; but after events confirmed their statement. The terrible visits, burnings, and robberies ceased; the roads again became safe. According to another report, Doubrovsky had fled to some foreign country.

THE QUEEN OF SPADES

CHAPTER I

There was a card party at the rooms of Naroumoff of the Horse Guards. The long winter night passed away imperceptibly, and it was five o'clock in the morning before the company sat down to supper. Those who had won, ate with a good appetite; the others sat staring absently at their empty plates. When the champagne appeared, however, the conversation became more animated, and all took a part in it.

"And how did you fare, Sourin?" asked the host.

"Oh, I lost, as usual. I must confess that I am unlucky: I play mirandole, I always keep cool, I never allow anything to put me out, and yet I always lose!"

"And you did not once allow yourself to be tempted to back the red?... Your firmness astonishes me."

"But what do you think of Hermann?" said one of the guests, pointing to a young Engineer: "he has never had a card in his hand in his life, he has never in his life laid a wager, and yet he sits here till five o'clock in the morning watching our play."

"Play interests me very much," said Hermann: "but I am not in the position to sacrifice the necessary in the hope of winning the superfluous."

"Hermann is a German: he is economical—that is all!" observed Tomsky. "But if there is one person that I cannot understand, it is my grandmother, the Countess Anna Fedorovna."

"How so?" inquired the guests.

"I cannot understand," continued Tomsky, "how it is that my grandmother does not punt."

"What is there remarkable about an old lady of eighty not punting?" said Naroumoff.

"Then you do not know the reason why?"

"No, really; haven't the faintest idea."

"Oh! then listen. You must know that, about sixty years ago, my grandmother went to Paris, where she created quite a sensation. People used to run after her to catch a glimpse of the 'Muscovite Venus.' Richelieu made love to her, and my grandmother maintains that he almost blew out his brains in consequence of her cruelty. At that time ladies used to play at faro. On one occasion at the Court, she lost a very considerable sum to the Duke of Orleans. On returning home, my grandmother removed the patches from her

167

face, took off her hoops, informed my grandfather of her loss at the gaming-table, and ordered him to pay the money. My deceased grandfather, as far as I remember, was a sort of house-steward to my grandmother. He dreaded her like fire; but, on hearing of such a heavy loss, he almost went out of his mind; he calculated the various sums she had lost, and pointed out to her that in six months she had spent half a million of francs, that neither their Moscow nor Saratoff estates were in Paris, and finally refused point blank to pay the debt. My grandmother gave him a box on the ear and slept by herself as a sign of her displeasure. The next day she sent for her husband, hoping that this domestic punishment had produced an effect upon him, but she found him inflexible. For the first time in her life, she entered into reasonings and explanations with him, thinking to be able to convince him by pointing out to him that there are debts and debts, and that there is a great difference between a Prince and a coachmaker. But it was all in vain, my grandfather still remained obdurate. But the matter did not rest there. My grandmother did not know what to do. She had shortly before become acquainted with a very remarkable man. You have heard of Count St. Germain, about whom so many marvellous stories are told. You know that he represented himself as the Wandering Jew, as the discoverer of the elixir of life, of the philosopher's stone, and so forth. Some laughed at him as a charlatan; but Casanova, in his memoirs, says that he was a spy. But be that as it may, St. Germain, in spite of the mystery surrounding him, was a very fascinating person, and was much sought after in the best circles of society. Even to this day my grandmother retains an affectionate recollection of him, and becomes quite angry if anyone speaks disrespectfully of him. My grandmother knew that St. Germain had large sums of money at his disposal. She resolved to have recourse to him, and she wrote a letter to him asking him to come to her without delay. The queer old man immediately waited upon her and found her overwhelmed with grief. She described to him in the blackest colours the barbarity of her husband, and ended by declaring that her whole hope depended upon his friendship and amiability.

"St. Germain reflected.

"'I could advance you the sum you want,' said he; 'but I know that you would not rest easy until you had paid me back, and I should not like to bring fresh troubles upon you. But there is another way of getting out of your difficulty: you can win back your money.'

"'But, my dear Count,' replied my grandmother, 'I tell you that I haven't any money left.'

"'Money is not necessary,' replied St. Germain: 'be pleased to listen to me.'

"Then he revealed to her a secret, for which each of us would give a good deal...."

The young officers listened with increased attention. Tomsky lit his pipe, puffed away for a moment and then continued:

"That same evening my grandmother went to Versailles to the jeu de la reine. The Duke of Orleans kept the bank; my grandmother excused herself in an off-handed manner for not having yet paid her debt, by inventing some little story, and then began to play against him. She chose three cards and played them one after the other: all three won sonika,[78] and my grandmother recovered every farthing that she had lost."

"Mere chance!" said one of the guests.

"A tale!" observed Hermann.

"Perhaps they were marked cards!" said a third.

"I do not think so," replied Tomsky gravely.

"What!" said Naroumoff, "you have a grandmother who knows how to hit upon three lucky cards in succession, and you have never yet succeeded in getting the secret of it out of her?"

"That's the deuce of it!" replied Tomsky: "she had four sons, one of whom was my father; all four were determined gamblers, and yet not to one of them did she ever reveal her secret, although it would not have been a bad thing either for them or for me. But this is what I heard from my uncle, Count Ivan Hitch, and he assured me, on his honour, that it was true. The late Chaplitsky—the same who died in poverty after having squandered millions—once lost, in his youth, about three hundred thousand roubles—to Zoritch, if I remember rightly. He was in despair. My grandmother, who was always very severe upon the extravagance of young men, took pity, however, upon Chaplitsky. She gave him three cards, telling him to play them one after the other, at the same time exacting from him a solemn promise that he would never play at cards again as long as he lived. Chaplitsky then went to his victorious opponent, and they began a fresh game. On the first card he staked fifty thousand roubles and won sonika; he doubled the stake and won again, till at last, by pursuing the same tactics, he won back more than he had lost....

"But it is time to go to bed: it is a quarter to six already."

And indeed it was already beginning to dawn: the young men emptied their glasses and then took leave of each other.

---

[78] Said of a card when it wins or loses in the quickest possible time.

CHAPTER II

The old Countess A—— was seated in her dressings room in front of her looking-glass. Three waiting maids stood around her. One held a small pot of rouge, another a box of hair-pins, and the third a tall cap with bright red ribbons. The Countess had no longer the slightest pretensions to beauty, but she still preserved the habits of her youth, dressed in strict accordance with the fashion of seventy years before, and made as long and as careful a toilette as she would have done sixty years previously. Near the window, at an embroidery frame, sat a young lady, her ward.

"Good morning, grandmamma," said a young officer, entering the room. "Bonjour, Mademoiselle Lise. Grandmamma, I want to ask you something."

"What is it, Paul?"

"I want you to let me introduce one of my friends to you, and to allow me to bring him to the ball on Friday."

"Bring him direct to the ball and introduce him to me there. Were you at B——'s yesterday?"

"Yes; everything went off very pleasantly, and dancing was kept up until five o'clock. How charming Eletskaia was!"

"But, my dear, what is there charming about her? Isn't she like her grandmother, the Princess Daria Petrovna? By the way, she must be very old, the Princess Daria Petrovna."

"How do you mean, old?" cried Tomsky thoughtlessly; "she died seven years ago."

The young lady raised her head and made a sign to the young officer. He then remembered that the old Countess was never to be informed of the death of any of her contemporaries, and he bit his lips. But the old Countess heard the news with the greatest indifference.

"Dead!" said she; "and I did not know it. We were appointed maids of honour at the same time, and when we were presented to the Empress...."

And the Countess for the hundredth time related to her grandson one of her anecdotes.

"Come, Paul," said she, when she had finished her story, "help me to get up. Lizanka,[79] where is my snuff-box?"

And the Countess with her three maids went behind a screen to finish her toilette. Tomsky was left alone with the young lady.

---

[79] Diminutive of Lizaveta (Elizabeth).

"Who is the gentleman you wish to introduce to the Countess?" asked Lizaveta Ivanovna in a whisper.

"Naroumoff. Do you know him?"

"No. Is he a soldier or a civilian?"

"A soldier."

"Is he in the Engineers?"

"No, in the Cavalry. What made you think that he was in the Engineers?"

The young lady smiled, but made no reply.

"Paul," cried the Countess from behind the screen, "send me some new novel, only pray don't let it be one of the present day style."

"What do you mean, grandmother?"

"That is, a novel, in which the hero strangles neither his father nor his mother, and in which there are no drowned bodies. I have a great horror of drowned persons."

"There are no such novels nowadays. Would you like a Russian one?"

"Are there any Russian novels? Send me one, my dear, pray send me one!"

"Good-bye, grandmother: I am in a hurry.... Goodbye, Lizaveta Ivanovna. What made you think that Naroumoff was in the Engineers?"

And Tomsky left the boudoir.

Lizaveta Ivanovna was left alone: she laid aside her work and began to look out of the window. A few moments afterwards, at a corner house on the other side of the street, a young officer appeared. A deep blush covered her cheeks; she took up her work again and bent her head down over the frame. At the same moment the Countess returned completely dressed.

"Order the carriage, Lizaveta," said she; "we will go out for a drive."

Lizaveta arose from the frame and began to arrange her work.

"What is the matter with you, my child, are you deaf?" cried the Countess. "Order the carriage to be got ready at once."

"I will do so this moment," replied the young lady, hastening into the ante-room.

A servant entered and gave the Countess some books from Prince Paul Alexandrovitch.

"Tell him that I am much obliged to him," said the Countess. "Lizaveta! Lizaveta! where are you running to?"

"I am going to dress."

"There is plenty of time, my dear. Sit down here. Open the first volume and read to me aloud."

171

Her companion took the book and read a few lines.

"Louder," said the Countess. "What is the matter with you, my child? Have you lost your voice? Wait—give me that footstool—a little nearer—that will do!"

Lizaveta read two more pages. The Countess yawned.

"Put the book down," said she: "what a lot of nonsense! Send it back to Prince Paul with my thanks.... But where is the carriage?"

"The carriage is ready," said Lizaveta, looking out into the street.

"How is it that you are not dressed?" said the Countess: "I must always wait for you. It is intolerable, my dear!"

Liza hastened to her room. She had not been there two minutes, before the Countess began to ring with all her might. The three waiting-maids came running in at one door and the valet at another.

"How is it that you cannot hear me when I ring for you?" said the Countess. "Tell Lizaveta Ivanovna that I am waiting for her."

Lizaveta returned with her hat and cloak on.

"At last you are here!" said the Countess. "But why such an elaborate toilette? Whom do you intend to captivate? What sort of weather is it? It seems rather windy."

"No, Your Ladyship, it is very calm," replied the valet.

"You never think of what you are talking about. Open the window. So it is: windy and bitterly cold. Unharness the horses. Lizaveta, we won't go out—there was no need for you to deck yourself like that."

"What a life is mine!" thought Lizaveta Ivanovna.

And, in truth, Lizaveta Ivanovna was a very unfortunate creature. "The bread of the stranger is bitter," says Dante, "and his staircase hard to climb." But who can know what the bitterness of dependence is so well as the poor companion of an old lady of quality? The Countess A—— had by no means a bad heart, but she was capricious, like a woman who had been spoilt by the world, as well as being avaricious and egotistical, like all old people who have seen their best days, and whose thoughts are with the past and not the present. She participated in all the vanities of the great world, went to balls, where she sat in a corner, painted and dressed in old-fashioned style, like a deformed but indispensable ornament of the ball-room; all the guests on entering approached her and made a profound bow, as if in accordance with a set ceremony, but after that nobody took any further notice of her. She received the whole town at her house, and observed the strictest etiquette, although she could no longer recognize the faces of people. Her numerous domestics, growing fat and old in her ante-chamber and servants' hall, did just as they liked, and vied with each other in robbing the aged Countess in the most bare-faced manner. Lizaveta Ivanovna was the martyr of the household. She made tea, and was reproached with using too much sugar; she read novels aloud to the Countess, and the faults of the author were visited upon her head; she accompanied the Countess in her walks, and was held answerable for the weather or the state of the pavement. A salary was attached to the post, but she very rarely received it, although she was expected to dress like everybody else, that is to say, like very few indeed. In society she played the most pitiable rôle. Everybody knew her, and nobody paid her any attention. At balls she danced only when a partner was wanted, and ladies would only take hold of her arm when it was necessary to lead her out of the room to attend to their dresses. She was very self-conscious, and felt her position keenly, and she looked about her with impatience for a deliverer to come to her rescue; but the young men, calculating in their giddiness, honoured her with but very little attention, although Lizaveta Ivanovna was a hundred times prettier than the bare-faced and cold-hearted marriageable girls around whom they hovered. Many a time did she quietly slink away from the glittering but wearisome drawing-room, to go and cry in her own poor little room, in which stood a screen, a chest of drawers, a looking-glass and a painted bedstead, and where a tallow candle burnt feebly in a copper candle-stick.

One morning—this was about two days after the evening party described at the beginning of this story, and a week previous to the scene at which we have just assisted—Lizaveta Ivanovna was seated near the window at her embroidery frame, when, happening to look out into the street, she caught sight of a young Engineer officer, standing motionless with his eyes fixed upon her window. She lowered her head and went on again with her work. About five minutes afterwards she looked out again—the young officer was still standing in the same place. Not being in the habit of coquetting with passing officers, she did not continue to gaze out into the street, but went on sewing for, a couple of hours, without raising her head. Dinner was announced. She rose up and began to put her embroidery away, but glancing casually out of the window, she perceived the officer again. This seemed to her very strange. After dinner she went to the window with a certain feeling of uneasiness, but the officer was no longer there—and she thought no more about him.

A couple of days afterwards, just as she was stepping into the carriage with the Countess, she saw him again. He was standing close behind the door, with his face half-concealed by his fur collar, but his dark eyes sparkled beneath his cap. Lizaveta felt alarmed, though she knew not why, and she trembled as she seated herself in the carriage.

On returning home, she hastened to the window—the officer was standing in his accustomed place, with his eyes fixed upon her. She drew back, a prey to curiosity and agitated by a feeling which was quite new to her.

From that time forward' not a day passed without the young officer making his appearance under the window at the customary hour, and between him and her there was established a sort of mute acquaintance. Sitting in her place at work, she used to feel his approach; and raising her head, she would look at him longer and longer each day. The young man seemed to be very grateful to her: she saw with the sharp eye of youth, how a sudden flush covered his pale cheeks each time that their glances met. After about a week she commenced to smile at him....

When Tomsky asked permission of his grandmother the Countess to present one of his friends to her, the young girl's heart beat violently. But hearing that Naroumoff was not an Engineer, she regretted that by her thoughtless question, she had betrayed her secret to the volatile Tomsky.

Hermann was the son of a German who had become a naturalized Russian, and from whom he had inherited a small capital. Being firmly convinced of the necessity of preserving his independence, Hermann did not touch his private income, but lived on his pay, without allowing himself the slightest luxury. Moreover, he was reserved and ambitious, and his companions rarely had an opportunity of making merry at the expense of his extreme parsimony. He had strong passions and an ardent imagination, but his firmness of disposition preserved him from the ordinary errors of young men. Thus, though a gamester at heart, he never touched a card, for he considered his position did not allow him—as he said—"to risk the necessary in the hope of winning the superfluous," yet he would sit for nights together at the card table and follow with feverish anxiety the different turns of the game.

The story of the three cards had produced a powerful impression upon his imagination, and all night long he could think of nothing else. "If," he thought to himself the following evening, as he walked along the streets of St. Petersburg, "if the old Countess would but reveal her secret to me! if she would only tell me the names of the three winning cards. Why should I not try my fortune? I must get introduced to her and win her favour—become her lover.... But all that will take time, and she is eighty-seven years old: she might be dead in a week, in a couple of days even!... But the story itself: can it really be true?... No! Economy, temperance and industry: those are my three winning cards; by means of them I shall be able to double my capital—increase it sevenfold, and procure for myself ease and independence."

Musing in this manner, he walked on until he found himself in one of the principal streets of St. Petersburg, in front of a house of antiquated architecture. The street was blocked with equipage; carriages one after the other drew up in front of the brilliantly illuminated doorway. At one moment there stepped out on to the pavement the well-shaped little foot of some young beauty, at another the heavy boot of a cavalry officer, and then the silk stockings and shoes of a member of the diplomatic world. Furs and cloaks passed in rapid succession before the gigantic porter at the entrance.

Hermann stopped. "Who's house is this?" he asked of the watchman at the corner.

"The Countess A——'s," replied the watchman.

Hermann started. The strange story of the three cards again presented itself to his imagination. He began walking up and down before the house, thinking of its owner and her strange secret. Returning late to his modest lodging, he could not go to sleep for a long time, and when at last he did doze off, he could dream of nothing but cards, green tables, piles of banknotes and heaps of ducats. He played one card after the other, winning uninterruptedly, and then he gathered up the gold and filled his pockets with the notes. When he woke up late the next morning, he sighed over the loss of his imaginary wealth, and then sallying out into the town, he found himself once more in front of the Countess's residence. Some unknown power seemed to have attracted him thither. He stopped and looked up at the windows. At one of these he saw a head with luxuriant black hair, which was bent down probably over some book or an embroidery frame. The head was raised. Hermann saw a fresh complexion and a pair of dark eyes. That moment decided his fate.

CHAPTER III

Lizaveta Ivanovna had scarcely taken off her hat and cloak, when the Countess sent for her and again ordered her to get the carriage ready. The vehicle drew up before the door, and they prepared to take their seats. Just at the moment when two footmen were assisting the old lady to enter the carriage, Lizaveta saw her Engineer standing close beside the wheel; he grasped her hand; alarm caused her to lose her presence of mind, and the young man disappeared—but not before he had left a letter between her fingers. She concealed it in her glove, and during the whole of the drive she neither saw nor heard anything. It was the custom of the Countess, when out for an airing in her carriage, to be constantly asking such questions as: "Who was that person that met us just now? What is the name of this bridge? What is written on that signboard?" On this occasion, however, Lizaveta returned such vague and absurd answers, that the Countess became angry with her.

"What is the matter with you, my dear?" she exclaimed. "Have you taken leave of your senses, or what is it? Do you not hear me or understand what I say?... Heaven be thanked, I am still in my right mind and speak plainly enough!"

Lizaveta Ivanovna did not hear her. On returning home she ran to her room, and drew the letter out of her glove: it was not sealed. Lizaveta read it. The letter contained a declaration of love; it was tender, respectful, and copied word for word from a German novel. But Lizaveta did not know anything of the German language, and she was quite delighted.

For all that, the letter caused her to feel exceedingly uneasy. For the first time in her life she was entering into secret and confidential relations with a young man. His boldness alarmed her. She reproached herself for her imprudent behaviour, and knew not what to do. Should she cease to sit at the window and, by assuming an appearance of indifference towards him, put a check upon the young officer's desire for further acquaintance with her? Should she send his letter back to him, or should she answer him in a cold and decided manner? There was nobody to whom she could turn in her perplexity, for she had neither female friend nor adviser.... At length she resolved to reply to him.

She sat down at her little writing-table, took pen and paper, and began to think. Several times she began her letter, and then tore it up: the way she had expressed herself seemed to her either too inviting or too cold and decisive. At last she succeeded in writing a few lines with which she felt satisfied.

"I am convinced," she wrote, "that your intentions are honourable, and that you do not wish to offend me by any imprudent behaviour, but our acquaintance must not begin in such a manner. I return you your letter, and I hope that I shall never have any cause to complain of this undeserved slight."

The next day, as soon as Hermann made his appearance,

Lizaveta rose from her embroidery, went into the drawing-room, opened the ventilator and threw the letter into the street, trusting that the young officer would have the perception to pick it up.

Hermann hastened forward, picked it up and then repaired to a confectioner's shop. Breaking the seal of the envelope, he found inside it his own letter and Lizaveta's reply. He had expected this, and he returned home, his mind deeply occupied with his intrigue.

Three days afterwards, a bright-eyed young girl from a milliner's establishment brought Lizaveta a letter. Lizaveta opened it with great uneasiness, fearing that it was a demand for money, when suddenly she recognized Hermann's handwriting.

"You have made a mistake, my dear," said she: "this letter is not for me."

"Oh, yes, it is for you," replied the girl, smiling very knowingly. "Have the goodness to read it."

Lizaveta glanced at the letter. Hermann requested an interview.

"It cannot be," she cried, alarmed at the audacious request, and the manner in which it was made. "This letter is certainly not for me."

And she tore it into fragments.

"If the letter was not for you, why have you torn it up?" I said the girl. "I should have given it back to the person who sent it."

"Be good enough, my dear," said Lizaveta, disconcerted by this remark, "not to bring me any more letters for the future, and tell the person who sent you that he ought to be ashamed...."

But Hermann was not the man to be thus put off. Every day Lizaveta received from him a letter, sent now in this way, now in that. They were no longer translated from the German. Hermann wrote them under the inspiration of passion, and spoke in his own language, and they bore full testimony to the inflexibility of his desire and the disordered condition of his uncontrollable imagination. Lizaveta no longer thought of sending them back to him: she became intoxicated with them and began to reply to them, and little by little her answers became longer and more affectionate. At last she threw out of the window to him the following letter:

"This evening there is going to be a ball at the Embassy. The Countess will be there. We shall remain until two o'clock. You have now an opportunity of seeing me alone. As soon as the Countess is gone, the servants will very probably go out, and there will be nobody left but the Swiss, but he usually goes to sleep in his lodge. Come about half-past eleven. Walk straight upstairs. If you meet anybody in the ante-room, ask if the Countess is at home. You will be told 'No,' in which case there will be nothing left for you to do but to go away again. But it is most probable that you will meet nobody.

177

The maidservants will all be together in one room. On leaving the ante-room, turn to the left, and walk straight on until you reach the Countess's bedroom. In the bedroom, behind a screen, you will find two doors: the one on the right leads to a cabinet, which the Countess never enters; the one on the left leads to a corridor, at the end of which is a little winding staircase; this leads to my room."

Hermann trembled like a tiger, as he waited for the appointed time to arrive. At ten o'clock in the evening he was already in front of the Countess's house. The weather was terrible; the wind blew with great violence; the sleety snow fell in large flakes; the lamps emitted a feeble light, the streets were deserted; from time to time a sledge, drawn by a sorry-looking hack, passed by, on the look-out for a belated passenger. Hermann was enveloped in a thick overcoat, and felt neither wind nor snow.

At last the Countess's carriage drew up. Hermann saw two footmen carry out in their arms the bent form of the old lady, wrapped in sable fur, and immediately behind her, clad in a warm mantle, and with her head ornamented with a wreath of fresh flowers, followed Lizaveta. The door was closed. The carriage rolled away heavily through the yielding snow. The porter shut the street-door; the windows became dark.

Hermann began walking up and down near the deserted house; at length he stopped under a lamp, and glanced at his watch: it was twenty minutes past eleven. He remained standing under the lamp, his eyes fixed upon the watch, impatiently waiting for the remaining minutes to pass. At half-past eleven precisely, Hermann ascended the steps of the house, and made his way into the brightly-illuminated vestibule. The porter was not there. Hermann hastily ascended the staircase, opened the door of the ante-room and saw a footman sitting asleep in an antique chair by the side of a lamp. With a light firm step Hermann passed by him. The drawing-room and dining-room were in darkness, but a feeble reflection penetrated thither from the lamp in the ante-room.

Hermann reached the Countess's bedroom. Before a shrine, which was full of old images, a golden lamp was burning. Faded stuffed chairs and divans with soft cushions stood in melancholy symmetry around the room, the walls of which were hung with China silk. On one side of the room hung two portraits painted in Paris by Madame Lebrun. One of these represented a stout, red-faced man of about forty years of age in a bright-green uniform and with a star upon his breast; the other—a beautiful young woman, with an aquiline nose, forehead curls and a rose in her powdered hair. In the corners stood porcelain shepherds and shepherdesses, dining-room clocks from the workshop of the celebrated Lefroy, bandboxes, roulettes, fans and the various playthings for the amusement of ladies that were in vogue at the end of the last century, when Montgolfier's balloons and Mesmer's magnetism were the rage. Hermann stepped behind the screen. At the back of it stood a little iron bedstead; on the right was the door which led to the cabinet; on the left—the other which led to the corridor. He opened the latter, and saw the little winding staircase which led to the room of the poor companion.... But he retraced his steps and entered the dark cabinet.

The time passed slowly. All was still. The clock in the drawing-room struck twelve; the strokes echoed through the room one after the other, and everything was quiet again. Hermann stood leaning against the cold stove. He was calm; his heart beat regularly, like that of a man resolved upon a dangerous but inevitable undertaking. One o'clock in the morning struck; then two; and he heard the distant noise of carriage-wheels. An involuntary agitation took possession of him. The carriage drew near and stopped. He heard the sound of the carriage-steps' being let down. All was bustle within the house. The servants were running hither and thither, there was a confusion of voices, and the rooms were lit up. Three antiquated chamber-maids entered the bedroom, and they were shortly afterwards followed by the Countess who, more dead than alive, sank into a Voltaire armchair. Hermann peeped through a chink. Lizaveta Ivanovna passed close by him, and he heard her hurried steps as she hastened up the little spiral staircase. For a moment his heart way assailed by something like a pricking of conscience, but the emotion was only transitory, and his heart became petrified as before.

The Countess began to undress before her looking-glass. Her rose-bedecked cap was taken off, and then her powdered wig was removed from off her white and closely-cut hair. Hairpins fell in showers around her. Her yellow satin dress, brocaded with silver, fell down at her swollen feet Hermann was a witness of the repugnant mysteries of her toilette; at last the Countess was in her night-cap and dressing-gown, and in this costume, more suitable to her age, she appeared less hideous and deformed.

Like all old people in general, the Countess suffered from sleeplessness. Having undressed, she seated herself at the window in a Voltaire armchair and dismissed her maids. The candles were taken away, and once more the room was left with only one lamp burning in it. The Countess sat there looking quite yellow, mumbling with her flaccid lips and swaying to and fro. Her dull eyes expressed complete vacancy of mind, and, looking at her, one would have thought that the rocking of her body was not a voluntary action

179

of her own, but was produced by the action of some concealed galvanic mechanism.

Suddenly the death-like face assumed an inexplicable expression. The lips ceased to tremble, the eyes became animated: before the Countess stood an unknown man.

"Do not be alarmed, for Heaven's sake, do not be alarmed!" said he in a low but distinct voice. "I have no intention of doing you any harm, I have only come to ask a favour of you."

The old woman looked at him in silence, as if she had not heard what he had said. Hermann thought that she was deaf, and, bending down towards her ear, he repeated what he had said. The aged Countess remained silent as before.

"You can insure the happiness of my life," continued Hermann, "and it will cost you nothing. I know that you can name three cards in order——"

Hermann stopped. The Countess appeared now to understand what he wanted; she seemed as if seeking for words to reply.

"It was a joke," she replied at last: "I assure you it was only a joke."

"There is no joking about the matter," replied Hermann angrily. "Remember Chaplitsky, whom you helped to win."

The Countess became visibly uneasy. Her features expressed strong emotion, but they quickly resumed their former immobility.

"Can you not name me these three winning cards?" continued Hermann.

The Countess remained silent; Hermann continued:

"For whom are you preserving your secret? For your grandsons? They are rich enough without it; they do not know the worth of money. Your cards would be of no use to a spendthrift. He who cannot preserve his paternal inheritance, will die in want, even though he had a demon at his service. I am not a man of that sort; I know the value of money. Your three cards will not be thrown away upon me. Come!"...

He paused and tremblingly awaited her reply. The Countess remained silent; Hermann fell upon his knees.

"If your heart has ever known the feeling of love," said he, "if you remember its rapture, if you have ever smiled at the cry of your new-born child, if any human feeling has ever entered into your breast, I entreat you by the feelings of a wife, a lover, a mother, by all that is most sacred in life, not to reject my prayer. Reveal to me your secret. Of what use is it to you?... May be it is connected with some terrible sin, with the loss of eternal salvation, with some bargain with the devil.... Reflect,—you are old; you have not long to live—I am ready to take your sins upon my soul. Only reveal to me

180

your secret. Remember that the happiness of a man is in your hands, that not only I, but my children, and grandchildren will bless your memory and reverence you as a saint...."

The old Countess answered not a word.

Hermann rose to his feet.

"You old hag!" he exclaimed, grinding his teeth, "then I will make you answer!"

With these words he drew a pistol from his pocket.

At the sight of the pistol, the Countess for the second time exhibited strong emotion. She shook her head and raised her hands as if to protect herself from the shot ... then she fell backwards and remained motionless.

"Come, an end to this childish nonsense!" said Hermann, taking hold of her hand. "I ask you for the last time: will you tell me the names of your three cards, or will you not?"

The Countess made no reply. Hermann perceived that she was dead!

CHAPTER IV

Izaveta Ivanovna was sitting in her room, still in her ball dress, lost in deep thought. On returning home, she had hastily dismissed the chambermaid who very reluctantly came forward, to assist her, saying that she would undress herself, and with a trembling heart had gone up to her own room, expecting to find Hermann there, but yet hoping not to find him. At the first glance she convinced herself that he was not there, and she thanked her fate for having prevented him keeping the appointment. She sat down without undressing, and began to recall to mind all the circumstances which in so short a time had carried her so far. It was not three weeks since the time when she first saw the young officer from the window—and yet she was already in correspondence with him, and he had succeeded in inducing her to grant him a nocturnal interview! She knew his name only through his having written it at the bottom of some of his letters; she had never spoken to him, had never heard his voice, and had never heard him spoken of until that evening. But, strange to say, that very evening at the ball, Tomsky, being piqued with the young Princess Pauline N——, who, contrary to her usual custom, did not flirt with him, wished to revenge himself by assuming an air of indifference: he therefore engaged Lizaveta Ivanovna and danced an endless mazurka with her. During the whole of the time he kept teasing her about her partiality for Engineer officers; he assured her that he knew far more than she imagined, and some of his jests were so happily aimed, that Lizaveta thought several times that her secret was known to him.

"From whom have you learnt all this?" she asked, smiling.

"From a friend of a person very well known to you," replied Tomsky, "from a very distinguished man."

"And who is this distinguished man?"

"His name is Hermann."

Lizaveta made no reply; but her hands and feet lost all sense of feeling.

"This Hermann," continued Tomsky, "is a man of romantic personality. He has the profile of a Napoleon, and the soul of a Mephistopheles. I believe that he has at least three crimes upon his conscience.... How pale you have become!"

"I have a headache.... But what did this Hermann—or whatever his name is—tell you?"

"Hermann is very much dissatisfied with his friend: he says that in his place he would act very differently ... I even think that Hermann himself has designs upon you; at least, he listens very attentively to all that his friend has to say about you."

"And where has he seen me?"

"In church, perhaps; or on the parade—God alone knows where. It may have been in your room, while you were asleep, for there is nothing that he——"

Three ladies approaching him with the question: "oubli ou regret?" interrupted the conversation, which had become so tantalizingly interesting to Lizaveta.

The lady chosen by Tomsky was the Princess Pauline herself. She succeeded in effecting a reconciliation with him during the numerous turns of the dance, after which he conducted her to her chair. On returning to his place, Tomsky thought no more either of Hermann or Lizaveta. She longed to renew the interrupted conversation, but the mazurka came to an end, and shortly afterwards the old Countess took her departure.

Tomsky's words were nothing more than the customary small talk of the dance, but they sank deep into the soul of the young dreamer. The portrait, sketched by Tomsky, coincided with the picture she had formed within her own mind, and thanks to the latest romances, the ordinary countenance of her admirer became invested with attributes capable of alarming her and fascinating her

182

imagination at the same time. She was now sitting with her bare arms crossed and with her head, still adorned with flowers, sunk upon her uncovered bosom. Suddenly the door opened and Hermann entered. She shuddered.

"Where were you?" she asked in a terrified whisper.

"In the old Countess's bedroom," replied Hermann: "I have just left her. The Countess is dead."

"My God! What do you say?"

"And I am afraid," added Hermann, "that I am the cause of her death."

Lizaveta looked at him, and Tomsky's words found an echo in her soul: "This man has at least three crimes upon his conscience!" Hermann sat down by the window near her, and related all that had happened.

Lizaveta listened to him in terror. So all those passionate letters, those ardent desires, this bold obstinate pursuit—all this was not love! Money—that was what his soul yearned for! She could not satisfy his desire and make him happy! The poor girl had been nothing but the blind tool of a robber, of the murderer of her aged benefactress!... She wept bitter tears of agonized repentance. Hermann gazed at her in silence: his heart, too, was a prey to violent emotion, but neither the tears of the poor girl, nor the wonderful charm of her beauty, enhanced by her grief, could produce any impression upon his hardened soul. He felt no pricking of conscience at the thought of the dead old woman. One thing only grieved him: the irreparable loss of the secret from which he had expected to obtain great wealth.

"You are a monster!" said Lizaveta at last.

"I did not wish for her death," replied Hermann: "my pistol was not loaded."

Both remained silent.

The day began to dawn. Lizaveta extinguished her candle: a pale light illumined her room. She wiped her tear-stained eyes and raised them towards Hermann: he was sitting near the window, with his arms crossed and with a fierce frown upon his forehead. In this attitude he bore a striking resemblance to the portrait of Napoleon. This resemblance struck Lizaveta even.

"How shall I get you out of the house?" said she at last. "I thought of conducting you down the secret staircase, but in that case it would be necessary to go through the Countess's bedroom, and I am afraid."

"Tell me how to find this secret staircase—I will go alone."

Lizaveta arose, took from her drawer a key, handed it to Hermann and gave him the necessary instructions. Hermann pressed her cold, powerless hand, kissed her bowed head, and left the room.

He descended the winding staircase, and once more entered the Countess's bedroom. The dead old lady sat as if petrified; her face expressed profound tranquillity. Hermann stopped before her, and gazed long and earnestly at her, as if he wished to convince himself of the terrible reality; at last he entered the cabinet, felt behind the tapestry for the door, and then began to descend the dark staircase, filled with strange emotions. "Down this very staircase," thought he, "perhaps coming from the very same room, and at this very same hour sixty years ago, there may have glided, in an embroidered coat, with his hair dressed à l'oiseau royal and pressing to his heart his three-cornered hat, some young gallant who has long been mouldering in the grave, but the heart of his aged mistress has only to-day ceased to beat...."

At the bottom of the staircase Hermann found a door, which he opened with a key, and then traversed a corridor which conducted him into the street.

CHAPTER V

Three days after the fatal night, at nine o'clock in the morning, Hermann repaired to the Convent of where the last honours were to be paid to the mortal remains of the old Countess. Although feeling no remorse, he could not altogether stifle the voice of conscience, which said to him: "You are the murderer of the old woman!" In spite of his entertaining very little religious belief, he was exceedingly superstitious; and believing that the dead Countess might exercise an evil influence on his life, he resolved to be present at her obsequies in order to implore her pardon.

The church was full. It was with difficulty that Hermann made his way through the crowd of people. The coffin was placed upon a rich catafalque beneath a velvet baldachin. The deceased Countess lay within it, with her hands crossed upon her breast, with a lace cap upon her head and dressed in a white satin robe. Around the catafalque stood the members of her household: the servants in black caftans, with armorial ribbons upon their shoulders, and candles in their hands; the relatives—children, grandchildren, and great-grandchildren—in deep mourning.

Nobody wept; tears would have been une affectation. The Countess was so old, that her death could have surprised nobody, and her relatives had long looked upon her as being out of the world. A famous preacher pronounced the funeral sermon. In simple and touching words he described the peaceful passing away of the righteous, who had passed long years in calm preparation for a Christian end. "The angel of death found her," said the orator, "engaged in pious meditation and waiting for the midnight bridegroom."

The service concluded amidst profound silence. The relatives went forward first to take farewell of the corpse. Then followed the numerous guests, who had come to render the last homage to her who for so many years had been a participator in their frivolous amusements. After these followed the members of the Countess's household. The last of these was an old woman of the same age as the deceased. Two young women led her forward by the hand. She had not strength enough to bow down to the ground—she merely shed a few tears and kissed the cold hand of her mistress.

Hermann now resolved to approach the coffin. He knelt down upon the cold stones and remained in that position for some minutes; at last he arose, as pale as the deceased Countess herself; he ascended the steps of the catafalque and bent over the corpse.... At that moment it seemed to him that the dead woman darted a mocking look at him and winked with one eye. Hermann started back, took a false step and fell to the ground. Several persons hurried forward and raised him up. At the same moment Lizaveta Ivanovna was borne fainting into the porch of the church. This episode disturbed for some minutes the solemnity of the gloomy ceremony. Among the congregation arose a deep murmur, and a tall thin chamberlain, a near relative of the deceased, whispered, in the ear of an Englishman who was standing near him, that the young officer was a natural son of the Countess, to which the Englishman coldly replied: "Oh!"

During the whole of that day, Hermann was strangely excited. Repairing to an out-of-the-way restaurant to dine, he drank a great deal of wine, contrary to his usual custom, in the hope of deadening his inward agitation. But the wine only served to excite his imagination still more. On returning home, he threw himself upon his bed without undressing, and fell into a deep sleep.

When he woke up it was already night, and the moon was shining into the room. He looked at his watch: it was a quarter to three. Sleep had left him; he sat down upon his bed and thought of the funeral of the old Countess.

At that moment somebody in the street looked in at his

window, and immediately passed on again. Hermann paid no attention to this incident. A few moments afterwards he heard the door of his ante-room open. Hermann thought that it was his orderly, drunk as usual, returning from some nocturnal expedition, but presently he heard footsteps that were unknown to him: somebody was walking softly over the floor in slippers. The door opened, and a woman dressed in white, entered the room. Hermann mistook her for his old nurse, and wondered what could bring her there at that hour of, the night. But the white woman glided rapidly across the room and stood before him and Hermann recognized the Countess!

"I have come to you against my wish," she said in a firm voice: "but I have been ordered to grant your request. Three, seven, ace, will win for you if played in succession, but only on these conditions: that you do not play more than one card in twenty-four hours, and that you never play again during the rest of your life. I forgive you my death, on condition that you marry my companion, Lizaveta Ivanovna."

With these words she turned round very quietly, walked with a shuffling gait towards the door and disappeared. Hermann heard the street-door open and shut, and again he saw someone look in at him through the window.

For a long time Hermann could not recover himself. He then rose up and entered the next room. His orderly was lying asleep upon the floor, and he had much difficulty in waking him. The orderly was drunk as usual, and no information could be obtained from him. The street-door was locked. Hermann returned to his room, lit his candle, and wrote down all the details of his vision.

CHAPTER VI

Two fixed ideas can no more exist together in the moral world than two bodies can occupy one and the same place in the physical world. "Three, seven, ace" soon drove out of Hermann's mind the thought of the dead countess. "Three, seven, ace" were perpetually running through his head and continually being repeated by his lips, If he saw a young girl, he would say: "How slender she is! quite like the three of hearts." If anybody asked: "What is the time?" he would reply: "Five minutes to seven." Every stout man that he saw reminded him of the ace. "Three, seven, ace" haunted him in his sleep, and assumed all possible shapes. The threes bloomed before him in the storms of magnificent flowers, the sevens were represented by gothic portals, and the aces became transformed into gigantic spiders. One thought alone occupied his whole mind—to make a profitable use of the secret which he had purchased so dearly. He thought of applying for a furlough so as to travel abroad. He wanted to go to Paris and tempt fortune in some of the public gambling-houses that abounded there. Chance spared him all this rouble.

There was in Moscow a society of rich gamesters, presided over by the celebrated Chekalinsky, who had passed all his life at the card-table and had amassed millions, accepting bills of exchange for his winnings and paying is losses in ready money. His long experience secured for him the confidence of his companions, and his open house, his famous cook, and his agreeable and fascinating manners gained for him the respect of the public. He came to St. Petersburg. The young men of the capital flocked to his rooms, forgetting balls for cards, and preferring the emotions of faro to the seductions of flirting. Naroumoff conducted Hermann to Chekalinsky's residence.

They passed through a suite of magnificent rooms, filled with attentive domestics. The place was crowded. Generals and Privy Counsellors were playing at whist; young men were lolling carelessly upon the velvet-covered sofas, eating ices and smoking pipes. In the drawing-room, at the head of a long table, around which were assembled about a score of players, sat the master of the house keeping the bank. He was a man of about sixty years of age, of a very dignified appearance; his head was covered with silvery-white hair; his full, florid countenance expressed good-nature, and his eyes twinkled with a perpetual smile. Naroumoff introduced Hermann to him. Chekalinsky shook him by the hand in a friendly manner, requested him not to stand on ceremony, and then went on dealing.

The game occupied some time. On the table lay more, than thirty cards. Chekalinsky paused after each throw, in order to give the players time to arrange their cards and note down their losses, listened politely to their requests, and more politely still, put straight the corners of cards that some player's hand had chanced to bend. At last the game was finished. Chekalinsky shuffled the cards and prepared to deal again.

"Will you allow me to take a card?" said Hermann, stretching out his hand from behind a stout gentleman who was punting.

Chekalinsky smiled and bowed silently, as a sign of

187

acquiescence. Naroumoff laughingly congratulated Hermann on his abjuration of that abstention from cards which he had practised for so long a period, and wished him a lucky beginning.

"Stake!" said Hermann, writing some figures with chalk on the back of his card.

"How much?" asked the banker, contracting the muscles of his eyes; "excuse me, I cannot see quite clearly."

"Forty-seven thousand roubles," replied Hermann.

At these words every head in the room turned suddenly round, and all eyes were fixed upon Hermann.

"He has taken leave of his senses!" thought Naroumoff.

"Allow me to inform you," said Chekalinsky, with his eternal smile, "that you are playing very high; nobody here has ever staked more than two hundred and seventy-five roubles at once."

"Very well," replied Hermann; "but do you accept my card or not?"

Chekalinsky bowed in token of consent.

"I only wish to observe," said he, "that although I have the greatest confidence in my friends, I can only play against ready money. For my own part, I am quite convinced that your word is sufficient, but for the sake of the order of the game, and to facilitate the reckoning up, I must ask you to put the money on your card."

Hermann drew from his pocket a bank-note and handed it to Chekalinsky, who, after examining it in a cursory manner, placed it on Hermann's card.

He began to deal. On the right a nine turned up, and on the left a three.

"I have won!" said Hermann, showing his card.

A murmur of astonishment arose among the players. Chekalinsky frowned, but the smile quickly returned to his face.

"Do you wish me to settle with you?" he said to Hermann.

"If you please," replied the latter.

Chekalinsky drew from his pocket a number of banknotes and paid at once. Hermann took up his money and left the table. Naroumoff could not recover from his astonishment. Hermann drank a glass of lemonade and returned home.

The next evening he again repaired to Chekalinsky's. The host was dealing. Hermann walked up to the table; the punters immediately made room for him. Chekalinsky greeted him with a gracious bow.

Hermann waited for the next deal, took a card and placed upon it his forty-seven thousand roubles, together with his winnings of the previous evening.

188

Chekalinsky began to deal. A knave turned up on the right, a seven on the left.

Hermann showed his seven.

There was a general exclamation. Chekalinsky was evidently ill at ease, but he counted out the ninety-four thousand roubles and handed them over to Hermann, who pocketed them in the coolest manner possible and immediately left the house.

The next evening Hermann appeared again at the table. Everyone was expecting him. The generals and Privy Counsellors left their whist in order to watch such extraordinary play. The young officers quitted their sofas, and even the servants crowded into the room. All pressed round Hermann. The other players left off punting, impatient to see how it would end. Hermann stood at the table and prepared to play alone against the pale, but still smiling Chekalinsky. Each opened a pack of cards. Chekalinsky shuffled. Hermann took a card and covered it with a pile of bank-notes. It was like a duel. Deep silence reigned around.

Chekalinsky began to deal; his hands trembled. On the right a queen turned up, and on the left an ace. "Ace has won!" cried Hermann, showing his card.

"Your queen has lost," said Chekalinsky, politely.

Hermann started; instead of an ace, there lay before him the queen of spades! He could not believe his eyes, nor could he understand how he had made such a mistake.

At that moment it seemed to him that the queen of spades smiled ironically and winked her eye at him. He was struck by her remarkable resemblance....

"The old Countess!" he exclaimed, seized with terror.

Chekalinsky gathered up his winnings. For some time, Hermann remained perfectly motionless. When at last he left the table, there was a general commotion in the room.

"Splendidly punted!" said the players. Chekalinsky shuffled the cards afresh, and the game went on as usual.

Hermann went out o1 ms mind, and is now confined in room Number 17 of the Oboukhoff Hospital. He never answers any questions, but he constantly mutters with unusual rapidity: "Three, seven, ace! Three, scven, queen!"

Lizaveta Ivanovna has married a very amiable young man, a son of the former steward of the old Countess. He is in the service of the State somewhere, and is in receipt of a good income. Lizaveta is also supporting a poor relative.

Tomsky has been promoted to the rank of captain, and has become the husband of the Princess Pauline.

AN AMATEUR PEASANT GIRL

In one of our most distant governments was situated the domain of Ivan Petrovitch Berestoff. In his youth he had served in the Guards, but having quitted the service at the beginning of the year 1797, he repaired to his estate, and since that time he had not stirred away from it. He had married a poor but noble lady, who died in child-bed at a time when he was absent from home on a visit to one of the outlying fields of his domain. He soon found consolation in domestic occupations. He built a house on a plan of his own, established a cloth manufactory, made good use of his revenues, and began to consider himself the most sensible man in the whole country roundabout, and in this he was not contradicted by those of his neighbours who came to visit him with their families and their dogs. On week-days he wore a plush jacket, but on Sundays and holidays he appeared in a surtout of cloth that had been manufactured on his own premises. He himself kept an account of all his expenses, and he never read anything except the "Senate Gazette."

In general he was liked, although he was considered proud. There was only one person who was not on good terms with him, and that was Gregory Ivanovitch Mouromsky, his nearest neighbour. This latter was a genuine Russian noble of the old stamp. After having squandered in Moscow the greater part of his fortune, and having become a widower about the same time, he retired to his last remaining estate, where he continued to indulge in habits of extravagance, but of a new kind. He laid out an English garden, on which he expended nearly the whole of his remaining revenue. His grooms were dressed like English jockeys, his daughter had an English governess, and his fields were cultivated after the English method.

"But after the foreign manner Russian corn does not bear fruit," and in spite of a considerable reduction in his expenses, the revenues of Gregory Ivanovitch did not increase. He found means, even in the country, of contracting new debts. Nevertheless he was not considered a fool, for he was the first landowner in his government who conceived the idea of placing his estate under the safeguard of a council of tutelage—a proceeding which at that time was considered exceedingly complicated and venturesome. Of all those who censured him, Berestoff showed himself the most severe. Hatred of all innovation was a distinguishing trait in his character. He could not bring himself to speak calmly of the Anglomania of his

190

neighbour, and he constantly found occasion to criticise him. If he showed his possessions to a guest, in reply to the praises bestowed upon him for his economical arrangements, he would say with a sly smile:—

"Ah yes, it is not the same with me as with my neighbour Gregory Ivanovitch. What need have we to ruin ourselves in the English style, when we have enough to do to keep the wolf from the door in the Russian style?"

These, and similar sarcastic remarks, thanks to the zeal of obliging neighbours, did not fail to reach the ears of Gregory Ivanovitch greatly embellished. The Anglomaniac bore criticism as impatiently as our journalists. He became furious, and called his traducer a bear and a countryman.

Such were the relations between the two proprietors, when the son of Berestoff returned home to his father's estate. He had been educated at the University of ——, and was anxious to enter the military service, but to this his father would not give his consent. For the civil service the young man had not the slightest inclination, and as neither felt inclined to yield to the other, the young Alexei lived in; the meantime like a nobleman, and allowed his moustache to grow at all events.[80]

Alexei was indeed a fine young fellow, and it would really have been a pity were his slender figure never to be set off to advantage by a military uniform, and were he to be compelled to spend his youth in bending over the papers of the chancery office, instead of bestriding a gallant steed. The neighbours, observing how he was always first in the chase, and always out of the beaten tracks, unanimously agreed I, that he would never make a useful official. The young ladies gazed after him, and sometimes cast stolen glances at him, but Alexei troubled himself very little about them, and they attributed this insensibility to some secret love affair. Indeed, there passed from hand to hand a copy of the address of one of his letters: "To Akoulina Petrovna Kourotchkin, in Moscow, opposite the Alexeivsky Monastery, in the house of the coppersmith Saveleff, with the request that she will forward this letter to A. N. R."

Those of my readers who have never lived in the country, cannot imagine how charming these provincial young ladies are! Brought up in the pure air, under the shadow of the apple trees of their gardens, they derive their knowledge of the world and of life chiefly from books. Solitude, freedom, and reading develop very early within them sentiments and passions unknown to our town-

---

[80] It was formerly the custom in Russia for military men only to wear the moustache.

bred beauties. For the young ladies of the country the sound of the post-bell is an event; a journey to the nearest town marks an epoch in their lives, and the visit of a guest leaves behind a long, and sometimes an eternal recollection. Of course everybody is at liberty to laugh at some of their peculiarities, but the jokes of a superficial observer cannot nullify their essential merits, the chief of which is that personality of character, that individualité without which, in Jean Paul's opinion, there can be no human greatness. In the capitals, women receive perhaps a better instruction, but intercourse with the world soon levels the character and makes their souls as uniform as their head-dresses. This is said neither by way of praise nor yet by way of censure, but "nota nostra manet," as one of the old commentators writes.

It can easily be imagined what impression Alexei would produce among the circle of our young ladies. He was the first who appeared before them gloomy and disenchanted, the first who spoke to them of lost happiness and of his blighted youth; in addition to which he wore a mourning ring engraved with a death's head. All this was something quite new in that distant government. The young ladies simply went, out of their minds about him.

But not one of them felt so much interest in him as the daughter of our Anglomaniac Liza, or Betsy, as Gregory Ivanovitch usually called her. As their parents did not visit each other, she had not yet seen Alexei, even when he had become the sole topic of conversation among all the young ladies of the neighbourhood. She was seventeen years of age. Dark eyes illuminated her swarthy and exceedingly pleasant countenance. She was an only child, and consequently she was perfectly spoiled. Her wantonness and continual pranks delighted her father and filled with despair the heart of Miss Jackson, her governess, an affected old maid of forty, who powdered her face and darkened her eyebrows, read through "Pamela"[81] twice a year, for which she received two thousand roubles, and felt almost bored to death in this barbarous Russia of ours.

Liza was waited upon by Nastia, who, although somewhat older, was quite as giddy as her mistress. Liza was very fond of her, revealed to her all her secrets, and planned pranks together with her; in a word, Nastia was a far more important person in the village of Priloutchina, than the trusted confidante in a French tragedy.

"Will you allow me to go out to-day on a visit?" said Nastia one morning, as she was dressing her mistress.

"Very well; but where are you going to?"

---

[81] A novel written by Samuel Richardson, and first published in 1740.

"To Tougilovo, to the Berestoffs. The wife of their cook is going to celebrate her name-day to-day, and she came over yesterday to invite us to dinner."

"That's curious," said Liza: "the masters are at daggers drawn, but the servants fête each other."

"What have the masters to do with us?" replied Nastia. "Besides, I belong to you, and not to your papa. You have not had any quarrel with young Berestoff; let the old ones quarrel and fight, if it gives them any pleasure."

"Try and see Alexei Berestoff, Nastia, and then tell me what he looks like and what sort of a person he is."

Nastia promised to do so, and all day long Liza waited with impatience for her return. In the evening Nastia made her appearance.

"Well, Lizaveta Gregorievna," said she, on entering the room, "I have seen young Berestoff, and I had ample opportunity for taking a good look at him, for we have been together all day."

"How did that happen? Tell me about it, tell me everything about it."

"Very well. We set out, I, Anissia Egorovna, Nenila, Dounka...."

"Yes, yes, I know. And then?"

"With your leave, I will tell you everything in detail. We arrived just in time for dinner. The room was full of people. The Kolbinskys were there, as well as the Zakharevskys, the Khloupinskys, the bailiff's wife and her daughters...."

"Well, and Berestoff?"

"Wait a moment. We sat down to table; the bailiff's wife had the place of honour. I sat next to her ... the daughters pouted and didn't like it, but I didn't care about them...."

"Good heavens, Nastia, how tiresome you are with your never-ending details!"

"How impatient you are! Well, we rose from the table we had been sitting down for three hours, and the dinner was excellent: pastry, blanc-manges, blue, red and striped.... Well, we left the table and went into the garden to have a game at catching one another, and it was then that the young lord made his appearance."

"Well, and is it true that he is so very handsome?"

"Exceedingly handsome: tall, well-built, and with red cheeks...."

"Really? And I was under the impression that he was fair. Well, and how did he seem to you? Sad, thoughtful?"

"Nothing of the kind! I have never in my life seen such a frolicsome person. He wanted to join in the game with us."

"Join in the game with you? Impossible!"

193

"Not all impossible. And what else do you think he wanted to do? To kiss us all round!"

"With your permission, Nastia, you are talking nonsense."

"With your permission, I am not talking nonsense. I had the greatest trouble in the world to get away from him, He spent the whole day along with us."

"But they say that he is in love, and hasn't eyes for anybody."

"I don't know anything about that, but I know that he looked at me a good deal, and so he did at Tania, the bailiff's daughter, and at Pasha[82] Kolbinsky also. But it cannot be said that he offended anybody—he is so very agreeable."

"That is extraordinary! And what do they say about him in the house?"

"They say that he is an excellent master—so kind, so cheerful. They have only one fault to find with him: he is too fond of running after the young girls. But for my part, I don't think that is a very great fault: he will grow steady with age."

"How I should like to see him!" said Liza, with a sigh.

"What is there to hinder you from doing so? Tougilovo is not far from us—only about three versts. Go and take a walk in that direction, or a ride on horseback, and you will assuredly meet him. He goes out early every morning with his gun."

"No, no, that would not do. He might think that I was running after him. Besides, our fathers are not on good terms, so that I cannot make his acquaintance.... Ah! Nastia, do you know what I'll do? I will dress myself up as a peasant girl!"

"Exactly! Put on a coarse chemise and a sarafan, and then go boldly to Tougilovo; I will answer for it that Berestoff will not pass by without taking notice of you."

"And I know how to imitate the style of speech of the peasants about here. Ah, Nastia! my dear Nastia! what an excellent idea!"

And Liza went to bed, firmly resolved on putting her plan into execution.

The next morning she began to prepare for the accomplishment of her scheme. She sent to the bazaar and bought some coarse linen, some blue nankeen and some copper buttons, and with the help of Nastia she cut out for herself a chemise and sarafan. She then set all the female servants to work to do the necessary sewing, so that by the evening everything was ready. Liza tried on the new costume, and as she stood before the mirror, she confessed to herself that she had never looked so charming. Then she practised her part. As she walked she made a low bow, and then tossed her head several times,

---

[82] Diminutive of Praskovia.

after the manner of a china cat, spoke in the peasants' dialect, smiled behind her sleeve, and did everything to Nastia's complete satisfaction. One thing only proved irksome to her: she tried to walk barefooted across the courtyard, but the turf pricked her tender feet, and she found the stones and gravel unbearable. Nastia immediately came to her assistance. She took the measurement of Liza's foot, ran to the fields to find Trophim the shepherd, and ordered him to make a pair of bast shoes of the same measurement.

The next morning, almost before it was dawn, Liza was already awake. Everybody in the house was still asleep. Nastia went to the gate to wait for the shepherd. The sound of a horn was heard, and the village flock defiled past the manor-house. Trophim, on passing by Nastia, gave her a small pair of coloured bast shoes, and received from her a half-rouble in exchange. Liza quietly dressed herself in the peasant's costume, whispered her instructions to Nastia with reference to Miss Jackson, descended the back staircase and made her way through the garden into the field beyond.

The eastern sky was all aglow, and the golden lines of clouds seemed to be awaiting the sun, like courtiers await their monarch. The bright sky, the freshness of the morning, the dew, the light breeze, and the singing of the birds filled the heart of Liza with childish joy. The fear of meeting some acquaintance seemed to give her wings, for she flew rather than walked. But as she approached the wood which formed the boundary of her father's estate, she slackened her pace. Here she resolved to wait for Alexei.

Her heart beat violently, she knew not why; but is not the fear which accompanies our youthful escapades that which constitutes their greatest charm? Liza advanced into the depth of the wood. The deep murmur of the waving branches seemed to welcome the young girl. Her gaiety vanished. Little by little she abandoned herself to sweet reveries. She thought—but who cap say exactly what a young lady of seventeen thinks of, alone in a wood, at six o'clock of a spring morning? And so she walked musingly along the pathway, which was shaded on both sides by tall trees, when suddenly a magnificent hunting dog came barking and bounding towards her. Liza became alarmed and cried out. But at the same moment a voice called out: "Tout beau, Sbogar, ici!"... and a young hunter emerged from behind a clump of bushes.

"Don't be afraid, my dear," said he to Liza: "my dog does not bite."

Liza had already recovered from her alarm, and she immediately took advantage of her opportunity.

"But, sir," said she, assuming a half-frightened, half-bashful

195

expression, "I am so afraid; he looks so fierce—he might fly at me again."

Alexei—for the reader has already recognized him—gazed fixedly at the young peasant-girl.

"I will accompany you if you are afraid," said he to her: "will you allow me to walk along with you?"

"Who is to hinder you?" replied Liza. "Wills are free, and the road is open to everybody."

"Where do you come from?"

"From Priloutchina; I am the daughter of Vassili the blacksmith, and I am going to gather mushrooms." (Liza carried a basket on her arm.) "And you, sir? From Tougilovo, I have no doubt."

"Exactly so," replied Alexei: "I am the young master's valet-de-chambre."

Alexei wanted to put himself on an equality with her, but Liza looked at him and began to smile.

"That is a fib," said she: "I am not such a fool as you may think. I see very well that you are the young master himself."

"Why do you think so?"

"I think so for a great many reasons."

"But——"

"As if it were not possible to distinguish the master from the servant! You are not dressed like a servant, you do not speak like one, and you address your dog in a different way to us."

Liza began to please Alexei more and more. As he was not accustomed to standing upon ceremony with peasant girls, he wanted to embrace her; but Liza drew back from him, and suddenly assumed such a cold and severe look, that Alexei, although much amused, did not venture to renew the attempt.

"If you wish that we should remain good friends," said she with dignity, "be good enough not to forget yourself."

"Who taught you such wisdom?" asked Alexei, bursting into a laugh. "Can it be my friend Nastenka,[83] the chambermaid to your young mistress? See by what paths enlightenment becomes diffused!"

Liza felt that she had stepped out of her rôle, and she immediately recovered herself.

"Do you think," said she, "that I have never been to the manor-house? Don't alarm yourself; I have seen and heard a great many things.... But," continued she, "if I talk to you, I shall not gather my mushrooms. Go your way, sir, and I will go mine. Pray excuse me."

---

[83] Diminutive of Nastia.

And she was about to move off, but Alexei seized hold of her hand.

"What is your name, my dear?"

"Akoulina," replied Liza, endeavouring to disengage her fingers from his grasp: "but let me go, sir; it is time for me to return home."

"Well, my friend Akoulina, I will certainly pay a visit to your father, Vassili the blacksmith."

"What do you say?" replied Liza quickly: "for Heaven's sake, don't think of doing such a thing! If it were known at home that I had been talking to a gentleman alone in the wood, I should fare very badly,—my father, Vassili the blacksmith, would beat me to death."

"But I really must see you again."

"Well, then, I will come here again some time to gather mushrooms."

"When?"

"Well, to-morrow, if you wish it."

"My dear Akoulina, I would kiss you, but I dare not.... To-morrow, then, at the same time, isn't that so?"

"Yes, yes!"

"And you will not deceive me?"

"I will not deceive you."

"Swear it."

"Well, then, I swear by Holy Friday that I will come."

The young people separated. Liza emerged from the wood, crossed the field, stole into the garden and hastened to the place where Nastia awaited her. There she changed her costume, replying absently to the questions of her impatient confidante, and then she repaired to the parlour. The cloth was laid, the breakfast was ready, and Miss Jackson, already powdered and laced up, so that she looked like a wine-glass, was cutting thin slices of bread and butter.

Her father praised her for her early walk.

"There is nothing so healthy," said he, "as getting up at daybreak."

Then he cited several instances of human longevity, which he had derived from the English journals, and observed that all persons who had lived to be upwards of a hundred, abstained from brandy and rose at daybreak, winter and summer.

Liza did not listen to him. In her thoughts she was going over all the circumstances of the meeting of that morning, all the conversation of Akoulina with the young hunter, and her conscience began to torment her. In vain did she try to persuade herself that their conversation had not gone beyond the bounds of propriety, and that the frolic would be followed by no serious consequences—

her conscience spoke louder than her reason. The promise given for the following day troubled her more than anything else, and she almost felt resolved not to keep her solemn oath. But then, might not Alexei, after waiting for her in vain, make his way to the village and search out the daughter of Vassili the blacksmith, the veritable Akoulina—a fat, pockmarked peasant girl—and so discover the prank she had played upon him? This thought frightened Liza, and she resolved to repair again to the little wood the next morning in the same disguise as at first.

On his side, Alexei was in an ecstasy of delight. All day long he thought of his new acquaintance; and in his dreams at night the form of the dark-skinned beauty appeared before him. The morning had scarcely begun to dawn, when he was already dressed. Without giving himself time to load his gun, he set out for the fields with his faithful Sbogar, and hastened to the place of the promised rendezvous. A half hour of intolerable waiting passed by; at last he caught a glimpse of a blue sarafan between the bushes, and he rushed forward to meet his charming Akoulina. She smiled at the ecstatic nature of his thanks, but Alexei immediately observed upon her face traces of sadness and uneasiness. He wished to know the cause. Liza confessed to him that her act seemed to her very frivolous, that she repented of it, that this time she did not wish to break her promised word, but that this meeting would be the last, and she therefore entreated him to break off an acquaintanceship which could not lead to any good.

All this, of course, was expressed in the language of a peasant; but such thoughts and sentiments, so unusual in a simple girl of the lower class, struck Alexei with astonishment. He employed all his eloquence to divert Akoulina from her purpose; he assured her that his intentions were honourable, promised her that he would never give her cause to repent, that he would obey her in everything, and earnestly entreated her not to deprive him of the joy of seeing her alone, if only once a day, or even only twice a week. He spoke the language of true passion, and at that moment he was really in love. Liza listened to him in silence.

"Give me your word," said she at last, "that you will never come to the village in search of me, and that you will never seek a meeting with me except those that I shall appoint myself."

Alexei swore by Holy Friday, but she stopped him with a smile.

"I do not want you to swear," said she; "your mere word is sufficient."

After that they began to converse together in a friendly manner, strolling about the wood, until Liza said to him:

"It is time for me to return home."

198

They separated, and when Alexei was left alone, he could not understand how, in two interviews, a simple peasant girl had succeeded in acquiring such influence over him. His relations with Akoulina had for him all the charm of novelty, and although the injunctions of the strange young girl appeared to him to be very severe, the thought of breaking his word never once entered his mind. The fact was that Alexei, in spite of his fatal ring, his mysterious correspondence and his gloomy disenchantment, was a good and impulsive young fellow, with a pure heart capable of enjoying the pleasures of innocence.

Were I to listen to my own wishes only, I would here enter into a minute description of the interviews of the young people, of their growing passion for each other, their confidences, occupations and conversations; but I know that the greater part of my readers would not share my satisfaction. Such details are usually considered tedious and uninteresting, and therefore I will omit them, merely observing, that before two months had elapsed, Alexei was already hopelessly in love, and Liza equally so, though less demonstrative in revealing the fact. Both were happy in the present and troubled themselves little about the future.

The thought of indissoluble ties frequently passed through their minds, but never had they spoken to each other about the matter. The reason was plain: Alexei, however much attached he might be to his lovely Akoulina, could not forget the distance that separated him from the poor peasant girl; while Liza, knowing the hatred that existed between their parents, did not dare to hope for a mutual reconciliation. Moreover, her self-love was stimulated in secret by the obscure and romantic hope of seeing at last the proprietor of Tougilovo at the feet of the blacksmith's daughter of Priloutchina. All at once an important event occurred which threatened to interrupt their mutual relations.

One bright cold morning—such a morning as is very common during our Russian autumn—Ivan Petrovitch Berestoff went out for a ride on horseback, taking with him three pairs of hunting dogs, a gamekeeper and several stable-boys with clappers. At the same time, Gregory Ivanovitch Mouromsky, seduced by the beautiful weather, ordered his bob-tailed mare to be saddled, and started out to visit his domains cultivated in the English style. On approaching the wood, he perceived his neighbour, sitting proudly on his horse, in his cloak lined with fox-skin, waiting for a hare which his followers, with loud cries and the rattling of their clappers, had started out of a thicket. If Gregory Ivanovitch had foreseen this meeting, he would certainly have proceeded in another direction, but he came upon Berestoff so unexpectedly, that he suddenly found himself no farther than the distance of a pistol-shot away from him. There was no help for it: Mouromsky, like a civilized European, rode forward towards his adversary and politely saluted him. Berestoff returned the salute with the characteristic grace of a chained bear, who salutes the public in obedience to the order of his master.

At that moment the hare darted out of the wood and started off across the field. Berestoff and the gamekeeper raised a loud shout, let the dogs loose, and then galloped off in pursuit. Mouromsky's horse, not being accustomed to hunting, took fright and bolted. Mouromsky, who prided himself on being a good horseman, gave it full rein, and inwardly rejoiced at the incident which delivered him from a disagreeable companion. But the horse, reaching a ravine which it had not previously noticed, suddenly sprang to one side, and Mouromsky was thrown from the saddle. Striking the frozen ground with considerable force, he lay there cursing his bob-tailed mare, which, as if recovering from its fright, had suddenly come to a standstill as soon as it felt that it was without a rider.

Ivan Petrovitch hastened towards him and inquired if he had injured himself. In the meantime the gamekeeper had secured the guilty horse, which he now led forward by the bridle. He helped Mouromsky into the saddle, and Berestoff invited him to his house. Mouromsky could not refuse the invitation, for he felt indebted to him; and so Berestoff returned home, covered with glory for having hunted down a hare and for bringing with him his adversary wounded and almost a prisoner of war.

The two neighbours took breakfast together and conversed with each other in a very friendly manner. Mouromsky requested Berestoff to lend him a droshky, for he was obliged to confess that, owing to his bruises, he was not in a condition to return home on horseback. Berestoff conducted him to the steps, and Mouromsky did not take leave of him until he had obtained a promise from him that he would come the next day in company with Alexei Ivanovitch, and dine in a friendly way at Priloutchina. In this way was a deeply-rooted enmity of long standing apparently brought to an end by the skittishness of a bob-tailed mare.

Liza ran forward to meet Gregory Ivanovitch.

"What does this mean, papa?" said she with astonishment. "Why are you walking lame? Where is your horse? Whose is this droshky?"

"You will never guess, my dear," replied Gregory Ivanovitch; and then he related to her everything that had happened.

Liza could not believe her ears. Without giving her time to collect herself, Gregory Ivstpovitch then went on to inform her that the two Berestoffs—father and son—would dine with them on the following day.

"What do you say?" she exclaimed, turning pale. "The Berestoffs, father and son, will dine with us to-morrow! No, papa, you can do as you please, but I shall not show myself."

"Have you taken leave of your senses?" replied her father. "Since when have you been so bashful? Or do you cherish an hereditary hatred towards him like a heroine of romance? Enough, do not act the fool."

"No, papa, not for anything in the world, not for any treasure would I appear before the Berestoffs."

Gregory Ivanovitch shrugged his shoulders, and did not dispute with her any further, for he knew that by contradiction he would obtain nothing from her. He therefore went to rest himself after his remarkable ride.

Lizaveta Gregorievna repaired to her room and summoned Nastia. They both conversed together for a long time about the impending visit. What would Alexei think if, in the well-bred young lady, he recognized his Akoulina? What opinion would he have of her conduct, of her manners, of her good sense? On the other hand, Liza wished very much to see what impression would be produced upon him by a meeting so unexpected.... Suddenly an idea flashed through her mind. She communicated it to Nastia; both felt delighted with it, and they resolved to carry it into effect.

The next day at breakfast, Gregory Ivanovitch asked his daughter if she still intended to avoid the Berestoffs.

"Papa," replied Liza, "I will receive them if you wish it, but on one condition, and that is, that however I may appear before them, or whatever I may do, you will not be angry with me, or show the least sign of astonishment or displeasure."

"Some new freak!" said Gregory Ivanovitch, laughing. "Very well, very well, I agree; do what you like, my dark-eyed romp."

With these words he kissed her on the forehead, and Liza ran off to put her plan into execution.

At two o'clock precisely, a Russian calèche drawn by six horses, entered the courtyard and rounded the lawn. The elder Berestoff mounted the steps with the assistance of two lackeys in the Mouromsky livery. His son came after him on horseback, and both entered together into the dining-room, where the table was already laid. Mouromsky received his neighbours in the most gracious manner, proposed to them to inspect his garden and park before dinner, and conducted them along paths carefully kept and gravelled. The elder Berestoff inwardly deplored the time and labour wasted in such useless fancies, but he held his tongue out of politeness. His son shared neither the disapprobation of the economical landowner, nor the enthusiasm of the vain-glorious Anglomaniac, but waited with impatience for the appearance of his host's daughter, of whom he had heard a great deal; and although his heart, as we know, was already engaged, youthful beauty always had a claim upon his imagination.

Returning to the parlour, they all three sat down; and while the old men recalled their young days, and related anecdotes of their respective careers, Alexei considered in his mind what rôle he should play in the presence of Liza. He came to the conclusion that an air of cold indifference would be the most becoming under the circumstances, and he prepared to act accordingly. The door opened; he turned his head with such indifference, with such haughty carelessness, that the heart of the most inveterate coquette would inevitably have shuddered. Unfortunately, instead of Liza, it was old Miss Jackson, who, painted and bedecked, entered the room with downcast eyes and with a low bow, so that Alexei's dignified military salute was lost upon her. He had not succeeded in recovering from his confusion, when the door opened again, and this time it was Liza herself who entered.

All rose; her father was just beginning to introduce his guests, when suddenly he stopped short and bit his lips.... Liza, his dark-complexioned Liza, was painted white up to the ears, and was more bedizened than even Miss Jackson herself; false curls, much lighter than her own hair, covered her head like the perruque of Louis the Fourteenth; her sleeves à l'imbécile stood out like the hooped skirts of Madame de Pompadour; her figure was pinched in like the letter X, and all her mother's jewels, which had not yet found their way to the pawnbroker's, shone upon her fingers, her neck and in her ears.

Alexei could not possibly recognize his Akoulina in the grotesque and brilliant young lady. His father kissed her hand, and he followed his example, though much against his will; when he touched her little white fingers, it seemed to him that they trembled. In the meantime he succeeded in catching a glimpse of her little foot, intentionally advanced and set off to advantage by the most coquettish shoe imaginable. This reconciled him somewhat to the rest of her toilette. As for the paint and powder, it must be confessed that, in the simplicity of his heart, he had not noticed them at the first glance, and afterwards had no suspicion of them. Gregory Ivanovitch remembered his promise, and endeavoured not to show any astonishment; but his daughter's freak seemed to him so amusing, that he could scarcely contain himself. But the person who felt no inclination to laugh was the affected English governess. She had a shrewd suspicion that the paint and powder had been extracted from her chest of drawers, and the deep flush of anger was distinctly visible beneath the artificial whiteness of her face. She darted angry glances at the young madcap, who, reserving her explanations for another time, pretended that she did not notice them.

They sat down to table. Alexei continued to play his rôle of assumed indifference and absence of mind. Liza put on an air of affectation, spoke through her teeth, and only in French. Her father kept constantly looking at her, not understanding her aim, but finding it all exceedingly amusing. The English governess fumed with rage and said not a word. Ivan Petrovitch alone seemed at home: he ate, like two, drank heavily, laughed at his own jokes, and grew more talkative, and hilarious at every moment.

At last they all rose up from the table; the guests took their departure, and Gregory Ivanovitch gave free vent to his laughter and to his interrogations.

"What put the idea into your head of acting the fool like that with them?" he said to Liza. "But do you know what? The paint suits you admirably. I do not wish to fathom the mysteries of a lady's toilette, but if I were in your place, I would very soon begin to paint; not too much, of course, but just a little."

Liza was enchanted with the success of her stratagem. She embraced her father, promised him that she would consider his advice, and then hastened to conciliate the indignant Miss Jackson, who, with great reluctance consented to open the door and listen to her explanations. Liza was ashamed to appear before strangers with her dark complexion; she had not dared to ask she felt sure that dear, good Miss Jackson would pardon her, etc., etc. Miss Jackson, feeling convinced that Liza had not wished to make her a laughing-stock by imitating her, calmed down, kissed her, and as a token of reconciliation, made her a present of a small pot of English paint, which Liza accepted with every appearance of sincere gratitude.

The reader will readily imagine that Liza lost no time in repairing to the rendezvous in the little wood the next morning.

"You were at our master's yesterday," she said at once to Alexei: "what do you think of our young mistress?"

Alexei replied that he had not observed her.

"That's a pity!" replied Liza.

"Why so?" asked Alexei.

"Because I wanted to ask you if it is true what they say——"

"What do they say?"

"Is it true, as they say, that I am very much like her?"

"What nonsense! She is a perfect monstrosity compared with you."

"Oh, sir, it is very wrong of you to speak like that. Our young mistress is so fair and so stylish! How could I be compared wither!"

Alexei vowed to her that she was more beautiful than all the fair young ladies in creation, and in order to pacify her completely, he began to describe her mistress in such comical terms, that Liza laughed heartily.

"But," said she with a sigh, "even though our young mistress may be ridiculous, I am but a poor ignorant thing in comparison with her."

"Oh!" said Alexei; "is that anything to break your heart about? If you wish it, I will soon teach you to read and write."

"Yes, indeed," said Liza, "why should I not try?"

"Very well, my dear; we will commence at once."

They sat down. Alexei drew from his pocket a pencil and note-book, and Akoulina learnt the alphabet with astonishing rapidity. Alexei could not sufficiently admire her intelligence. The following morning she wished to try to write. At first the pencil refused to obey her, but after a few minutes she was able to trace the letters with tolerable accuracy.

"It is really wonderful!" said Alexei. "Our method certainly produces quicker results than the Lancaster system."[84]

And indeed, at the third lesson Akoulina began to spell through "Nathalie the Boyard's Daughter," interrupting her reading by observations which really filled Alexei with astonishment, and she filled a whole sheet of paper with aphorisms drawn from the same story.

A week went by, and a correspondence was established between them. Their letter-box was the hollow of an old oak-tree, and Nastia acted as their messenger. Thither Alexei carried his letters written in a bold round hand, and there he found on plain blue paper the delicately-traced strokes of his beloved. Akoulina perceptibly began to acquire an elegant style of expression, and her mental faculties commenced to develop themselves with astonishing rapidity.

Meanwhile, the recently-formed acquaintance between Ivan Petrovitch Berestoff and Gregory Ivanovitch Mouromsky soon became transformed into a sincere friendship, under the following circumstances. Mouromsky frequently reflected that, on the death of Ivan Petrovitch, all his possessions would pass into the hands of Alexei Ivanovitch, in which case the latter would be one of the wealthiest landed proprietors in the government, and there would be nothing to hinder him from marrying Liza. The elder Berestoff,

---

[84] An allusion to the system of education introduced into England by Joseph Lancaster at the commencement of the present century.

on his side, although recognizing in his neighbour a certain extravagance (or, as he termed it, English folly), was perfectly ready to admit that he possessed many excellent qualities, as for example, his rare tact. Gregory Ivanovitch was closely related to Count Pronsky, a man of distinction and of great influence. The Count could be of great service to Alexei, and Mouromsky (so thought Ivan Petrovitch) would doubtless rejoice to see his daughter marry so advantageously. By dint of constantly dwelling upon this idea, the two old men came at last to communicate their thoughts to one another. They embraced each other, both promised to do their best to arrange the matter, and they immediately set to work, each on his own side. Mouromsky foresaw that he would have some difficulty in persuading his Betsy to become more intimately acquainted with Alexei, whom she had not seen since the memorable dinner. It seemed to him that they had not been particularly well pleased with each other; at least Alexei had not paid any further visits to Priloutchina, and Liza had retired to her room every time that Ivan Petrovitch had honoured them with a visit.

"But," thought Gregory Ivanovitch, "if Alexei came to see us every day, Betsy could not help falling in love with him. That is the natural order of things. Time will settle everything."

Ivan Petrovitch was no less uneasy about the success of his designs. That same evening he summoned his son into his cabinet, lit his pipe, and, after a long pause, said:

"Well, Alesha,[85] what do you think about doing? You have not said anything for a long time about the military service. Or has the Hussar uniform lost its charm for you?"

"No, father," replied Alexei respectfully; "but I see that you do not like the idea of my entering the Hussars, and it is my duty to obey you."

"Good," replied Ivan Petrovitch; "I see that you are an obedient son; that is very consoling to me.... On my side, I do not wish to compel you; I do not want to force you to enter ... at once ... into the civil service, but, in the meanwhile, I intend you to get married."

"To whom, father?" asked Alexei in astonishment.

"To Lizaveta Gregorievna Mouromsky," replied Ivan Petrovitch. "She is a charming bride, is she not?"

"Father, I have not thought of marriage yet."

"You have not thought of it, and therefore I have thought of it for you."

"As you please, but I do not care for Liza Mouromsky in the least."

---

[85] Diminutive of Alexei (Alexis).

"You will get to like her afterwards. Love comes with time."

"I do not feel capable of making her happy."

"Do not distress yourself about making her happy. What? Is this how you respect your father's wish? Very well!"

"As you please. I do not wish to marry, and I will not marry."

"You will marry, or I will curse you; and as for my possessions, as true as God is holy, I will sell them and squander the money, and not leave you a farthing. I will give you three days to think about the matter; and in the meantime, don't show yourself in my sight."

Alexei knew that when his father once took an idea into his head, a nail even would not drive it out, as Taras Skotinin[86] says in the comedy. But Alexei took after his father, and was just as headstrong as he was. He went to his room and began to reflect upon the limits of paternal authority; Then his thoughts reverted to Lizaveta Gregorievna, to his father's solemn vow to make him a beggar, and last of all to Akoulina. For the first time he saw clearly that he was passionately in love with her; the romantic idea of marrying a peasant girl and of living by the labour of their hands came into his head, and the more he thought of such a decisive step, the more reasonable did it seem to him. For some time the interviews in the wood had ceased on account of the rainy weather. He wrote to Akoulina a letter in his most legible handwriting, informing her of the misfortune that threatened them, and offering her his hand. He took the letter at once to the post-office in the wood, and then went to bed, well satisfied with himself.

The next day Alexei, still firm in his resolution, rode over early in the morning to visit Mouromsky, in order to explain matters frankly to him. He hoped to excite his generosity and win him over to his side.

"Is Gregory Ivanovitch at home?" asked he, stopping his horse in front of the steps of the Priloutchina mansion.

"No," replied the servant; "Gregory Ivanovitch rode out early this morning, and has not yet returned."

"How annoying!" thought Alexei.... "Is Lizaveta Gregorievna at home, then?" he asked.

"Yes, sir."

Alexei sprang from his horse, gave the reins to the lackey, and entered without being announced.

"Everything is now going to be decided," thought he, directing his steps towards the parlour: "I will explain everything to Lizaveta herself."

He entered ... and then stood still as if petrified! Liza ... no ...

---

[86] A character in "Nedorosl," a comedy by Denis Von Vizin.

Akoulina, dear, dark-haired Akoulina, no longer in a sarafan, but in a white morning robe, was sitting in front of the window, reading his letter; she was so occupied that she had not heard him enter.

Alexei could not restrain an exclamation of joy. Liza started, raised her head, uttered a cry, and wished to fly from the room. But he threw himself before her and held her back.

"Akoulina! Akoulina!"

Liza endeavoured to liberate herself from his grasp.

"Mais laissez-moi donc, Monsieur! ... Mais êtes-vous fou?" she said, twisting herself round.

"Akoulina! my dear Akoulina!" he repeated, kissing her hand.

Miss Jackson, a witness of this scene, knew not what to think of it. At that moment the door opened, and Gregory Ivanovitch entered the room.

"Ah! ah!" said Mouromsky; "but it seems that you have already arranged matters between you."

The reader will spare me the unnecessary obligation of describing the dénouement.

THE SHOT

CHAPTER I

We were stationed in the little town of N——. The life of an officer in the army is well known. In the morning, drill and the riding-school; dinner with the Colonel or at a Jewish restaurant; in the evening, punch and cards. In N—— there was not one open house, not a single marriageable girl. We used to meet in each other's rooms, where, except our uniforms, we never saw anything.

One civilian only was admitted into our society. He was about thirty-five years of age, and therefore we looked upon him as an old fellow. His experience gave him great advantage over us, and his habitual taciturnity, stern disposition and caustic tongue produced a deep impression upon our young minds. Some mystery surrounded his existence; he had the appearance of a Russian, although his name was a foreign one. He had formerly served in the Hussars, and with distinction. Nobody knew the cause that had induced him to retire from the service and settle in a wretched little village, where he lived poorly and, at the same time, extravagantly. He always went on foot, and constantly wore a shabby black overcoat, but the officers of our regiment were ever welcome at his table. His dinners, it is true, never consisted of more than two or three dishes, prepared by a retired soldier, but the champagne flowed like water. Nobody knew what his circumstances were, or what his income was, and nobody dared to question him about them. He had a collection of books, consisting chiefly of works on military matters and a few novels. He willingly lent them to us to read, and never asked for them back; on the other hand, he never returned to the owner the books that were lent to him. His principal amusement was shooting with a pistol. The walls off his room were riddled with bullets, and were as full of holes as a honey-comb. A rich collection of pistols was the only luxury in the humble cottage where he lived. The skill which he had acquired with his favourite weapon was simply incredible; and if he had offered to shoot a pear off somebody's forage-cap, not a man in our regiment would have hesitated to place the object upon his head.

Our conversation often turned upon duels. Silvio—so I will call him—never joined in it. When asked if he had ever fought, he drily replied that he had; but he entered into no particulars, and it was evident that such questions were not to his liking. We came to the conclusion that he had upon his conscience the memory of some unhappy victim of his terrible skill. Moreover, it never entered into the head of any of us to suspect him of anything like cowardice. There are persons whose mere look is sufficient to repel such a suspicion. But an unexpected incident-occurred which astounded us all.

One day, about ten of our officers dined with Silvio. They drank as usual, that is to say, a great deal. After dinner we asked our host to hold the bank for a game at faro. For a long time he refused, for he hardly ever played, but at last he ordered cards to be brought, placed half a hundred ducats upon the table, and sat down to deal. We took our places round him, and the play began. It was Silvio's custom to preserve a complete silence when playing. He never disputed, and never entered into explanations. If the punter made a mistake in calculating, he immediately paid him the difference or noted down the surplus. We were acquainted with this habit of his, and we always allowed him to have his own way; but among us on this occasion was an officer who had only recently been transferred to our regiment. During the course of the game, this officer absently scored one point too many. Silvio took the chalk and noted down the correct account according to his usual custom. The officer, thinking that he had made a mistake, began to enter into explanations. Silvio continued dealing in silence. The officer, losing patience, took the brush and rubbed out what he considered was wrong. Silvio took the chalk and corrected the score again. The officer, heated with wine, play, and the laughter of his comrades, considered himself grossly insulted, and in his rage he seized a brass candle-stick from the table, and hurled it at Silvio, who barely succeeded in avoiding the missile. We were filled with consternation. Silvio rose, white with rage, and with gleaming eyes, said:

"My dear sir, have the goodness to withdraw, and thank God that this has happened in my house."

None of us entertained the slightest doubt as to what the result would be, and we already looked upon our new comrade as a dead man. The officer withdrew, saying that he was ready to answer for his offence in whatever way the banker liked. The play went on for a few minutes longer, but feeling that our host was no longer interested in the game, we withdrew one after the other, and repaired to our respective quarters, after having exchanged a few words upon the probability of there soon being a vacancy in the regiment.

The next day, at the riding-school, we were already asking each other if the poor lieutenant was still alive, when he himself appeared among us. We put the same question to him, and he replied that he had not yet heard from Silvio. This astonished us. We went to Silvio's house and found him in—the courtyard shooting bullet after bullet into an ace pasted upon the gate. He received us as usual, but did not utter a word about the event of the previous evening. Three days passed, and the lieutenant was still alive. We asked each other in astonishment: "Can it be possible that Silvio is not going to fight?"

Silvio did not fight. He was satisfied with a very lame explanation, and became reconciled to his assailant.

This lowered him very much in the opinion of all our young fellows. Want of courage is the last thing to be pardoned by young men, who usually look upon bravery as the chief of all human virtues, and the excuse for every possible fault. But, by degrees, everything became forgotten, and Silvio regained his former influence.

I alone could not approach him on the old footing. Being endowed by nature with a romantic imagination, I had become attached more than all the others to the man whose life was an enigma, and who seemed to me the hero of some mysterious drama. He was fond of me; at least, with me alone did he drop his customary sarcastic tone, and converse on different subjects in a simple and unusually agreeable manner. But after this unlucky evening, the thought that his honour had been tarnished, and that the stain had been allowed to remain upon it in accordance with his own wish, was ever present in my mind, and prevented me treating him as before. I was ashamed to look at him. Silvio was too intelligent and experienced not to observe this and guess the cause of it. This seemed to vex him; at least I observed once or twice a desire on his part to enter into an explanation with me, but I avoided such opportunities, and Silvio gave up the attempt. From that time forward I saw him only in the presence of my comrades, and our confidential conversations came to an end.

The inhabitants of the capital, with minds occupied by so many matters of business and pleasure, have no idea of the many sensations so familiar to the inhabitants of villages and small towns, as, for instance, the awaiting the arrival of the post. On Tuesdays and Fridays our regimental bureau used to be filled with officers: some expecting money, some letters, and others newspapers. The packets were usually opened on the spot, items of news were communicated from one to another, and the bureau used to present a very animated picture. Silvio used to have his letters addressed to our regiment, and he was generally there to receive them.

One day he received a letter, the seal of which he broke with a look of great impatience. As he read the contents, his eyes sparkled.

The officers, each occupied with his own letters, did not observe anything.

"Gentlemen," said Silvio, "circumstances demand my immediate departure; I leave to-night. I hope that you will not refuse to dine with me for the last time. I shall expect you, too," he added, turning towards me. "I shall expect you without fail."

With these words he hastily departed, and we, after agreeing to meet at Silvio's, dispersed to our various quarters.

I arrived at Silvio's house at the appointed time, and found nearly the whole regiment there. All his things were already packed; nothing remained but the bare, bullet-riddled walls. We sat down to table. Our host was in an excellent humour, and his gaiety was quickly communicated to the rest. Corks popped every moment, glasses foamed incessantly, and, with the utmost warmth, we wished our departing friend a pleasant journey and every happiness. When we rose from the table it was already late in the evening After having wished everybody good-bye, Silvio took me by the hand and detained me just at the moment when I was preparing to depart.

"I want to speak to you," he said in a low voice.

I stopped behind.

The guests had departed, and we two were left alone. Sitting down opposite each other, we silently lit our pipes. Silvio seemed greatly troubled; not a trace remained of his former convulsive gaiety. The intense pallor of his face, his sparkling eyes, and the thick smoke issuing from his mouth, gave him a truly diabolical appearance. Several minutes elapsed, and then Silvio broke the silence.

"Perhaps we shall never see each other again," said he; "before we part, I should like to have an explanation with you. You may have observed that I care very little for the opinion of other people, but I like you, and I feel that it would be painful to me to leave you with a wrong impression upon your mind."

He paused, and began to knock the ashes out of his pipe. I sat gazing silently at the ground.

"You thought it strange," he continued, "that I did not demand satisfaction from that drunken idiot R——. You will admit, however, that having the choice of weapons, his life was in my hands, while my own was in no great danger. I could ascribe my forbearance to generosity alone, but I will not tell a lie. If I could have chastised R—— without the least risk to my own life, I should never have pardoned him."

I looked at Silvio with astonishment. Such a confession completely astounded me. Silvio continued:

211

"Exactly so: I have no right to expose myself to death. Six years ago I received a slap in the face, and my enemy still lives."

My curiosity was greatly excited.

"Did you not fight with him?" I asked. "Circumstances probably separated you."

"I did fight with him," replied Silvio: "and here is a souvenir of our duel."

Silvio rose and took from a cardboard box a red cap with a gold tassel and embroidery (what the French call a bonnet de police); he put in on a bullet had passed through it about an inch above the forehead.

"You know," continued Silvio, "that I served in one of the Hussar regiments. My character is well-known to you: I am accustomed to taking the lead. From my youth this has been my passion. In our time dissoluteness was the fashion, and I was the most outrageous man in the army. We used to boast of our drunkenness: I beat in a drinking bout the famous Bourtsoff,[87] of whom Denis Davidoff[88] has sung. Duels in our regiment were constantly taking place, and in all of them I was either second or principal. My comrades adored me, while the regimental commanders, who were constantly being changed, looked upon me as a necessary evil.

"I was calmly enjoying my reputation, when a young man belonging to a wealthy and distinguished family—I will not mention his name—joined our regiment. Never in my life have, I met with such a fortunate fellow! Imagine to yourself youth, wit, beauty, unbounded gaiety, the most reckless bravery, a famous name, untold wealth—imagine all these, and you can form some idea of the effect that he would be sure to produce among us. My supremacy was shaken. Dazzled by my reputation, he began to seek my friendship, but I received him coldly, and without the least regret he held aloof from me. I took a hatred to him. His success in the regiment and in the society of ladies brought me to the verge of despair. I began to seek a quarrel with him; to my epigrams he replied with epigrams which always seemed to me more spontaneous and more cutting than mine, and which were decidedly more amusing, for he joked while I fumed. At last, at a ball given by a Polish landed proprietor, seeing him the object of the attention of all the ladies, and especially of the mistress of the house, with whom I was upon very good terms, I whispered some grossly insulting remark in his ear. He flamed up and gave me a slap in the face. We

---

[87] A military poet who flourished in the reign of Alexander L I.
[88] A cavalry officer, notorious for his drunken escapades.

grasped our swords; the ladies fainted; we were separated; and that same night we set out to fight.

"The dawn was just breaking. I was standing at the appointed place with my three seconds. With inexplicable impatience I awaited my opponent. The spring sun rose, and it was already growing hot. I saw him coming in the distance. He was walking on foot, accompanied by one second. We advanced to meet him. He approached, holding his cap filled with black cherries. The seconds measured twelve paces for us. I had to fire first, but my agitation was so great, that I could not depend upon the steadiness of my hand; and in order to give myself time to become calm, I ceded to him the first shot. My adversary would not agree to this. It was decided that we should cast lots. The first number fell to him, the constant favourite of fortune. He took aim, and his bullet went through my cap. It was now my turn. His life at last was in my hands; I looked at him eagerly, endeavouring to detect if only the faintest shadow of uneasiness. But he stood in front of my pistol, picking out the ripest cherries from his cap and spitting out the stones, which flew almost as far as my feet. His indifference annoyed me beyond measure. 'What is the use,' thought I, 'of depriving him of life, when he attaches no value whatever to it?' A malicious thought flashed through my mind. I lowered my pistol.

"'You don't seem to be ready for death just at present,' I said to him: 'you wish to have your breakfast; I do not wish to hinder you.'

"'You are not hindering me in the least,' replied he. 'Have the goodness to fire, or just as you please—the shot remains yours; I shall always be ready at your service.'

"I turned to the seconds, informing them that I had no intention of firing that day, and with that the duel came to an end.

"I resigned my commission and retired to this little place. Since then, not a day has passed that I have not thought of revenge. And now my hour has arrived."

Silvio took from his pocket the letter that he had received that morning, and gave it to me to read. Someone (it seemed to be his business agent) wrote to him from Moscow, that a certain person was going to be married to a young and beautiful girl.

"You can guess," said Silvio, "who the certain person is I am going to Moscow. We shall see if he will look death in the face with as much indifference now, when he is on the eve of being married, as he did once with his cherries!"

With these words, Silvio rose, threw his cap upon the floor, and began pacing up and down the room like a tiger in his cage. I had listened to him in silence; strange conflicting feelings agitated me.

The servant entered and announced that the horses were ready.

Silvio grasped my hand tightly, and we embraced each other. He seated himself in his telega, in which lay two trunks, one containing his pistols, the other his effects. We said good-bye once more, and the horses galloped off.

CHAPTER II

Several years passed, and family circumstances compelled me to settle in the poor little village of M——. Occupied with agricultural pursuits, I ceased not to sigh in secret for my former noisy and careless life. The most difficult thing of all was having to accustom myself to passing the spring and winter evenings in perfect solitude. Until the hour for dinner I managed to pass away the time somehow or other, talking with the bailiff, riding about to inspect the work, or going round to look at the new buildings; but as soon as it began to get dark, I positively did not know what to do with myself. The few books that I had found in the cupboards and store-rooms, I already knew by heart. All the stories that my housekeeper Kirilovna could I remember, I had heard over and over again. The songs of the peasant women made me feel depressed. I tried drinking spirits, but it made my head ache; and moreover, I confess I was afraid of becoming a drunkard from mere chagrin, that is to say, the saddest kind of drunkard, of which I had seen many examples in our district.

I had no near neighbours, except two or three topers, whose conversation consisted for the most part of hiccups and sighs. Solitude was preferable to their society. At last I decided to go to bed as early as possible, and to dine as late as possible; in this way I shortened the evening and lengthened out the day, and I found that the plan answered very well.

Four versts from my house was a rich estate belonging to the Countess B——; but nobody lived there except the steward. The Countess had only visited her estate once, in the first year of her married life, and then she had remained there no longer than a month. But in the second spring of my hermitical life, a report was circulated that the Countess, with her husband, was coming to spend the summer on her estate. The report turned out to be true, for they arrived at the beginning of June.

214

The arrival of a rich neighbour is an important event in the lives of country people. The landed proprietors and the people of their household talk about it for two months beforehand, and for three years afterwards. As for me, I must confess that the news of the arrival of a young and beautiful neighbour affected me strongly. I burned with impatience to see her, and the first Sunday after her arrival I set out after dinner for the village of A——, to pay my respects to the Countess and her husband, as their nearest neighbour and most humble servant.

A lackey conducted me into the Count's study, and then went to announce me. The spacious apartment was furnished with every' possible luxury. Around the walls were cases filled with books and surmounted by bronze busts; over the marble mantelpiece was a large mirror; on the floor was a green cloth covered with carpets. Unaccustomed to luxury in my own poor corner, and not having seen the wealth of other people for a long time, I awaited the appearance of the Count with some little trepidation, as a suppliant from the provinces awaits the arrival of the minister. The door opened, and a handsome-looking man, of about thirty-two years of age, entered the room. The Count approached me with a frank and friendly air: I endeavoured to be self-possessed and began to introduce myself, but he anticipated me. We sat down. His conversation, which was easy and agreeable, soon dissipated my awkward bashfulness; and I was already beginning to recover my usual composure, when the Countess suddenly entered, and I became more confused than ever. She was indeed beautiful. The Count presented me. I wished to appear at ease, but the more I tried to assume an air of unconstraint, the more awkward I felt. They, in order to give me time to recover myself and to become accustomed to my new acquaintances, began to talk to each other, treating me as a good neighbour, and without ceremony. Meanwhile, I walked about the room, examining the books and pictures. I am no judge of pictures, but one of them attracted my attention. It represented some view in Switzerland, but it was not the painting that struck me, but the circumstance that the canvas was shot through by two bullets, one planted just above the other.

"A good shot, that!" said I, turning to the Count.

"Yes," replied he, "a very remarkable shot.... Do you shoot well?" he continued.

"Tolerably," replied I, rejoicing that the conversation had turned at last upon a subject that was familiar to me. "At thirty paces I can manage to hit a card without fail,—I mean, of course, with a pistol that I am used to."

"Really?" said the Countess, with a look of the greatest interest. "And you, my dear, could you hit a card at thirty paces?"

"Some day," replied the Count, "we will try. In my time I did not shoot badly, but it is now four years since I touched a pistol."

"Oh!" I observed, "in that case, I don't mind laying a wager that Your Excellency will not hit the card at twenty paces: the pistol demands practice every day. I know that from experience. In our regiment I was reckoned one of the best shots. It once happened that I did not touch a pistol for a whole month, as I had sent mine to be mended; and would you believe it, Your Excellency, the first time I began to shoot again, I missed a bottle four times in succession at twenty paces! Our captain, a witty and amusing fellow, happened to be standing by, and he said to me: 'It is evident, my friend, that your hand will not lift itself against the bottle,' No, Your Excellency, you must not neglect to practise, or your hand will soon lose its cunning. The best shot that I ever met used to shoot at least three times every day before dinner. It was as much his custom to do this, as it was to drink his daily glass of brandy."

The Count and Countess seemed pleased that I had begun to talk.

"And what sort of a shot was he?" asked the Count.

"Well, it was this way with him, Your Excellency: if he saw a fly settle on the wall—you smile, Countess, but, before Heaven, it is the truth. If he saw a fly, he would call out: 'Kouzka, my pistol!' Kouzka would bring him a loaded pistol—bang! and the fly would be crushed against the wall."

"Wonderful!" said the Count. "And what was his name?"

"Silvio, Your Excellency."

"Silvio!" exclaimed the Count, starting up. "Did you know Silvio?"

"How could I help knowing him, Your Excellency: we were intimate friends; he was received in our regiment like a brother officer, but it is now five years since I had any tidings of him. Then Your Excellency also knew him?"

"Oh, yes, I knew him very well. Did he ever tell you of one very strange incident in his life?"

"Does Your Excellency refer to the slap in the face that he received from some blackguard at a ball?"

"Did he tell you the name of this blackguard?"

"No, Your Excellency, he never mentioned his name.... Ah! Your Excellency!" I continued, guessing the truth: "pardon me ... I did not know ... could it really have been you?"

"Yes, I myself," replied the Count, with a look of extraordinary

216

agitation; "and that bullet-pierced picture is a memento of our last meeting."

"Ah, my dear," said the Countess, "for Heaven's sake, do not speak about that; it would be too terrible for me to listen to."

"No," replied the Count: "I will relate everything. He knows how I insulted his friend, and it is only right that he should know how Silvio revenged himself."

The Count pushed a chair towards me, and with the liveliest interest I listened to the following story:

"Five years ago I got married. The first month—the honeymoon—I spent here, in this village. To this house I am indebted for the happiest moments of my life, as well as for one of its most painful recollections.

"One evening we went out together for a ride on horseback. My wife's horse became restive; she grew frightened, gave the reins to me, and returned home on foot. I rode on before. In the courtyard I saw a travelling carriage, and I was told that in my study sat waiting for me a man, who would not give his name, but who merely said that he had business with me. I entered the room and saw in the darkness a man, covered with dust and wearing a beard of several days' growth. He was standing there, near the fireplace. I approached him, trying to remember his features.

"'You do not recognize me, Count?' said he, in a quivering voice.

"'Silvio!' I cried, and I confess that I felt as if my hair had suddenly stood on end.

"'Exactly,' continued he. 'There is a shot due to me, and I have come to discharge my pistol. Are you ready?'

"His pistol protruded from a side pocket. I measured twelve paces and took my stand there in that corner, begging him to fire quickly, before my wife arrived. He hesitated, and asked for a light. Candles were brought in. I closed the doors, gave orders that nobody was to enter, and again begged him to fire. He drew out his pistol and took aim.... I counted the seconds ... I thought of her.... A terrible minute passed! Silvio lowered his hand.

"'I regret,' said he, 'that the pistol is not loaded with cherry-stones ... the bullet is heavy. It seems to me that this is not a duel, but a murder. I am not accustomed to taking aim at unarmed men. Let us begin all over again; we will cast lots as to who shall fire first.'

"My head went round ... I think I raised some objection.... At last we loaded another pistol, and rolled up two pieces of paper. He placed these latter in his cap—the same through which I had once sent a bullet—and again I drew the first number.

"'You are devilish lucky, Count,' said he, with a smile that I shall never forget.

"I don't know what was the matter with me, or how it was that he managed to make me do it ... but I fired and hit that picture."

The Count pointed with his finger to the perforated picture; his face glowed like fire; the Countess was whiter than her own handkerchief; and I could not restrain an exclamation.

"I fired," continued the Count, "and, thank Heaven, missed my aim. Then Silvio ... at that moment he was really terrible.... Silvio raised his hand to take aim at me. Suddenly the door opens, Masha rushes into the room, and with a loud shriek throws herself upon my neck. Her presence restored to me all my courage.

"'My dear,' said I to her, 'don't you see that we are joking? How frightened you are! Go and drink a glass of water and then come back to us; I will introduce you to an old friend and comrade.'

"Masha still doubted.

"'Tell me, is my husband speaking the truth?' said she, turning to the terrible Silvio: 'is it true that you are only joking?'

"'He is always joking, Countess,' replied Silvio: 'once he gave me a slap in the face in a joke; on another occasion he sent a bullet through my cap in a joke; and just now, when he fired at me and missed me, it was all in a joke. And, now I feel inclined for a joke.'

"With these words he raised his pistol to take aim at me—right before her! Masha threw herself at his feet.

"'Rise, Masha; are you not ashamed!' I cried in a rage: 'and you, sir, will you cease to make fun of a poor woman? Will you fire or not?'

"'I will not,' replied Silvio: 'I am satisfied. I have seen your confusion, your alarm. I forced you to fire at me. That is sufficient. You will remember me. I leave you to your conscience.'

"Then he turned to go, but pausing in the doorway, and looking at the picture that my shot had passed through, he fired at it almost without taking aim, and disappeared. My wife had fainted away; the servants did not venture to stop him, the mere look of him filled them with terror. He went out upon the steps, called his coachman, and drove off before I could recover myself."

The Count was silent. In this way I learned the end of the story, whose beginning had once made such a deep impression upon me. The hero of it I never saw again. It is said that Silvio commanded a detachment of Hetairists during the revolt under Alexander Ipsilanti, and that he was killed in the battle of Skoulana.

THE SNOWSTORM

Towards the end of the year 1811, a memorable period for us, the good Gavril Gavrilovitch R—— was living on his domain of Nenaradova. He was celebrated throughout the district for his hospitality and kind-heartedness. The neighbours were constantly visiting him: some to eat and drink; some to play at five copeck "Boston" with his wife, Praskovia Petrovna; and some to look at their daughter, Maria Gavrilovna, a pale, slender girl of seventeen. She was considered a wealthy match, and many desired her for themselves or for their sons.

Maria Gavrilovna had been brought up on French novels, and consequently was in love. The object of her choice was a poor sublieutenant in the army, who was then on leave of absence in his village. It need scarcely be mentioned that the young man returned her passion with equal ardour, and that the parents of his beloved one, observing their mutual inclination, forbade their daughter to think of him, and received him worse than a discharged assessor.

Our lovers corresponded with one another and daily saw each other alone in the little pine wood or near the old chapel. There they exchanged vows of eternal love, lamented their cruel fate, and formed various plans. Corresponding and conversing in this way, they arrived quite naturally at the following conclusion:

If we cannot exist without each other, and the will of hard-hearted parents stands in the way of our happiness, why cannot we do without them?

Needless to mention that this happy idea originated in the mind of the young man, and that it was very congenial to the romantic imagination of Maria Gavrilovna.

The winter came and put a stop to their meetings, but their correspondence became all the more active. Vladimir Nikolaievitch in every letter implored her to give herself up to him, to get married secretly, to hide for some time, and then throw themselves at the feet of their parents, who would, without any doubt, be touched at last by the heroic constancy and unhappiness of the lovers, and would infallibly say to them: "Children, come to our arms!"

Maria Gavrilovna hesitated for a long time, and several plans for a flight were rejected. At last she consented: on the appointed day she was not to take supper, but was to retire to her room under the pretext of a headache. Her maid was in the plot; they were both to go into the garden by the back stairs, and behind the garden they would find ready a sledge, into which they were to get, and then drive straight to the church of Jadrino, a village about five versts from Nenaradova, where Vladimir would be waiting for them.

On the eve of the decisive day, Maria Gavrilovna did not sleep the whole night; she packed and tied up her linen and other articles of apparel, wrote a long letter to a sentimental young lady, a friend of hers, and another to her parents. She took leave of them in the most touching terms, urged the invincible strength of passion as an excuse for the step she was taking, and wound up with the assurance that she should consider it the happiest moment of her life, when she should be allowed to throw herself at the feet of her dear parents.

After having sealed both letters with a Toula seal, upon which were engraved two flaming hearts with a suitable inscription, she threw herself upon her bed just before daybreak, and dozed off: but even then she was constantly being awakened by terrible dreams. First it seemed to her that at the very moment when she seated herself in the sledge, in order to go and get married, her father stopped her, dragged her over the snow with fearful rapidity, and threw her into a dark bottomless abyss, down which she fell headlong with an indescribable sinking of the heart. Then she saw Vladimir lying on the grass, pale and bloodstained. With his dying breath he implored her in a piercing voice to make haste and marry him.... Other fantastic and senseless visions floated before her one after another. At last she arose, paler than usual, and with an unfeigned headache. Her father and mother observed her uneasiness; their tender solicitude and incessant inquiries: "What is the matter with you, Masha? Are you ill, Masha?" cut her to the heart. She tried to reassure them and to appear cheerful, but in vain.

The evening came. The thought, that this was the last day she would pass in the bosom of her family, weighed upon her heart. She was more dead than alive. In secret she took leave of everybody, of all the objects that surrounded her.

Supper was served; her heart began to beat violently. In a trembling voice she declared that she did not want any supper, and then took leave of her father and mother. They kissed her and blessed her as usual, and she could hardly restrain herself from weeping.

On reaching her own room, she threw herself into a chair and burst into tears. Her maid urged her to be calm and to take courage. Everything was ready. In half an hour Masha would leave for ever her parents' house, her room, and her peaceful girlish life....

Out in the courtyard the snow was falling heavily; the wind howled, the shutters shook and rattled, and everything seemed to her to portend misfortune.

220

Soon all was quiet in the house: everyone was asleep. Masha wrapped herself in a shawl, put on a warm cloak, took her small box in her hand, and went down the back staircase. Her maid followed her with two bundles.' They descended into the garden. The snowstorm had not subsided; the wind blew in their faces, as if trying to stop the young criminal. With difficulty they reached the end of the garden. In the road a sledge awaited them. The horses, half-frozen with the cold, would not keep still; Vladimir's coachman was walking up and down in front of them, trying to restrain their impatience. He helped the young lady and her maid into the sledge, placed the box and the bundles in the vehicle, seized the reins, and the horses dashed off.

Having intrusted the young lady to the care of fate and to the skill of Tereshka the coachman, we will return to our young lover.

Vladimir had spent the whole of the day in driving about. In the morning he paid a visit to the priest of Jadrino, and having come to an agreement with him after a great deal of difficulty, he then set out to seek for witnesses among the neighbouring landowners. The first to whom he presented himself, a retired cornet of about forty years of age, and whose name was Dravin, consented with pleasure. The adventure, he declared, reminded him of his young days and his pranks in the Hussars. He persuaded Vladimir to stay to dinner with him, and assured him that he would have no difficulty in finding the other two witnesses. And, indeed, immediately after dinner, appeared the surveyor Schmidt, with moustache and spurs, and the son of the captain of police, a lad of sixteen years of age, who had recently entered the Uhlans. They not only accepted Vladimir's proposal, but even vowed that they were ready to sacrifice their lives for him. Vladimir embraced them with rapture, and returned home to get everything ready.

It had been dark for some time. He dispatched his faithful Tereshka to Nenaradova with his sledge and with detailed instructions, and ordered for himself the small sledge with one horse, and set out alone, without any coachman, for Jadrino, where Maria Gavrilovna ought to arrive in about a couple of hours. He knew the road well, and the journey would only occupy about twenty minutes altogether.

But scarcely had Vladimir issued from the paddock into the open field, when the wind rose and such a snowstorm came on that he could see nothing. In one minute the road was completely hidden; all surrounding objects disappeared in a thick yellow fog, through which fell the white flakes of snow; earth and sky became confounded. Vladimir found himself in the middle of the field, and tried in vain to find the road again. His horse went on at random,

221

and at every moment; kept either stepping into a snowdrift or stumbling into a hole, so that the sledge was constantly being overturned.. Vladimir endeavoured not to lose the right direction. But it seemed to him that more than half an hour had already passed, and he had not yet reached the Jadrino wood. Another ten minutes elapsed—still no wood was to be seen. Vladimir drove across a field intersected by deep ditches. The snowstorm did not abate, the sky did not become any clearer. The horse began to grow tired, and the perspiration rolled from him in great drops, in spite of the fact that he was constantly being half-buried in the snow.

At last Vladimir perceived that he was going in the wrong direction. He stopped, began to think, to recollect, and compare, and he felt convinced that he ought to have turned to the right. He turned to the right now. His horse could scarcely move forward. He had now been on the road for more than an hour. Jadrino could not be far off. But on and on he went, and still no end to the field— nothing but snowdrifts and ditches. The sledge was constantly being overturned, and as constantly being set right again. The time was passing: Vladimir began to grow seriously uneasy.

At last something dark appeared in the distance. Vladimir directed his course towards it. On drawing near, he perceived that it was a wood.

"Thank Heaven!" he thought, "I am not far off now."

He drove along by the edge of the wood, hoping by-and-by to fall upon the well-known road or to pass round the wood: Jadrino was situated just behind it. He soon found the road, and plunged into the darkness of the wood, now denuded of leaves by the winter. The wind could not rage here; the road was smooth; the horse recovered courage, and Vladimir felt reassured.

But he drove on and on, and Jadrino was not to be seen; there was no end to the wood. Vladimir discovered with horror that he had entered an unknown forest. Despair took possession of him. He whipped the horse; the poor animal broke into a trot, but it soon slackened its pace, and in about a quarter of an hour it was scarcely able to drag one leg after the other, in spite of all the exertions of the unfortunate Vladimir.

Gradually the trees began to get sparser, and Vladimir emerged from the forest; but Jadrino was not to be seen. It must now have been about midnight. Tears gushed from his eyes; he drove on at random. Meanwhile the storm had subsided, the clouds dispersed, and before him lay a level plain covered with a white undulating carpet The night was tolerably clear. He saw, not far off, a little village, consisting of four or five houses. Vladimir drove towards it. At the first cottage he jumped out of the sledge, ran to the window and began to knock. After a few minutes, the wooden shutter was raised, and an old man thrust out his grey beard.

"What do you want?"

"Is Jadrino far from here?"

"Is Jadrino far from here?"

"Yes, yes! Is it far?"

"Not far; about ten versts."

At this reply, Vladimir grasped his hair and stood motionless, like a man condemned to death.

"Where do you come from?" continued the old man. Vladimir had not the courage to answer the question.

"Listen, old man," said he: "can you procure me horses to take me to Jadrino?"

"How should we have such things as horses?" replied the peasant.

"Can I obtain a guide? I will pay him whatever he pleases."

"Wait," said the old man, closing the shutter; "I will send my son out to you; he will guide you."

Vladimir waited. But a minute had scarcely elapsed when he began knocking again. The shutter was raised, and the beard again appeared.

"What do you want?"

"What about your son?"

"He'll be out presently; he is putting on his boots. Are you cold? Come in and warm yourself."

"Thank you; send your son out quickly."

The door creaked: a lad came out with a cudgel and went on in front, at one time pointing out the road, at another searching for it among the drifted snow.

"What is the time?" Vladimir asked him.

"It will soon be daylight," replied the young peasant. Vladimir spoke not another word.

The cocks were crowing, and it was already light when they reached Jadrino. The church was closed. Vladimir paid the guide and drove into the priest's courtyard. His sledge was not there. What news awaited him! But let us return to the worthy proprietors of Nenaradova, and see what is happening there.

Nothing.

The old people awoke and went into the parlour, Gavril Gavrilovitch in a night-cap and flannel doublet, Praskovia; Petrovna in a wadded dressing-gown. The tea-urn was brought in, and Gavril Gavrilovitch sent a servant to ask Maria Gavrilovna how she was and how she had passed the night. The servant returned, saying that the young lady had not slept very well, but that she felt better now, and that she would come down presently into the parlour. And indeed, the door opened and Maria Gavrilovna entered the room and wished her father and mother good morning.

"How is your head, Masha?" asked Gavril Gavrilovitch.

"Better, papa," replied Masha.

"Very likely you inhaled the fumes from the charcoal yesterday," said Praskovia Petrovna.

"Very likely, mamma," replied Masha.

The day passed happily enough, but in the night Masha was taken ill. A doctor was sent for from the town. He arrived in the evening and found the sick girl delirious. A violent fever ensued, and for two weeks the poor patient hovered on the brink of the grave.

Nobody in the house knew anything about her flight. The letters, written by her the evening before, had been burnt; and her maid, dreading the wrath of her master, had not whispered a word about it to anybody. The priest, the retired cornet, the moustached surveyor, and the little Uhlan were discreet, and not without reason. Tereshka, the coachman, never uttered one word too much about it, even when he was drunk. Thus the secret was kept by more than half-a-dozen conspirators.

But Maria Gavrilovna herself divulged her secret during her delirious ravings. But her words were so disconnected, that her mother, who never left her bedside, could only understand from them that her daughter was deeply in love with Vladimir Nikolaievitch, and that probably love was the cause of her illness. She consulted her husband and some of her neighbours, and at last it was unanimously decided that such was evidently Maria Gavrilovna's fate, that a woman cannot ride away from the man who is destined to be her husband, that poverty is not a crime, that one does not marry wealth, but a man, etc., etc. Moral proverbs are wonderfully useful in those cases where we can invent little in our own justification.

In the meantime the young lady began to recover. Vladimir had not been seen for a long time in the house of Gavril Gavrilovitch. He was afraid of the usual reception. It was resolved to send and announce to him an unexpected piece of good news: the consent of Maria's parents to his marriage with their daughter. But what was the astonishment of the proprietor of Nenaradova, when, in reply to their invitation, they received from him a half-insane letter. He informed them that he would never set foot in their house again, and begged-them to forget an unhappy creature whose only hope was in death. A few days afterwards they heard that Vladimir had joined the army again. This was in the year 1812.

224

For a long time they did not dare to announce this to Masha, who was now convalescent. She never mentioned the name of Vladimir. Some months afterwards, finding his name in the list of those who had distinguished themselves and been severely wounded at Borodino,[89] she fainted away, and it was feared that she would have another attack of fever. But, Heaven be thanked! the fainting fit had no serious consequences.

Another misfortune fell upon her: Gavril Gavrilovitch died, leaving her the heiress to all his property. But the inheritance did not console her; she shared sincerely the grief of poor Praskovia Petrovna, vowing that she would never leave her. They both quitted Nenaradova, the scene of so many sad recollections, and went to live on another estate.

Suitors crowded round the young and wealthy heiress, but she gave not the slightest hope to any of them. Her mother sometimes exhorted her to make a choice; but Maria Gavrilovna shook her head and became pensive. Vladimir no longer existed: he had died in Moscow on the eve of the entry of the French. His memory seemed to be held sacred by Masha; at least she treasured up everything that could remind her of him: books that he had once read, his drawings, his notes, and verses of poetry that he had copied out for her. The neighbours, hearing of all this, were astonished at her constancy, and awaited with curiosity the hero who should at last triumph over the melancholy fidelity of this virgin Artemisia.

Meanwhile the war had ended gloriously. Our regiments returned from abroad, and the people went out to meet them. The bands played the conquering songs: "Vive Henri-Quatre," Tyrolese waltzes and airs from "Joconde." Officers, who had set out for the war almost mere lads, returned grown men, with martial air, and their breasts decorated with crosses. The soldiers chatted gaily among themselves, constantly mingling French and German words in their speech. Time never to be forgotten! Time of glory and enthusiasm! How throbbed the Russian heart at the word "Fatherland!" How sweet were the tears of meeting! With what unanimity did we unite feelings of national pride with love for the Czar! And for him—what a moment!

The women, the Russian women, were then incomparable. Their usual coldness disappeared. Their enthusiasm was truly intoxicating, when welcoming the conquerors they cried "Hurrah!"

[89] A village about fifty miles from Moscow, and the scene of a sanguinary battle between the French and Russian forces during the invasion of Russia by Napoleon I.

"And threw their caps high in the air!"[90]

What officer of that time does not confess that to the Russian women he was indebted for his best and most precious reward?

At this brilliant period Maria Gavrilovna was living with her mother in the province of ——, and did not see how both capitals celebrated the return of the troops. But in the districts and villages the general enthusiasm was, if possible, even still greater. The appearance of an officer in those places was for him a veritable triumph, and the lover in a plain coat felt very ill at ease in his vicinity.

We have already said that, in spite of her coldness, Maria Gavrilovna was, as before, surrounded by suitors. But all had to retire into the background when the wounded Colonel Bourmin of the Hussars, with the Order of St. George in his button-hole, and with an "interesting pallor," as the young ladies of the neighbourhood observed, appeared at the castle. He was about twenty-six years of age. He had obtained leave of absence to visit his estate, which was contiguous to that of Maria Gavrilovna. Maria bestowed special attention upon him. In his presence her habitual pensiveness disappeared. It cannot be said that she coquetted with him, but a poet, observing her behaviour, would have said:

"Se amor non è che dunque?"

Bourmin was indeed a very charming young man. He possessed that spirit which is eminently pleasing to women: a spirit of decorum and observation, without any pretensions, and yet not without a slight tendency towards careless satire. His behaviour towards Maria Gavrilovna was simple and frank, but whatever she said or did, his soul and eyes followed her. He seemed to be of a quiet and modest disposition, though report said that he had once been a terrible rake; but this did not injure him in the opinion of Maria Gavrilovna, who—like all young ladies in general—excused with pleasure follies that gave indication of boldness and ardour of temperament.

But more than everything else—more than his tenderness, more than his agreeable conversation, more than his interesting pallor, more than his arm in a sling,—the silence of the young Hussar excited her curiosity and imagination. She could not but confess that he pleased her very much; probably he, too, with his perception and experience, had already observed that she made a distinction between him and others; how was it then that she had not yet seen him at her feet or heard his declaration? What restrained him? Was it timidity, inseparable from true love, or pride, or the coquetry of a

---

[90] Griboiedoff.

226

crafty wooer? It was an enigma to her. After long reflection, she came to the conclusion that timidity alone was the cause of it, and she resolved to encourage him by greater attention and, if circumstances should render it necessary, even by an exhibition of tenderness. She prepared a most unexpected dénouement, and waited with impatience for the moment of the romantic explanation. A secret, of whatever nature it may be, always presses heavily upon the female heart. Her stratagem had the desired success; at least Bourmin fell into such a reverie, and his black eyes rested with such fire upon her, that the decisive moment seemed close at hand. The neighbours spoke about the marriage as if it were a matter already decided upon, and good Praskovia Petrovna rejoiced that her daughter had at last found a lover worthy of her.

On one occasion the old lady was sitting alone in the parlour, amusing herself with a pack of cards, when Bourmin entered the room and immediately inquired for Maria Gavrilovna.

"She is in the garden," replied the old lady: "go out to her, and I will wait here for you."

Bourmin went, and the old lady made the sign of the cross and thought: "Perhaps the business will be settled to-day!"

Bourmin found Maria Gavrilovna near the pond, under a willow-tree with a book in her hands, and in a white dress: a veritable heroine of romance. After the first few questions and observations, Maria Gavrilovna purposely allowed the conversation to drop, thereby increasing their mutual embarrassment, from which there was no possible way of escape except only by a sudden and decisive declaration.

And this is what happened: Bourmin, feeling the difficulty of his position, declared that he had long sought for an opportunity to open his heart to her, and requested a moment's attention. Maria Gavrilovna closed her book and cast down her eyes, as a sign of compliance with his request.

"I love you," said Bourmin: "I love you passionately...."

Maria Gavrilovna blushed and lowered her head still more. "I have acted imprudently in accustoming myself to the sweet pleasure of seeing and hearing you daily...." Maria Gavrilovna recalled to mind the first letter of St. Preux.[91] "But it is now too late to resist my fate; the remembrance of you, your dear incomparable image, will henceforth be the torment and the consolation of my life, but there still remains a grave duty for me to perform—to reveal to you a terrible secret which will place between us an insurmountable barrier...."

---

[91] In "La Nouvelle Héloise," by Jean-Jacques Rousseau.

"That barrier has always existed," interrupted Maria Gavrilovna hastily: "I could never be your wife."

"I know," replied he calmly: "I know that you once loved, but death and three years of mourning.... Dear, kind Maria Gavrilovna, do not try to deprive me of my last consolation: the thought that you would have consented to make me happy, if——"

"Don't speak, for Heaven's sake, don't speak. You torture me."

"Yes, I know, I feel that you would have been mine, but—I am the most miserable creature under the sun—I am already married!"

Maria Gavrilovna looked at him in astonishment.

"I am already married," continued Bourmin: "I have been married four years, and I do not know who is my wife, or where she is, or whether I shall ever see her again!"

"What do you say?" exclaimed Maria Gavrilovna. "How very strange! Continue: I will relate to you afterwards.... But continue, I beg of you."

"At the beginning of the year 1812," said Bourmin, "I was hastening to Vilna, where my regiment was stationed. Arriving late one evening at one of the post-stations, I ordered the horses to be got ready as quickly as possible, when suddenly a terrible snowstorm came on, and the postmaster and drivers advised me to wait till it had passed over. I followed their advice, but an unaccountable uneasiness took possession of me: it seemed as if someone were pushing me forward. Meanwhile the snowstorm did not subside; I could endure it no longer, and again ordering out the horses, I started off in the midst of the storm. The driver conceived the idea of following the course of the river, which would shorten our journey by three versts. The banks were covered with snow: the driver drove past the place where we should have come out upon the road, and so we found ourselves in an unknown part of the country.... The storm did not cease; I saw a light in the distance, and I ordered the driver to proceed towards it. We reached a village; in the wooden church there was a light. The church was open. Outside the railings stood several sledges, and people were passing in and out through the porch.

"'This way! this way!' cried several voices.

"I ordered the driver to proceed.

"'In the name of Heaven, where have you been loitering' said somebody to me. 'The bride has fainted away; the pope does not know what to do, and we were just getting ready to go back. Get out as quickly as you can.'

"I got out of the sledge without saying a word, and went into the church, which was feebly lit up by two or three tapers. A young girl was sitting on a bench in a dark corner of the church; another girl was rubbing her temples.

"'Thank God!' said the latter, 'you have come at last. You have almost killed the young lady.'

"The old priest advanced towards me, and said:

"'Do you wish me to begin?'

"'Begin, begin, father,' replied I, absently.

"The young girl was raised up. She seemed to me not at all bad-looking.... Impelled by an incomprehensible, unpardonable levity, I placed myself by her side in front of the pulpit; the priest hurried on; three men and a chambermaid supported the bride and only occupied themselves with her. We were married.

"'Kiss each other!' said the witnesses to us.

"My wife turned her pale face towards me. I was about to kiss her, when she exclaimed: 'Oh! it is not he! it is not he!' and fell senseless.

"The witnesses gazed at me in alarm. I turned round and left the church without the least hindrance, flung myself into the kibitka and cried: 'Drive off!'"

"My God!" exclaimed Maria Gavrilovna. "And you do not know what became of your poor wife?"

"I do not know," replied Bourmin; "neither do I know the name of the village where I was married, nor the poststation where I set out from. At that time I attached so little importance to my wicked prank, that on leaving the church, I fell asleep, and did not awake till the next morning after reaching the third station. The servant, who was then with me, died during the campaign, so that I have no hope of ever discovering the woman upon whom I played such a cruel joke, and who is now so cruelly avenged."

"My God! my God!" cried Maria Gavrilovna, seizing him by the hand: "then it was you! And you do not recognize me?"

Bourmin turned pale—and threw himself at her feet.

THE POSTMASTER

Who has not cursed postmasters, who has not quarrelled with them? Who, in a moment of anger, has not demanded from them the fatal book in order to record in it unavailing complaints of their extortions, rudeness and unpunctuality? Who does not look upon them as monsters of the human race, equal to the defunct attorneys, or, at least, the brigands of Mourom? Let us, however, be just; let us place ourselves in their position, and perhaps we shall begin to judge them with more indulgence. What is a postmaster? A veritable martyr of the fourteenth class,[92] only protected by his rank from blows, and that not always (I appeal to the conscience of my readers). What is the function of this dictator, as Prince Viazemsky jokingly calls him? Is he not an actual galley-slave? He has no rest either day or night. All the vexation accumulated during the course of a wearisome journey the traveller vents upon the postmaster. Should the weather prove intolerable, the road abominable, the driver obstinate, the horses ungovernable—the postmaster is to blame. Entering into his poor abode, the traveller looks upon him as an enemy, and the postmaster is fortunate if he succeeds in soon getting rid of his uninvited guest; but if there should happen to be no horses!... Heavens! what volleys of abuse, what threats are showered upon his head! In rain and sleet he is compelled to go out into the courtyard; during times of storm and nipping frost, he is glad to seek shelter in the vestibule, if only to enjoy a minute's repose from the shouting and jostling of incensed travellers.

A general arrives: the trembling postmaster gives him the two last troikas, including that intended for the courier. The general drives off without uttering a word of thanks. Five minutes afterwards—a bell!... and a courier throws down upon the table before him his order for fresh post-horses!... Let us bear all this well in mind, and, instead of anger, our hearts will be filled with sincere compassion. A few words more. During a period of twenty years I have traversed Russia in every direction; I know nearly all the post roads, and I have made the acquaintance of several generations of drivers. There are very few postmasters that I do not know personally, and few with whom I have not had business relations. In the course of time I hope to publish some curious observations that I have noted down during my travels. For the present I will only say

---

[92] The Chinnovniks, or official nobles of Russia, are divided into fourteen classes, the fourteenth being the lowest. The members of this latter class were formerly little removed from serfs.

that the body of postmasters is presented to the public in a very false light. These much-calumniated officials are generally very peaceful persons, obliging by nature, disposed to be sociable, modest in their pretensions and not too much addicted to the love of money. From their conversation (which travelling gentlemen very unreasonably despise) much may be learnt that is both interesting and instructive. For my own part, I confess that I prefer their talk to that of some official of the sixth class travelling on government business.

It may easily be supposed that I have friends among the honourable body of postmasters. Indeed, the memory of one of them is dear to me. Circumstances once brought us together, and it is of him that I now intend to tell my amiable readers.

In the month of May of the year 1816, I happened to be travelling through the Government of N——, upon a road now destroyed. I then held an inferior rank, and I travelled by post stages, paying the fare for two horses. As a consequence, the postmasters treated me with very little ceremony, and I often had to take by force what, in my opinion, belonged to me by right. Being young and passionate, I was indignant at the baseness and cowardice of the postmaster, when the latter harnessed to the caliche of some, official noble, the horses prepared for me. It was a long time, too, before I could get accustomed to being served out of my turn by a discriminating servant at the governor's dinner. To-day the one and the other seem to me to be in the natural order of things. Indeed, what would become of us, if, instead of the generally observed rule: "Let rank honour rank," another were to be brought into use, as for example: "Let mind honour mind?" What disputes would arise! And with whom would the servants begin in serving the dishes? But to return to my story.

The day was hot. About three versts from A——, a drizzling rain came on, and in a few minutes it began to pour down in torrents and I was drenched to the skin. On arriving at the station, my first care was to change my clothes as quickly as possible, my second to ask for some tea.

"Hi! Dounia!"[93] cried the Postmaster: "prepare the tea-urn and go and get some cream."

At these words, a young girl of about fourteen years of age appeared from behind the partition, and ran out into the vestibule. Her beauty struck me.

"Is that your daughter?" I inquired of the Postmaster.

---

[93] Diminutive of Avdotia.

"That is my daughter," he replied, with a look of gratified pride; "and she is so sharp and sensible, just like her late mother."

Then he began to register my travelling passport, and I occupied myself with examining the pictures that adorned his humble abode. They illustrated the story of the Prodigal Son. In the first, a venerable old man, in a night-cap and dressing-gown, is taking leave of the restless youth, who is eagerly accepting his blessing and a bag of money. In the next picture, the dissipated life of the young man is depicted in vivid colours: he is represented sitting at a table surrounded by false friends and shameless women. Further on, the ruined youth, in rags and a three-cornered hat, is tending swine and sharing with them their food: on his face is expressed deep grief and repentance. The last picture represented his return to his father: the good old man, in the same night-cap and dressing-gown, runs forward to meet him; the prodigal son falls on his knees; in the distance the cook is killing the fatted calf, and the elder brother is asking the servants the cause of all the rejoicing. Under each picture I read some suitable German verses. All this I have preserved in my memory to the present day, as well as the little pots of balsams, the bed with speckled curtains, and the other objects with which I was then surrounded. I can see at the present moment the host himself, a man of about fifty years of age, fresh and strong, in his long green surtout with three medals on faded ribbons.

I had scarcely settled my account with my old driver, when Dounia returned with the tea-urn. The little coquette saw at the second glance the impression she had produced upon me; she lowered her large blue eyes; I began to talk to her; she answered me without the least timidity, like a girl who has seen the world. I offered her father a glass of punch, to Dounia herself I gave a cup of tea, and then the three of us began to converse together, as if we were old acquaintances.

The horses had long been ready, but I felt reluctant to take leave of the Postmaster and his daughter. At last I bade them good-bye, the father wished me a pleasant journey, the daughter accompanied me to the telega. In the vestibule I stopped and asked her permission to kiss her; Dounia consented.... I can reckon up a great many kisses since that time, but not one which has left behind such a long, such a pleasant recollection.

Several years passed, and circumstances led me to the same road, and to the same places.

"But," thought I, "perhaps the old Postmaster has been changed, and Dounia may already be married."

The thought that one or the other of them might be dead also

flashed through my mind, and I approached the station of A——
with a sad presentiment. The horses drew up before the little post-
house. On entering the room, I immediately recognized the pictures
illustrating the story of the prodigal son. The table and the bed
stood in the same places as before, but the flowers were no longer
on the window-sills, and everything around indicated decay and
neglect.

The Postmaster was asleep under his sheep-skin pelisse; my
arrival awoke him, and he rose up.... It was certainly Simeon Virin,
but how aged! While he was preparing to register my travelling
passport, I gazed at his grey hairs, the deep wrinkles upon his face,
that had not been shaved for a long time, his bent back, and I was
astonished to see how three or four years had been able to
transform a strong and active individual into a feeble old man.

"Do you recognize me?" I asked him: "we are old
acquaintances."

"May be," replied he mournfully; "this is a high road, and many
travellers have stopped here."

"Is your Dounia well?" I continued.

The old man frowned.

"God knows," he replied.

"Probably she is married?" said I.

The old man pretended not to have heard my question, and
went on reading my passport in a low tone. I ceased questioning
him and ordered some tea. Curiosity began to torment me, and I
hoped that the punch would loosen the tongue of my old
acquaintance.

I was not mistaken; the old man did not refuse the proffered
glass. I observed that the rum dispelled his mournfulness. At the
second glass he began to talk; he remembered me, or appeared as if
he remembered me, and I heard from him a story, which at the
time, deeply interested and affected me.

"So you knew my Dounia?" he began. "But who did not know
her? Ah, Dounia, Dounia! What a girl she was! Everybody who
passed this way praised her; nobody had a word to say against her.
The ladies used to give her presents—now a handkerchief, now a
pair of earrings. The gentlemen used to stop intentionally, as if to
dine or to take supper, but in reality only to take a longer look at
her. However angry a gentleman might be, in her presence he grew
calm and spoke graciously to me. Would you believe it, sir: couriers
and Court messengers used to talk to her for half-hours at a stretch.
It was she who kept the house; she put everything in order, got
everything ready, and looked after everything. And I, like an old
fool, could not look at her enough, could not idolize her enough. Did

233

I not love my Dounia? Did I not indulge my child? Was not her life a happy one? But no, there is no escaping misfortune: there is no evading what has been decreed." Then he began to tell me his sorrow in detail. Three years before, one winter evening, when the Postmaster was ruling a new book, and his daughter behind the partition was sewing a dress, a troika drove up, and a traveller in a Circassian cap and military cloak, and enveloped in a shawl, entered the room and demanded horses. The horses were all out. On being told this, the traveller raised his voice and whip; but Dounia, accustomed to such scenes, ran out from behind the partition and graciously inquired of the traveller whether he would not like something to eat and drink.

The appearance of Dounia produced the usual effect. The traveller's anger subsided; he consented to wait for horses, and ordered supper. Having taken off his wet shaggy cap, and divested himself of his shawl and cloak, the traveller was seen to be a tall, young Hussar with a black moustache He made himself comfortable with the Postmaster, and began to converse in a pleasant manner with him and his daughter. Supper was served. Meanwhile the horses returned, and the Postmaster ordered them, without being fed, to be harnessed immediately to the traveller kibitka. But on returning to the room, he found the young man lying almost unconscious on the bench; he had come over faint, his head ached, it was impossible for him to continue his journey. What was to be done? The Postmaster gave up his own bed to him, and it was decided that if the sick man did not get better, they would send next day to C—— for the doctor.

The next day the Hussar was worse. His servant rode to the town for the doctor. Dounia bound round his head a handkerchief steeped in vinegar, and sat with her needlework beside his bed. In the presence of the Postmaster, the sick man sighed and scarcely uttered a word; but he drank two cups of coffee, and, with a sigh, ordered dinner. Dounia did not quit his side. He constantly asked for something to drink, and Dounia gave him a jug of lemonade prepared by herself. The sick man moistened his lips, and each time, on returning the jug, he feebly pressed Dounia's hand in token of gratitude.

About dinner time the doctor arrived. He felt the sick man's pulse, spoke to him in German, and declared in Russian that he only needed rest, and that in about a couple of days he would be able to set out on his journey. The Hussar gave him twenty-five roubles for his visit, and invited him to dinner; the doctor accepted the invitation. They both ate with a good appetite, drank a bottle of wine, and separated very well satisfied with each other.

Another day passed, and the Hussar felt quite himself again. He was extraordinarily lively, joked unceasingly, now with Dounia, now with the Postmaster, whistled tunes, chatted with the travellers, copied their passports into the post-book, and so won upon the worthy Postmaster, that when the third day arrived, it was with regret that he parted with his amiable guest.

The day was Sunday; Dounia was preparing to go to mass. The Hussar's kibitka stood ready. He took leave of the Postmaster, after having generously recompensed him for his board and lodging, bade farewell to Dounia, and offered to drive her as far as the church, which was situated at the end of the village. Dounia hesitated.

"What are you afraid of?" asked her father. "His Excellency is not a wolf: he won't eat you. Drive with him as far as the church."

Dounia seated herself in the kibitka by the side of the Hussar, the servant sprang upon the box, the driver whistled, and the horses started off at a gallop.

The poor Postmaster could not understand how he could have allowed his Dounia to drive off with the Hussar, how he could have been so blind, and what had become of his senses at that moment. A half-hour had not elapsed, before his heart began to grieve, and anxiety and uneasiness took possession of him to such a degree, that he could contain himself no longer, and started off for mass himself. On reaching the church, he saw that the people were already beginning to disperse, but Dounia was neither in the churchyard nor in the porch. He hastened into the church: the priest was leaving the altar, the clerk was extinguishing the candles, two old women were still praying in a corner, but Dounia was not in the church. The poor father was scarcely able to summon up sufficient resolution to ask the clerk if she had been to mass. The clerk replied that she had not. The Postmaster returned home neither alive nor dead. One hope alone remained to him: Dounia, in the thoughtlessness of youth, might have taken it into her head to go on as far as the next station, where her godmother lived. In agonizing agitation he awaited the return of the troika in which he had let her set out. The driver did not return. At last, in the evening, he arrived alone and intoxicated, with the terrible news that Dounia had gone on with the Hussar at the other station.

The old man could not bear his misfortune: he immediately took to that very same bed where, the evening before, the young deceiver had lain. Taking all the circumstances into account, the Postmaster now came to the conclusion that the illness had been a mere pretence. The poor man fell ill with a violent fever; he was removed to C——, and in his place another person was appointed for

235

the time being. The same doctor, who had attended the Hussar, attended him also. He assured the Postmaster that the young man had been perfectly well, and that at the time of his visit he had suspected him of some evil intention, but that he had kept silent through fear of his whip. Whether the German spoke the truth or only wished to boast of his perspicacity, his communication afforded no consolation to the poor invalid. Scarcely had the latter recovered from his illness, when he asked the Postmaster of C——for two months' leave of absence, and without saying a word to anybody of his intention, he set out on foot in search of his daughter.

From the travelling passport he found out that Captain Minsky was journeying from Smolensk to St. Petersburg. The yemshik[94] who drove him, said that Dounia had wept the whole of the way, although she seemed to go of her own free will.

"Perhaps," thought the Postmaster, "I shall bring back home my erring ewe-lamb."

With this thought he reached St. Petersburg, stopped at the barracks of the Ismailovsky Regiment, in the quarters of a retired non-commissioned officer, an old comrade of his, and then began his search. He soon discovered that Captain Minsky was in St. Petersburg, and was living at the Demoutoff Hotel. The Postmaster resolved to call upon him.

Early in the morning he went to Minsky's ante-chamber, and requested that His Excellency might be informed that an old soldier wished to see him. The military servant, who was cleaning a boot on a boot-tree, informed him that his master was still asleep, and that he never received anybody before eleven o'clock. The Postmaster retired and returned at the appointed time. Minsky himself came out to him in his dressing-gown and red skull-cap.

"Well, my friend, what do you want?" he asked.

The old man's heart began to boil, tears started to his eyes, and he was only able to say in a trembling voice:

"Your Excellency!... do me the divine favour!..."

Minsky glanced quickly at him, grew confused, took him by the hand, led him into his cabinet and locked the door.

"Your Excellency!" continued the old man: "what has fallen from the load is lost; give me back at least my poor Dounia. You have made her your plaything; do not ruin her entirely."

"What is done cannot be undone," said the young man, in the utmost confusion; "I am guilty before you, and am ready to ask your pardon, but do not think that I could forsake Dounia: she shall be

---

[94] Driver.

happy, I give you my word of honour. Why do you want her? She loves me; she has become disused to her former existence. Neither you nor she will forget what has happened."

Then, pushing something up the old man's sleeve, he opened the door, and the Postmaster, without remembering how, found himself in the street again.

For a long time he stood immovable; at last he observed in the cuff of his sleeve a roll of papers; he drew them out and unrolled several fifty rouble notes. Tears again filled his eyes, tears of indignation! He crushed the notes into a ball, flung them upon the ground, stamped upon them with the heel of his boot, and then walked away.... After having gone a few steps, he stopped, reflected, and returned ... but the notes were no longer there. A well-dressed young man, observing him, ran towards a droshky, jumped in hurriedly, and cried to the driver: "Go on!"

The Postmaster did not pursue him. He resolved to return home to his station, but before doing so he wished to see his poor Dounia once more. For that purpose, he returned to Minsky's lodgings a couple of days afterwards, but the military servant told him roughly that his master received nobody, pushed him out of the ante-chamber and slammed the door in his face. The Postmaster stood waiting for a long time, then he walked away.

That same day, in the evening, he was walking along the Liteinaia, having been to a service at the Church of the Afflicted. Suddenly a stylish droshky flew past him, and the Postmaster recognized Minsky. The droshky stopped in front of a three-storeyed house, close to the entrance, and the Hussar ran up the steps. A happy thought flashed through the mind of the Postmaster. He returned, and, approaching the coachman:

"Whose horse is this, my friend?" asked he: "Doesn't it belong to Minsky?"

"Exactly so," replied the coachman: "what do you want?"

"Well, your master ordered me to carry a letter to his Dounia, and I have forgotten where his Dounia lives."

"She lives here, on the second floor. But you are late with your letter, my friend; he is with her himself just now."

"That doesn't matter," replied the Postmaster, with an inexplicable beating of the heart. "Thanks for your information, but I shall know how to manage my business." And with these words he ascended the staircase.

The door was locked; he rang. There was a painful delay of several seconds. The key rattled, and the door was' opened.

"Does Avdotia Simeonovna live here?" he asked.

"Yes," replied a young female servant: "what do you want with her?"

The Postmaster, without replying, walked into the room.

"You mustn't go in, you mustn't go in!" the servant cried put after him: "Avdotia Simeonovna has visitor."

But the Postmaster, without heeding her, walked straight on. The first two rooms were dark; in the third there was a light. He approached the open door and paused. In the room, which was beautifully furnished, sat Minsky in deep thought. Dounia, attired in the most elegant fashion, was sitting upon the arm of his chair, like a lady rider upon her English saddle. She was gazing I tenderly at Minsky, and winding his black curls round her sparkling fingers. Poor Postmaster! Never had his daughter seemed to him so beautiful; he admired her against his will.

"Who is there?" she asked, without raising her head.

He remained silent. Receiving no reply, Dounia raised her head.... and with a cry she fell upon the carpet. The alarmed Minsky hastened to pick her up, but suddenly catching sight of the old Postmaster in the doorway, he left Dounia and approached him, trembling with rage.

"What do you want?" he said to him, clenching his teeth. "Why do you steal after me everywhere, like a thief? Or do you want to murder me? Be off!" and with a powerful hand he seized the old man by the collar and pushed him down the stairs.

The old man returned to his lodging. His friend advised him to lodge a complaint, but the Postmaster reflected, waved his hand, and resolved to abstain from taking any further steps in the matter. Two days afterwards he left St. Petersburg and returned to his station to resume his duties.

"This is the third year," he concluded, "that I have been living without Dounia, and I have not heard a word about her. Whether she is alive or not—God only knows. So many things happen. She is not the first, nor yet the last, that a travelling scoundrel has seduced, kept for a little while, and then forsaken. There are many such young fools in St. Petersburg, to-day in satin and velvet, and to-morrow sweeping the streets along with the wretched hangers-on of the dram-shops. Sometimes, when I think that Dounia also may come to such an end, then, in spite of myself, I sin and wish her in her grave...."

Such was the story of my friend, the old Postmaster, a story more than once interrupted by tears, which he picturesquely wiped away with the skirt of his coat, like the zealous Terentitch in Dmitrieff's beautiful ballad. These tears were partly induced by the punch, of which he had drunk five glasses during the course of his

238

narrative, but for all that, they produced a deep impression upon my heart After taking leave of him, it was a long time before I could forget the old Postmaster, and for a long time I thought of poor Dounia....

Passing through the little town of a short time ago, I remembered my friend. I heard that the station, over which he ruled, had been abolished. To my question: "Is the old Postmaster still alive?" nobody could give me a satisfactory reply. I resolved to pay a visit to the well-known place, and having hired horses, I set out for the village of N——.

It was in the autumn. Grey clouds covered the sky; a cold wind blew across the reaped fields, carrying along with it the red and yellow leaves from the trees that it encountered. I arrived in the village at sunset, and stopped at the little post-house. In the vestibule (where Dounia had once kissed me) a stout woman came out to meet me, and in answer to my questions replied, that the old Postmaster had been dead for about a year, that his house was occupied by a brewer, and that she was the brewer's wife. I began to regret my useless journey, and the seven roubles that I had spent in vain.

"Of what did he die?" I asked the brewer's wife.

"Of drink, little father," replied she.

"And where is he buried?"

"On the outskirts of the village, near his late wife."

"Could somebody take me to his grave?"

"To be sure! Hi, Vanka,[95] you have played with that cat long enough. Take this gentleman to the cemetery, and show him the Postmaster's grave."

At these words a ragged lad, with red hair, and a cast in his eye, ran up to me and immediately began to lead the way towards the burial-ground.

"Did you know the dead man?" I asked him on the road.

"Did I not know him! He taught me how to cut blowpipes. When he came out of the dram-shop (God rest his soul!) we used to run after him and call out: 'Grandfather! grandfather! some nuts!' and he used to throw nuts to us. He always used to play with us."

"And do the travellers remember him?"

"There are very few travellers now; the assessor passes this way sometimes, but he doesn't trouble himself about dead people. Last summer a lady passed through here, and she asked after the old Postmaster, and went to his grave."

"What sort of a lady?" I asked with curiosity.

---

[95] One of the many diminutives of Ivan.

"A very beautiful lady," replied the lad. "She was in a carriage with six horses, and had along with her three little children, a nurse, and a little black dog; and when they told her that the old Postmaster was dead, she began to cry, and said to the children: 'Sit still, I will go to the cemetery.' I offered to show her the way. But the lady said: 'I know the way.' And she gave me a five-copeck piece.... such a kind lady!"

We reached the cemetery, a dreary place, not inclosed in the least; it was sown with wooden crosses, but there was not a single tree to throw a shade over it. Never in my life had I seen such a dismal cemetery.

"This is the old Postmaster's grave," said the lad to me, leaping upon a heap of sand, in which was planted a black cross with a copper image.

"And did the lady come here?" asked I.

"Yes," replied Vanka; "I watched her from a distance. She lay down here, and remained lying down for a long time. Then she went back to the village, sent for the pope, gave him some money and drove off, after giving me a five-copeck piece.... such an excellent lady!"

And I, too, gave the lad a five-copeck piece, and I no longer regretted the journey nor the seven roubles that I had spent on it.

THE COFFIN-MAKER

The last of the effects of the coffin-maker, Adrian Prokhoroff, were placed upon the hearse, and a couple of sorry-looking jades dragged themselves along for the fourth time from Basmannaia to Nikitskaia, whither the coffin-maker was removing with all his household. After locking up the shop, he posted upon the door a placard announcing that the house was to be let or sold, and then made his way on foot to his new abode. On approaching the little yellow house, which had so long captivated his imagination, and which at last he had bought for a considerable sum, the old coffin-maker was astonished to find that his heart did not rejoice. When he crossed the unfamiliar threshold and found his new home in the greatest confusion, he sighed for his old hovel, where for eighteen years the strictest order had prevailed. He began to scold his two daughters and the servant for their slowness, and then set to work to help them himself. Order was soon established; the ark with the sacred images, the cupboard with the crockery, the table, the sofa, and the bed occupied the corners reserved for them in the back room; in the kitchen and parlour were placed the articles comprising the stock-in-trade of the master—coffins of all colours and of all sizes, together with cupboards containing mourning hats, cloaks and torches.

Over the door was placed a sign representing a fat Cupid with an inverted torch in his hand and bearing this inscription: "Plain and coloured coffins sold and lined here; coffins also let out on hire, and old ones repaired."

The girls retired to their bedroom; Adrian made a tour of inspection of his quarters, and then sat down by the window and ordered the tea-urn to be prepared.

The enlightened reader knows that Shakespeare and Walter Scott have both represented their grave-diggers as merry and facetious individuals, in order that the contrast might more forcibly strike our imagination. Out of respect for the truth, we cannot follow their example, and we are compelled to confess that the disposition of our coffin-maker was in perfect harmony with his gloomy occupation. Adrian Prokhoroff was usually gloomy and thoughtful. He rarely opened his mouth, except to scold his daughters when he found them standing idle and gazing out of the window at the passers by, or to demand for his wares an exorbitant price from those who had the misfortune—and sometimes the good fortune—to need them. Hence it was that Adrian, sitting near the

241

window and drinking his seventh cup of tea, was immersed as usual in melancholy reflections. He thought of the pouring rain which, just a week before, had commenced to beat down during the funeral of the retired brigadier. Many of the cloaks had shrunk in consequence of the downpour, and many of the hats had been put quite out of shape. He foresaw unavoidable expenses, for his old stock of funeral dresses was in a pitiable condition. He hoped to compensate himself for his losses by the burial of old Trukhina, the shopkeeper's wife, who for more than a year had been upon the point of death. But Trukhina lay dying at Rasgouliai, and Prokhoroff was afraid that her heirs, in spite of their promise, would not take the trouble to send so far for him, but would make arrangements with the nearest undertaker.

These reflections were suddenly interrupted by three masonic knocks at the door.

"Who is there?" asked the coffin-maker.

The door opened, and a man, who at the first glance could be recognized as a German artisan, entered the room, and with a jovial air advanced towards the coffin-maker.

"Pardon me, respected neighbour," said he in that Russian dialect which to this day we cannot hear without a smile: "pardon me for disturbing you.... I wished to make your acquaintance as soon as possible. I am a shoemaker, my name is Gottlieb Schultz, and I live across the street, in that little house just facing your windows. To-morrow I am going to celebrate my silver wedding, and I have come to invite you and your daughters to dine with us."

The invitation was cordially accepted. The coffin-maker asked the shoemaker to seat himself and take a cup of tea, and thanks to the open-hearted disposition of Gottlieb Schultz, they were soon engaged in friendly conversation.

"How is business with you?" asked Adrian.

"Just so so," replied Schultz; "I cannot complain. My wares are not like yours: the living can do without shoes, but the dead cannot do without coffins."

"Very true," observed Adrian; "but if a living person hasn't anything to buy shoes with, you cannot find fault with him, he goes about barefooted; but a dead beggar gets his coffin for nothing."

In this manner the conversation was carried on between them for some time; at last the shoemaker rose and took leave of the coffin-maker, renewing his invitation.

The next day, exactly at twelve o'clock, the coffin-maker and his daughters issued from the doorway of their newly-purchased residence, and directed their steps towards the abode of their neighbour. I will not stop to describe the Russian caftan of Adrian

Prokhoroff, nor the European toilettes of Akoulina and Daria, deviating in this respect from the usual custom of modern novelists. But I do not think it superfluous to observe that they both had on the yellow cloaks and red shoes, which they were accustomed to don on solemn occasions only.

The shoemaker's little dwelling was filled with guests, consisting chiefly of German artisans with their wives and foremen. Of the Russian officials there was present but one, Yourko the Finn, a watchman, who, in spite of his humble calling, was the special object of the host's attention. For twenty-five years he had faithfully discharged the duties of postilion of Pogorelsky. The conflagration of 1812, which destroyed the ancient capital, destroyed also his little yellow watch-house. But immediately after the expulsion of the enemy, a new one appeared in its place, painted grey and with white Doric columns, and Yourko began again to pace to and fro before it, with his axe and grey coat of mail. He was known to the greater part of the Germans who lived near the Nikitskaia Gate, and some of them had even spent the night from Sunday to Monday beneath his roof.

Adrian immediately made himself acquainted with him, as with a man whom, sooner or later, he might have need of, and when the guests took their places at the table, they sat down beside each other. Herr Schultz and his wife, and their daughter Lotchen, a young girl of seventeen, did the honours of the table and helped the cook to serve. The beer flowed in streams; Yourko ate like four, and Adrian in no way yielded to him; his daughters, however, stood upon their dignity. The conversation, which was carried on in German, gradually grew more and more boisterous. Suddenly the host requested a moment's attention, and uncorking a sealed bottle, he said with a loud voice in Russian:

"To the health of my good Louise!"

The champagne foamed. The host tenderly kissed the fresh face of his partner, and the guests drank noisily to the health of the good Louise.

"To the health of my amiable guests!" exclaimed the i host, uncorking a second bottle; and the guests thanked him by draining their glasses once more.

Then followed a succession of toasts. The health of each I individual guest was drunk; they drank to the health of Moscow and to quite a dozen little German towns; they drank to the health of all corporations in general and of each in particular; they drank to the health of the masters and foremen. Adrian drank with enthusiasm and became so merry, that he proposed a facetious toast to himself.

243

Suddenly one of the guests, a fat baker, raised his glass and exclaimed:

"To the health of those for whom we work, our customers!"

This proposal, like all the others, was joyously and unanimously received. The guests began to salute each other; the tailor bowed to the shoemaker, the shoemaker to the tailor, the baker to both, the whole company to the baker, and so on. In the midst of these mutual congratulations, Yourko exclaimed, turning to his neighbour:

"Come, little father! Drink to the health of your corpses!"

Everybody laughed, but the coffin-maker considered himself insulted, and frowned. Nobody noticed it, the guests continued to drink, and the bell had already rung for vespers when they rose from the table.

The guests dispersed at a late hour, the greater part of them in a very merry mood. The fat baker and the bookbinder, whose face seemed as if bound in red morocco, linked their arms in those of Yourko and conducted him back to his little watch-house, thus observing the proverb: "One good turn deserves another."

The coffin-maker returned home drunk and angry.

"Why is it," he exclaimed aloud, "why is it that my trade is not as honest as any other? Is a coffin-maker brother to the hangman? Why did those heathens laugh? Is a coffin-maker a buffoon? I wanted to invite them to my new dwelling and give them a feast, but now I'll do nothing of the kind. Instead of inviting them, I will invite those for whom I work: the orthodox dead."

"What is the matter, little father?" said the servant, who was engaged at that moment in taking off his boots: "why do you talk such nonsense? Make the sign of the cross! Invite the dead to your new house! What folly!"

"Yes, by the Lord! I will invite them," continued Adrian, "and that, too, for to-morrow!... Do me the favour, my benefactors, to come and feast with me to-morrow evening; I will regale you with what God has sent me."

With these words the coffin-maker turned into bed and soon began to snore.

It was still dark when Adrian was awakened out of his sleep. Trukhina, the shopkeeper's wife, had died during the course of that very night, and a special messenger was sent off on horseback by her bailiff to carry the news to Adrian. The coffin-maker gave him ten copecks to buy brandy with, dressed himself as hastily as possible, took a droshky and set out for Rasgouliai. Before the door of the house in which the deceased lay, the police had already taken their stand, and the trades-people were passing backwards and forwards, like ravens that smell a dead body. The deceased lay upon a table, yellow as wax, but not yet disfigured by decomposition. Around her stood her relatives, neighbours and domestic servants. All the windows were open; tapers were burning; and the priests were reading the prayers for the dead. Adrian went up to the nephew of Trukhina, a young shopman in a fashionable surtout, and informed him that the coffin, wax candles, pall, and the other funeral accessories would be immediately delivered with all possible exactitude. The heir thanked him in an absent-minded manner, saying that he would not bargain about the price, but would rely upon him acting in everything according to his conscience. The coffin-maker, in accordance with his usual custom, vowed that he would not charge him too much, exchanged significant glances with the bailiff, and then departed to commence operations.

The whole day was spent in passing to and fro between Rasgouliai and the Nikitskaia Gate. Towards evening everything was finished, and he returned home on foot, after having dismissed his driver. It was a moonlight night. The coffin-maker reached the Nikitskaia Gate in safety. Near the Church of the Ascension he was hailed by our acquaintance Yourko, who, recognizing the coffin-maker, wished him good-night. It was late. The coffin-maker was just approaching his house, when suddenly he fancied he saw some one approach his gate, open the wicket, and disappear within.

"What does that mean?" thought Adrian. "Who can be wanting me again? Can it be a thief come to rob me? Or have my foolish girls got lovers coming after them? It means no good, I fear!"

And the coffin-maker thought of calling his friend Yourko to his assistance. But at that moment, another person approached the wicket and was about to enter, but seeing the master of the house hastening towards him, he stopped and took off his three-cornered hat. His face seemed familiar to Adrian, but in his hurry he had not been able to examine it closely.

"You are favouring me with a visit," said Adrian, out of breath. "Walk in, I beg of you."

"Don't stand on ceremony, little father," replied the other, in a hollow voice; "you go first, and show your guests the way."

Adrian had no time to spend upon ceremony. The wicket was open; he ascended the steps followed by the other. Adrian thought he could hear people walking about in his rooms.

"What the devil does all this mean!" he thought to himself, and he hastened to enter. But the sight that met his eyes caused his legs to give way beneath him.

The room was full of corpses. The moon, shining through the windows, lit up their yellow and blue faces, sunken mouths, dim, half-closed eyes, and protruding noses. Adrian, with horror, recognized in them people that he himself had buried, and in the guest who entered with him, the brigadier who had been buried during the pouring rain. They all, men and women, surrounded the coffin-maker, with bowings and salutations, except one poor fellow lately buried gratis, who, conscious and ashamed of his rags, did not venture to approach, but meekly kept aloof in a corner. All the others were decently dressed: the female corpses in caps and ribbons, the officials in uniforms, but with their beards unshaven, the tradesmen in their holiday caftans.

"You see, Prokhoroff," said the brigadier in the name of all the honourable company, "we have all risen in response to your invitation. Only those have stopped at home who were unable to come, who have crumbled to pieces and have nothing left but fleshless bones. But even of these there was one who hadn't the patience to remain behind—so much did he want to come and see you...."

At this moment a little skeleton pushed his way through the crowd and approached Adrian. His fleshless face smiled affably at the coffin-maker. Shreds of green and red cloth and rotten linen hung on him here and there as on a pole, and the bones of his feet rattled inside his big jack-boots, like pestles in mortars.

"You do not recognize me, Prokhoroff," said the skeleton. "Don't you remember the retired sergeant of the Guards, Peter Petrovitch Kourilkin, the same to whom, in the year 1799, you sold your first coffin, and that, too, of deal instead of oak?"

With these words the corpse stretched out his bony arms towards him; but Adrian, collecting all his strength, shrieked and pushed him from him. Peter Petrovitch staggered, fell, and crumbled all to pieces. Among the corpses arose a murmur of indignation; all stood up for the honour of their companion, and they overwhelmed Adrian with such threats and imprecations, that the poor host, deafened by their shrieks and almost crushed to death, lost his presence of mind, fell upon the bones of the retired sergeant of the Guards, and swooned away.

For some time the sun had been shining upon the bed on which lay the coffin-maker. At last he opened his eyes and saw before him the servant attending to the tea-urn. With horror, Adrian recalled all the incidents of the previous day. Trukhina, the brigadier, and the sergeant, Kourilkin, rose vaguely before his imagination. He waited in silence for the servant to open the conversation and inform him of the events of the night.

"How you have slept, little father Adrian Prokhorovitch!" said Aksinia, handing him his dressing-gown. "Your neighbour, the tailor, has been here, and the watchman also called to inform you that to-day is his name-day; but you were so sound asleep, that we did not wish to wake you." "Did anyone come for me from the late Trukhina?"

"The late? Is she dead, then?"

"What a fool you are! Didn't you yourself help me yesterday to prepare the things for her funeral?"

"Have you taken leave of your senses, little father, or have you not yet recovered from the effects of yesterday's drinking-bout? What funeral was there yesterday? You spent the whole day feasting at the German's, and then came home drunk and threw yourself upon the bed, and have slept till this hour, when the bells have already rung for mass."

"Really!" said the coffin-maker, greatly relieved.

"Yes, indeed," replied the servant.

"Well, since that is the case, make the tea as quickly as possible and call my daughters."

KIRDJALI

Kirdjali was by birth a Bulgarian. Kirdjali, in the Turkish language, signifies a knight-errant, a bold fellow. His real name I do not know.

Kirdjali with his acts of brigandage brought terror upon the whole of Moldavia. In order to give some idea of him, I will relate one of his exploits. One night he and the Arnout Mikhaelaki fell together upon a Bulgarian village. They set it on fire at both ends, and began to go from hut to hut. Kirdjali dispatched the inmates, and Mikhaelaki carried off the booty. Both cried: "Kirdjali! Kirdjali!" The whole village took to flight.

When Alexander Ipsilanti[96] proclaimed the revolt and began to collect his army, Kirdjali brought to him some of his old companions. The real object of the revolt was but ill understood by them, but war presented an opportunity for getting rich at the expense of the Turks, and perhaps of the Moldavians, and that was object enough in their eyes.

Alexander Ipsilanti was personally brave, but he did not possess the qualities necessary for the rôle which he had assumed with such ardour and such a want of caution. He did not know how to manage the people over whom he was obliged to exercise control. They had neither respect for him nor confidence in him. After the unfortunate battle, in which perished the flower of Greek youth, Iordaki Olimbioti persuaded him to retire, and he himself took his place. Ipsilanti escaped to the borders of Austria, and thence sent his curses to the people whom he termed traitors, cowards and scoundrels. These cowards and scoundrels for the most part perished within the walls of the monastery of Seko, or on the banks of the Pruth, desperately defending themselves against an enemy ten times their number.

Kirdjali found himself in the detachment of George Kantakuzin, of whom might be repeated the same that has been said of Ipsilanti. On the eve of the battle near Skoulana, Kantakuzin asked permission of the Russian authorities to enter our lines. The detachment remained without a leader, but Kirdjali, Saphianos, Kantagoni, and others stood in no need whatever of a leader.

The battle near Skoulana does not seem to have been described by anybody in all its affecting reality. Imagine seven hundred men—

---

[96] The chief of the Hetairists (Philiké Hetairia), whose object was the liberation of Greece from the Turkish yoke.

Arnouts, Albanians, Greeks, Bulgarians and rabble of every kind—with no idea of military art, retreating in sight of fifteen thousand Turkish cavalry. This detachment hugged the bank of the Pruth, and placed in front of themselves two small cannons, found at Jassy, in the courtyard of the Governor, and from which salutes used to be fired on occasions of rejoicing. The Turks would have been glad to make use of their cartridges, but they dared not without the permission of the Russian authorities: the shots would infallibly have flown over to our shore. The commander of our lines (now deceased), although he had served forty years in the army, had never in his life heard the whistle of a bullet, but Heaven ordained that he should hear it then. Several of them whizzed past his ears. The old man became terribly angry, and abused the major of the Okhotsky infantry regiment, who happened to be in advance of the lines. The major, not knowing what to do, ran towards the river, beyond which some of the mounted insurgents were caracoling about, and threatened them with his finger. The insurgents, seeing this, turned round and galloped off, with the whole Turkish detachment after them. The major, who had threatened them with his finger, was called Khortcheffsky. I do not know what became of him.

The next day, however, the Turks attacked the Hetairists. Not daring to use bullets or cannon-balls, they resolved, contrary to their usual custom, to employ cold steel. The battle was a fiercely-contested one. Yataghans[97] were freely used. On the side of the Turks were seen lances, which had never been employed by them till then; these lances were Russian: Nekrassovists fought in their ranks. The Hetairists, by permission of our Emperor, were allowed to cross the Pruth and take refuge within our lines. They began to cross over. Kantagoni and Saphianos remained last upon the Turkish bank. Kirdjali, wounded the evening before, was already lying within our lines. Saphianos was killed. Kantagoni, a very stout man, was wounded in the stomach by a lance. With one hand he raised his sword, with the other he seized the hostile lance, thrust it further into himself, and in that manner was able to reach his murderer with his sword, when both fell together.

All was over. The Turks remained victorious. Moldavia was swept clear of insurrectionary bands. About six hundred Arnouts were dispersed throughout Bessarabia; and though not knowing how to support themselves, they were yet grateful to Russia for her protection. They led an idle life, but not a licentious one. They could always be seen in the coffee-houses of half Turkish Bessarabia, with

[97] Long Turkish daggers.

long pipes in their mouths, sipping coffee grounds out of small cups. Their figured jackets and red pointed slippers were already beginning to wear out, but their tufted skullcaps were still worn on the side of the head, and yataghans and pistols still protruded from under their broad sashes. Nobody complained of them. It was impossible to imagine that these poor, peaceably-disposed men were the notorious insurgents of Moldavia, the companions of the ferocious Kirdjali, and that he himself was among them.

The Pasha in command at Jassy became informed of this, and in virtue of treaty stipulations, requested the Russian authorities to deliver up the brigand.

The police instituted a search. They discovered that Kirdjali was really in Kishineff. They captured him in the house of a fugitive monk in the evening, when he was having supper, sitting in the dark with seven companions.

Kirdjali was placed under arrest. He did not try to conceal the truth; he acknowledged that he was Kirdjali.

"But," he added, "since I crossed the Pruth, I have not touched a hair of other people's property, nor imposed upon even a gipsy. To the Turks, to the Moldavians and to the Wallachians I am undoubtedly a brigand, but to the Russians I am a guest. When Saphianos, having fired off all his cartridges, came over into these lines, collecting from the wounded, for the last discharge, buttons, nails, watch-chains and the knobs of yataghans, I gave him twenty beshliks, and was left without money. God knows that I, Kirdjali, lived by alms. Why then do the Russians now deliver me into the hands of my enemies?"

After that, Kirdjali was silent, and tranquilly awaited the decision that was to determine his fate. He did not wait long. The authorities, not being bound to look upon brigands from their romantic side, and being convinced of the justice of the demand, ordered Kirdjali to be sent to Jassy.

A man of heart and intellect, at that time a young and unknown official, but now occupying an important post, vividly described to me his departure.

At the gate of the prison stood a karoutsa.... Perhaps you do not know what a karouisa is. It is a low, wicker vehicle, to which, not very long since, used generally to be yoked six or eight sorry jades. A Moldavian, with a moustache and a sheepskin cap, sitting astride one of them, incessantly shouted and cracked his whip, and his wretched animals ran on at a fairly sharp trot. If one of them began to slacken its pace, he unharnessed it with terrible oaths and left it upon the road, little caring what might be its fate. On the return journey he was sure to find it in the same place, quietly grazing upon the green steppe. It not unfrequently happened that a traveller, starting from one station with eight horses, arrived at the next with a pair only. It used to be so about fifteen years ago. Nowadays in Russianized Bessarabia they have adopted Russian harness and Russian telegas.

Such a karoutsa stood at the gate of the prison in the year 1821, towards the end of the month of September. Jewesses in loose sleeves and slippers down at heel, Arnouts in their ragged and picturesque attire, well-proportioned Moldavian women with black-eyed children in their arms, surrounded the karoutsa. The men preserved silence, the women were eagerly expecting something.

The gate opened, and several police officers stepped out into the street; behind them came two soldiers leading the fettered Kirdjali.

He seemed about thirty years of age. The features of his swarthy face were regular and harsh. He was tall, broad-shouldered, and seemed endowed with unusual physical strength. A variegated turban covered the side of his head, and a broad sash encircled his slender waist. A dolman of thick, dark-blue cloth, the broad folds of his shirt falling below the knee, and handsome slippers composed the remainder of his costume. His look was proud and calm....

One of the officials, a red-faced old man in a threadbare uniform, three buttons of which were dangling down, with a pair of pewter spectacles pinching the purple knob that served him for a nose, unrolled a paper and, in a snuffling tone, began to read in the Moldavian tongue. From time to time he glanced haughtily at the fettered Kirdjali, to whom apparently the paper referred. Kirdjali listened to him attentively. The official finished his reading, folded up the paper and shouted sternly at the people, ordering them to give way and the karoutsa to be driven up. Then Kirdjali turned to him and said a few words to him in Moldavian; his voice trembled, his countenance changed, he burst into tears and fell at the feet of the police official, clanking his fetters. The police official, terrified, started back; the soldiers were about to raise Kirdjali, but he rose up himself, gathered up his chains, stepped into the karoutsa and cried: "Drive on!" A gendarme took a seat beside him, the Moldavian cracked his whip, and the karoutsa rolled away.

"What did Kirdjali say to you?" asked the young official of the police officer.

"He asked me," replied the police officer, smiling, "to look after his wife and child, who lived not far from Kilia, in a Bulgarian village: he is afraid that they may suffer through him. The mob is so stupid!"

The young official's story affected me deeply. I was sorry for

251

poor Kirdjali. For a long time I knew nothing of his fate. Some years later I met the young official. We began to talk about the past.

"What about your friend Kirdjali?" I asked. "Do you know what became of him?"

"To be sure I do," replied he, and he related to me the following.

Kirdjali, having been taken to Jassy, was brought before the Pasha, who condemned him to be impaled. The execution was deferred till some holiday. In the meantime he was confined in jail.

The prisoner was guarded by seven Turks (common people, and in their hearts as much brigands as Kirdjali himself); they respected him and, like all Orientals, listened with avidity to his strange stories.

Between the guards and the prisoner an intimate acquaintance sprang up. One day Kirdjali said to them: "Brothers! my hour is near. Nobody can escape his fate. I shall soon take leave of you. I should like to leave you something in remembrance of me."

The Turks pricked up their ears.

"Brothers," continued Kirdjali, "three years ago, when I was engaged in plundering along with the late Mikhaelaki, we buried on the steppes, not from Jassy, a kettle filled with money. Evidently, neither I nor he will make use of the hoard. Be it so; take it for yourselves and divide it in a friendly manner."

The Turks almost took leave of their senses. The question was, how were they to find the blessed spot? They thought and thought and finally resolved that Kirdjali himself should conduct them to the place.

Night came on. The Turks removed the irons from the feet of the prisoner, tied his hands with a rope, and, leaving the town, set out with him for the steppe.

Kirdjali led them, keeping on in one direction from one mound to another. They walked on for a long time. At last Kirdjali stopped near a broad stone, measured twelve paces towards the south, stamped and said: "Here."

The Turks began to make their arrangements. Four of them took out their yataghans and commenced digging the earth. Three remained on guard. Kirdjali sat down upon the stone and watched them at their work.

"Well, how much longer are you going to be?" he asked; "haven't you come to it?"

"Not yet," replied the Turks, and they worked away with such ardour, that the perspiration rolled from them like hail.

Kirdjali began to show signs of impatience.

"What people!" he exclaimed: "they do not even know how to

252

dig decently. I should have finished the whole business in a couple of minutes. Children! untie my hands and give me a yataghan."

The Turks reflected and began to take counsel together. "What harm would there be?" reasoned they. "Let us untie his hands and give him a yataghan. He is only one, we are seven."

And the Turks untied his hands and gave him a yataghan.

At last Kirdjali was free and armed. What must he have felt at that moment!.... He began digging quickly, the guard helping him.... Suddenly he plunged his yataghan into one of them, and, leaving the blade in his breast, he snatched from his belt a couple of pistols.

The remaining six, seeing Kirdjali armed with two pistols, ran off.

Kirdjali is now carrying on the profession of brigand near Jassy. Not long ago he wrote to the Governor, demanding from him five thousand levs,[98] and threatening, in the event of the money not being paid, to set fire to Jassy and to reach the Governor himself. The five thousand levs were handed over to him!

Such is Kirdjali!

---

[98] A lev is worth about ten-pence.

THE EGYPTIAN NIGHTS

CHAPTER I

Charsky was one of the native-born inhabitants of St. Petersburg. He was not yet thirty years of age; he was not married; the service did not oppress him too heavily. His late uncle, having been a vice-governor in the good old times, had left him a respectable estate. His life was a very agreeable one, but he had the misfortune to write and print verses. In the journals he was called "poet," and in the ante-rooms "author."

In spite of the great privileges which verse-makers enjoy (we must confess that, except the right of using the accusative instead of the genitive, and other so-called poetical licenses of a similar kind, we fail to see what are the particular privileges of Russian poets), in spite of their every possible privilege, these persons are compelled to endure a great deal of unpleasantness. The bitterest misfortune of all, the most intolerable for the poet, is the appellation with which he is branded, and which will always cling to him. The public look upon him as their own property; in their opinion, he was created for their especial benefit and pleasure. Should he return from the country, the first person who meets him accosts him with:

"Haven't you brought anything new for us?"

Should the derangement of his affairs, or the illness of some being dear to him, cause him to become lost in thoughtful reflection, immediately a trite smile accompanies the trite exclamation:

"No doubt he is composing something!"

Should he happen to fall in love, his beauty purchases an album at the English warehouse, and expects an elegy.

Should he call upon a man whom he hardly knows, to talk about serious matters of business, the latter quickly calls his son and compels him to read some of the verses of so-and-so, and the lad regales the poet with some of his lame productions. And these are but the flowers of, the calling; what then must be the fruits! Charsky acknowledged that the compliments, the questions, the albums, and the little boys bored him to such an extent, that he was constantly compelled to restrain himself from committing some act of rudeness.

Charsky used every possible endeavour to rid himself of the intolerable appellation. He avoided the society of his literary brethren, and preferred to them the men of the world, even the most shallow-minded: but that did not help him. His conversation was of the most commonplace character, and never turned upon literature. In his dress he always observed the very latest fashion, with the timidity and superstition of a young Moscovite arriving in St. Petersburg for the first time in his life. In his study, furnished like a lady's bedroom, nothing recalled the writer; no books littered the table; the divan was not stained with ink; there was none of that disorder which denotes the presence of the Muse and the absence of broom and brush. Charsky was in despair if any of his worldly friends found him with a pen in his hand. It is difficult to believe to what trifles a man, otherwise endowed with talent and soul, can descend. At one time he pretended to be a passionate lover of horses, at another a desperate gambler, and at another a refined gourmet, although he was never able to distinguish the mountain breed from the Arab, could never remember the trump cards, and in secret preferred a baked potato to all the inventions of the French cuisine. He led a life of unbounded pleasure, was seen at all the balls, gormandized at all the diplomatic dinners, and appeared at all the soirees as inevitably as the Rezan ices. For all that, he was a poet, and his passion was invincible. When he found the "silly fit" (thus he called the inspiration) coming upon him, Charsky would shut himself up in his study, and write from morning till late into the night. He confessed to his genuine friends that only then did he know what real happiness was. The rest of his time he strolled about, dissembled, and was assailed at every step by the eternal question:

"Haven't you written anything new?"

One morning, Charsky felt that happy disposition of soul, when the illusions are represented in their brightest colours, when vivid, unexpected words present themselves for the incarnation of one's visions, when verses flow easily from the pen, and sonorous rhythms fly to meet harmonious thoughts. Charsky was mentally plunged into a sweet oblivion... and the world, and the trifles of the world, and his own particular whims no longer existed for him. He was writing verses.

Suddenly the door of his study creaked, and the unknown head of a man appeared. Charsky gave a sudden start and frowned.

"Who is there?" he asked with vexation, inwardly cursing his servants, who were never in the ante-room when they were wanted.

The unknown entered. He was of a tall, spare figure, and appeared to be about thirty years of age. The features of his swarthy face were very expressive: his pale, lofty forehead, shaded by dark locks of hair, his black, sparkling eyes, aquiline nose, and thick beard surrounding his sunken, tawny cheeks, indicated him to be a foreigner. He was attired in a black dress-coat, already whitened at the seams, and summer trousers (although the season was well into the autumn); under his tattered black cravat, upon a yellowish shirt-front, glittered a false diamond; his shaggy hat seemed to have seen rain and bad weather. Meeting such a man in a wood, you would have taken him for a robber; in society—for a political conspirator; in an ante-room—for a charlatan, a seller of elixirs and arsenic.

"What do you want?" Charsky asked him in French.

"Signor," replied the foreigner in Italian, with several profound bows: "Lei voglia perdonar mi, si ..." (Please pardon me, if....)

Charsky did not offer him a chair, and he rose himself: the conversation was continued in Italian.

"I am a Neapolitan artist," said the unknown: "circumstances compelled me to leave my native land; I have, come to Russia, trusting to my talent."

Charsky thought that the Italian was preparing to give some violoncello concerts and was disposing of his tickets from house to house. He was just about to give him twenty-five roubles in order to get rid of him as quickly as possible, but the unknown added:

"I hope, signor, that you will give a friendly support to your confrère, and introduce me into the houses to which, you have access."

It was impossible to offer a greater affront to Charsky's vanity. He glanced haughtily at the individual who called himself his confrère.

"Allow me to ask, what are you, and for whom do you take me?" he said, with difficulty restraining his indignation.

The Neapolitan observed his vexation.

"Signor," he replied, stammering: "Ho creduto ... ho sentito ... la vostra Eccelenza ... mi ferdonera..." (I believed ... I felt ... Your Excellency ... will pardon me....)

"What do you want?" repeated Charsky drily.

"I have heard a great deal of your wonderful talent; I am sure that the gentlemen of this place esteem it an honour to extend every possible protection to such an excellent poet," replied the Italian: "and that is why I have ventured to present myself to you...."

"You are mistaken, signor," interrupted Charsky. "The calling of poet does not exist among us. Our poets do not solicit the protection of gentlemen; our poets are gentlemen themselves, and if our Maecenases (devil take them!) do not know that, so much the worse for them. Among us there are no ragged abbés, whom a musician would take out of the streets to compose a libretto. Among us, poets do not go on foot from house to house, begging for help. Moreover, they must have been joking, when they told you that I was a great poet. It is true that I once wrote some wretched epigrams, but thank God, I haven't anything in common with messieurs les poètes, and do not wish to have."

The poor Italian became confused. He looked around him. The pictures, marble statues, bronzes, and the costly baubles on Gothic what-nots, struck him. He understood that between the haughty dandy, standing before him in a tufted brocaded cap, gold-embroidered nankeen dressing-gown and Turkish sash,—and himself, a poor wandering artist, in tattered cravat and shabby dress-coat—there was nothing in common. He stammered out some unintelligible excuses, bowed, and wished to retire. His pitiable appearance touched Charsky, who, in spite of the defects in his character, had a good and noble heart. He felt ashamed of his irritated vanity.

"Where are you going?" he said to the Italian. "Wait ... I was compelled to decline an unmerited title and confess to you that I was not a poet. Now let us speak about your business. I am ready to serve you, if it be in my power to do so. Are you a musician?"

"No, Eccelenza," replied the Italian; "I am a poor improvisatore."

"An improvisatore!" cried Charsky, feeling all the cruelty of his reception. "Why didn't you say sooner that you were an improvisatore?"

And Charsky grasped his hand with a feeling of sincere regret.

His friendly manner encouraged the Italian. He spoke naïvely of his plans. His exterior was not deceptive. He was in need of money, and he hoped somehow in Russia to improve his domestic circumstances. Charsky listened to him with attention.

"I hope," said he to the poor artist, "that you will have success; society here has never heard an improvisatore. Curiosity will be awakened. It is true that the Italian language is not in use among us; you will not be understood, but that will be no great misfortune; the chief thing is that you should be in the fashion."

"But if nobody among you understands Italian," said the improvisatore, becoming thoughtful, "who will come to hear me?"

"Have no fear about that—they will come: some out of curiosity, others to pass away the evening somehow or other, others to show that they understand Italian. I repeat, it is only necessary that you should be in the fashion, and you will be in the fashion—I give you my hand upon it."

Charsky dismissed the improvisatore very cordially, after having taken his address, and the same evening he set to work to do what he could for him.

CHAPTER II

The next day, in the dark and dirty corridor of a tavern, Charsky discovered the number 35. He stopped at the door and knocked. It was opened by the Italian of the day before.

"Victory!" said Charsky to him: "your affairs are in a good way. The Princess N——, offers you her salon; yesterday, at the rout, I succeeded in enlisting the half of St. Petersburg; get your tickets and announcements printed. If I cannot guarantee a triumph for you, I'll answer for it that you will at least be a gainer in pocket...."

"And that is the chief thing," cried the Italian, manifesting his delight in a series of gestures that were characteristic of his southern origin. "I knew that you would help me. Corpo di Baccol You are a poet like myself, and there is no denying that poets are excellent fellows! How can I show my gratitude to you? Stop.... Would you like to hear an improvisation?"

"An improvisation!... Can you then do without public, without music, and without sounds of applause?"

"And where could I find a better public? You are a poet: you understand me better than they, and your quiet approbation will be dearer to me than whole storms of applause.... Sit down somewhere and give me a theme." "Here is your theme, then," said Charsky to him: "the poet himself should choose the subject of his songs; the crowd has not the right to direct his inspirations." The eyes of the Italian sparkled: he tried a few chords, raised his head proudly, and passionate verses—the expression of instantaneous sentiment—fell in cadence from his lips....

The Italian ceased.... Charsky remained silent, filled with delight and astonishment.

"Well?" asked the improvisatore.

Charsky seized his hand and pressed it firmly.

"Well?" asked the improvisatore.

"Wonderful!" replied the poet. "The idea of another has scarcely reached your ears, and already it has become your own, as if you had nursed, fondled and developed it for a long time. And so for you there exists neither difficulty nor discouragement, nor that uneasiness which precedes inspiration? Wonderful, wonderful!"

The improvisatore replied: "Each talent is inexplicable. How does the sculptor see, in a block of Carrara marble, the hidden Jupiter, and how does he bring it to light with hammer and chisel by chipping off its envelope? Why does the idea issue from the poet's head already equipped with four rhymes, and arranged in measured

258

and harmonious feet? Nobody, except the improvisatore himself, can understand that rapid impression, that narrow link between inspiration proper and a strange exterior will; I myself would try in vain to explain it. But ... I must think of my first evening. What do you think? What price could I charge for the tickets, so that the public may not be too exacting, and so that, at the same time, I may not be out of pocket myself? They say that La Signora Catalani[99] took twenty-five roubles. That is a good price...."

It was very disagreeable to Charsky to fall suddenly from the heights of poesy down to the bookkeeper's desk, but he understood very well the necessities of this world, and he assisted the Italian in his mercantile calculations. The improvisator, during this part of the business, exhibited such savage greed, such an artless love of gain, that he disgusted Charsky, who hastened to take leave of him, so that he might not lose altogether the feeling of ecstasy awakened within him by the brilliant improvisation. The Italian, absorbed in his calculations, did not observe this change, and he conducted Charsky into the corridor and out to the steps, with profound bows and assurances of eternal gratitude.

CHAPTER III

The salon of Princess N—— had been placed at the disposal of the improvisatore; a platform had been erected, and the chairs were arranged in twelve rows. On the appointed day, at seven o'clock in the evening, the room was illuminated; at the door, before a small table, to sell and receive tickets, sat a long-nosed old woman, in a grey cap with broken feathers, and with rings on all her fingers. Near the steps stood gendarmes.

The public began to assemble. Charsky was one of the first to arrive. He had contributed greatly to the success of the representation, and wished to see the improvisatore, in order to know if he was satisfied with everything. He found the Italian in a side room, observing his watch with impatience. The improvisatore

---

[99] A celebrated Italian vocalist, whose singing created an unprecedented sensation in the principal European capitals during the first quarter of the present century.

259

was attired in a theatrical costume. He was dressed in black from head to foot. The lace collar of his shirt was thrown back; his naked neck, by its strange whiteness, offered a striking contrast to his thick black beard; his hair was brought forward, and overshadowed his forehead and eyebrows.

All this was not very gratifying to Charsky, who did not care to see a poet in the dress of a wandering juggler. After a short conversation, he returned to the salon, which was becoming more and more crowded. Soon all the rows of seats were occupied by brilliantly-dressed ladies: the gentlemen stood crowded round the sides of the platform, along the walls, and behind the chairs at the back; the musicians, with their music-stands, occupied two sides of the platform.

In the middle, upon a table, stood a porcelain vase.

The audience was a large one. Everybody awaited the commencement with impatience. At last, at half-past seven o'clock, the musicians made a stir, prepared their bows, and played the overture from "Tancredi." All took their places and became silent. The last sounds of the overture ceased.... The improvisatore, welcomed by the deafening applause which rose from every side, advanced with profound bows to the very edge of the platform.

Charsky waited with uneasiness to see what would be the first impression produced, but he perceived that the costume, which had seemed to him so unbecoming, did not produce the same effect upon the audience; even Charsky himself found nothing ridiculous in the Italian, when he saw him upon the platform, with his pale face brightly illuminated by a multitude of lamps and candles. The applause subsided; the sound of voices ceased....

The Italian, expressing himself in bad French, requested the gentlemen present to indicate some themes, by writing them upon separate pieces of paper. At this unexpected invitation, all looked at one another in silence, and nobody made reply. The Italian, after waiting a little while, repeated his request in a timid and humble voice. Charsky was standing right under the platform; a feeling of uneasiness took possession of him; he had a presentiment that the business would not be able to go on without him, and that he would be compelled to write his theme. Indeed, several ladies turned their faces towards him and began to pronounce his name, at first in a low tone, then louder and louder. Hearing his name, the improvisatore sought him with his eyes, and perceiving him at his feet, he handed him a pencil and a piece of paper with a friendly smile. To play a rôle in this comedy seemed very disagreeable to Charsky, but there was no help for it: he took the pencil and paper from the hands of the Italian and wrote some words. The Italian, taking the vase from the table, descended from the platform and presented it to Charsky, who deposited within it his theme. His example produced an effect: two journalists, in their quality as literary men, considered it incumbent upon them to write each his theme; the secretary of the Neapolitan embassy, and a young man recently returned from a journey to Florence, placed in the urn their folded papers. At last, a very plain-looking girl, at the command of her mother, with tears in her eyes, wrote a few lines in Italian and, blushing to the ears, gave them to the improvisatore, the ladies in the meantime regarding her in silence, with a scarcely perceptible smile. Returning to the platform, the improvisatore placed the urn upon the table, and began to take out the papers one after the other, reading each aloud:

"La famiglia del Cenci. ... L'ultimo giorno di Pompeia ... Cleopatra e i suoi amanti. ... La primavera veduta da una prigione. ... Il trionfo di Tasso."

"What does the honourable company command?" asked the Italian humbly. "Will it indicate itself one of the subjects proposed, or let the matter be decided by lot?"

"By lot!" said a voice in the crowd.... "By lot, by lot!" repeated the audience.

The improvisatore again descended from the platform, holding the urn in his hands, and casting an imploring glance along the first row of chairs, asked:

"Who will be kind enough to draw out the theme?"

Not one of the brilliant ladies, who were sitting there, stirred. The improvisatore, not accustomed to Northern indifference, seemed greatly disconcerted.... Suddenly he perceived on one side of the room a small white-gloved hand held up: he turned quickly and advanced towards a tall young beauty, seated at the end of the second row. She rose without the slightest confusion, and, with the greatest simplicity in the world, plunged her aristocratic hand into the urn and drew out a roll of paper.

"Will you please unfold it and read," said the improvisatore to her.

The young lady unrolled the paper and read aloud:

"Cleopatra e i suoi amanti."

These words were uttered in a gentle voice, but such a deep silence reigned in the room, that everybody heard them. The improvisatore bowed profoundly to the young lady, with an air of the deepest gratitude, and returned to his platform.

"Gentlemen," said he, turning to the audience: "the lot has indicated as the subject of improvisation: 'Cleopatra and her lovers,' I humbly request the person who has chosen this theme, to explain

261

to me his idea: what lovers is it here a question of, perchè la grande regina haveva molto?"

At these words, several gentlemen burst out laughing. The improvisatore became somewhat confused.

"I should like to know," he continued, "to what historical feature does the person, who has chosen this theme, allude?... I should feel very grateful if he would kindly explain."

Nobody hastened to reply. Several ladies directed their glances towards the plain-looking girl who had written a theme at the command of her mother. The poor girl observed this hostile attention, and became so confused, that the tears came into her eyes.... Charsky could not endure this, and turning to the improvisatore, he said to him in Italian:

"It was I who proposed the theme. I had in view a passage in Aurelius Victor, who speaks as if Cleopatra used to name death as the price of her love, and yet there were found adorers whom such a condition neither frightened nor repelled. It seems to me, however, that the subject is somewhat difficult.... Could you not choose another?"

But the improvisatore already felt the approach of the god.... He gave a sign to the musicians to play. His face became terribly pale; he trembled as if in a fever; his eyes sparkled with a strange fire; he raised with his hand his dark hair, wiped with his handkerchief his lofty forehead, covered with beads of perspiration.... then suddenly stepped forward and folded his arms across his breast.... the musicians ceased.... the improvisation began:

> "The palace glitters; the songs of the choir
> Echo the sounds of the flute and lyre;
> With voice and glance the stately Queen
> Gives animation to the festive scene,
> And eyes are turned to her throne above,
> And hearts beat wildly with ardent love.
> But suddenly that brow so proud
> Is shadowed with a gloomy cloud,
> And slowly on her heaving breast,
> Her pensive head sinks down to rest.
> The music ceases, hushed is each breath,
> Upon the feast falls the lull of death;"[100]

*****

---

[100] The story is incomplete in the original.—Translator.

CHAPTER I

Among the number of young men sent abroad by Peter the Great for the acquisition of knowledge indispensable to a country in a state of transition, was his godson, the negro, Ibrahim. After being educated in the Military School at Paris, which he left with the rank of Captain of Artillery, he distinguished himself in the Spanish War of Succession, but having been severely wounded, he returned to Paris. The Emperor, in the midst of his extensive labours, never ceased to inquire after his favourite and he always received flattering accounts of his progress and conduct. Peter was exceedingly pleased with him, and more than once requested him to return to Russia, but Ibrahim was in no hurry. He excused himself under various pretexts: now it was his wound, now it was a wish to complete his education, now a want of money; and Peter indulgently complied with his wishes, begged him to take care of his health, thanked him for his zeal in the pursuit of knowledge, and although extremely parsimonious in his own expenses, he did not spare his exchequer when his favourite was concerned, and the ducats were generally accompanied by fatherly advice and words of admonition.

According to the testimony of all historical accounts, nothing could be compared with the frivolity, folly and luxury of the French of that period. The last years of the reign of Louis the Fourteenth, remarkable for the strict piety, gravity, and decorum of the court, had left no traces behind. The Duke of Orleans, uniting many brilliant qualities with vices of every kind, unfortunately did not possess the slightest shadow of hypocrisy. The orgies of the Palais Royal were no secret in Paris; the example was infectious. At that time Law[102] appeared upon the scene; greed for money was united to the thirst for pleasure and dissipation; estates were squandered, morals perished, Frenchmen laughed and calculated, and the kingdom fell to pieces to the music of satirical vaudevilles.

In the meantime society presented a most remarkable picture.

---

[101] Although this story was unfortunately left unfinished, it has been included in this collection, as, apart from its intrinsic merit, it throws an interesting light upon the history of Poushkin's African ancestor.—The real name of the hero was Hannibal.—Translator.

[102] John Law, the famous projector of financial schemes.

Culture and the desire for amusement brought all ranks together. Wealth, amiability, renown, talent, even eccentricity—everything that satisfied curiosity or promised amusement, was received with the same indulgence. Literature, learning and philosophy forsook their quiet studies and appeared in the circles of the great world to render homage to fashion and to obey its decrees. Women reigned, but no longer demanded adoration. Superficial politeness was substituted for the profound respect formerly shown to them. The pranks of the Duke de Richelieu, the Alcibiades of modern Athens, belong to history, and give an idea of the morals of that period.

> "Temps fortuné, marqué par la licence,
> Où la folie, agitant son grelot,
> D'un pied leger parcourt toute la France,
> Où nul mortel ne daigne être dévot,
> Où l'on fait tout excepté pénitence."

The appearance of Ibrahim, his bearing, culture and natural intelligence excited general attention in Paris. All the ladies were anxious to see "le négre du Czar" at their houses, and vied with each other in their attentions towards him. The Regent invited him more than once to his merry evening parties; he assisted at the suppers animated by the youth of Arouet,[103] the old age of Chaulieu, and the conversations of Montesquieu and Fontenelle. He did not miss a single ball, fête or first representation, and he gave himself up to the general whirl with all the ardour of his years and nature. But the thought of exchanging these delights, these brilliant amusements for the simplicity of the Petersburg Court was not the only thing that dismayed Ibrahim; other and stronger ties bound him to Paris. The young African was in love.

The Countess L——, although no longer in the first bloom of youth, was still renowned for her beauty. On leaving the convent at the age of seventeen, she was married to a man whom she had not succeeded in loving, and who later on did not take the trouble to gain her love. Report assigned several lovers to her, but thanks to the indulgent views entertained by the world, she enjoyed a good reputation, for nobody was able to reproach her with any ridiculous or scandalous adventure. Her house was one of the most fashionable, and the best Parisian society made it their rendezvous. Ibrahim was introduced to her by young Merville, who was generally looked upon as her latest lover,—and who did all in his power to obtain credit for the report.

---

[103] Voltaire.

The Countess received Ibrahim politely, but without any particular attention: this made him feel flattered. Generally the young negro was regarded in the light of a curiosity; people used to surround him and overwhelm him with compliments and questions—and this curiosity, although concealed by a show of graciousness, offended his vanity. The delightful attention of women, almost the sole aim of our exertions, not only afforded him no pleasure, but even filled him with bitterness and indignation. He felt that he was for them a kind of rare beast, a peculiar creature, accidentally brought into the world, but having with it nothing in common. He even envied people who remained unnoticed, and considered them fortunate in their insignificance.

The thought, that nature had not created him for the inspiring of a passion, emancipated him from self-assertion and vain pretensions, and added a rare charm to his behaviour towards women. His conversation was simple and dignified; he found great favour in the eyes of the Countess L——, who had grown tired of the pronounced jests and pointed insinuations of French wit. Ibrahim frequently visited her. Little by little she became accustomed to the young negro's appearance, and even began to find something agreeable in that curly head, that stood out so black in the midst of the powdered perukes in her reception-room (Ibrahim had been wounded in the head, and wore a bandage instead of a peruke). He was twenty-seven years of age, and was tall and slender, and more than one beauty glanced at him with a feeling more flattering than simple curiosity. But the prejudiced Ibrahim either did not observe anything of this or merely looked upon it as coquetry. But when his glances met those of the Countess, his distrust vanished. Her eyes expressed such winning kindness, her manner towards him was so simple, so unconstrained, that it was impossible to suspect her of the least shadow of coquetry or raillery.

The thought of love had not entered his head, but to see the Countess each day had become a necessity to him. He tried to meet her everywhere, and every meeting with her seemed an unexpected favour from heaven. The Countess guessed his feelings before he himself did. There is no denying that a love, which is without hope and which demands nothing, touches the female heart more surely than all the devices of the libertine. In the presence of Ibrahim, the Countess followed all his movements, listened to every word that he said; without him she became thoughtful, and fell into her usual absence of mind. Merville was the first to observe this mutual inclination, and he congratulated Ibrahim. Nothing inflames love so much as the approving observations of a bystander: love is blind, and, having no trust in itself, readily grasps hold of every support.

Merville's words roused Ibrahim. The possibility of possessing the woman that he loved had never till then occurred to his mind; hope suddenly dawned upon his soul; he fell madly in love. In vain did the Countess, alarmed by the ardour of his passion, wish to combat his vehemence with friendly warnings and wise counsels, she herself was beginning to waver....

Nothing is hidden from the eyes of the observing world. The Countess's new inclination was soon known by everybody. Some ladies were amazed at her choice; to many it seemed quite natural. Some laughed; others regarded her conduct as unpardonably indiscreet. In the first intoxication of passion, Ibrahim and the Countess observed nothing, but soon the equivocal jokes of the men and the sarcastic observations of the women began to reach their ears. Ibrahim's cold and serious manner had hitherto protected him from such attacks; he bore them with impatience, and knew not how to retaliate. The Countess, accustomed to the respect of the world, could not calmly bear to see herself an object of calumny and ridicule. With tears in her eyes she complained to Ibrahim, now bitterly reproaching him, now imploring him not to defend her, lest by some useless brawl she should be completely ruined.

A new circumstance tended to make her position still more difficult: the result of imprudent love began to be noticeable. The Countess in despair informed Ibrahim of the matter. Consolation, advice, proposals—all were exhausted and all rejected. The Countess saw that her ruin was inevitable, and in despair awaited it.

As soon as the condition of the Countess became known, gossip began again with renewed vigour; sentimental women gave vent to exclamations of horror; and epigrams were disseminated with reference to her husband, who alone in all Paris knew nothing and suspected nothing.

The fatal moment approached. The condition of the Countess was terrible. Ibrahim visited her every day. He saw her mental and physical strength gradually giving way. Her tears and her terror were renewed every moment Measures were hastily taken. Means were found for getting the Count out of the way. The doctor arrived. Two days before this a poor woman had been persuaded to resign into the hands of strangers her new-born infant; for this a confidential person was sent. Ibrahim was in the room adjoining the bedchamber where lay the unhappy Countess.... Suddenly he heard the weak cry of a child—and, unable to repress his delight, he rushed into the Countess's room.... A black baby lay upon the bed at her feet. Ibrahim approached it. His heart beat violently. He blessed his son with a trembling hand. The Countess smiled faintly and stretched out to him her feeble hand, but the doctor, fearing that the excitement might be too great for the patient, dragged Ibrahim away from her bed. The new-born child was placed in a covered basket, and carried out of the house by a secret staircase. Then the other child was brought in, and its cradle placed in the bedroom. Ibrahim took his departure, feeling very ill at ease. The Count was expected. He returned late, heard of the happy deliverance of his wife, and was much gratified. In this way the public, which had been expecting a great scandal, was deceived in its hope, and was compelled to console itself with slandering. Everything resumed its usual course.

But Ibrahim felt that there would have to be a change in his lot, and that sooner or later his relations with the Countess would come to the knowledge of her husband. In that case, whatever might happen, the ruin of the Countess was inevitable. Ibrahim loved passionately and was passionately loved in return, but the Countess was wilful and light-minded; it was not the first time that she had loved. Disgust, and even hatred might replace in her heart the most tender feelings. Ibrahim already foresaw the moment of her coolness. Hitherto he had not known jealousy, but with dread he now felt a presentiment of it; he thought that the pain of separation would be less distressing, and he resolved to break off the unhappy connection, leave Paris, and return to Russia, whither Peter and a vague sense of duty had been calling him for a long time.

CHAPTER II

Days, months passed, and the enamoured Ibrahim could not resolve to leave the woman that he had seduced. The Countess grew more and more attached to him. Their son was being brought up in a distant province. The slanders of the world were beginning to subside, and the lovers began to enjoy greater tranquillity, silently remembering the past storm and endeavouring not to think of the future.

One day Ibrahim was in the lobby of the Duke of Orleans' residence. The Duke, passing by him, stopped, and handing him a letter, told him to read it at his leisure. It was a letter from Peter the First. The Emperor, guessing the true cause of his absence, wrote to the Duke that he had no intention of compelling Ibrahim, that he left it to his own free will to return to Russia or not, but that in any case he would never abandon his former foster-child. This letter touched Ibrahim to the bottom of his heart. From that moment his resolution was taken. The next day he informed the Regent of his intention to set out immediately for Russia.

"Reflect upon what you are going to do," said the Duke to him: "Russia is not your native country. I do not think that you will ever again see your torrid home, but your long residence in France has made you equally a stranger to the climate and the ways of life of semi-civilized Russia. You were not born a subject of Peter. Listen to my advice: take advantage of his magnanimous permission, remain in France, for which you have already shed your blood, and rest assured that here your services and talents will not remain unrewarded."

Ibrahim thanked the Duke sincerely, but remained firm in his resolution.

"I feel very sorry," said the Regent: "but perhaps you are right."

He promised to let him retire from the French service, and wrote a full account of the matter to the Czar.

Ibrahim was soon ready for the journey. On the eve of his departure he spent the evening as usual at the house of the Countess L——. She knew nothing. Ibrahim had not the courage to inform her of his intention. The Countess was calm and cheerful. She several times called him to her and joked about his thoughtfulness. After supper the guests departed. The Countess, her husband, and Ibrahim were left alone in the parlour. The unhappy man would have given everything in the world to have been left alone with her; but Count L—— seemed to have seated himself so comfortably beside the fire, that it appeared useless to hope that he would leave the room. All three remained silent.

"Bonne nuit!" said the Countess at last.

A pang passed through Ibrahim's heart, and he suddenly felt all the horrors of parting. He stood motionless.

"Bonne nuit, messieurs!" repeated the Countess.

Still he remained motionless.... At last his eyes became dim, his head swam round, and he could scarcely walk out of the room. On reaching home, he wrote, almost unconsciously, the following letter:

"I am going away, dear Leonora; I am leaving you for ever. I am writing to you, because I have not the strength to inform you otherwise.

"My happiness could not continue: I have enjoyed it against fate and nature. You must have ceased to love me; the enchantment must have vanished. This thought has always pursued me, even in those moments when I have seemed to forget everything, when at

268

your feet I have been intoxicated by your passionate self-denial, by your unbounded tenderness.... The thoughtless world unmercifully runs down that which it permits in theory; its cold irony sooner or later would have vanquished you, would have humbled your ardent soul, and at last you would have become ashamed of your passion.... What would then have become of me? No, it were better that I should die, better that I should leave you before that terrible moment.

"Your tranquillity is dearer to me than everything: you could not enjoy it while the eyes of the world were fixed upon you. Think of all that you have suffered, all your wounded self-love, all the tortures of fear; remember the terrible birth of our son. Think: ought I to expose you any longer to such agitations and dangers? Why should I endeavour to unite the fate of such a tender, beautiful creature to the miserable fate of a negro, of a pitiable being, scarce worthy of the name of man?

"Farewell, Leonora; farewell, my dear and only friend. I am leaving you, I am leaving the first and last joy of my life. I have neither fatherland nor kindred; I am going to Russia, where my utter loneliness will be a consolation to me. Serious business, to which from this time forth I devote myself, if it will not stifle, will at least divert painful recollections of the days of rapture and bliss.... Farewell, Leonora! I tear myself away from this letter, as if from your embrace. Farewell, be happy, and think sometimes of the poor negro, of your faithful Ibrahim."

That same night he set out for Russia.

The journey did not seem to him as terrible as he had expected. His imagination triumphed over the reality. The further he got from Paris, the more vivid and nearer rose up before him the objects he was leaving for ever.

Before he was aware of it he had crossed the Russian frontier. Autumn had already set in, but the postilions, in spite of the bad state of the roads, drove him with the speed of the wind, and on the seventeenth day of his journey he arrived at Krasnoe Selo, through which at that time the high road passed.

It was still a distance of twenty-eight versts to Petersburg. While the horses were being changed, Ibrahim entered the post-house. In a corner, a tall man, in a green caftan and with a clay pipe in his mouth, was leaning with his elbows upon the table reading the "Hamburg Gazette," Hearing somebody enter, he raised his head.

"Ah, Ibrahim!" he exclaimed, rising from the bench. "How do you do, godson?"

Ibrahim recognized Peter, and in his delight was about to rush towards him, but he respectfully paused. The Emperor approached, embraced him and kissed him upon the forehead.

"I was informed of your coming," said Peter, "and set off to meet you. I have been waiting for you here since yesterday."

Ibrahim could not find words to express his gratitude.

"Let your carriage follow on behind us," continued the Emperor, "and you take your place by my side and ride along with me."

The Czar's carriage was driven up; he took his seat with Ibrahim, and they set off at a gallop. In about an hour and a half they reached Petersburg. Ibrahim gazed with curiosity at the new-born city which had sprung up at the beck of his master. Bare banks, canals without quays, wooden bridges everywhere testified to the recent triumph of the human will over the hostile elements. The houses seemed to have been built in a hurry. In the whole town there was nothing magnificent but the Neva, not yet ornamented with its granite frame, but already covered with warships and merchant vessels. The imperial carriage stopped at the palace, i.e., at the Tsaritsin Garden. On the steps Peter was met by a woman of about thirty-five years of age, handsome, and dressed in the latest Parisian fashion. Peter kissed her and, taking Ibrahim by the hand, said:

"Do you recognize my godson, Katinka?[104] I beg you to love and favour him as formerly."

Catherine fixed on him her dark piercing eyes, and stretched out her hand to him in a friendly manner. Two young beauties, tall, slender, and fresh as roses, stood behind her and respectfully approached Peter.

"Liza," said he to one of them, "do you remember the little negro who stole my apples for you at Oranienbaum? Here he is; I introduce him to you."

The Grand Duchess laughed and blushed. They went into the dining-room. In expectation of the Emperor the table had been laid. Peter sat down to dinner with all his family, and invited Ibrahim to sit down with them. During the course of the dinner the Emperor conversed with him on various subjects, questioned him about the Spanish war, the internal affairs of France and the Regent, whom he liked, although he blamed him for many things. Ibrahim possessed an exact and observant mind. Peter was very pleased with his replies. He recalled to mind some features of Ibrahim's childhood, and related them with such good-humour and gaiety, that nobody

---

[104] Diminutive of Catherine.

could have suspected this kind and hospitable host to be the hero of Poltava,[105] the powerful and terrible reformer of Russia.

After dinner the Emperor, according to the Russian custom, retired to rest. Ibrahim remained with the Empress and the Grand Duchesses. He tried to satisfy their curiosity, described the Parisian way of life, the holidays that were kept there, and the changeable fashions. In the meantime, some of the persons belonging to the Emperor's suite had assembled in the palace. Ibrahim recognized the magnificent Prince Menshikoff, who, seeing the negro conversing with Catherine, cast an arrogant glance at him; Prince Jacob Dolgorouky, Peter's stern counsellor; the learned Bruce,[106] who had acquired among the people the name of the "Russian Faust"; the young Ragouzinsky, his former companion, and others who had come to bring reports to the Emperor and to await his orders.

In about two hours' time the Emperor appeared.

"Let us see," said he to Ibrahim, "if you have forgotten your old duties. Take a slate and follow me."

Peter shut himself up in his work-room and busied himself with state affairs. He worked in turns with Bruce, with Prince Dolgorouky, and with General Police-master Devier, and dictated to Ibrahim several ukases and decisions. Ibrahim could not help feeling astonished at the quickness and firmness of his understanding, the strength and pliability of his powers of observation, and the variety of his occupations. When the work was finished, Peter drew out a pocket-book in order to see if all that he had proposed to do that day had been accomplished. Then, issuing from the work-room, he said to Ibrahim:

"It is late; no doubt you are tired,—sleep here to-night, as you used to do in the old times; to-morrow I will wake you."

Ibrahim, on being left alone, could hardly collect his thoughts. He found himself in Petersburg; he saw again the great man, near whom, not yet knowing his worth, he had passed his childhood. Almost with regret he confessed to himself that the Countess L——, for the first time since their separation, had not been his sole thought during the whole of the day. He saw that the new mode of life which awaited him,—the activity and constant occupation,— would revive his soul, wearied by passion, idleness and secret grief. The thought of being a fellow-worker with the great man, and, in conjunction with him, of influencing the fate of a great nation,

---

[105] A town in the Ukraine, where, in 1709, the Swedes, under Charles XII., were completely routed by the Russians under Peter the Great.
[106] Peter the Great encouraged foreigners of ability to settle in Russia.

aroused within him for the first time the noble feeling of ambition. In this disposition of mind he lay down upon the camp bed prepared for him, and then the usual dreams carried him back to far-off Paris, to the arms of his dear Countess.

CHAPTER III

The next morning, Peter, according to his promise, awoke Ibrahim and congratulated him on his elevation to the rank of Captain-lieutenant of the Grenadier company of the Preobrajensky Regiment,[107] in which he himself was Captain. The courtiers surrounded Ibrahim, each in his way trying to flatter the new favourite. The haughty Prince Menshikoff pressed his hand in a friendly manner; Sheremetieff inquired after his Parisian acquaintances, and Golovin invited him to dinner. Others followed the example of the latter, so that Ibrahim received invitations for at least a whole month.

Ibrahim now began to lead a monotonous but busy life, consequently did not feel at all dull. From day to day he became more attached to the Emperor, and was better able to estimate his lofty soul. To follow the thoughts of a great man is a very interesting study. Ibrahim saw Peter in the Senate disputing with Boutourlin and Dolgorouky, in the Admiralty College discussing the naval power of Russia; in his hours of leisure he saw him with Feophan, Gavril Boujinsky, and Kopievitch, examining translations from foreign publications, or visiting the manufactory of a merchant, the workshop of a mechanic, or the study of some learned man. Russia presented to Ibrahim the appearance of a huge workshop, where machines alone move, where each workman, subject to established rules, is occupied with his own particular business. He felt within himself that he ought to work at his own bench also, and endeavour to regret as little as possible the gaieties of his Parisian life. But it was more difficult for him to drive from his mind that other dear recollection: he often thought of the Countess L——, and pictured to himself her just indignation, her tears and her grief.... But sometimes a terrible thought oppressed him: the seductions of the

---

[107] One of the "crack" regiments of the Russian Army.

great world, a new tie, another favourite—he shuddered; jealousy began to set his African blood in a ferment, and hot tears were ready to roll down his swarthy face.

One morning he was sitting in his study, surrounded by business papers, when suddenly he heard a loud greeting in French. Ibrahim turned round quickly, and young Korsakoff, whom he had left in Paris in the whirl of the great world, embraced him with joyful exclamations.

"I have only just arrived," said Korsakoff, "and I have come straight to you. All our Parisian acquaintances send their greetings to you, and regret your absence. The Countess L ordered me to summon you to return without fail, and here is her letter to you."

Ibrahim seized it with a trembling hand and looked at the well-known handwriting of the address, not daring to believe, his eyes.

"How glad I am," continued Korsakoff, "that you have not yet died of ennui in this barbarous Petersburg! What do people do here? How do they occupy themselves? Who is your tailor? Have they established an opera?" Ibrahim absently replied that probably the Emperor was just then at work in the dockyard.

Korsakoff laughed.

"I see," said he, "that you do not want me just now; some other time we will have a long chat together; I am now going to pay my respects to the Emperor."

With these words he turned on his heel and hastened out of the room.

Ibrahim, left alone, hastily opened the letter. The Countess tenderly complained to him, reproaching him with dissimulation and distrustfulness.

"You say," wrote she, "that my tranquillity is dearer to you than everything in the world. Ibrahim, if this were the truth, would you have brought me to the condition to which I was reduced by the unexpected news of your departure? You were afraid that I might have detained you. Be assured that, in spite of my love, I should have known how to sacrifice it for your happiness and for what you consider your duty."

The Countess ended the letter with passionate assurances of love, and implored him to write to her, if only now and then, even though there should be no hope of their ever seeing each other again.

Ibrahim read this letter through twenty times, kissing the priceless lines-with rapture. He was burning with impatience to hear something about the Countess, and he was just preparing to set out for the Admiralty, hoping to find Korsakoff still there, when the door opened, and Korsakoff himself appeared once more. He had

273

already paid his respects to the Emperor, and as was usual with him, he seemed very well satisfied with himself.

"Entre nous," he said to Ibrahim, "the Emperor is a very strange man. Just fancy, I found him in a sort of linen under-vest, on the mast of a new ship, whither I was compelled to climb with my dispatches. I stood on the rope ladder, and had not sufficient room to make a suitable bow, and so I became completely confused, a thing that had never happened to me in my life before. However, when the Emperor had read my letter, he looked at me from head to foot, and no doubt was agreeably struck by the taste and splendour of my attire; at any rate he smiled and invited me to to-day's assembly. But I am a perfect stranger in Petersburg; during the course of my six years' absence I have quite forgotten the local customs; pray be my mentor; come with me and introduce me."

Ibrahim agreed to do so, and hastened to turn the conversation to a subject that was more interesting to him.

"Well, and how about the Countess L——"

"The Countess? Of course, at first she was very much grieved on account of your departure; then, of course, little by little, she grew reconciled and took unto herself a new lover: do you know whom? The long-legged Marquis R——. Why do you show the whites of your negro eyes in that manner? Does it seem strange to you? Don't you know that lasting grief is not in human nature, particularly in feminine nature? Think over this well, while I go and rest after my journey, and don't forget to come and call for me."

What feelings filled the soul of Ibrahim? Jealousy? Rage? Despair? No, but a deep, oppressing sorrow. He repeated to himself: "I foresaw it, it had to happen." Then he opened the Countess's letter, read it again, hung his head and wept bitterly. He wept for a long time. The tears relieved his heart. Looking at the clock, he perceived that it was time to set out. Ibrahim would have been very glad to stay away, but the assembly was a matter of duty, and the Emperor strictly demanded the presence of his retainers. He dressed himself and started out to call for Korsakoff.

Korsakoff was sitting in his dressing-gown, reading a French book.

"So early?" he said to Ibrahim, on seeing him.

"Pardon me," the latter replied; "it is already half-past five, we shall be late; make haste and dress and let us go."

Korsakoff started up and rang the bell with all his might; the servants came running in, and he began hastily to dress, himself. His French valet gave him shoes with red heels, blue velvet breeches, and a red caftan embroidered with spangles. His peruke was hurriedly powdered in the antechamber and brought in to him.

Korsakoff placed it upon his cropped head, asked for his sword and gloves, turned round about ten times before the glass, and then informed Ibrahim that he was ready. The footmen handed them their bearskin cloaks, and they set out for the Winter Palace.

Korsakoff overwhelmed Ibrahim with questions: Who was the greatest beauty in Petersburg? Who was supposed to be the best dancer? Which dance was just then the rage? Ibrahim very reluctantly gratified his curiosity. Meanwhile they reached the palace. A great number of long sledges, old-fashioned carriages, and gilded coaches already stood on the lawn. Near the steps were crowded coachmen in liveries and moustaches; running footmen glittering with tinsel and feathers, and bearing staves; hussars, pages, and clumsy servants loaded with the cloaks and muffs of their masters—a train indispensable according to the notions of the gentry of that time. At the sight of Ibrahim, a general murmur arose: "The negro, the negro, the Czar's negro!" He hurriedly conducted Korsakoff through this motley crowd. The Court lackey opened wide the doors to them, and they entered the hall. Korsakoff was dumfounded.... In the large room, illuminated by tallow candles, which burnt dimly amidst clouds of tobacco smoke, magnates with blue ribbons across their shoulders, ambassadors, foreign merchants, officers of the Guards in green uniforms, ship-masters in jackets and striped trousers, moved backwards and forwards in crowds to the uninterrupted sound of the music of wind instruments. The ladies sat against the walls, the young ones being decked out in all the splendour of the prevailing fashion. Gold and silver glittered upon their dresses; out of monstrous farthingales their slender forms rose like flower stalks; diamonds sparkled in their ears, in their long curls, and around their necks. They glanced gaily about to the right and to the left, waiting for their cavaliers and for the dancing to begin. The elderly ladies craftily endeavoured to combine the new style of dress with that of the past; their caps were made to resemble the small sable head-dress of the Empress Natalia Kirilovna,[108] and their gowns and mantles recalled the sarafan and doushegreika.[109] They seemed to take part in these newly introduced amusements more with astonishment than pleasure, and cast looks of resentment at the wives and daughters of the Dutch skippers, who, in dimity skirts and red jackets, knitted their stockings and laughed and chatted among themselves as if they were at home.

[108] The mother of Peter the Great.
[109] A short sleeveless jacket.

Observing new arrivals, a servant approached them with beer and glasses on a tray. Korsakoff was completely bewildered.

"Que diable est ce que tout cela?" he said in a whisper to Ibrahim.

Ibrahim could not repress a smile. The Empress and the Grand Duchesses, dazzling in their beauty and their attire, walked through the rows of guests, conversing affably with them. The Emperor was in another room. Korsakoff, wishing to show himself to him, with difficulty succeeded in pushing his way thither through the constantly moving crowd. In this room were chiefly foreigners, solemnly smoking their clay pipes and drinking out of earthenware jugs. On the tables were bottles of beer and wine, leather pouches with tobacco, glasses of punch, and some chessboards. At one of these Peter was playing at chess with a broad-shouldered English skipper. They zealously saluted one another with whiffs of tobacco smoke, and the Emperor was so occupied with an unexpected move that had been made by his opponent, that he did not observe Korsakoff, as he smirked and capered about them. Just then a stout gentleman, with a large bouquet upon his breast, rushed hurriedly into the room and announced in a loud voice that the dancing had commenced, and immediately retired. A large number of the guests followed him, Korsakoff being among the number.

An unexpected scene filled him with astonishment. Along the whole length of the ball-room, to the sound of the most mournful music, the ladies and gentlemen stood in two rows facing each other; the gentlemen bowed low, the ladies curtsied still lower, first to the front, then to the right, then to the left, then again to the front, again to the right, and so on. Korsakoff, gazing at this peculiar style of amusement, opened wide his eyes and bit his lips. The curtseying and bowing continued for about half an hour; at last they ceased, and the stout gentleman with the bouquet announced that the ceremonial dances were ended, and ordered the musicians to play a minuet. Korsakoff felt delighted, and prepared-to shine. Among the young ladies was one in particular whom he was greatly charmed with. She was about sixteen years of age, was richly dressed, but with taste, and sat near an elderly gentleman of stern and dignified appearance. Korsakoff approached her and asked her to do him the honour of dancing with him. The young beauty looked at him in confusion, and did not seem to know what to say to him. The gentleman sitting near her frowned still more. Korsakoff awaited her decision, but the gentleman with the bouquet came up to him, led him to the middle of the room, and said in a pompous manner:

276

"Sir, you have done wrong. In the first place, you approached this young person without making the three necessary reverences to her, and in the second place, you took upon yourself to choose her, whereas, in the minuet that right belongs to the lady, and not to the gentleman. On that account you must be severely, punished, that is to say, you must drain the goblet of the Great Eagle."

Korsakoff grew more and more astonished. In a moment the guests surrounded him, loudly demanding the immediate fulfilment of the law. Peter, hearing the laughter and the cries, came out of the adjoining room, as he was very fond of being present in person at such punishments. The crowd divided before him, and he entered the circle, where stood the culprit and before him the marshal of the Court holding in his hands a huge goblet filled with malmsey wine. He was trying in vain to persuade the offender to comply willingly with the law.

"Aha!" said Peter, seeing Korsakoff: "you are caught, my friend. Come now, monsieur, drink up and no frowning about it."

There was no help for it: the poor beau, without pausing to take breath, drained the goblet to the dregs and returned it to the marshal.

"Hark you, Korsakoff," said Peter to him: "those breeches of yours are of velvet, such as I myself do not wear, and I am far richer than you. That is extravagance; take care that I do not fall out with you."

Hearing this reprimand, Korsakoff wished to make his way out of the circle, but he staggered and almost fell, to the indescribable delight of the Emperor and all the merry company. This episode not only did not spoil the unison and interest of the principal performance, but even enlivened it. The gentlemen began to scrape and bow, and the ladies to curtsey and knock their heels with great zeal, and this time without paying the least attention to the time of the music. Korsakoff could not take part in the general gaiety. The lady, whom he had chosen, by the order of her father, Gavril Afanassievitch Rjevsky, approached Ibrahim, and, dropping her blue eyes, timidly gave him her hand. Ibrahim danced the minuet with her and led her back to her former place, then sought out Korsakoff, led him out of the ball-room, placed him in the carriage and drove home. On the way Korsakoff began to mutter in an incoherent manner: "Accursed assembly!... accursed goblet of the Great Eagle!"... but he soon fell into a sound sleep, and knew not how he reached home, nor how he was undressed and put into bed: and he awoke the next day with a headache, and with a dim recollection of the scraping, the curtseying, the tobacco-smoke, the gentleman with the bouquet, and the goblet of the Great Eagle.

CHAPTER IV

I must now introduce the gracious reader to Gavril Afanassievitch Rjevsky. He was descended from an ancient noble family, possessed vast estates, was hospitable, loved falconry, and had a large number of domestics,—in a word, he was a genuine Russian nobleman. To use his own expression, he could not endure the German spirit, and he endeavoured to preserve in his home the ancient customs that were so dear to him. His daughter was in her seventeenth year. She had lost her mother while she was yet in her infancy, and she had been brought up in the old style, that is to say, she was surrounded by governesses, nurses, playfellows, and maidservants, was able to embroider in gold, and could neither read nor write. Her father, notwithstanding his dislike to everything foreign, could not oppose her wish to learn German dances from a captive Swedish officer, living in their house. This deserving dancing-master was about fifty years of age; his right foot had been shot through at Narva,[110] and consequently he was not very well suited for minuets and courantes, but the left executed with wonderful ease and agility the most difficult steps. His pupil did honour to his teaching. Natalia Gavrilovna was celebrated for being the best dancer at the assemblies, and this was partly the cause of the mistake made by Korsakoff, who came the next day to apologize to Gavril Afanassievitch; but the airiness and elegance of the young fop did not find favour in the eyes of the proud noble, who wittily nicknamed him the French monkey.

It was a holiday. Gavril Afanassievitch expected some relatives and friends. In the ancient hall a long table was laid. The guests arrived with their wives and daughters, who had at last been set free from domestic imprisonment by the decree of the Emperor and by his own example.[111] Natalia Gavrilovna carried round to each guest a silver tray laden with golden cups, and each man, as he drained his,

---

[110] A town on the southern shore of the Gulf of Finland, and the scene of a great battle in 1700, when the Russians were completely routed by the Swedes under Charles XII.

[111] Previous to the reign of Peter the Great, the Russian women lived in almost Oriental seclusion, and it was for the purpose of abolishing this custom that Peter established his famous "assemblies."

regretted that the kiss, which it was customary to receive on such occasions in the olden times, had gone out of fashion.

They sat down to table. In the first place, next to the host, sat his father-in-law, Prince Boris Alexeievitch Likoff, a boyar[112] of seventy years of age; the other guests ranged themselves according to the antiquity of their family, thus recalling the happy times when respect for age was observed. The men sat on one side, the women on the other. At the end of the table, the housekeeper in her old-fashioned costume—a little woman of thirty, affected and wrinkled—and the captive dancing-master, in his faded blue uniform, occupied their accustomed places. The table, which was covered with a large number of dishes, was surrounded by an anxious crowd of domestics, among whom was distinguishable the house-steward, with his severe look, big paunch and lofty immobility. The first few minutes of dinner were devoted entirely to the productions of our old cookery; the noise of plates and the rattling of spoons alone interrupted the general silence. At last the host, seeing that the time had arrived for amusing the guests with agreeable conversation, turned round and asked:

"But where is Ekemovna? Summon her hither."

Several servants were about to rush off in different directions, but at that moment an old woman, painted white and red, decorated with flowers and tinsel, in a silk gown with a low neck, entered, singing and dancing. Her appearance produced general satisfaction.

"Good-day, Ekemovna," said Prince Likoff: "how do you do?"

"Quite well and happy, gossip: still singing and dancing and looking out for sweethearts."

"Where have you been, fool?" asked the host.

"Decorating myself, gossip, for the dear guests, for this holy day, by order of the Czar, by command of my master, to be a laughing-stock for everybody after the German manner."

At these words there arose a loud burst of laughter, and the fool took her place behind the host's chair.

"A fool talks nonsense, but sometimes speaks the truth," said Tatiana Afanassievna, the eldest sister of the host, and for whom he entertained great respect. "As a matter of fact, the present fashion must seem ridiculous in the eyes of everybody. But since you, gentlemen, have shaved off your beards[113] and put on short caftans, it is, of course, useless to talk about women's rags, although it is

---

[112] A noble of the second degree.
[113] In his zeal to introduce into his empire the customs of Western Europe, Peter the Great issued an order that all Russians were to shave off their beards.

279

really a pity about the sarafan, the maiden's ribbons, and the povoinik![114] It is pitiable and at the same time laughable, to see the beauties of to-day: their hair frizzed like tow, greased and covered with French powder; the waist drawn in to such a degree, that it is almost on the point of breaking in two; their petticoats are distended with hoops, so that they have to enter a carriage sideways; to go through a door they are obliged to stoop down; they can neither stand, nor sit, nor breathe—real martyrs, the poor doves!"

"Oh, little mother Tatiana Afanassievna!" said Kirila Petrovitch T——, a former governor of Riazan, where he acquired three thousand serfs and a young wife, both by somewhat dishonourable means, "as far as I am concerned, my wife may do as she pleases, and wear what she likes, provided that she does not order new dresses every month and throw away the former ones that are nearly new. In former times the grandmother's sarafan formed part of the granddaughter's dowry, but nowadays all that is changed: the dress, that the mistress wears to-day, you will see the servant wearing to-morrow. What is to be done? It is the ruin of the Russian nobility, alas!"

At these words he sighed and looked at his Maria Ilienishna, who did not seem at all to like either his praises of the past or his disparagement of the latest customs. The other young ladies shared her displeasure, but they remained silent, for modesty was then considered an indispensable attribute in young women.

"And who is to blame?" said Gavril Afanassievitch, filling a tankard with an effervescing beverage. "Isn't it our own fault? The young women play the fool, and we encourage them."

"But what can we do, when our wishes are not consulted?" replied Kirila Petrovitch. "One would be glad to shut his wife up in an attic, but with beating of drums she is summoned to appear at the assemblies. The husband goes after the whip, but the wife after dress. Oh, those assemblies! The Lord has sent them upon us as a punishment for our sins."

Maria Ilienishna sat as if upon needles; her tongue itched to speak. At last she could restrain herself no longer, and turning to her husband, she asked him with an acid smile, what he found wrong in the assemblies.

"This is what I find wrong in them," replied the provoked husband: "since the time when they commenced, husbands have been unable to manage their wives; wives have forgotten the words of the Apostle: 'Let the wife reverence her husband'; they no longer

---

[114] The national head-dress of the Russian women.

busy themselves about domestic affairs, but about new dresses; they do not think of how to please their husbands, but how to attract the attention of frivolous officers. And is it becoming, Madame, for a Russian lady to associate with German smokers and their work-women? And was ever such a thing heard of, as dancing and talking with young men till far into the night? It would be all very well if it were with relatives, but with strangers, with people that they are totally unacquainted with!"

"I would say just a word, but there is a wolf not far off," said Gavril Afanassievitch, frowning. "I confess that these assemblies are not to my liking: before you know where you are, you knock against some drunkard, or are made drunk yourself to become the laughing-stock of others. Then you must keep your eyes open lest some good-for-nothing fellow should act the fool with your daughter; the young men nowadays are so spoilt, that they cannot be worse. Look, for example, at the son of the late Evgraf Sergeievitch Korsakoff, who at the last assembly made so much noise about Natasha, that it brought the blood to my cheeks. The next day I see somebody driving straight into my courtyard; I thought to myself, who in the name of Heaven is it, can it be Prince Alexander Danilovitch? But no: it was Ivan Evgrafovitch! He could not stop at the gate and make his way on foot to the steps, not he! He flew in, bowing and chattering, the Lord preserve us! The fool Ekemovna mimics him very amusingly: by the way, fool, give us an imitation of the foreign monkey."

The fool Ekemovna seized hold of a dish-cover, placed it under her arm like a hat, and began twisting, scraping, and bowing in every direction, repeating: "monsieur ... mamselle ... assemble ... pardon." General and prolonged laughter again testified to the delight of the guests.

"Just like Korsakoff," said old Prince Likoff, wiping away the tears of laughter, when calmness was again restored. "But why conceal the fact? He is not the first, nor will he be the last, who has returned from abroad to holy Russia a buffoon. What do our children learn there? To scrape with their feet, to chatter God knows in what gibberish, to treat their elders with disrespect, and to dangle after other men's wives. Of all the young people who have been educated abroad (the Lord forgive me!) the Czar's negro most resembles a man."

"Oh, Prince," said Tatiana Afanassievna: "I have seen him, I have seen him quite close: what a frightful muzzle he has! He quite terrified me!"

"Of course," observed Gavril Afanassievitch: "he is a sober, decent man, and not a mere weathercock.... But who is it that has just driven through the gate into the courtyard? Surely it cannot be that foreign monkey again? Why do you stand gaping there, beasts?" he continued, turning to the servants: "run and stop him from coming in, and for the future...."

"Old beard, are you dreaming?" interrupted Ekemovna the fool, "or are you blind? It is the imperial sledge—the Czar has come."

Gavril Afanassievitch rose hastily from the table; everybody rushed to the window, and sure enough they saw the Emperor ascending the steps, leaning on the shoulder of his servant. A great confusion arose. The host rushed to meet Peter; the servants ran hither and thither as if they had gone crazy; the guests became alarmed; some even thought how they might hasten home as quickly as possible. Suddenly the thundering voice of Peter resounded in the ante-room; all became silent, and the Czar entered, accompanied by his host, who was beside himself with joy.

"Good day, gentlemen!" said Peter, with a cheerful countenance.

All made a profound bow. The sharp eyes of the Czar sought out in the crowd the young daughter of the host; he called her to him. Natalia Gavrilovna advanced boldly enough, but she blushed not only to the ears but even to the shoulders.

"You grow more beautiful every day," said the Emperor to her, and according to his usual custom he kissed her upon the head; then turning to the guests, he added: "I have disturbed you? You were dining? Pray sit down again, and give me some aniseed brandy, Gavril Afanassievitch."

The host rushed to the stately house-steward, snatched from his hand a tray, filled a golden goblet himself, and gave it with a bow to the Emperor. Peter drank the brandy, ate a biscuit, and for the second time requested the guests to continue their dinner. All resumed their former places, except the dwarf and the housekeeper, who did not dare to remain at a table honoured by the presence of the Czar. Peter sat down by the side of the host and asked for some soup. The Emperor's servant gave him a wooden spoon mounted with ivory, and a knife and fork with green bone handles, for Peter never used any other knives, forks and spoons but his own. The dinner, which a moment before had been so noisy and merry, was now continued in silence and constraint. The host, through respect and delight, ate nothing; the guests also stood upon ceremony and listened with respectful attention, as the Emperor discoursed in German with the captive Swede about the campaign of 1701. The fool Ekemovna, several times questioned by the Emperor, replied with a sort of timid coldness, which, be it remarked, did not at all

282

prove her natural stupidity. At last the dinned came to an end. The Emperor rose, and after him all the guests.

"Gavril Afanassievitch!" he said to the host: "I want to say a word with you alone;" and, taking him by the arm, he led him into the parlour and locked the door. The guests remained in the dining-room, talking in whispers about the unexpected visit, and, afraid of being indiscreet, they soon dispersed one after another, without thanking the host for his hospitality. His father-in-law, daughter, and sister conducted them very quietly to the door, and remained alone in the dining-room, awaiting the issue of the Emperor.

CHAPTER V

About half an hour afterwards the door opened and Peter issued forth. With a dignified inclination of the head he replied to the threefold bow of Prince Likoff, Tatiana Afanassievna and Natasha, and walked straight out into the ante-room. The host handed him his red cloak, conducted him to the sledge, and on the steps thanked him once more for the honour he had shown him.

Peter drove off.

Returning to the dining-room, Gavril Afanassievitch seemed very much troubled; he angrily ordered the servants to clear the table as quickly as possible, sent Natasha to her own room, and, informing his sister and father-in-law that he must talk with them, he led them into the bedroom, where he usually rested after dinner. The old Prince lay down upon the oak bed; Tatiana Afanassievna sat down in the old silk-lined armchair, and placed her feet upon the footstool; Gavril Afanassievitch locked the doors, sat down upon the bed at the feet of Prince Likoff, and in a low voice began:

"It was not for nothing that the Emperor paid me a visit to-day: guess what he wanted to talk to me about."

"How can we know, brother?" said Tatiana Afanassievna.

"Has the Czar appointed you to some government?" said his father-in-law:—"it is quite time enough that he did so. Or has he offered an embassy to you? Why not? That need not mean being a mere secretary—distinguished people are sent to foreign monarchs."

"No," replied his son-in-law, frowning. "I am a man of the old school, and our services nowadays are of no use, although, perhaps, an orthodox Russian nobleman is worth more than these modern upstarts, bakers and heathens. But this is a different matter altogether."

"Then what is it, brother?" said Tatiana Afanassievna. "Why was he talking with you for such a long time? Can it be that you are threatened with some misfortune? The Lord save and defend us!"

"No misfortune, certainly, but I confess that it is a matter for reflection."

"Then what is it, brother? What is the matter about?"

"It is about Natasha: the Czar came to ask for her hand."

"God be thanked!" said Tatiana Afanassievna, crossing herself. "The maiden is of a marriageable age, and as the matchmaker is, so must the bridegroom be. God give them love and counsel, the honour is great. For whom does the Czar ask her hand?"

"H'm!" exclaimed Gavril Afanassievitch: "for whom? That's just it for whom!"

"Who is it, then?" repeated Prince Likoff, already beginning to doze off to sleep.

"Guess," said Gavril Afanassievitch.

"My dear brother," replied the old lady: "how can we guess? There are a great number of marriageable men at Court, each of whom would be glad to take your Natasha for his wife. Is it Dolgorouky?"

"No, it is not Dolgorouky."

"God be with him: he is too overbearing. Schein? Troekouroff?"

"No, neither the one nor the other."

"I do not care for them either; they are flighty, and too much imbued with the German spirit. Well, is it Miloslavsky?"

"No, not he."

"God be with him, he is rich and stupid. Who then? Eletsky? Lvoff? It cannot be Ragouzinsky? I cannot think of anybody else. For whom, then, does the Czar want Natasha?"

"For the negro Ibrahim."

The old lady uttered a cry and clasped her hands. Prince Likoff raised his head from the pillow, and with astonishment repeated:

"For the negro Ibrahim?"

"My dear brother!" said the old lady in a tearful voice: "do not destroy your dear child, do not deliver poor little Natasha into the clutches of that black devil."

"How?" replied Gavril Afanassievitch: "refuse the Emperor, who promises in return to bestow his favour upon us and all our house."

"What!" exclaimed the old Prince, who was now wide awake: "Natasha, my granddaughter, to be married to a bought negro."

"He is not of common birth," said Gavril Afanassievitch: "he is the son of a negro Sultan. The Mussulmen took him prisoner and sold him in Constantinople, and our ambassador bought him and presented him to the Czar. The negro's eldest brother came to Russia with a considerable ransom and——"

"We have heard the story of Bova Korolevitch and Erouslana Lazarevitch."[115]

"My dear Gavril Afanassievitch!" interrupted the old lady, "tell us rather how you replied to the Emperor's proposal."

"I said that we were under his authority, and that it was our duty to obey him in all things."

At that moment a noise was heard behind the door. Gavril Afanassievitch went to open it, but felt some obstruction. He pushed against it with increased force, the door opened, and they saw Natasha lying in a swoon upon the blood-stained floor.

Her heart sank within her, when the Emperor shut himself up with her father; some presentiment whispered to her that the matter concerned her, and when Gavril Afanassievitch ordered her to withdraw, saying that he wished to speak to her aunt and grandfather, she could not resist the instinct of feminine curiosity, stole quietly along through the inner rooms to the bedroom door, and did not miss a single word of the whole terrible conversation; when she heard her father's last words, the poor girl lost consciousness, and falling, struck her head against an iron-bound chest, in which was kept her dowry.

The servants hastened to the spot; Natasha was lifted up, carried to her own room, and placed in bed. After a little time she regained consciousness, opened her eyes, but recognized neither father nor aunt. A violent fever set in; she spoke in her delirium about the Czar's negro, about marriage, and suddenly cried in a plaintive and piercing voice:

"Valerian, dear Valerian, my life, save me! there they are, there they are...."

Tatiana Afanassievna glanced uneasily at her brother, who turned pale, bit his lips, and silently left the room. He returned to the old Prince, who, unable to mount the stairs, had remained below.

"How is Natasha?" asked he.

"Very bad," replied the grieved father: "worse than I thought; she is delirious, and raves about Valerian."

"Who is this Valerian?" asked the anxious old man. "Can it be that orphan, the archer's son, whom you brought up in your house?"

---

[115] The two principal characters in one of the legendary stories of Russia.

"The same, to my misfortune!" replied Gavril Afanassievitch. "His father, at the time of the rebellion, saved my life, and the devil induced me to take the accursed young wolf into my house. When, two years ago, he was enrolled in the regiment at his own request, Natasha, on taking leave of him, shed bitter tears, and he stood as if petrified. This seemed suspicious to me, and I spoke about it to my sister. But since that time Natasha has never mentioned his name, and nothing whatever has been heard of him. I thought that she had forgotten him, but it is evident that such is not the case. But it is decided: she shall marry the negro."

Prince Likoff did not contradict him: it would have been useless. He returned home; Tatiana Afanassievna remained by the side of Natasha's bed; Gavril Afanassievitch, having sent for the doctor, locked himself in his room, and in his house all was still and sad.

The unexpected proposal astonished Ibrahim quite as much as Gavril Afanassievitch. This is how it happened. Peter, being engaged in business with Ibrahim, said to him:

"I perceive, my friend, that you are downhearted; speak frankly, what is it you want?"

Ibrahim assured the Emperor that he was very well satisfied with his lot, and wished for nothing better.

"Good," said the Emperor: "if you are dull without any cause, I know how to cheer you up."

At the conclusion of the work, Peter asked Ibrahim:

"Do you like the young lady with whom you danced the minuet at the last assembly?"

"She is very charming, Your Majesty, and seems to be a good and modest girl."

"Then I shall take it upon myself to make you better acquainted with her. Would you like to marry her?"

"I, Your Majesty?"

"Listen, Ibrahim: you are a man alone in the world, without birth and kindred, a stranger to everybody, except myself. Were I to die to-day, what would become of you to-morrow, my poor negro? You must get settled while there is yet time, find support in new ties, become connected by marriage with the Russian nobility."

"Your Majesty, I am happy under your protection, and in the possession of your favour. God grant that I may not survive my Czar and benefactor—I wish for nothing more; but even if I had any idea of getting married, would the young lady and her relations consent? My appearance——"

"Your appearance? What nonsense! A clever fellow like you, too! A young girl must obey the will of her parents, and we will see what old Gavril Rjevsky will say, when I myself will be your matchmaker."

With these words the Emperor ordered his sledge, and left Ibrahim sunk in deep reflection.

"Get married?" thought the African: "why not? Am I to be condemned to pass my life in solitude, and not know the greatest pleasure and the most sacred duties of man, just because I was born beneath the torrid zone? I cannot hope to be loved: a childish objection! Is it possible to believe in love? Does it then exist in the frivolous heart of woman? As I have renounced for ever such alluring errors, I must devote my attention to ideas of a more practical nature. The Emperor is right: I must think of my future. Marriage with the young Rjevsky will connect me with the proud Russian nobility, and I shall cease to be a sojourner in my new fatherland. From my wife I shall not require love: I shall be satisfied with her fidelity; and her friendship I will acquire by constant tenderness, confidence and devotion."

Ibrahim, according to his usual custom, wished to occupy himself with work, but his imagination was too excited. He left the papers and went for a stroll along the banks of the Neva. Suddenly he heard the voice of Peter; he looked round and saw the Emperor, who, dismissing his sledge, advanced towards him with a beaming countenance.

"It is all settled, my friend!" said Peter, taking him by the arm: "I have affianced you. To-morrow, go and visit your father-in-law, but see that you humour his boyar pride: leave the sledge at the gate, go through the courtyard on foot, talk to him about his services and distinctions, and he will be perfectly charmed with you.... And now," continued he, shaking his cudgel, "lead me to that rogue Danilitch, with whom I must confer about his recent pranks."

Ibrahim thanked Peter heartily for his fatherly solicitude on his account, accompanied him as far as the magnificent palace of Prince Menshikoff, and then returned home.

CHAPTER VI

Dimly burnt the lamp before the glass case in which glittered the gold and silver frames of the sacred images. The flickering light

287

faintly illuminated the curtained bed and the little table set out with labelled medicine-bottles. Near the stove sat a servant-maid at her spinning-wheel, and the subdued noise of the spindle was the only sound that broke the silence of the room.

"Who is there?" asked a feeble voice.

The servant-maid rose immediately, approached the bed, and gently raised the curtain.

"Will it soon be daylight?" asked Natalia.

"It is already midday," replied the maid.

"Oh, Lord of Heaven! and why is it so dark?"

"The shutters are closed, miss."

"Help me to dress quickly."

"You must not do so, miss; the doctor has forbidden it." "Am I ill then? How long have I been so?"

"About a fortnight."

"Is it possible? And it seems to me as if it were only yesterday that I went to bed...."

Natasha became silent; she tried to collect her scattered thoughts. Something had happened to her, but what it was she could not exactly remember. The maid stood before her, awaiting her orders. At that moment a dull noise was heard below.

"What is that?" asked the invalid.

"The gentlemen have finished dinner," replied the maid: "they are rising from the table. Tatiana Afanassievna will be here presently."

Natasha seemed pleased at this; she waved her feeble hand. The maid dropped the curtain and seated herself again at the spinning-wheel.

A few minutes afterwards, a head in a broad white cap with dark ribbons appeared in the doorway and asked in a low voice:

"How is Natasha?"

"How do you do, auntie?" said the invalid in a faint voice, and Tatiana Afanassievna hastened towards her.

"The young lady has regained consciousness," said the maid, carefully drawing a chair to the side of the bed. The old lady, with tears in her eyes, kissed the pale, languid face of her niece, and sat down beside her. Just behind her came a German doctor in a black caftan and learned wig. He felt Natalia's pulse, and announced in Latin, and then in Russian, that the danger was over. He asked for paper and ink, wrote out a new prescription, and departed. The old lady rose, kissed Natalia once more, and immediately hurried down with the good news to Gavril Afanassievitch.

In the parlour, in uniform, with sword by his side and hat in his hand, sat the Czar's negro, respectfully talking with Gavril

288

Afanassievitch. Korsakoff, stretched out upon a soft couch, was listening to their conversation, and teasing a venerable greyhound. Becoming tired of this occupation, he approached the mirror, the usual refuge of the idle, and in it he saw Tatiana Afanassievna, who through the doorway was making unnoticed signs to her brother.

"Someone is calling you, Gavril Afanassievitch," said Korsakoff, turning round to him and interrupting Ibrahim's speech.

Gavril Afanassievitch immediately went to his sister and closed the door behind him.

"I am astonished at your patience," said Korsakoff to Ibrahim. "For a full hour you have been listening to a lot of nonsense about the antiquity of the Likoff and Rjevsky families, and have even added your own moral observations! In your place j'aurais planté là the old babbler and all his race, including Natalia Gavrilovna, who is an affected girl, and is only pretending to be ill—une petite santé. Tell me candidly: do you really love this little mijaurée?"

"No," replied Ibrahim: "I am certainly not going to marry, out of love, but out of prudence, and then only if she has no decided aversion to me."

"Listen, Ibrahim," said Korsakoff, "follow my advice this time; in truth, I am more discreet than I seem. Get this foolish idea out of your head—don't marry. It seems to me that your bride has no particular liking for you. Do not a few things happen in this world? For instance: I am certainly not a very bad sort of fellow myself, but yet it has happened to me to deceive husbands, who, by the Lord, were in no way worse than me. And you yourself ... do you remember our Parisian friend, Count L—-? There is no dependence to be placed upon a woman's fidelity; happy is he who can regard it with indifference. But you!... With your passionate, pensive and suspicious nature, with your flat nose, thick lips, and shaggy head, to rush into all the dangers of matrimony!...."

"I thank you for your friendly advice," interrupted Ibrahim coldly; "but you know the proverb: 'It is not your duty to rock other people's children.'"

"Take care, Ibrahim," replied Korsakoff, laughing, "that you are not called upon some day to prove the truth of that proverb in the literal sense of the word."

Meanwhile the conversation in the next room became? very heated.

"You will kill her," the old lady was saying: "she cannot bear the sight of him."

"But judge for yourself," replied her obstinate brother. "For a fortnight he has been coming here as her bridegroom, and during that time he has not once seen his bride. He may think at last that

289

her illness is a mere invention and that we are only seeking to gain time in order to rid ourselves of him in some way. And what will the Czar say? He has already sent three times to ask after the health of Natalia. Do as you like, but I have no intention of quarrelling with him."

"My Lord God!" said Tatiana Afanassievna: "what, will become of the poor child! At least let me go and prepare her for such a visit."

Gavril Afanassievitch consented, and then returned, to the parlour.

"Thank God!" said he to Ibrahim: "the danger is over. Natalia is much better. Were it not that I do not like to leave my dear guest Ivan Evgrafovitch here alone, I would take you upstairs to have a glimpse of your bride."

Korsakoff congratulated Gavril Afanassievitch, asked him not to be uneasy on his account, assured him that he was compelled to go at once, and rushed out into the hall, without allowing his host to accompany him.

Meanwhile Tatiana Afanassievna hastened to prepare the invalid for the appearance of the terrible guest. Entering the room, she sat down breathless by the side of the bed, and took Natasha by the hand; but before she, was able to utter a word, the door opened.

Natasha asked: "Who has come in?"

The old lady turned faint. Gavril Afanassievitch drew back the curtain, looked coldly at the sick girl, and asked how she was. The invalid wanted to smile at him, but could not. Her father's stern look struck her, and unease took possession of her. At that moment it seemed to her that someone was standing at the head of her bed. She raised her head with an effort and suddenly recognized the czar's negro. Then she remembered everything, and the horror of the future presented itself before her. But exhausted nature received no perceptible shock. Natasha dropped her head down again upon the pillow and closed her eyes,... her heart beat painfully within her. Tatiana Afanassievna made a sign to her brother that the invalid wanted to go to sleep, and all quitted the room very quietly, except the maid, who resumed her seat at the spinning-wheel.

The unhappy beauty opened her eyes, and no longer seeing anybody by her bedside, called the maid and sent her for the nurse. But at that moment a round, old creature like a ball, rolled up to her bed. Lastotchka (for so nurse was called) with all the speed of her short legs, had followed Gavril Afanassievitch and Ibrahim up the stairs, and concealed herself behind the door, in accordance to the promptings of that curiosity which is inborn in the fair sex. Natasha, seeing her, sent the maid away, and the nurse sat down upon a stool by the bedside.

Never had so small a body contained within itself so much energy of soul. She intermeddled in everything, knew everything, and busied herself about everything. By cunning and insinuating ways she had succeeded in gaining the love of her masters, and the hatred of all the household, which she controlled in the most arbitrary manner. Gavril Afanassievitch listened to her reports, complaints, and petty requests. Tatiana Afanassievna constantly asked her opinion, followed her advice, and Natasha had the most unbounded affection for her, and confided to her all the thoughts, all the emotions of her sixteen-year old heart.

"Do you know, Lastotchka," said she, "my father is going to marry me to the negro."

The nurse sighed deeply, and her wrinkled face became still more wrinkled.

"Is there no hope?" continued Natasha: "Will my father not take pity upon me?"

The nurse shook her cap.

"Will not my grandfather or my aunt intercede for me?"

"No, miss; during your illness the negro succeeded in bewitching everybody. The master is out of his mind about him, the Prince raves about him alone, and Tatiana Afanassievna says it a pity that he is a negro, as a better bridegroom we could not wish for."

"My God, my God!" moaned poor Natasha.

"Do not grieve, my pretty one," said the nurse, kissing her feeble hand. "If you are to marry the negro, you will have your own way in everything. Nowadays it is not as it was in the olden times: husbands no longer keep their wives under lock and key; they say the negro is rich; your house will be like a full cup—you will lead a merry life."

"Poor Valerian!" said Natasha, but so softly that the nurse could only guess what she said, as she did not hear the words.

"That is just it, miss," said she, mysteriously lowering her voice; "if you thought less of the archer's orphan you would not rave about him in your illness, and your father would not be angry."

"What!" said the alarmed Natasha: "I have raved about Valerian? And my father heard it? And my father is angry?"

"That is just the misfortune," replied the nurse. "Now if you were to ask him not to marry you to the negro he would think that Valerian was the cause. There is nothing to be done; submit to the will of your parents, for what is to be will be."

Natasha did not reply. The thought that the secret of her heart was known to her father, produced a powerful effect upon her imagination. One hope alone remained, the hope to die before the completion of the odious marriage. This thought consoled her. Weak and sad at heart she resigned herself to her fate.

CHAPTER VII

In the house of Gavril Afanassievitch, to the right vestibule, was a narrow room with one window. There stood a simple bed covered with a woollen counter. In front of the bed was a small deal table, on which a candle was burning, and some sheets of music lay. On the wall hung an old blue uniform and its contemporary, a three-cornered hat; above it, fastened by three nails hung a rude picture representing Charles XII on horseback. The notes of a flute resounded through this humble mansion. The captive dancing-master, its lonely occupant in night-cap and nankeen dressing-gown, was relieving the dulness of a winter's evening, by playing some old Swedish marches. After devoting two whole hours to this exercise, the Swede took his flute to pieces, placed it in a box and began to undress....

www.ingramcontent.com/pod-product-compliance
Lightning Source LLC
Chambersburg PA
CBHW010805250626
47156CB00010B/2997